What people are saying about …

Two Crosses and Two Testaments

"One intriguing era in France's history, one unforgettable cast of characters, and one of the best writers in the CBA today all add up to one incredible read! In *Two Crosses*, Elizabeth Musser has achieved another literary triumph."

Ann Tatlock, award-winning author
of *Promises to Keep*

"Elizabeth Musser reminds me of Francine Rivers. The characters are real, the drama is gripping, and the Spirit rises up from the grass roots of the story. You'll love *Two Crosses*."

Creston Mapes, best-selling
author of *Nobody*

"In a novel rich in historical detail, Elizabeth Musser spins an intriguing story of the lives and loves of young people caught up in the Algerian revolution to win independence from France in 1954–1962. It was a costly conflict, and we are invited to see it through the eyes of those living on both sides of the Mediterranean. Christian convictions and patriotic loyalties are put to the test, as

God works His plans for individuals and nations. I enjoyed this book and look forward to reading the rest of the trilogy."

Ruth Stewart, AWM missionary for forty years to Algeria and France

"In this delightful story, the sounds, scents, and scenery of France and Algeria come alive. *Two Crosses* untangles the complicated history of Algeria's war for independence from France. You feel as though you know the characters. The surprising twists in the story never stop. As the book comes to an end, you are ready to immediately pick up *Two Testaments*."

Margaret Haines, former missionary with over thirty years of missionary experience among the Algerians and French in North Africa during the end of the war

Two Crosses

OTHER BOOKS BY ELIZABETH MUSSER

The Swan House
The Dwelling Place
Searching for Eternity
Words Unspoken
The Sweetest Thing

THE SECRETS OF THE CROSS TRILOGY

Two Crosses
Two Testaments
Two Destinies [coming September 2012]

ELIZABETH MUSSER

Two Crosses

—— A NOVEL ——

SECRETS OF
THE CROSS
TRILOGY

I

David C Cook®

transforming lives together

TWO CROSSES
Published by David C Cook
4050 Lee Vance View
Colorado Springs, CO 80918 U.S.A.

David C Cook Distribution Canada
55 Woodslee Avenue, Paris, Ontario, Canada N3L 3E5

David C Cook U.K., Kingsway Communications
Eastbourne, East Sussex BN23 6NT, England

The graphic circle C logo is a registered trademark of David C Cook.

This story is a work of fiction. Characters and events are the product of the author's
imagination. Any resemblance to any person, living or dead, is coincidental.

All Scripture quotations in the story are taken from the King James Version
of the Bible. (Public Domain.) Scripture quotation in the acknowledgments
is taken from the New American Standard Bible®, Copyright © 1960, 1995
by The Lockman Foundation. Used by permission. (www.Lockman.org.)

LCCN 2012930188
ISBN 978-0-7814-0500-3
eISBN 978-1-4347-0500-6

© 1996, 2012 Elizabeth Musser
The author is represented by MacGregor Literary.
First edition published by Victor Books in 1996
© Elizabeth Musser, ISBN 1-56476-577-6.

The Team: Don Pape, LB Norton, Amy Konyndyk, Jack Campbell, Karen Athen
Cover Design: Nick Lee
Cover Photos: stock.xchng by jvangalen, flaivoloka, kitenellie, breizh;
iStockphoto

Printed in the United States of America
Second Edition 2012

1 2 3 4 5 6 7 8 9 10

032312

This story is dedicated to my beloved grandmother,
Allene Massey Goldsmith,
with thankfulness for all the wonderful afternoons we shared
together, sitting on the wicker love seat on your porch.
For as long as I can remember, you have listened,
encouraged, cared, and believed.
You are one of God's greatest gifts to me.
Thanks for finding a face in each pansy. I love you.

Acknowledgments

This new edition: It is rare for an author to have the chance to reedit a novel. In a sweet story of God's timing, David C Cook has come alongside me in getting *Two Crosses* back in print.

I send my warmest *merci* to Don Pape, who read this novel years ago and decided it needed another chance.

My wonderful editor and friend, LB Norton, is responsible for my serendipitous meeting with Don. She also walked me through the editing of *Two Crosses* sixteen years ago, and she's been with me in the process again. We've had such fun together, and I raise my glass to you, LB, and say *merci*.

Thanks, too, to the great staff at David C Cook. What a pleasure to be working together.

The first edition: It seems all of my life I have been writing stories in my head. To have one in book form, after all these years, is a testimony to the Lord's goodness and timing. "Faithful is He who calls you, and He also will bring it to pass."

To my parents, Barbara and Jere Goldsmith, I owe a lifetime of thanks for encouraging me and allowing me to pursue my dreams. You are truly two of the most generous people on the face of this earth.

To my grandmother, Allene Goldsmith, I say again thank you for caring and spending time with me.

To all my friends here in France who so willingly gave me information about events that were often painful memories, *merci mille fois*!

To all of our prayer partners on the other side of the ocean who have read my letters throughout our years of ministry in France, thank you for your prayers and for encouraging me in my writing.

To Dave Horton, my friend, editor, and fellow French enthusiast, I am deeply grateful to you for making this book happen, for giving patient advice, and for reminding me of the intrigue of the Huguenot cross.

To LoraBeth Norton, for your careful editing and expert eye, I am glad to have had the opportunity to work together.

To Trudy Owens and Cathy Carmeni, for reading and rereading the manuscript and offering helpful advice, I appreciate it.

To my teammates, Howard and Trudy Owens and Odette Beauregard, who have been cheerleaders, babysitters, soul mates, and family away from home, *je vous embrasse avec tout mon coeur.*

To Andrew and Christopher, my precious sons, who have been so patient while Mommy sat at the computer and who have served as role models for the children in this book, I give you a heart full of hugs.

And mostly to my husband, Paul, who has laughed and cried in all the right places year after year, I can never say it enough: *je t'aime.*

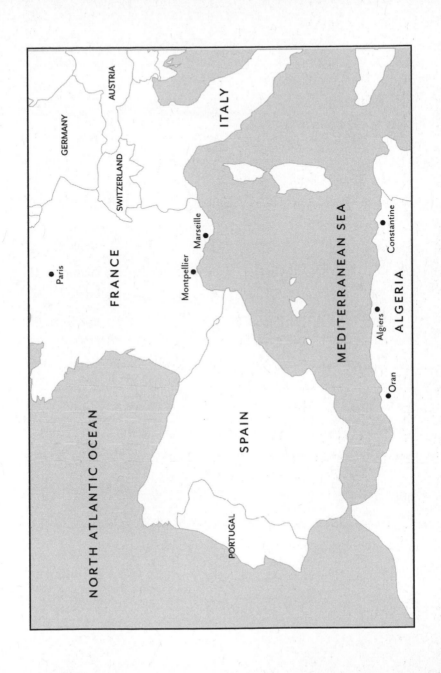

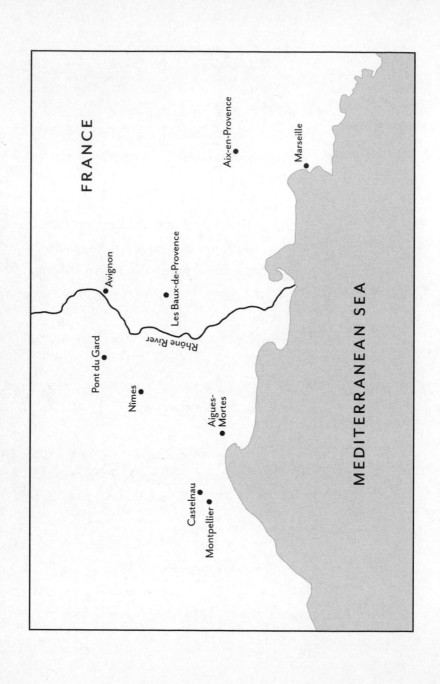

Glossary

Casbah—the old part of Algiers, named for the Turkish-built sixteenth-century fortress that dominated the quarter. It was also the headquarters for the FLN.

FLN—Front de Libération Nationale (National Liberation Front), socialist political party in Algeria. It was organized on November 1, 1954, from a merger of small political groups that sought independence for Algeria from France.

harki—an Algerian soldier who remained loyal to the French army and therefore fought against his fellow Algerians.

Le Monde—*The World*, a French daily newspaper.

OAS—Organisation de l'Armée Secrète (Organization of the Secret Army), a French far-right nationalist militant and underground organization during the Algerian War (1954–62) whose goal was to prevent Algeria's independence.

petits blancs—the poorest of the Europeans in Algeria.

pied-noir—a European living in Algeria.

1

September 1961
Castelnau, France

The sun rose softly on the lazy town of Castelnau in the south of France. Gabriella quietly slipped out of bed, stretched, and ran her fingers through her thick mane of red hair. The tile floor felt cool to her bare feet. Peering down from her tiny room, she watched the empty streets begin to fill with people. Mme Leclerc, her landlady, was the first to enter the *boulangerie* just in view down the street to buy *baguettes* and *gros pain*, the bread essential for breakfast for her three boarding students.

She watched a moment longer, until a lanky young man in his midtwenties walked briskly up the street. There was no mistaking the next client who entered the *boulangerie*. Gabriella had recognized him the first time she saw him buying bread a few days earlier, from the description of the other boarders. This was David Hoffmann, the university's handsome American instructor. Gabriella strained to get a closer look.

Castelnau was a pleasant town, she thought as she moved away from the window. She pulled the duvet up from the end of the bed and lightly fluffed her pillow. It wasn't a bit like Dakar, or any other part of Senegal—except, of course, that the beach and ocean were not far away. Only here it was the Mediterranean Sea.

She tied back her unruly hair with a large ribbon and then washed her face in the small porcelain sink that stood neatly in the corner of the room. Opening a large oak armoire, she removed a freshly pressed blouse and a simple straight-lined navy skirt. As she dressed, she noted that the skirt hung loosely around her waist—in spite of the boulangerie's bread and pastries.

She had come to Castelnau only two weeks earlier, excited and confident, ready to discover a new land and people. But as the days between her and her family lengthened, pangs of homesickness caught her by surprise. In the midst of a walk through town she would notice a woman with hair like her mother's, or two lithe, tanned girls, carefree and laughing, like Jessica and Henrietta.

By afternoon she knew it would be blistering hot outside, but the morning was bright and crisp, with a hint of autumn in the air. At home there would be no fall smells. And at home she would not yet be starting her first day at university. But here, in this small French village separated by a sea from the African world she loved, Gabriella knew she must push away thoughts of the past. At twenty-one, she should know that no good would come from giving in to homesickness.

She reached for the large leather-bound Bible sitting on her wooden nightstand and leafed familiarly through the pages until she found the place she was seeking. Ten minutes later, as she carefully laid the book back on the nightstand, a letter fell from the Bible. She reached down and retrieved it, and as she tucked it back into the book, a line caught her eye: *I give you this cross, which has always been for me a symbol of forgiveness and love.*

A shadow swept across her. Instinctively she reached to touch the gold chain that hung around her neck. Paying no attention to the cold, hard tile beneath her bare knees, she knelt on the floor and propped her folded hands on the side of the bed. She moved her lips without a sound escaping. It was only later, when she rose to her feet and smoothed her skirt, that she noticed her hands were wet from her warm tears.

Gabriella finished her breakfast of bread, butter, and jelly dipped into a huge bowl of rich hot chocolate. The first morning, she had barely managed to choke down the strong coffee the French drank in their wide bowls, diluting it with plenty of cream and four cubes of sugar. After that disaster, Mme Leclerc had offered her hot chocolate instead. Gabriella smiled now as she remembered her embarrass-ment, then swept the bread crumbs from her skirt, cleared the table, and let the dishes rattle in the small sink.

"Gabriella, please. You are always the last one, helping an old lady like me. But today you mustn't be late. *Allez!* Go along now and catch up with the others." Mme Leclerc shooed her out of the house.

Stephanie and Caroline, the two other boarders, had hurried off minutes before, and Gabriella appreciated Mme Leclerc's friendly dismissal. She grabbed her small satchel that lay by the entrance of the apartment. Opening the door, she turned back and said "*Au revoir,*" then placed the expected quick kisses on her landlady's cheeks. "And *merci!*"

She made her way down the dark, narrow staircase. On a good day Gabriella could descend the stairs two at a time, race back up, and come down again before the automatic light in the stairwell went off. It was her own childish game, played only when others weren't present. Today, however, she did not press the shining orange button. She needed these few seconds of darkness to collect her thoughts.

At the bottom of the staircase, a massive oak door opened onto the street. She stepped out into the sunlight and blinked. Quickly she trotted down the sidewalk, past the *boulangerie* with its smells of fresh bread, past the *café*, where paunchy men were already sipping an early-morning *apéritif* and women chatted noisily as their dogs strained on leashes. She liked the short walk through the village that led to the small yet imposing Church of St. Joseph. The church was built in the Romanesque style and seemed to Gabriella like a benevolent father surrounding a houseful of children, saying nothing but ever present and knowing.

She stepped through the red-washed wooden side door and down the steps into the hollow nave, where flickering candles testified to the early-morning fidelity of a few parishioners. The church was slowly filling up with young women. Gabriella took a seat on a wooden pew near the front, next to Stephanie.

"You made it!" her housemate said, too loudly. "I thought you'd be late."

Gabriella smiled. "Fortunately it's a short walk."

"I've heard the first day is a little boring," Stephanie said. Her husky voice echoed in the hollow room.

Gabriella nodded and put a finger to her lips.

By now many young women were scattered throughout the twenty rows of pews. A small woman wearing a black nun's habit walked up the aisle and stood before them. Gabriella had heard that she was over seventy, but the nun's green eyes were lively. She spoke in English, with a heavy French accent.

"Good morning, *mesdemoiselles*, and welcome to the Church of St. Joseph. I am Mother Griolet, the director of the Franco-American exchange program here in Castelnau. As you have already discovered during your week of orientation, this church is where you will meet each morning at eight thirty for announcements, after which you will go to your morning classes.

"This is my fourteenth year of working with the program, and by now I have, shall we say, gotten used to the ways of American women." She lifted her eyebrows, and muffled laughter echoed through the church. "We try not to have too many rules, for we want you to soak up this region of France and learn the language. However, we do expect you to act becoming of your age and remember that you are representing your country.

"As is my custom, I will give a brief history of St. Joseph. The church dates back to the thirteenth century. The parsonage, as you call it, was added in the eighteenth century, as were the classrooms, refectory, and dormitory. At one time St. Joseph was used as a parochial school for French women. I came here in 1917 as a teacher and also opened a small orphanage at that time, which continues to function—I'm sure you have noticed the children about.

"During World War II the school was abandoned, though the church and orphanage remained open. After the war, with the help of some businessmen from America, St. Joseph was transformed into a school that offered classes in both French and English—an exchange program for young women during their university education.

"In 1947 I assumed the position of director and had to brush up on my English a bit." She emphasized her last phrase with an exaggerated accent, and the young women laughed. "As I like to tell your parents, who are paying, as you say, 'through the nose' for you to be here, the school's location on the Mediterranean offers an ideal setting for your cultural advancement. Several excursions are planned each quarter to visit the historical sites of the region. And there is, of course, springtime in Paris. Two weeks to soak up the charm of the city, lose oneself in the museums, and join the students from the Sorbonne in a café on the Left Bank. Doesn't it sound grand?"

Gabriella and Stephanie nodded at Mother Griolet's romantic description.

"This year there are forty-two of you representing seven different universities and three countries. Many of you are taking *demi-pension*, living with a French family and eating one meal a day with them. Others are housed at the university in Montpellier, only fifteen minutes away by bus. I hope you have already begun to meet one another.

"I would now like to introduce our professors." She addressed the woman and three men seated in the front row. "If you will please stand after I introduce you. First, M. Claude Brunet, who will teach all three levels of French grammar, as well as the conversation class." A thin, tall middle-aged man with an enormous mustache and heavy eyebrows rose and nodded slightly.

"They say he had an affair with a girl from Rhode Island last year. He's a real playboy," Stephanie whispered.

Gabriella gave her a look of disbelief, but Stephanie just shrugged.

"Next, M. Jean-Louis Vidal." A balding man with wire glasses and a generous stomach, who looked at least sixty, stood quickly, a slightly flustered expression on his face. "M. Vidal will teach all of you European history—in French, of course."

"Boring," was Stephanie's comment.

Mother Griolet continued. "We are privileged to have a professor from the Faculté des Lettres in Montpellier teaching eighteenth-century French literature and twentieth-century French novel. Madame Josephine Resch." A woman of about thirty-five with black blunt-cut hair stood, looking poised and cool in her lightweight suit.

"She's supposed to be tough but good," came the running commentary from Stephanie.

"And finally, M. David Hoffmann, who will be teaching a course he first presented at St. Joseph last year: 'Visions of Man, Past and Present.' M. Hoffmann will teach in both French and English, since his course deals with art, history, and literature from both France and England."

When David Hoffmann rose to his feet, every eye in the church followed him. His frame was lean and athletic, and his hair and eyes were jet black. He appeared calm and sophisticated for such a young professor.

Stephanie jabbed Gabriella in the ribs. "He is one charming man, I heard. But very distant."

Mother Griolet thanked the professors, then turned her attention once again to the young women. "We are delighted to have you with us for the school year. I believe you have all received your course schedules and know where the classrooms are. I will end by saying that I am an old woman and have seen many things. Young ladies can get into all kinds of trouble. I cannot prevent it, but my office is open for a friendly chat if you should happen to need it. You are dismissed."

She left the podium, her face a picture of joviality dusted with friendly concern. The girls offered a smattering of polite applause

before they stood up and filed out of the church and into the adjoining building.

Gabriella liked the firm yet humorous style of the director. *I can
see why Mother grew so fond of her*, she thought. Then she hurried
after Stephanie to find a place in the classroom of M. Hoffmann.

Mother Griolet closed the door to her small office and sat down
behind the mahogany desk. She picked up the list in front of her,
cursorily reading the forty-two girls' names. Over the next few
months they would become as familiar to her as her own. But one
she already knew. *Gabriella Madison*. She closed her eyes and saw this
now-grown young woman with the fiery hair as a child of six, trembling and sobbing, her face dirty as she clung to Mother Griolet's
black skirts.

Mother Griolet did not cry often, but the memory of that scene
brought an unexpected sting to her green eyes and sent a sudden chill
through her small frame.

"Dear child. Why did you come back here?" She was sure it was
a mistake. She was equally sure that she would pray night and day
that Gabriella Madison would never discover the story that an old
nun had kept to herself for so long.

2

David Hoffmann stood before his class, a hint of a smile on his lips. The young women scurried excitedly into the room, clearly nervous in spite of their efforts to look mature and appealing. The rumors doubtless were the same as last year: M. Hoffmann would be a perfect match for one of these up-and-coming debutantes.

"*Mesdemoiselles*," he said sternly, "please be seated. You may discuss the shortcomings of your *professeurs* later."

Nervous laughter, and a few raised eyebrows.

"I have the distinct pleasure of presiding over this most fascinating course, 'Visions of Man: Past and Present.' It is a composite of several subject areas and will test your minds in the areas of French and English literature, poetry, the history of art, and the psychology of learning. You will soon see how marvelously these subjects flow together. Is that not right, Mlle Loudermilk?"

An impeccably dressed blonde in the third row looked up, surprised, and then beamed back. "Of course, M. Hoffmann. It sounds enchanting."

Good, he thought. *They aren't quite sure what to think of me.* But his eyes kept straying to the young woman sitting like a statue to his right. He had noticed her at once: mounds of red hair curling wildly about her head and bright, clear blue eyes with an innocence and luminosity that shone like an angel from one of Raphael's paintings. In contrast to the other girls, she seemed childlike and fragile. *An angel*, he thought. *A Raphaelite angel.*

He realized then who she must be, so out of place among these sophisticated socialites-in-training. Yes, this must be the daughter of missionaries from the west coast of Africa. A wealthy relative was paying for her junior year abroad before she continued her education at a college in the States. That was the story, anyway. The poor girl was probably scared stiff.

Clearing his throat, David came around to the front of his desk and sat lightly on it. His dark eyes flashed as he began to recite:

"Know then thyself, presume not God to scan

The proper study of Mankind is Man ...

Created half to rise, and half to fall;

Great lord of all things, yet a prey to all;

Sole judge of Truth, in endless Error hurl'd:

The glory, jest, and riddle of the world!"

When he finished, he returned to the other side of his desk and stared at the mesmerized girls, who seemed not to have understood a word of his soliloquy but nonetheless appreciated his charm and talent. "*Mesdemoiselles*, please! Who can tell me the poet's name and the title of the work?"

Forty-two heads looked around nervously.

Then a hand went up. He almost didn't see it, so little did he expect an answer. "Yes, Miss ..." His voice trailed off as he searched the roll for the missionary girl's name.

"Madison. Gabriella Madison." Her voice was soft but calm.

Gabriella! Even the name of an angel.

"Why, it's from Alexander Pope's 'Essay on Man'!" she exclaimed excitedly, as if she were delighted to find someone else who shared her enthusiasm for the poet.

David felt himself blush, then regained his composure and began his lecture. But after class, his thoughts returned to the angel on his right. Worth investigating, this Gabriella Madison.

Everything in France seemed to close between noon and two. Gabriella had observed the daily routine: shop owners covered their windows with corrugated aluminum and locked their doors, and workers passed one another on the cobblestones in the center of town as they headed toward their homes.

The main meal of the day lasted two full hours and was eaten in leisurely fashion with plenty of bread and wine accompanying each of the four courses. Gabriella blushed slightly as she remembered her first taste of wine at Mme Leclerc's dinner table.

"*Mais, bien sûr*, you must try a little red wine, *ma chérie*," the proprietor had insisted. "What is a meal without wine?"

To be polite, Gabriella had lifted the glass to her lips and sipped the rich red liquid. It had burned her mouth and caused her eyes to fill with tears, and she coughed uncontrollably. Mme Leclerc, Stephanie, and Caroline had laughed loudly.

"The first sip is always surprising. But do not worry, *ma chérie*. You will come to appreciate it, I assure you."

So far, all that Gabriella had come to appreciate about the red wine and ample noontime meal was how hard it was for her to keep her eyes open the rest of the afternoon. She did not want to fall asleep in her first European history class. Stephanie had reported that the history teacher

spoke in a slow, droning voice that would lull even the staunchest teeto-
taler into dreamland. If only she had M. Hoffmann after lunch! No one
in her right mind could have heavy eyes in his class.

She had found it hard to concentrate on his lecture that morning. He had seemed discerning and profound, and his dark, deep-set
eyes made her feel uncomfortable. Were they dark blue or coffee
brown or jet black? In any case, they were penetrating. The other girls
called him handsome and mysterious, but Gabriella saw something
different. Brilliant and sad, was her conclusion.

"Miss Madison! May I have a word with you?"

Gabriella turned to see M. Hoffmann striding toward her. A feeling
of panic swept across her face, and she felt her cheeks turn crimson. What
could he want with her? Had he read her mind? She considered ignoring
his question and hurrying toward the door of Mme Leclerc's apartment. Instead, she slowed her step to let him catch up. The brightness
of the sun combined with her own embarrassment made her suddenly
feel light-headed and weak. She tripped on the cobblestone street and
stumbled awkwardly until M. Hoffmann's strong hand grasped her arm
and steadied her. She groaned inwardly. Every girl at school was longing
for a *tête-a-tête* with this man, and she, at this golden opportunity, could
only conduct herself like a clumsy adolescent.

He seemed unfazed as he matched her pace. "Where are you
going? You don't eat lunch at the cafeteria in town, I suppose?"

"Oh, no. I'm boarding with Mme Leclerc. We eat all our meals
with her. She says we keep her company. It's always delicious, but the
wine and food make me sleepy." She realized she was babbling.

He chuckled. "Bring some toothpicks, then, for M. Vidal's class. You'll need them to prop open your eyes!"

Although Gabriella disapproved of M. Hoffmann's cutting remark, she struggled to suppress a grin.

Again M. Hoffmann seemed oblivious to her uneasiness. "I was impressed that you knew Mr. Pope and his poem. I didn't expect anyone to recognize it … or to have any interest in my opening statement."

"Oh, I'm sure everyone was interested. They just weren't familiar with the work. My mother used to read to us all the time—classics, poetry, any books she could get her hands on. I mean, it was sometimes hard to have books … where we lived … in English." Rambling again. "Anyway, I really like Pope's poetry."

"You're from Africa, I hear. What do you think of St. Joseph and its charming young ladies?"

"I think it will be fine, interesting. Oh dear, there's Mme Leclerc looking out the window for me. Good-bye." With that she left his side and hurriedly walked toward her door. Racing up the stairs and entering the apartment, she caught a glimpse of her flushed face as she passed the mirror in the entranceway. Her heart was pounding so loudly she was sure the other girls would notice.

The first day of class at St. Joseph was over, and Mother Griolet slumped quietly into the black cushioned chair behind her desk. *That went well for a first day*, she concluded, satisfied. *Not a bit like*

the old days, with all the nuns scurrying about. Now most of the professors were male. At times she had wondered if hiring each of them had been a mistake.

M. Brunet was a womanizer and everyone knew it, but he taught grammar better than anyone else. M. Vidal had needed a job when he applied four years ago. He spoke a pitiful English, but his knowledge of European history was vast, and she allowed him to teach in French. A position at St. Joseph would pay his bills, if he could manage to stay away from the *café-bar* on his way home after class.

But it was not M. Vidal's drinking habits that bothered Mother Griolet today as she sat reflecting at her desk—it was the baffling personality of David Hoffmann. She had hired him on the spot eighteen months earlier. His references had been impeccable, a brilliant young man with an Ivy League education, twenty-three years old, the son of an ambassador. Well-traveled. Charming. Confident in his ability to assume his first teaching position. And in this, Mother Griolet had not been disappointed. Though he did not have the degrees to match the other professors, he was a gifted teacher. And it seemed to her as if he felt that he *needed* to be here.

Now, however, she suspected that David Hoffmann was not teaching at St. Joseph as an end in itself. He spoke beautiful French; his manners were polite, though aloof. But she sensed that he was hiding something....

The bells in the chapel chimed five o'clock. She stood up, smoothed the black robe that had been her daily wardrobe for the past fifty years, and walked out the door and down the hall.

David walked briskly down the dark street, the click of his heels reverberating on the deserted cobblestones. He slipped into a phone booth, plunked a *franc* piece into the open slot, and dialed a number.

"It's me," he whispered. "I'll be there. And listen, I'm bringing a girl."

"A girl! Are you crazy? The last thing we need is someone else involved."

"Don't worry, she'll be a perfect cover for us. It will work out beautifully."

"I'm not convinced."

"Don't worry, she doesn't know a thing." He continued quickly, not allowing the voice on the other end to interrupt. "We'll be in Aigues-Mortes in two weeks. Oh, and my friend has red hair. Lots of it. *A bientôt, mon ami.*" He returned the receiver to its hook, then walked back up the street, deep in thought.

3

Paris, France

In the streets beyond the Seine on the Left Bank of Paris, a young child played alone while her mother looked on from their third-floor apartment. "Be careful, Ophélie!" called the woman, glancing down the street to where three men waited at the corner. Students from the Sorbonne, foreigners perhaps. The men began to move in her direction.

"Dinnertime, *ma chérie*," said the mother. "*Vite!* Come upstairs quickly."

"But, Mama," the child protested, "you said I could play a while longer. The sun has not yet closed his eyes. A few more minutes, please, Mama?"

The young woman coughed weakly. Her face was pale and thin, and her dark, almost black, eyes, framed by rich, thick lashes, mirrored intense pain. Again she coughed and pleaded, "*Now*, Ophélie, you must come now."

The three men drew closer, and she recognized their faces. Fear erased the pain in her eyes. "*Now!*"

Ophélie glanced over her shoulder at the men half a block away. For a moment, a look of fear flitted across her innocent face. Then she replaced it with a smile as she tossed her long brown hair over her shoulders. "*Oui, Mama*. I'm coming."

Like an actress poised before her audience, she turned to face the shadows of the strangers. Ophélie would play her part well. For the sake of Mama, she would not be afraid. She would know nothing, no matter what they asked. If, of course, they came to the door, as so many others had done before in her short life.

She skipped into the apartment building, as if she hadn't a care in the world, then ran up the stairs.

"You must leave at once, *ma chérie*," whispered Mama as she pulled Ophélie inside the apartment and bolted the door. She handed her daughter the precious little blue sack that had been stored away, waiting for this fateful day. "Go out the secret way, Ophélie. Run fast to M. Gady's shop. Tell him you must stay with him until I come. He will understand. Now go quickly."

As Ophélie prepared to leave, her mother caught her up in her arms and hugged her fiercely against her breast. "Always you know that Mama loves you. Always. You're a wonderful girl."

Mother and child ran to the back bedroom, and Mama opened the window. Ophélie perched on the sill for only a moment, like a baby swallow before its first flight. Then, with the small sack crossed over her neck, she grabbed the thick rope her mother had tied to the outside railing months ago. The rope fell to the ground and Ophélie shimmied down gracefully, just as she had done in their many "secret practice sessions," as Mama called them. Ophélie had felt a sense of adventure and excitement as she practiced for some unknown day. But as dusk settled in and she touched the cement of the street below, she knew that tonight was not a practice. She looked up for one last glimpse of Mama pulling in the rope and closing the window.

"*Au revoir, Mama. A bientôt,*" whispered Ophélie as she rushed down the side street and lost herself in the teeming crowd of the Left Bank of Paris at sunset.

Anne-Marie Duchemin could hear their footsteps as the three men raced up the stairs to her apartment. *Oh, God, this is it.* She would not let them find her daughter. She would delay them for the precious few minutes Ophélie needed to reach M. Gady's shop. They would never find her there ... unless they forced Anne-Marie to talk.

She had no doubt that she might talk if she were tortured. It had happened before. But this time she was prepared. Her life did not matter anymore.

Anne-Marie would not die for a lofty cause that, however important, was very flawed. No, she had discovered that there was only one cause worth dying for—love. She felt the tiny bottle sewn inside her sleeve. If necessary, she could slip a pill under her tongue, and she would reveal nothing.

She quickly untied the escape rope, fingers trembling, and ran to the kitchen, where she opened the small metal trash chute. Silently she let the rope fall into the trash bin in the basement.

By now the men were banging on the door, cursing loudly in Arabic. Anne-Marie stood frozen in the hallway. *Only a few seconds now, and she will be safe.* Again with shaking fingers, she unbolted the brass lock and grasped the door handle. Immediately two dark-skinned Arab men rushed in, shoving Anne-Marie aside. As Anne-Marie caught herself on a small table in the hall, she recognized the third man, who entered slowly.

"Moustafa!" she whispered.

The man lowered his head as she said his name. Anne-Marie read the look of guilt and sorrow in his eyes: *I had no choice.* She knew it was true. They had forced him to talk, and he was ashamed.

"Where is the girl? Bring her here now." The tallest of the three directed the second man, whose young face was badly scarred, toward the kitchen.

Moustafa stood, riveted in his place, dark panic in his eyes.

"You coward! Help Rachid. Go find the girl!" The tall man pushed Moustafa down the hallway.

Anne-Marie followed Moustafa as he obediently, like a whipped puppy, walked toward the back of the apartment and briefly glanced around the sparse bedroom. It held an old mattress with springs but no headboard, two chairs with worn material, a cheap armoire, and a small bedside table. Moustafa stopped by the window to look out at the street below. The curtain fluttered slightly, and Anne-Marie saw that the window was not completely closed. Quietly Moustafa pushed it shut and turned the handle to lock it.

"There is nothing back here, Ali. She is not here," he reported.

Ali turned his rage-filled face to Anne-Marie. "Where is your daughter? We have seen her. We know she is near."

Anne-Marie said nothing, but she was sure her terror showed in her eyes. She remembered too well Ali's penchant for sadistic pleasure.

He reached for her face, grabbing her chin. "Tell me, woman." His voice filled with hatred. "I can make you talk." He swung his other hand and hit her fiercely across the cheek.

Anne-Marie cried out as she fell backward, and Moustafa caught her. "Please." She was on her knees. "You don't need her. I'll go with you! She's nothing to you." She was sobbing now, and Ali pulled her to her feet. He looked as if he might strike her again, but Moustafa interrupted.

"Ali, sir, I have seen them often at the meat stand, as I told you. The girl is only six. She knows nothing."

"And have you lived with them?" He turned angrily to glare at Moustafa, relaxing his grip on Anne-Marie. "Have you heard every conversation? Of course not! You do not know. There is a war in your country. Algeria will be independent! And you would protect a disgusting whore and her bastard instead of the cause. You will die with them, fool."

Finishing his search of the small apartment, the young man called Rachid came back to the hall. "Ali! Calm yourself. You will kill her, and then we'll never find the others. Moustafa is right. What would a scared child know? Bring along the woman. She will talk. She's talked before."

Ophélie waited for her mother at M. Gady's shop until well past dark. Each time a customer came through the doorway, pushing aside the long strands of colorful beads, she glanced up hopefully. But it was never Mama. They came and bought flour and couscous and rice from Thailand and hot little peppers. They laughed and joked with the stooped, graying shopkeeper. He winked back and shuffled behind the counter. Ophélie sat on a small stool and watched each face. She grew angry that they could laugh and joke while her life had stopped abruptly. She wondered when M. Gady would close the store. Her stomach rumbled, and she knew it must be past dinnertime.

As if reading her thoughts, M. Gady said, "Ah, little Ophélie, we will lock the store soon and have our supper, *n'est-ce pas?* Oh, such sadness in your big brown eyes! Come now, little one, do not worry. M. Gady will care for you. And your mother will come soon. You will see."

But Ophélie read the fear in his tired eyes. She had seen such lines of concern often on Mama's face. No, something was wrong.

The small blue velvet bag still hung on the white cord around her neck, hidden beneath her dress. She found an excuse to leave the watchful eye of M. Gady and go to the back of the shop and up the narrow steps that led to his apartment. Mama had said she should give the bag to M. Gady immediately, but she could not. What if he didn't give it back? Then all that mattered would be lost, and she would not carry even the memory of her mother with her. Quickly she removed the bag from around her neck. Reaching inside, she fumbled through two folded envelopes until she touched a thin necklace at the bottom. Bringing it out, she examined the small gold cross that hung on the chain. She lifted it to her lips and kissed it gently, then put it away.

She crept back down the stairs as darkness closed its heavy curtain over the busy city. Out in the dust of the street behind the shop, she bent down and with her finger drew a crude picture of the cross she had just held. It was a thick cross, with a dove hanging below the lowest branch. "For you, Mama," she whispered. "Here is hope." Then she stood and brushed away the picture with the sole of her shoe.

Although only forty-six years of age, Ali Boudani looked more like a man of sixty. His face was weathered and his teeth crooked and broken. He carried his tall, lean frame with steely confidence, a look he had acquired through thirty years in the armed service. He was the spitting image of his father, whose military progress he had watched proudly at the end of World War I, when Ali was only four.

The musty basement where he paced back and forth was occupied by a handful of somber men, several of them dark-skinned Arabs like himself. Two others were unmistakably French.

Ali addressed the group. "Today, right here in Paris, we have found the woman we have been hunting these months. Anne-Marie Duchemin." The face of a woman, delicate and beautiful, appeared on a screen at the front of the room. "We must thank our new friend, Moustafa, for this prize." Ali chuckled as he pointed to the young man seated in the back of the small, smoke-filled room.

"A foolish woman. A disgusting *pied-noir*. Her parents were killed in the massacre of 1958. A most unfortunate accident." A smile played around his lips. "Anne-Marie was of great help to us. She had the little child, and Jean-Claude was so kind to her."

The men quietly laughed and nodded their heads. A few of the Arabs patted a handsome young Frenchman on the back.

"Very helpful, this woman, until she left Algeria six months ago. She wanted to protect her daughter, you understand. Perhaps she has succeeded in that for now. We did not find the child." Another picture flashed on the screen: a young girl, fine and graceful, a reflection of a younger Anne-Marie, brown hair pulled back in a long braid, and a carefree smile on her face.

"We believe that Anne-Marie has information about the disturbing smuggling activities we have recently learned of and has had close ties in the past with several informers. We will have this information soon. We will take her back to Algeria with us." He clicked off the projector, and the men rose to leave. "Jean-Claude and Emile. You will stay in France. There is work for you here."

Bachir Karel crept through the streets of Algiers as the sun yawned and left a shimmering whisper across the face of the waters in the port. Its fading brilliance caught the silver on the *Capitaine* and sent a sharp glare out from the boat. Bachir crouched in the shadows and waited impatiently for darkness.

He glanced down at the slip of paper in his hand. A strange cross was scribbled in the top left-hand corner. It was a thick cross, with four arrows pointing inward and a bird drawn from the bottom arrow. Bachir reread the message scrawled on the paper: *vendredi 20H15.*

He stiffened as he heard a slight noise. Heart pounding, he pulled himself behind a small sailboat and watched. Silence. Only ten more minutes, and he would climb aboard the *Capitaine* and head to France. Ten more minutes to safety.

The boy had prepared the speech in his head. *My father served your army well in the Second World War and Indochina. Now he has been killed by the Front de Libération Nationale. They called him a traitor. He was a harki. I am his son. We are on your side in this war. Please. My family have all been murdered. I am fleeing Algeria with only the clothes on my back. I was told by a friend that here I would be safe.*

He knew the French did not want refugees, especially Algerian ones. They only wanted out of the war that was claiming their sons' lives. Twenty years of fighting had taken their toll on France. First World War II, then Indochina, now Algeria.

But someone will understand, he thought. He would start a new life in France. He looked at the sky. Black. Now was the time!

Slowly Bachir left the cover of the small sailboat. Crouching, he hurried along the dock. Four hundred yards to freedom.

Out of the darkness another form appeared, blocking his way. A low laugh echoed in the stillness of the night. "And where do you think you are going, Bachir?"

The boy froze, then looked frantically about him. He dashed toward a small fishing rig, hoping to jump into the water. But even as he moved, a shot rang out. Pain seared through his chest as he fell back onto the planks. Still conscious, he pulled his body toward

the water. Another shot. One foot from the edge of the dock, he
stopped. Bachir Karel never moved again.

The dark form of a man bent down over the body. "Fool! No one
escapes Ali! Now your whole family has paid for the traitorous act
of your father." He searched the body and found nothing of impor-
tance in Bachir's pant pockets. He pried open the dead boy's fist and
smiled. "Thank you, Bachir. This is exactly what I was looking for.
Ali will be most pleased."

He shoved the body into the cool waters and walked back toward
the lights of the city, while the *Capitaine* waited and waited in the
dark.

4

The bell rang out from atop the Church of St. Joseph as the young women hurried to the stone house behind the church. Gabriella slowed down when she reached the steps leading to the classroom on the second floor. Recalling her brief conversation with M. Hoffmann after yesterday's class, she felt strangely embarrassed to see him again.

She took a seat next to Stephanie, who was stuffing the last of a *pain au chocolat* into her mouth.

"Did you read that poetry stuff for today?" Not waiting for Gabriella's reply, Stephanie continued. "Analyzing John Donne! It's pure nonsense to me."

M. Hoffmann entered the classroom and strode smoothly to the podium, where he placed his notes and book. "*Mesdemoiselles*, please open your anthologies to page 1182. We will be considering the poetry and prose of John Donne, one of the wittiest and most spiritual men of the early seventeenth century, at once a scandalous young cavalier and a passionate, intellectual preacher.

"Mlle Madison"—M. Hoffmann turned his dark eyes toward Gabriella—"could you please tell us your impressions of a man who could write both sensual love poems and profound sermons?"

Gabriella was petrified, and she knew the teacher could see it—and he was pleased. *He wants to prove he knows more than I do. So let him.*

But she was too proud to let this man win a battle of wits. So with only a moment's hesitation, she expounded her thoughts on a man who happened to be one of her favorite poets.

"You were great, Gabriella," Stephanie enthused after class. "Next thing you know, M. Hoffmann will be asking you to teach." She scurried out of the room as the teacher approached.

"Miss Madison?"

"Yes?" Gabriella looked up at him without smiling.

"Would you care to join me for a stroll on the place de la Comédie this afternoon? It's a wonderful spot for people watching. I'd like to hear about your years in Africa."

"Well, I suppose I could for a little while. I need to study, of course, so I couldn't spend all day, but—"

M. Hoffmann chuckled. "It is not a date, *mademoiselle*. Just a conversation in broad daylight. There's no need to worry about my intentions." He winked at her and bent down to retrieve his leather briefcase. "I'll meet you outside the church at four thirty."

He left her standing in the middle of the empty classroom, fuming at his arrogance in not even waiting for her answer.

M. Hoffmann led Gabriella through the tiny backstreets of Montpellier until suddenly they entered a vast open square surrounded by old majestic buildings. In the center the Three Graces fountain sprayed water around students who hovered near it.

"It's beautiful!"

"Isn't it? La place de la Comédie is a favorite spot for students. They waste their days away at little outdoor cafés around here. Speaking of which, will you join me for a drink?"

The sun was hot and the sky a fierce bright blue. Gabriella felt beads of perspiration on her forehead and wished she had tied back her hair. "A drink would be great," she said.

M. Hoffmann led her across the vast square. "Montpellier has been called the Oxford of France," he commented. "The university has been around since the thirteenth century."

Gabriella nodded, enchanted by the huge gathering spot of multicolored youths. Beside a movie theater a violinist played, his open case collecting franc pieces from appreciative passers-by.

"Vivaldi's 'Autumn,'" reflected Gabriella, charmed by the poignant melody.

"Ah, the missionary is not only well read, she also knows classical music." He feigned astonishment. "Have a seat, *mademoiselle*." He offered her a chair at a small round table overlooking the Comédie.

To her right Gabriella saw more spewing fountains and a wide, long tree-lined park where people walked slowly beside gardens overflowing with impatiens and begonias.

Following her gaze, he said, "That's the Esplanade, a lovely little plot of earth filled with centuries' worth of history and splattered in bygone years with the blood of your beloved Protestants."

"What do you mean?"

"She can quote Pope and Donne and dance to Vivaldi, but she doesn't know the history of her own rich Protestant roots in this town? 'Tis strange, methinks."

His tone was again theatrical, but Gabriella sensed that he only was looking for a friendly argument.

"If you mean the history of the Huguenots, I am quite aware of the courageous stand they took after the revocation of the Edict of Nantes in 1685. I know they hid in the Cévennes mountains north of here, and I hope I will get to see Aigues-Mortes where the women were imprisoned. But if you mean what happened right here where we sit, Sir Historian, I'm all ears. Please enlighten me."

"*Touché!*" M. Hoffmann replied. "When Louis XIV was in power, the despicable Nicolas Basville was overseeing life in this region, and he ordered many Huguenots to be killed. They were martyred for their faith right here on the Esplanade, where we sit, and thousands turned out to watch the bloody deeds."

A waiter hovered over them, interrupting her professor's sordid tale.

"Yes, I'll have a *pastis*, if you please, and the lady ..."

He looked inquiringly at Gabriella, who blushed and said, "*Un citron pressé, s'il vous plaît.*"

"Wonderful! A lemonade for the lady."

Gabriella squinted up at him. "Do go on with your story."

"Ah, with the bloody deeds? Well, Claude Brousson was a brilliant lawyer and also a Protestant pastor. He was torn apart alive on the wheel, right here on the Esplanade." He paused as if to let the gruesome words sink in. "And why? Because he didn't agree with His Majesty and the pope. And then there was Pierre Durand. He was hung from the gallows as people like us stood and watched. It's a terrible waste, wouldn't you say? These intellectuals came to study at the great University of Montpellier and were killed for what they believed."

Gabriella didn't reply.

"That's why I don't believe anything, Miss Madison. You would tell me there is a God up there? What was He doing while His people argued over petty doctrine and ripped each other apart? Such a waste, religion. A curse for those who are born under its roof." M. Hoffmann spoke with passion now, continuing his soliloquy.

"Look at Algeria today, with its Muslims and Catholics and Protestants and Jews. They lived together in peace until somebody thought Algeria needed its precious freedom. Then suddenly they started hating each other and killing and torturing their neighbors just because they were forced to take sides. The war is over independence, but still religion divides. It's pointless."

Gabriella looked up as the waiter placed their drinks on the table, spilling a bit of the citron pressé and rushing off to another table with two frothy mugs of beer.

She spoke with mock admiration. "My, you know a lot about history. But with such cynical views, why are you so concerned with the Algerian War? Which side do you pick to win?"

"That's a very good question, and one I'm not prepared to answer. It's rather complicated, after all. On the one side you have the Algerian extremists who launched this crazy war in 1954. They want Algeria to be independent of France. The Front de Libération Nationale—the FLN—is a fanatical group, though of course they have their reasons. Most of the Arab population of Algeria, nearly ten million strong, agree with them.

"Then you have the pied-noirs—the French citizens born in Algeria. Many of these families trace their heritage back to when Algeria first became a French colony in 1830. There are maybe a million of them, and naturally they don't want to leave what they consider their homeland."

"Why are they called pied-noirs—'black feet'?" Gabriella interrupted.

"Oh, there are lots of explanations. The most colorful is that the first French citizens who settled in Algeria came as farmers and wore big black boots to work the land. The Algerians had never seen boots; they worked the land barefoot. So they called the foreigners *pied-noir*. Now, of course, it just means a French citizen who was born in Algeria."

She smiled, but he was already resuming his lecture.

"You also have the French army in Algeria, who originally came to keep Algeria French and ward off the FLN. In military power, they have all but won this war. But politically no one is satisfied, and the FLN, though small in numbers, is strong in persuasion through fear."

Gabriella wrinkled her brow, trying to keep up with this man who suddenly seemed lost in a world of his own.

"Back in 1958, the whole country, both Arab and French, demanded that General de Gaulle return to power in France, seeing him as the only man capable of settling this gory war. But the pied-noirs and many in his own army now see him as betraying them, as it becomes more apparent that he will give Algeria its independence.

"So now there are those in the French army, some very important men, who are against de Gaulle and have formed the OAS—Organisation de l'Armée Secrète, France's own secret terrorist group. They are determined to keep Algeria French and resort to the same barbaric measures as the FLN.

"Perhaps the most pitiful are the *harkis*—the Arab military who have remained loyal to France. They, of course, are seen as traitors to their country by the FLN, which takes great delight in slitting their throats from ear to ear if they are captured.

"And in the middle of this complicated mess you have a lot of innocent people getting killed. It's the same in every war." His voice betrayed a deep-set bitterness.

"It sounds, as you say, terribly confusing," Gabriella admitted, although she was still thinking of the Huguenots.

They sat for a long time without speaking. Gabriella stared down the Esplanade and pictured the men of yesterday screaming their pain and love to God as they were martyred. She reached up her hand to touch the small cross that hung around her neck beneath her blouse.

M. Hoffmann broke the silence with a question. "Miss Madison, don't you agree that religion brings despair? If there were a God up there, why would He sit silently by while His devoted followers tear each other apart?"

"I believe that God looks after His children," she replied.

"His children! Ha! I love it! Aren't the Jews His children? And didn't your God look after them well as they were marched off to death camps and put in gas chambers? What a great father!" His eyes flashed angrily.

"Tell me about your father, Miss Madison. What is he like?"

Gabriella looked puzzled for a moment, then brightened. "My father is a very kind, wise, and loving man. He gets along great with all kinds of people. He's not pretentious. He's ... he's humble, but smart...."

"Yes, you have a nice father, and so you believe in a nice God—a daddy God. Well, I'm not interested in a God who will be my father. The one I have just about killed me."

"I-I'm sorry. I didn't know you'd had such a terrible experience."

"No, Miss Madison, I'm not interested in your God. David Hoffmann believes only in David Hoffmann." He scowled. Then his face softened, and for a moment he seemed to want desperately for her to understand. "You were raised in a family that believed in an omniscient, loving higher being. It's easy for you to believe as your parents do. You Christians say something is an answer to prayer. I take the same circumstance and say it's coincidence. Prove to me a prayer was answered in your neat little religious way. I'll show you it was not."

Gabriella was silent, contemplating his challenge. Why was this man she barely knew challenging her with such angry intensity? Finally she spoke. "M. Hoffmann, I cannot prove that prayers are answered or that God is above if you do not want to believe it. But that isn't my business anyway. It is God's. He's the one who changes hearts. I dare you to ask *Him* to prove Himself to you."

M. Hoffmann laughed loudly. "Miss Madison, you are rarely at a loss for words, are you?" He reached out and touched her hand.

She met his gaze and pulled her hand away. Ironically she could think of nothing more to say, and so again they sat in silence.

Presently he spoke, "'I will lift up mine eyes unto the hills, from whence cometh my help....'" He continued reciting. "'The Lord shall preserve thy going out and thy coming in from this time forth, and even for evermore.' Aren't you impressed, Miss Madison? I know that psalm and many others by heart. But you will wait a very long time if you hope to hear me claim it as my own prayer."

Gabriella had been put on the defensive long enough. "I thought you asked me here to talk of my life in Senegal, not to criticize my religion," she snapped.

"Forgive me, that was my original intention. It was thinking of the poor Huguenots that got me on another tangent. And now I'm afraid it's time to go back. I wouldn't want your landlady to disapprove." For a moment he seemed genuinely disappointed. "But never mind. We'll be seeing each other often. You'll have plenty of time to tell me all about your life on the Dark Continent." He got to his feet, then took Gabriella's arm to help her up.

She brushed away his hand. "If you don't mind, I think I'll stay here a little longer." With a touch of sarcasm, she added, "And don't worry about my getting home. I'm a big girl."

He kept his composure. "As you wish. Good afternoon, Miss Madison." He walked across the wide, open square and turned down an adjoining street toward the bus stop.

If he asks me to do something again, I'll say no, she promised herself. But she knew it was a promise she wouldn't keep. The heat of the sun began to fade and shadows spread out along the Comédie, but she did not move from her seat at the café until she was sure that David Hoffmann was a long way away.

Gabriella sat at the small wooden desk in her room, books spread out in front of her. In her mind she saw again David Hoffmann's dark eyes taunting her and heard his voice reciting Psalm 121 with all the conviction of a true believer.

The man was so angry. Still, Gabriella was convinced that there was something more to him, behind his cynical eyes and proud exterior. Something worth discovering.

She imagined again the French Protestants being tortured and killed for their faith, and she pulled the cross out from under her blouse. Holding it gently in her hand, she traced its outline with her fingers. The points of four thick arrows turned inward toward the center, with a *fleur-de-lis* embedded within each corner of the cross. A small dove dangled below the bottom arrow. In Montpellier had lived the people who wore this cross. And wearing it, they had lived and died for their faith.

She opened her Bible and leafed through the pages until she found Psalm 121. In the margin Gabriella had scribbled the words *This is Your promise to me, God*. How ironic that M. Hoffmann had quoted the very psalm she had claimed for herself upon leaving Senegal for France.

She didn't fall asleep until long after the moon had risen to its full height. The warm wind of September teased the olive tree outside her window, causing its leaves to brush against the windowpane and taunt her with a whisper of love and hope.

5

The boat rocked wildly on the waves of the Mediterranean. Dawn had not yet come, and the wind blew cool. Far off, Anne-Marie could see the flickering lights of the shore. Her eyes gazed out from a face swollen and bruised.

"Oh, Ophélie," she murmured. "I'm glad you can't see Mama now. It's better that you think I'm dead. God be with you, Ophélie. The God of Papy be with you!"

The sheets rustled on the bunk above, where Moustafa sat in a crouched position, his head skimming the ceiling of the tiny compartment.

"We'll be there soon." His voice was gruff, and Anne-Marie felt the anger and bitterness in his words. Moustafa would not help her now. He had been beaten into submission. He was theirs.

She didn't blame him. It was her life or his. Only for love did one give his life for another, and there was no love in this war. Only wild extremists who sacrificed everything for the cause of independence. And a crazy man who sought a terrifying revenge.

What had happened to the Algeria she had known and loved? The joyful days of her childhood when she played in the street with friends, French and Algerian, Muslim and Catholic, Protestant and Jew, now seemed like a dream.

"Get up, Anne-Marie! We're going to debark." Moustafa climbed down the ladder and waited for her to rise.

She stood shakily and for a moment thought she would faint,

but Moustafa's hand steadied her and firmly led her through the door and down the dark corridor. Ali and Rachid waited impatiently by the door.

"Here, put this on," Ali hissed, thrusting a white lace scarf into her hands. "Welcome home, little tramp!" He pushed her forward toward the railing as the boat lurched and made its way into the port.

Anne-Marie stepped from the crowded bus into the streets of Algiers. Before her loomed rows and rows of buildings stacked up like a deck of cards on a hill. No one needed to tell her where she was; they were entering the Casbah. This was the old part of the city, named for the Turkish-built sixteenth-century fortress that dominated the quarter. It was also the headquarters for the FLN.

They walked past stalls where merchants were selling fruits, vegetables, and other wares in front of a row of low arches. Anne-Marie pulled the scarf tightly around her face so that only her eyes were visible. It was a death sentence for a pied-noir to be spotted in this neighborhood. Even in France she had heard of the young pied-noir girl raped and beaten to death here a few months earlier.

Keep walking or they will kill you right here, she told herself. Her skin was not as dark as that of the Algerians, but her black hair and dark eyes and the traditional Algerian scarf covering her face helped to conceal her identity.

Moustafa was by her side, pushing her along in front of Ali and Rachid. They started up the hill toward the mountain of apartments that stretched out before them in haphazard fashion. It was true what people said: the Casbah was a labyrinth. Once you were inside, it was impossible to find the way out unless you lived there.

Anne-Marie wished desperately for a drink of water, but she dared not ask. The sound of her dry cough echoed again and again as they continued up the road. She glanced over at Moustafa and pitied him. Her danger in the Casbah was great, but what about his? He was twice a traitor, and nowhere would be safe for him. Yet he didn't look afraid. His face was set in determination and hate—so different from the face of the trusted friend she had known almost all her life.

Just eight months earlier she and Ophélie had crossed the Mediterranean with him, escaping from Algeria. A pied-noir woman, her fatherless child, and the son of a harki. *Harki!* It was an explosive word in these days of war.

Moustafa had come to her, eyes wide with fear. "The FLN killed my father, Anne-Marie. They slit his throat. I must leave or they'll kill me. You must go too. It's much too dangerous for Ophélie … and for you."

She had known he was right. Life in Algeria was dangerous enough for a son of a harki and a pied-noir who at one time had given information to the FLN. If only their crime stopped there. But it was much worse. So they had fled from their homeland in the middle of a bitter night in January in search of safety in France.

"In here." Ali's voice interrupted her thoughts. "This is where you'll stay."

Rachid shoved Anne-Marie into the darkness of a drab cement building, and Moustafa followed.

"Touching, isn't it, to see these friends reunited in their lovely Algeria," Ali crooned. He entered the dark room and grabbed

Moustafa's shirt, pulling him around. "Explain the rules to her carefully. Remind her what happens to beautiful women who do not
talk! To disgusting pied-noir trash! Though I would be surprised if
she has forgotten so soon." He pushed Moustafa back into the darkness. "We'll be back shortly."

Ali and Rachid left. Anne-Marie, sobbing, felt about in the
blackness and found a chair.

Moustafa paced back and forth in the small room. "Stop crying!"
he whispered angrily. "I can't think if you cry."

She turned toward him. "You won't betray Ophélie, Moustafa?"

"You are foolish, Anne-Marie. They'll find Ophélie and bring
her back here with the information. There is hope that you may both
live, if you will only talk. Otherwise you will die. And they'll still find
Ophélie, and it will be much worse for her."

Anne-Marie held her head in her hands. She didn't believe him.
She felt certain that he too would be eliminated as soon as Ali had
gotten all the information he wanted.

At least by now M. Gady had the little blue bag, and Ophélie
was safe, hidden away. All Anne-Marie had to do was reveal a part of
the truth. They would go to M. Gady's shop and search, but no one
would be there.

She turned to Moustafa, a hopeful tone in her voice. "Don't
worry, Moustafa. I'll talk." But in spite of her resolve, she touched
the tiny bottle sewn into her sleeve and smiled to herself. Ophélie
would be safe.

Ophélie sat on a mattress in the upstairs office of M. Gady's shop. She could hear the old man breathing deeply in the bedroom next door. She was glad he was asleep. Twice that day he had questioned her.

"You are sure you have nothing for me, little one? Nothing from your mother?"

Each time Ophélie had shaken her head. How could she trust him? There was no one to trust.

The old man had looked disappointed and concerned. He had hovered by the radio all day, cursing and repeating, "Crazy war, crazy war."

Now, in the quiet of night, Ophélie carefully switched on the desk lamp and again emptied out the contents of the blue bag. The cross fell lightly onto the desk, along with a worn photograph and two small sealed envelopes. On one envelope was a simple word written in Mama's hand. She knew what it said. *Ophélie.* Silently she unsealed the envelope and spread out the letter before her.

Three pink pages written in Mama's smooth script. At the top of the first page she again read her name. She turned to the last piece of paper and saw the word *Mama.* These two words she knew. But the rest of the letter was a mysterious blend of lines falling up and down.

How could she ever know what Mama wished to tell her if she couldn't read? She began to cry. She couldn't tell M. Gady. *Please don't be mad, Mama, but I cannot give him the bag.*

She reached for the cross and slipped it around her neck and fastened it in the back. Mama had said the cross was good luck. Ophélie would wear it, and then Grandpapy's God would bring her good luck. She put the letter and the other envelope back into the sack, pausing only to look at a small photo of Mama holding her in her arms. "Please, Mama, don't die. I'll learn how to read, and then I'll know. Wait for me, Mama, wherever you are."

Rachid El Drissi watched from his window as Ali approached his apartment, walking easily through the maze of buildings in the Casbah. The night was black, but Rachid knew that Ali could find his way through this neighborhood blindfolded. Ali slipped onto the outside stairwell and climbed it, crouching like a cat ready to pounce on an unsuspecting sparrow. On the second floor he stepped through the window and pulled it closed behind him. The September air was heavy, suffocating, even at this late hour. Soundlessly he switched on the light, nodded to Rachid, and seated himself at an old, worn desk. He took out a manila folder.

"It must be done on Tuesday night. Look." Ali put his finger on a hand-sketched map of several areas of Algiers. "Monoprix is here at the corner of the road."

Rachid nodded. Everyone knew where the large department store was located.

"The bomb must go off here." Ali drew a red circle around the street that ran in front of the store. "Everyone will be asleep, but word will travel quickly nonetheless. They will panic and run, and then *boom*!" He laughed. "It will be very convincing, yes?"

Again Rachid nodded, the sleepiness gone from his eyes. Tuesday he would test another of his little bombs. Small but effective. "Don't worry, Ali. It's no trouble."

Ali turned to leave. As he closed the window behind him, Rachid brushed his fingers through his coarse hair and chuckled softly to himself. "Boom," he whispered.

6

A lone swallow flew low to the ground outside Mme Leclerc's apartment. From her second-story window, Gabriella watched as other birds joined their companion in weaving up into the air and swooping down to almost touch the ground. She thought of the French proverb she had learned in her childhood in Senegal: There's sure to be rain if the swallow flies low. But she wished the rain would not come today.

David Hoffmann had asked her to join him for a picnic on the beach, with perhaps a ride on horseback through the marshes afterward. "The Camargue ponies are sturdy and sure-footed, even if you've never been on a horse," he had said.

Gabriella had not mentioned that she once had a horse in West Africa; she only replied that she would go. She wanted to refuse, after their miserable afternoon on the Comédie, but she couldn't. She felt drawn to him, as if he somehow needed her. "But I will watch what I say," she told herself.

In spite of the ominous rumbling of clouds in a darkening sky, at precisely eleven the doorbell rang. The eager Mme Leclerc buzzed in their visitor, and Gabriella joined her teacher at the front door.

"*Enchanté, Mademoiselle Madison*," he greeted her. Moments later he was hurrying her along the cobblestones to his car, an old pale blue *deux chevaux* that, he told her, did fine on flat ground but could not climb a hill. If he was aware that his every movement was being observed, he gave no hint of it to the three women watching from the boarding-house windows upstairs.

The sun poked its face through the disturbing gray clouds as M. Hoffmann spread out an old blanket on the sand and motioned for Gabriella to sit down. He placed a basket beside him and took out sandwiches, cheese, fruit, fresh vegetables drenched in vinaigrette, and a bottle of red wine.

"I wish you would have let me fix something, M. Hoffmann," Gabriella said.

"Don't think that I am the preparer of such a feast. Mme Pons, with whom I board, is determined to marry me off and insists on fixing everything *comme il faut* for a proper picnic. Can't beat a ham and Emmental cheese on a French baguette."

He opened the wine and set the bottle in the sand. "And please, call me David ... outside of class."

For a moment he stared so intently into her blue eyes that Gabriella wondered what he was trying to see. She blushed and turned her head quickly away to gaze out on the Mediterranean.

"But I don't want to talk about myself today. I want to hear about you. It must be quite a shock to find yourself among these prim and proper socialites after being raised among the savages."

Gabriella gasped and turned toward him, anger and indignation sparkling in her eyes. "How dare you—" she began fiercely, only to stop when she saw the amusement on his face.

"I'm sorry, Miss Madison. I just can't resist getting a reaction whenever possible. I'm glad to see the missionary has a bit of fire in her character!"

Gabriella did not mean to start crying; it just happened. Tears burned her face as she stood and glared at him. "Why did you invite me out today? Didn't you criticize me enough on the Comédie? If you're just going to make fun of me, I'd rather go back to Mme Leclerc's. Right now!" And after a moment's silence she added, "Please."

David's strong hand found hers and led her back down.

"Forgive me, Miss Madison," he said, and his voice sounded genuine for the first time. "You're right. It's very rude to invite a girl out and criticize her from the start. It's just my style, you see. Please don't cry." He pulled a clean white handkerchief from the pocket of his khaki pants. "Here. Dry your eyes. And please stay. I can't eat all this food alone, and Mme Pons would be furious to know that I had ruined my chances with yet another lovely lady."

Gabriella wiped her eyes and removed her hand from his grasp. "I'll stay," she stated flatly. "But only for the sake of the food and Mme Pons. And, of course, because I don't want to get on the bad side of my distinguished professor." She was surprised at her own biting tone.

"*Chapeau*, Miss Madison. I stand rebuked. Let's talk about something else. I really would like to know about a young woman who can quote Pope and Donne and who has lived a life so different from that of the other girls at St. Joseph. They only want to talk of shopping and marriage and sex."

Gabriella's eyes met his without blinking. "Trying to get another reaction, *monsieur*?" But this time she was smiling too.

She looked again toward the dark blue of the sea and spoke as if to the rolling waves that lapped upon the fine, dusty sand. "I loved my life in Senegal. My parents moved there years ago, before I was even a thought. They gave up a lot of luxuries like modern transportation, a life free from malaria, because they believed in what they were doing.

"I grew up with the nationals and felt quite at home as the only white-skinned child, besides my sisters. I learned several tribal languages because we moved four different times. And I learned French, the trade language." Gabriella's voice grew vibrant as she spoke about the life she had left only a month earlier.

"I had a small mare. I loved galloping down the beach on her. We could ride for hours without meeting another soul. And always, when we turned around to ride back home, the hoofprints were gone, washed away like a forgotten memory. When I told my father this one day, he made a lesson of it. He said, 'There are some footprints that never disappear. You must leave footprints that are worthy of being followed.'

"I often think of Daddy's words, because I'm not sure anybody would want to follow in my steps."

David was staring at her with the same fixed gaze that had caused her to feel uncomfortable when they had first arrived at the beach. But now she understood what she read in his eyes. It was admiration.

He leaned forward, almost touching her hands with his, and asked, "What do your friends call you, Miss Madison?"

Instinctively she shifted her weight back, away from him. "I'm always introduced as Gabriella. I love long names, and I don't want to give mine up. But friends can call me whatever they want. That's the privilege of friendship, isn't it?"

"Then, if we can be friends, I shall call you Gabby."

David swallowed the last sip of wine in his glass. "You are sure you don't want any?"

"No, thank you, really. I'm not used to wine. I don't like the way it makes me feel." She raised her eyebrows and waited for his reaction.

He laughed. "Ah, Gabby. Did your mother warn you of what dashing young intellectuals might try to do to a beautiful idealist when she came to France? You are right to be on your guard."

"I have a question for you, the wise teacher."

"I can't wait to hear it." He scooted closer and stretched out his long frame on the blanket, resting his chin in his hands. He looked up at her, squinting at the sun behind her head. "From this position I have the feeling that I'm in the presence of an angel. Your hair is magnificent." He paused, then said softly, "You are magnificent."

"Please don't, David," she replied, hesitantly using his given name. "I know your game. You're afraid of my question, so you're trying to divert my attention by embarrassing me. Well, it won't work. So tell me this … you admire the poets who had such great faith, like Pope and Donne and Herrick. How can you admire their work and yet deny their God?"

David was sifting sand through his fingers and didn't answer immediately. "I have a question for you. How can you admire a 'wise teacher' and yet deny his advances?"

He reached toward her playfully, but she turned away, disappointed.

The clouds had returned. Gabriella stood up and said, "It's time to go home."

"It is indeed. We'll save the Camargue ponies for another day."

Quickly they filled the picnic basket with leftovers as the sky grumbled impatiently. Heavy drops of rain began to fall, and David took Gabriella's arm and hurried her up the beach until they passed the dunes and came to the road where the deux chevaux was parked. By the time they reached the car, they were drenched.

David laughed, holding his arms out to catch the rain. "Isn't it wonderful!"

Gabriella smiled and brushed the rain off her face as she climbed into the car. Her hair clung to her like a mass of wet noodles. "I'm afraid your poor car is in for a treat."

"Never mind. This old beater has seen worse."

Gabriella did not speak on the way home, but she counted the rushing beat of her heart and wished with all her might that she were safe in her small room behind a closed door where David Hoffmann could not read her tumultuous thoughts.

The rain had stopped, and the air was muggy and thick and still unbearably hot. Beads of perspiration ran down David's face. He studied the hand-drawn map that had arrived in the mail and cursed. "Right in the middle of Aigues-Mortes. Just as he said."

He sat lost in thought for several minutes. What did he feel? The months of planning might at last bring results. Vital results— the kind that could perhaps touch even David Hoffmann's hard heart. Yes, he felt excitement, as well as anger and that old enemy—fear.

He thought of his afternoon on the beach with Gabriella. He truly liked the girl, innocent though she was. *So why am I dragging her into this?* he argued with himself. Of course he could do it alone. Yet he wanted to take her with him.

Slowly he lit a match and held it to the map until the paper disintegrated before him. "May your God be with you, dear Gabriella. You may need Him."

7

Monique Pons brought two cups of steaming coffee into the parlor, where her friend Yvette Leclerc sat at the table perusing a basket full of fruits and vegetables.

"The pears were not a bit pretty today at the *marché*, quite a pity, but the price of tomatoes was down twenty *centimes*! And such tomatoes. The last of the season, to be sure." Yvette accepted the *demitasse* of black coffee with a smile and sat back in her chair. There was nothing better than coffee and a chat at Monique's house. It had been their daily custom for over twenty years. Castelnau was a small town, but there was always news to give and receive.

"He came back from the beach sopping wet, but he was happy," Monique declared. "M. Hoffmann is a strange man. He rarely smiles. But I can tell when he is happy." She leaned forward, her cheeks rosy from the fresh air. "But that afternoon he was all smiles. Gave me a kiss on each cheek, he did, when he came in." She blushed, remembering. "Kissed me, and stood there dripping on my floor. *Ooh là là!*"

What extreme luck, that M. Hoffmann was interested in Yvette's own beautiful American boarder! When this romance blossomed, the two women would practically be related!

"And, Yvette, listen. He said he was so sorry that they hadn't eaten everything, but that they had been so busy talking. You would have thought a bird had been nibbling at my basket. And the wine bottle was still half full. Imagine! He said she didn't drink a drop.

No wine to make the heart gay, and still they talked and talked. It is surely a sign."

Yvette smiled and nodded. "She doesn't touch the wine, that Gabriella. She's an interesting girl. Smart as a whip, I tell you. As smart as that American professeur, I'm sure. But she's different, all right. Not looking for a free party in France with all the wine and … well, you know how the other girls are sometimes."

Their eyes met, and they laughed heartily. Oh, the troubles they'd had with some of these American girls. Oh, the scandals. But always the two aging widows had each other to confide in and commiserate with. In truth, they would admit occasionally, they loved the American girls—and the extra revenue they gave to a widow's pension.

Suddenly Yvette stopped laughing. "But truthfully, I can't imagine what Gabriella is doing with the likes of your M. Hoffmann. He is not her type." She leaned forward and lowered her voice. "You know, she is very religious."

Religion was fine, the women agreed—if it was the Catholic Church and Mass. But this Gabriella was Protestant.

"And not a Protestant like the other Americans I've seen. She reads her Bible! Every day, I think. And once, I caught her praying on her knees! Now what would a girl who prays on her knees see in your cold professeur?"

When they really thought about it, neither Monique nor Yvette could figure out why such a strange but fine young woman had gone to the beach with David Hoffmann.

Mother Griolet's small office was cozy and inviting. The bookshelves were stuffed with antique books in French and English by the saints of old. Gabriella lightly touched the worn volumes of *L'Imitation de Jesus-Christ* and *The Pilgrim's Progress*. Interspersed among the old classics were books on psychology, children, education, and theology. But remembering the reason for her visit, she left the bookshelves and settled into the dark wood chair that sat before Mother Griolet's desk.

The old nun smiled. "Ah, Gabriella Madison. You've grown up to be a very lovely young woman. Your parents must be proud."

Gabriella blushed. "Thank you, Mother Griolet. But I've come to see you about a ... a problem. I mean, it's not really a problem, but a question. Well, it's just an idea, and ... and I'd like your advice."

Mother Griolet waited patiently for Gabriella to explain. "Yes, my child. I'll be happy to help you in any way I can."

"It's about your work. Well, not exactly this work, but ..." She paused awkwardly, then began again. "Have you ever really wanted to do something great—not for yourself, I mean, but something that mattered, that helped others?"

Mother Griolet settled back into her large office chair. Her green eyes twinkled as she considered Gabriella's question. "I suppose when I was your age, I dreamed of doing something great for God and man. We all have dreams. And sometimes the dreams are selfless and good."

"Yes. I mean, I know some of my thoughts are wrong," Gabriella said. "I just wish I knew for certain what I should do with my life. Mother and Father were so sure that God had called them to Africa, and they were no older than I am. But I'm not even sure where I belong. Is Africa home? Is America? I barely know America. Or perhaps it doesn't matter."

"Dear child, you are wondering what the future holds. I wondered too at twenty-one. But I already had my orders as a nun. My friends were all getting married. They thought I was quite strange and devout."

"And didn't you want to marry, have a family?"

"How can I explain?" She rested her arms on the desk, fingers intertwined. "It was not so much that I didn't want a husband or a family as that I had the conviction that I must do something else. This." Her arm swept around the room. "I chose this life, and it didn't seem heavy or full of sacrifices at the time, because I loved what I did. I loved teaching the children. We had just come out of the Great War, and there were so many orphans. So we started a school and orphanage right here. I didn't have time to worry about a family."

"And that was enough? You never wanted to do something else? A higher position? A different town?"

"There were opportunities to leave Castelnau for something that sounded better. But I could not. God was working here. And of course, when the Second World War came and France fell in 1940, we had even more orphans. And we hid many Jewish children."

Gabriella was impressed. "It must have felt good to be helping like that. I mean ... it was dangerous."

"We each did our part. We weren't looking for honors. Just survival. I do not take sides in war. In the end, nobody wins. I prayed, and God showed me whom to help. By God's grace some children survived who would not have otherwise. I keep in touch with many.

You see, I do have a large family." She nodded to the far wall, which was covered with photographs of children.

"And how did you know all this was from God?"

"God is always at work around us, child. You have doubtless seen that in Senegal. Now the question is, will I join Him or will I ask Him to join me? One way works, the other does not. I found out long ago, the hard way, that God did not need my lofty plans. His are much better."

She paused for a moment, lost in some memory, and Gabriella regarded her with amazement. This woman over seventy had such a zest for life, such a sparkle and assurance. And a faith that was real. Without thinking, Gabriella blurted out, "And did you always agree with the Catholic Church?"

Again the elderly woman smiled. "I think I should rather say that they did not always agree with me. I seemed to be running ahead of them and teaching things that got me in all sorts of trouble. And kept me right here in lowly Castelnau." Another mischievous grin. "I knew I was obeying the Master, and I got my marching orders from His book. Ah well, it is not up to me to judge. Have you noticed that it is usually easier to judge than obey? Religious people are especially good at it. I tried not to get caught up in that destructive little game. God works. I obey. Not an easy life, Gabriella." She looked the young woman full in the face. "It is never easy to take orders from Him, but I can assure you, I have never been bored."

Gabriella contemplated Mother Griolet's words. "Mother says the same thing about her life. It's true. Our days were full and hard and exciting … and terribly painful …" She let her phrase dangle, and Mother Griolet nodded, understanding. "But if only I knew that being here was right and how I could help. I see you with the orphans, and I feel like that is what I want to do. Pour my life into children who have no life. To give them a future and a hope, as the verse says in Jeremiah." Now Gabriella's eyes were dancing, and an enthusiasm filled her voice. "I'm not good at much, but I am good with children. I've taught lots of things in Africa—Sunday school and crafts and sports and—"

"Gabriella, are you asking if you can help me with the orphans? Is that your question?" The nun seemed amused. "Because, my child, I will certainly not say no to that."

"Really, Mother Griolet? When may I start?"

"Come to the parsonage basement after your last class tomorrow," Mother Griolet said, "and I'll introduce you to the children."

By the end of the next afternoon Gabriella knew almost every child's name. She was winded after their game of *un, deux, trois soleil* in the church's garden. Now she took the chubby hand of little Christophe. Barely four, he was the youngest at the orphanage. He had bright-blue eyes and round rosy cheeks that gave him the appearance of a little cherub.

His six-year-old brother, André, came beside Gabriella on the other side. He was tall and thin for his age, a sharp contrast to his pudgy little brother. André said nothing but stared at Gabriella, his hazel eyes surrounded by long, delicate brown lashes. In their eyes Gabriella saw that these brothers, in fact all of the children, knew hurt and solitude, a painful wisdom beyond their years. But also a hope and longing that maybe, just maybe, this new *maîtresse* would have enough love to soothe their hurting hearts, like a lullaby before bedtime.

The story of the bombing in the street beside Monoprix made the front page of every Algerian newspaper. Seven Killed in Midnight Madness, the caption read. This time the victims were all pied-noirs, although the previous bomb had killed two Algerians. The nationality did not matter to the FLN. Their point was well taken: Watch out. No one is safe. And underneath the terror, whispering in the night to all those who still favored a French Algeria, was the veiled threat: *Get out while you can, or it will be too late.*

Ali was pleased with the front-page report. "Good work, Rachid. With results like this, you will soon have more important jobs. Perhaps a position in the new government! Independence is not far away, I tell you. Algeria will be free! The senseless pied-noirs will see soon enough what their holy General de Gaulle meant when he said, 'I understand you!'" He laughed dryly. "He meant he understands *us*! He understands that it is hopeless for the French. They can never win this war. Give up! We will be free!"

Rachid regarded his crazed leader with fear and admiration. It was true, he felt sure. The war that had already cost hundreds of thousands of lives and dragged on for seven years was nearing its end. But the death toll would surely climb, faster and faster, like a man escaping a fire only to find that the ladder led him nowhere except to thicker smoke and death itself.

The French had their own group of extremists who launched a campaign of counterterrorism against the FLN and their own French authorities. The brutality of the French OAS matched in every way the cruel schemes of the FLN. Rachid smiled at Ali. The end was in sight, but the war was just heating up.

"Anne-Marie has talked?" Rachid questioned, hoping that he would soon have an opportunity to use his vivid imagination to eliminate this woman and her harki friend.

Ali shook his head. "No. There has been more important business to handle. It is satisfying enough to see them huddle in fear in that stinking room every time we enter. But don't worry; their end will come soon enough. And the child will be found. We have someone watching. His eyes are very good."

Anne-Marie listened from her seat on the floor as Moustafa described the Monoprix bombing.

"Half the block was destroyed. Three women and four children dead. Several men are missing. All pied-noir."

"Of course. I know the neighborhood well." She sighed. "What is the point of so many innocent deaths?"

"The point is fear, Anne-Marie. Fear. So they will all pack up and leave just as we did. Ironic that we are back where we started from. Only worse off."

"We'll never be free of them, will we, Moustafa?"

He looked away. "No. They're convinced you have more information. Or that we both know about the little operation in the south of France." He met her eyes.

"Yes, we know. But only the names of the harki children leaving. Thank goodness I cannot tell anything else. Ophélie is surely gone from M. Gady's shop, and I have no idea where the bag is now."

"We must escape. They'll kill us soon, or worse ..." His eyes were tender again.

Anne-Marie knew what *worse* meant. She looked down. "They will not torture me, Moustafa. Not like before. They will not have me." She shuddered, remembering the night five years ago when they had come to take her. Seven Arab men. In the end, Jean-Claude had saved her from being killed. How was she to know that he worked for them too? How was she to know what he could do to a beautiful pied-noir girl who helped the French army?

"We were so foolish, you and I," she said. "We thought Algeria would stay French. We thought it would never change."

"You tried to help, Anne-Marie. You did what you thought was right. The pied-noir and harki children must flee to France. Ali's war is not only Algeria's war. He murders for pleasure and revenge. And we are in the way."

After a moment, Anne-Marie pulled out the little bottle inside her sleeve. "I have two. Cyanide. If we die now—"

Moustafa turned away. "Suicide! Your religion does not permit it, nor does mine! It's wrong, Anne-Marie."

"You know that I have no religion, Moustafa. My father was Protestant, my mother Catholic, but I follow neither. The church will not have a stained woman. A woman with a child and no husband. A woman who has slept with the enemy to save her skin. A woman who is pied-noir and has betrayed her heritage. My sins are too many for the church and its God. I'm not ashamed of suicide. Ophélie will have a different life. I'll save her by dying before they force me to talk."

"No!" Moustafa grasped her shoulders. "Not yet, Anne-Marie. Our fathers died at the hands of a murderer. Their blood runs in the trenches. Perhaps mine will too. But we cannot be cowards. I will die fighting, not by my own hand. Give me another day. Another day to live. For both of us to live." He held her in his arms, and she wept.

Jean-Claude Gachon stepped off the train in the small town of Aigues-Mortes, his muscular frame rippling underneath the deep-green shirt he had chosen that morning. The color brought out the intensity of his hazel eyes. His thick brown hair touched the shirt's collar.

The scent of seaweed and fish greeted him as he walked along the platform and out into the late-September morning sun. He stared across a canal to the stone tower rising imposingly before him, then walked toward the entrance to the fortified city. The surrounding stone wall, with its towers and drawbridge, made the city look like it belonged in a fairy tale. But Jean-Claude was no stranger to the history of his country, and he knew this city had existed long before the Grimm brothers penned their first story.

He walked briskly across a bridge and made his way through the city gates. In his pocket was a scrap of paper on which a picture of a cross was crudely scribbled—a strange cross, with a dove dangling from the tip. Underneath, written in a hurried manner, were the words *Found on body. What does it have to do with the operation? Something is going on in Aigues-Mortes on the 30th, according to our friend Moustafa. Find out what it is.*

As a *porteur de valise*, Jean-Claude had been working clandestinely for the FLN since the war began. There were many other French who, like him, supported the Algerians' desire for independence, giving their time, money, and brains to the cause. That was how he had met Ali, the brilliant, driven military man with a personal mission that intrigued Jean-Claude. It was a violent plan, and it paid well.

Jean-Claude pulled out the slip of paper and stared at it. So Ali was searching for crosses now. In his four years of working with this madman, Jean-Claude had never had such an easy assignment. He knew all about the Huguenot cross. He remembered seeing one sparkling around Anne-Marie's neck every night when she had lain close to him. And he could recall her words. *It was my father's. He was a Protestant, a descendant of the Huguenots. He told me how their pastors were tortured and killed and the women imprisoned in a tower in Aigues-Mortes....*

If something was happening in Aigues-Mortes today, Jean-Claude knew just where to look. He walked confidently into the bustling early-morning marché. At last, another assignment to keep him busy on this side of the Mediterranean until he could cross the sea and celebrate Algeria's victory with his friends.

"You see, Gabby, it's not a long drive at all," David remarked as his deux chevaux rumbled down the road past a small marker that read AIGUES-MORTES 5 KM.

"This is real swampland around here," she mused, observing the white gulls flying en masse toward the open sea far in the distance.

"Yes, well, we've followed the Mediterranean since we left Montpellier twenty minutes ago. You know what *Aigues-Mortes* means, don't you?"

"Dead waters?"

"Exactly. It's totally surrounded by lagoons. Saint Louis, France's crusading king, built it in the thirteenth century, making this a port and hoping to attract trade. After his death, his son Philippe the Bold built the walls—you'll see them in a minute. The Tower of Constance is nearly a hundred feet high and has walls twenty feet thick."

Gabriella gasped as the perfect walled city with the massive tower he had just described came into view, rising like a mirage on the flat horizon. "It's like something out of a storybook!"

David agreed. "It's one of the most handsome and well-preserved monuments from the Middle Ages. The tower is where the Huguenot women were imprisoned. Let's park the car and have a look around."

David found a parking spot just outside the city walls. They got out of the car and walked past the vendors selling their wares.

"Saturday morning is always busy. But the city is nothing of what it was back in the Middle Ages. Fifteen thousand inhabitants then, and a mere four thousand now. Marseille, of course, became France's great port, and the silt from the Rhône River eventually cut off access to Aigues-Mortes."

David took Gabriella's arm and guided her through the heavy wooden doors into the cobblestone streets. "We enter here by the Porte de la Gardette." He looked at his watch. "It's eleven now. You'll have plenty of time to visit the tower and walk on the ramparts before lunch." He grinned. "But be careful. The ramparts aren't protected. Don't slip off into some squire's home."

"You aren't coming with me?"

"After a while, even the most fascinating history loses its luster. I've been here five times and been through the tower and ramparts every time. You run on and enjoy. I'll meet you at the main gate in an hour. No, let's make it twelve thirty. Ah, but we should get the bread first. The boulangeries all close at noon. Here—" He put ten francs in her hand. "Get a *baguette* and a *ficelle*. Do you mind? There's a good little store with a green-and-white awning on the next road. I'll slip out to the marché and get us some fruit and cheese. What will you have?"

"A pear, please," she said, "and some Morbier. I'll see you back here in a sec."

Gabriella turned down the side street David had indicated and easily found the shop with its awning and the delicious smells escaping from its door. She slipped inside and waited behind two customers.

"*Bonjour, mademoiselle*," the hearty baker greeted her when her turn came.

"*Bonjour.* Yes, I'd like a baguette and, and a ... now what did he say? Oh yes, a ficelle! Yes, that's it."

The baker, dusted in flour, reached behind him to where loaves upon loaves of bread in all shapes and sizes stood lined neatly in wire racks. He retrieved an especially long and narrow one and placed it on the counter. "A ficelle, you said?" His heavy eyebrows rose.

Gabriella blushed. "Yes, a ficelle. And a baguette."

"You are sure?"

"Yes, quite." She placed the ten francs on the counter and waited for the change before picking up the loaves of bread, which the baker had wrapped together around the middle with a thin piece of tissue.

Moments later she and David met in the open square and compared their purchases.

"Well done, Gabby! Enjoy yourself, and when you return, I'll have the most delicious sandwich that your mouth has ever tasted waiting for you."

Gabriella walked across the drawbridge, which had once obviously led over a moat, and passed through the heavy gates of the tower. The main floor was empty except for a young man in a dark-green shirt. He stood in the center of the circular room looking up at the vaulted ceiling. Reading from her guidebook, Gabriella walked around the room and felt the cool stones. *A prison.*

She found some spiraling, narrow stone stairs and made her way up, letting her imagination take her back several centuries. The second floor was where the female prisoners were kept. In the medical school in Montpellier she'd seen a painting of the women huddling together on the tower roof, but standing here, it all seemed more real.

The room looked like an exact replica of the one below. In the middle of the floor was a round opening covered with steel grating. She sat down on a curb of raised stones surrounding the hole and ran her fingers along the top of the curb, noticing what seemed to be writing on one stone.

She let out a small cry. This was it! This was where Marie Durand had scratched the famous word with her fingernail in the stone: *Résistez.* Don't give up, hang on, endure to the end! Taken prisoner when she was nineteen years old, she lived in this tower for thirty-seven years, standing firm in her faith and encouraging the other women to do the same. Gabriella sat in awe. Marie Durand couldn't have imagined that her single word in a stone would outlive the cruelty of the kings who tortured and killed their subjects in Aigues-Mortes.

After a while Gabriella looked up and saw an old worn banner hanging against the rounded wall. In the center of the banner was the Huguenot cross. Instinctively she moved near it, pulling her own cross out from under her blouse and holding it delicately in her hand to inspect it.

It was the same, the thick sides of the cross turning inward like four arrows pointing to the center of a target. In between, touching the sides of the arrows, was a fleur-de-lis, the symbol of royalty. A dove hung from the southernmost arrow.

So engrossed was Gabriella in her thoughts that she didn't notice the young Frenchman until he stood inches behind her, peering over her shoulder at the cross in her hand.

"Interesting," he whispered in French.

Gabriella turned and let out a sharp cry. "Oh! You frightened me!" she said. "Excuse me, I shouldn't have screamed."

"On the contrary, *mademoiselle*, it is I who need to ask your pardon. I thought you heard me come up." They stood for a moment in awkward silence until the young man ventured, "I couldn't help but notice that you wear the same cross as the one on the banner. Such an unusual design. What does it mean?"

"Oh, yes ... it's the Huguenot cross." She talked quickly to cover her embarrassment. "Do you know the history of the Huguenots? They were hunted down and killed or imprisoned here in this tower after the revocation of the Edict of Nantes in 1685."

"Yes, of course. When our king decided everyone should be Catholic. But these Huguenots, what did they believe? Do you know, *mademoiselle*?"

"I don't have all the answers, but I know they believed much the same as the Protestants of today. They were followers of Calvin and the Reformation. They believed in Jesus and the Bible."

"*Mais, oui!* I see. And you have come from far away to visit this tower? A pilgrimage for your faith?"

"Oh, not so far. I just came over for the day from Montpellier. I mean, that's not where I'm from originally.... I'm just studying there."

"Then why do you wear this cross, if I may ask?"

Gabriella looked surprised. "Me? It was a gift from my mother. We're Protestants, and I suppose she knew of its history and wanted me to understand its symbolism."

The young man moved closer. "It is symbolic of what? Forgive me, but could I see your cross?"

Gabriella suddenly felt uneasy and stepped back, tripping on an uneven stone. "Oh, it's just the same as the one on the banner. Nothing unusual. I ... I must be going now."

She shifted her weight and walked toward the steps, but he caught her arm. "Please, *mademoiselle*. I only wish to know a few things about this history. Perhaps we could have lunch together? My treat."

"Oh, no. That is quite impossible, thank you. I have a friend waiting for me for lunch."

"This friend did not wish to visit the tower?"

"No, I'm afraid he doesn't have much interest in Protestants and Huguenot crosses." She laughed nervously, feeling, as she often did, that she had said too much. Another flirtatious Frenchman.

"Well, I think I will have a look around upstairs on the terrace—it gives a magnificent view of the village, I'm told. You're sure
you won't join me?" He moved toward her again.

"No, I need to be going now." Gabriella turned and walked
quickly down the winding stairs until she came to the large room
on the ground floor. She paused to listen for the young man, but he
did not follow. Again she touched the cross around her neck, then
carefully placed it back under her blouse.

She glanced at her watch. Eleven thirty. She still had plenty of
time to visit the ramparts. As she stepped across the drawbridge, she
turned to her right where a sign indicated the way. Several flights of
stone steps, worn lower in the middle through centuries of use, led to
the impressive walls of the city. She climbed the stairs until she stood
on the narrow walkway at the top of the wall. To her right she saw
a canal filled with fishing boats and happy sailors. The canal twisted
its way out to the Mediterranean Sea, barely visible on the horizon.
She stared for a moment at the quiet marshes and the white gulls that
flew toward the sun in search of an unknown destination.

The walkway along the wall was interspersed with many thick
towers, much smaller in size than the Tower of Constance. Gabriella
walked along, enchanted as she looked to her left into the interior
of the city. From the ramparts she had a bird's-eye view of the town
and its red-tiled roofs, which protected the streets from the sun like a
large sombrero. Occasionally the roofs would open to reveal a beautiful garden, perfectly manicured, with geraniums cascading down the
walls of a house. Olive, cedar, and magnolia trees rustled their leaves
to applaud an ancient city constructed with the same elaborate planning as the yards in which they stood.

Taken by the scenery, Gabriella barely noticed that she had already walked almost a third of the way around the ramparts. She stopped to peek inside a small vaulted room containing an ancient fireplace and three windows that gave a view onto the marshes and the water. She gathered her skirt under her and perched by a small open window to read more about the history of the city.

From the terrace above the Salle des Chevaliers, Jean-Claude Gachon could see for miles in every direction. A small plastic map erected for tourists indicated that Paris was eight hundred kilometers to the north and the great port of Marseille only a little over an hour to the east. Jean-Claude smiled. What luck to have met the red-haired beauty downstairs. And wearing the same cross! Surely it was not a coincidence.

He walked beside the turret to look down and out to the south and the sea. And eight hundred kilometers in that direction, if he looked with his imagination, he could see the city of Algiers and the fighting men and the explosions and the bodies. Algeria was where the action was ... and Jean-Claude wanted to be in the middle of it.

Still looking south, he had a complete view of the walled city that spread out below him like a huge parallelogram enclosing neat lines of streets and buildings. He reached into his leather shoulder bag and pulled out a small pair of binoculars. Putting them to his eyes, he let his gaze travel across the rooftops that baked in an undulating pattern in the warm sun. A few haphazard antennae thrust skinny arms to the sky, testimony to modern technology. An old man in a *casquette* knelt on a roof, repairing a broken tile. A red-haired girl on the ramparts climbed the stairs and disappeared into one of the towers in the wall—

The girl! So she *was* out on the ramparts. He laughed again at his good luck. And there was no way for her to escape. She must either retrace her steps or continue around the walls. Either way, he had plenty of time to reach her. Perhaps a subtle warning would do. Yes, Ali would appreciate that. A subtle warning to the girl with the flaming hair who wore a Huguenot cross around her neck. Jean-Claude replaced his binoculars in the leather sack and hurried down the winding steps.

It took him no more than five minutes to reach the tower where he had seen the girl disappear. The room was empty, but he was sure she had not come back out onto the ramparts. Then he saw a small staircase winding upward. He moved silently up the narrow stairs, placed his bag on a step, tiptoed back down, and waited just outside the room on the ramparts.

Soon he heard the sound of footsteps above him. The girl was skipping down the dark stairwell with ease. Suddenly there was a scream and the sound of falling. Jean-Claude waited a moment longer before coming into the room. The girl lay still at the foot of the stairs. Jean-Claude quickly stooped to retrieve his leather bag before coming to her side. Bending down in the shadows, he feigned concern. "*Mademoiselle*, are you all right? What happened?"

She grimaced as she sat up. "I think I'm okay. I just tripped on something coming down the steps."

Jean-Claude walked over and looked up the stairwell. "These steps are narrow and uneven."

"Yes, I suppose. I thought I stepped on something. You don't see anything?"

"Nothing, *mademoiselle*."

"Well, you're right. It's dark and the steps are uneven. Careless of me."

Jean-Claude helped her to her feet, but as she tried to stand alone, she stumbled and reached out for his arm. "Oh dear, I think I've sprained my ankle."

"Then I will help you back around."

She hobbled next to him as they retraced their steps off the ramparts. "My friend will be here soon," she assured him. "Thank you for helping me."

"It is nothing." He whispered, "You must be careful, *mademoiselle*. Huguenot crosses seem to bring bad luck to those who wear them."

He disappeared down a side street, grinning to himself. Nothing, indeed. A small accident. But there would be others.

David found Gabriella sitting on a step beside the entrance to the city. "There you are, Gabby! I was beginning to get worried. Thought you might have fallen off the ramparts."

She squinted, looking up at him. "Don't joke, please. I've done something nearly as stupid. I think I sprained my ankle."

David bent down and inspected her swollen leg. "Oh, Gabby, I'm sorry. What happened?"

"I'm just clumsy. I was walking on the ramparts and went into one of those towers over there." She pointed. "There was a neat little terrace up above, with a beautiful view of the Mediterranean. But the steps are narrow and uneven, and it's pitch-dark, and coming back down, I tripped and fell. If it hadn't been for that nice young Frenchman, I don't think I would have made it back."

"A young Frenchman? He was with you?"

Gabriella laughed. "No. I met him in the tower. Actually I thought he was trying to pick me up. He asked lots of questions. Anyway, I left to walk on the ramparts, and he must have come out there a little later, because he heard me scream and came to see if I was hurt. He brought me here, but I had to assure him I had a friend who would take care of me or he would have carried me off with him, I'm quite sure."

"I can imagine." He didn't question her further. "Here, let me help you up. You'll need some ice on that ankle. We'll just have to enjoy the sandwiches in the car."

"I'm so sorry for my bumbling. We can still picnic if you wish." But she winced as she stood up.

Impulsively David picked her up in his arms and carried her back to the car, in spite of her embarrassed protest.

He didn't talk much on the way home. He thought about the young Frenchman and the pretty redhead and the information tucked in the pocket of his leather jacket. It had turned out to be a very interesting day after all.

Gabriella sat on her bed, holding a pack of ice on her swollen ankle. Ice on the ankle! How Mme Leclerc had balked at the idea. And where would they get ice in this heat? But she had placed some water in the tiny freezer that hung inside the refrigerator and they had made a pack. Now she stood over Gabriella like a conscientious nursemaid.

"*Ooh là là. Ma pauvre petite fille!* Such a pity, this accident."

Gabriella tried to sound cheery. "I'll be fine. I promise."

After several more ooh là làs, the landlady left Gabriella alone with her thoughts. And they were black. It did not happen often, but when the dark mood came, she could not push it away.

She was angry that David had not been more sympathetic. He seemed distant and worried, but not worried for her. She was furious with herself for stumbling down the steps. And she felt uneasy when she thought of the young Frenchman helping her to her feet and whispering that strange comment about Huguenot crosses.

She missed her family. She longed to talk to her mother. The ice pack fell to the floor and slowly melted on the tiles as Gabriella turned over and cried herself to sleep.

9

September had closed its door to let October open its own, and with it the weather in Paris grew cooler. Ophélie stared out the window of M. Gady's apartment. Fall was in the air, and all the other children raced to school, giggling and chasing one another down the narrow streets. But not Ophélie.

"My dear," M. Gady had explained several weeks ago, "it isn't wise right now for you to be at school. Soon things will change. Soon."

But Ophélie knew that things would not change. Mama had promised the same, and yet their life had always been one of flight and fear. Mama called it adventure and tried to help Ophélie be brave. But Ophélie had known. It was not a child's adventure now.

It wasn't fair. She was tired of playing alone. School! First grade! She longed to run to class with the other children, to sit in the old wooden desks and learn to read. She knew she could learn fast, if only someone would help her. She *had* to learn how to read. The blue bag was tucked inside her pillowcase, and the letter in Mama's handwriting lay there, still a mystery.

Ophélie turned away from the window with its picture of happy schoolchildren.

Mama had not let her go to school when they first arrived in France, and the days had grown long for a six-year-old stuck in a tiny apartment with a mother who coughed all the time and looked at her with weak, tired eyes.

"Things will get better, *ma chérie*," Mama had promised.

But they were not better. They were much worse. Why didn't her mother come back? Ophélie hid her face in the pillow to muffle her sobs.

"Ophélie! Ophélie!" M. Gady's loud voice boomed up the stairwell, startling her. Usually she knew when he was coming. He talked in an animated way to all his clients downstairs in the *épicerie*, and she could hear every word. But today she had been crying and hadn't heard his footsteps on the stairs.

She wiped her eyes and came to the door. "*Oui*, M. Gady?"

"Ophélie, come down and see, my child. Mme Soliveau has brought us flowers!"

Slowly Ophélie came down the stairs. Her long brown hair was tousled.

"You are still in your nightgown, little one. You do not feel well?"

Ophélie shook her head but did not look at the old shopkeeper.

"It is the school again, *n'est-ce pas?*"

She nodded.

"I know it's hard for you to stay cooped up with this old man, like a chick with its mother." He reached out a wrinkled hand and placed it under Ophélie's chin, gently pulling her face up until their eyes met. "It's not easy, my child. I am only trying to do what is best." He looked away, then seemed to remember his reason for calling her. "But look. Today we will plant pansies! Mme Soliveau brought them for us to plant in the window boxes and hang on the balcony. Will you help me?"

Ophélie looked at the delicate, velvety flowers. White and bright-yellow, deep violet and amber, with a dark-purple center in each one. "They are pretty." Suddenly she had an idea. She looked up at him hopefully. "I'll help you plant the flowers. But will you help me, M. Gady? Will you help me learn to read?"

M. Gady's face broke into a relieved smile. "Ah, so this is why you miss school so much? Yes, yes, of course. A little girl must know how to read. Then she can travel many places, even if for now she must stay in an ugly apartment with an old man. Yes, I will teach you to read." Then his enthusiasm wavered, and he rubbed his forehead with a gnarled hand. "Hmm. Yes, but I'll have to find the right books. But don't worry. M. Gady has many friends. I'm sure someone will know just the right books for a little girl like you." Again he looked worried. "But no one can know that I am teaching you, that you do not attend the *école primaire*. It shall be our secret, *d'accord?*"

Ophélie nodded vigorously. "*Oh, oui, oui, monsieur!* I will not tell anyone. And may we start today? After we plant the pansies?"

After lunch M. Gady was snoring loudly on the couch in his little *salon*. The store would not open for a while, Ophélie knew. He always closed up, like everyone else in France, so that people could go home and eat lunch. Ophélie was not sure how much time she had, but she tiptoed down the steps.

Today she would slip out the door and go to the meat stand where Moustafa worked. Surely he would know about Mama. And she would be back before the old man opened his eyes or stumbled down the stairs to open the doors to the clients who bustled by, jolly and full after their noon meals.

Emile Torrès walked down the three flights of stairs and stepped into the bright October afternoon. He followed the same narrow streets through the Left Bank that he had walked every day for the previous three weeks. He was not in a hurry.

"Find the girl. She cannot be far away." The instructions from Ali had been simple. So simple to pay the rent on Anne-Marie Duchemin's vacant apartment, to sleep on her sagging bed, and to walk three times a day down the street, past the *boulangerie* to the *tabac*, where he bought a pack of Gitanes and a copy of *Le Monde*. Simple to turn from rue Jacob onto rue de l'Echaudé in the sixth *arrondissement* of Paris and find the meat stand where Moustafa had worked. Simple to wait at the café-bar across the street and read of the world as he puffed a cigarette.

Today the news on the third page brought a smile to Emile's young, hardened face. Seven pied-noirs killed in an explosion outside of Monoprix in the French section of Algiers. That was fine news. Emile relaxed in his chair in the smoky café-bar and watched the people hurrying by. Mostly students at this hour, laughing and hurling insults at one another, munching hot crepes bought from the vendor across the street. Not a bad job, to wait and watch.

A small girl came into view as she hurried into the *boucherie*. Her long brown hair looked unkempt, and she wore a plain blue dress that came above her knees. Emile sat up. He reached for an envelope from inside his jacket and pulled out a small photograph. The same. Ophélie Duchemin had walked into the butcher's store in plain daylight for all the world to see. Emile chuckled as he stood up, folded his newspaper under his arm, and left ten francs on the table beside his empty cup. He put out his cigarette in the ashtray and left the café-bar. So very simple after all.

Ophélie's face was pained as she talked to the heavyset man behind the counter. "You are sure he is not here? I must find Moustafa!" She blinked back tears.

The stocky butcher paused from slicing *Jambon de Paris* for another customer. "I'm sorry, *Mademoiselle Ophélie*, but I haven't seen Moustafa for three weeks. He's taken a long vacation without warning the boss. Not very good etiquette, I would say!"

He chuckled, but Ophélie could see the same worry lines in his face as she had seen in M. Gady's.

He leaned over the glass that enclosed the raw meats and lowered his voice. "Your mama, is she all right? I have not seen her lately either. You both have been sick maybe?"

Ophélie did not want to talk about Mama. Surely he would know she was lying if she said all was well. But she could not think of anything else to say. Her eyes pleaded with him to understand. "We are fine … only … I wanted to talk to Moustafa. I need to see him. Will you tell him that when he comes back?"

"Of course, little Ophélie. I'll tell him. Now you take care of yourself and your mama."

Ophélie left the store before he could question her further. She did not notice the man with the thin mustache who followed her as she ran all the way back to M. Gady's shop, letting the tears fall as she went. She opened the door to the darkened store and closed it quietly behind her. Standing on the chair she had used earlier, she bolted the lock shut. Then she tiptoed back upstairs and passed M. Gady, who continued to snore peacefully.

Once again she buried her head in the pillow and cried. She touched the blue bag and whispered, "Mama. Moustafa is gone, like you. But M. Gady is going to teach me to read."

His class was over for the day at St. Joseph. Jean-Louis Vidal packed up his worn-out briefcase and left the parsonage. He looked older than his fifty-five years, and everyone said it was because of the alcohol. His cheeks were a continuous deep cherry red, with little veins spreading across them like tiny roads on a map. The students whispered about his mismatched clothes with their pre–World War II styles, but he didn't care.

The café-bar at the corner of rue Bastide hadn't changed much in twenty-three years. Jean-Louis knew all the other men who congregated there in the late afternoons. Often, after a refreshing pastis, the men would head to the nearby sand court for an invigorating game of *pétanque*. The physical exercise involved was minimal, but Jean-Louis enjoyed the company.

"*Bonjour, Henri*," he greeted the bartender, who nodded without looking up. A few minutes later, Henri placed a tall glass of pastis diluted in water in front of the teacher. Jean-Louis sipped it thoughtfully. The licorice drink was a specialty of this region. And he for one wanted to be sure that the supply-and-demand curve stayed balanced: an occasional nip of wine in the morning, a half liter of the table *rouge* at lunch, and four glasses of pastis in the afternoon, with some good red wine for supper.

A graying man, thin, with a prominent nose, took a seat at his table. Jean-Louis greeted his friend, Pierre, a boulanger who occasionally slipped away from his bread store in the afternoons, leaving his wife to tend to the customers.

"*B'jour,*" he mumbled, offering his hand. "*Tu vas bien?*" His accent was thick and the words strung out.

Jean-Louis had never adopted the Southern French drawl, though he had lived in Castelnau for twenty-three years. His French was purely Parisian.

They chatted about the weather and the mistral, which had picked up the night before and blown tiles from the roofs of several houses in Teyran, ten minutes down the road.

"Must've been a hundred kilometers an hour, rushing down the Rhône Valley and spilling out to blow us away. First bad wind of the season. Right pleasant outside now."

Jean-Louis agreed with his tablemate, and they talked on.

"You'll be joining us for a game of pétanque this afternoon, Pierre?" Jean-Louis questioned.

"Don't mind if I do, don't mind if I do."

The two men walked out of the café-bar, nodding and gesturing, and sometime in the course of the afternoon, Jean-Louis put his hand in his tweed jacket pocket and touched an envelope that had not been there that morning.

Every evening at six thirty Mother Griolet took a stroll around the courtyard within the walls of the church. In the summer, when the sun was still high, she sometimes sat in a wicker chair and read from the Gospels. Now, in the early days of October, she pulled her navy cardigan over her nun's habit as a crisp breeze played in the leaves.

She walked for twenty minutes, time enough to make five laps around the courtyard, and as she walked, she prayed out loud. On the south side, by the church and parsonage, she prayed for some of the forty-two girls in the Franco-American program.

"Thank You, Lord, for sending me Gabriella. I was wrong to be afraid for her. You always know best. She is so good and gentle with the children. Please help her to discover who she is in You." Then, as if adding a postscript to a letter, she addressed the Lord again. "And do help her to be wise about M. Hoffmann. Oh yes, Lord. Open her eyes."

She passed the refectory, where the children would soon be eating dinner. The quiet in the hall would be shattered by happy little voices and clanking silverware. And singing. That was the best part, when the children sang the blessing in a round. For all the heartache and trouble of the orphanage, she thanked God for the cherubic voices.

"And do, please, Lord, take away little Christophe's rasping cough. It worries me, even though he looks quite healthy. And you remember, Lord, of course, that little Anne-Sophie has lost her *nounours*. You know how much that teddy bear means to her. And

Jérémie … *ooh là*! What will we do with Jérémie? He is so angry in that little heart of his.…"

By the time she reminded the Lord of the special needs of the orphans, she was on her third lap and just passing the dormitories. "And thank You, too, dear Lord, for Sister Rosaline and Sister Isabelle. They have been faithful to You and to me all these years. Help them now as they prepare the evening meal. Give them laughter as they work."

She leaned against the stone wall at the north end of the courtyard. The back of the church and the parsonage stood in front of her. To the left, the lights in the refectory shone into the courtyard. The dormitory lay dark on the right. Together the buildings joined to hold hands, making three quarters of a square, while the stone wall against which she leaned completed it. She loved this piece of earth. For forty-five years she had called this abbey her home. "And, Lord, this new little adventure that I'm involved in … it is a bit worrisome. I am getting older. Help me do my part well."

She walked straight across the courtyard and let herself in the back door of the parsonage that led into her modest den. The ground floor held her living quarters, a bedroom, office, den, dining room, and kitchen. Years ago she had transformed a second bedroom into a student lounge. It made for less privacy but gave the exchange students a place to gather and visit between classes. The second floor was reserved for classrooms and a language lab. The orphans had their schoolrooms in the basement. The old building had served the church well for over a hundred years, she reflected.

Mother Griolet unlocked the door to her office and stepped inside, then switched on a lamp. Her desk faced the south wall with its large window overlooking the courtyard. On both sides of the window were bookcases lined with aging volumes. The other walls were wallpapered with simply framed photographs. She settled into the large chair behind her desk.

A lone white envelope sat on the desk. There was no writing on the outside. She flipped it over and opened the seal, and a small piece of paper slipped out. In the top left-hand corner was scribbled the image of a Huguenot cross. In the middle of the page was typed *14h30JeudiSNCF*.

She breathed out heavily. "So, Lord, You answer an old woman's prayer quickly. But will I be ready? Thursday at two thirty. Less than a week away."

She tucked the slip of paper into the pocket of her dress and switched off the light. Closing the door behind her, she locked it and walked down the hallway, back into the courtyard and across to the dining hall. The children's voices were singing the blessing as she entered through the side door.

"Pour ce repas, pour toute joie,
Nous te louons, Seigneur."

She closed her eyes.

"Yes, Lord, for this food we give You thanks. And for the grace to meet each day's challenges."

By the time she took her tray and sat down with Sister Rosaline and Sister Isabelle at the head table, her face radiated peace, warmth, and composure. Someone else was looking after Mother Griolet's problems. That was good enough for her.

10

By mid-October all the girls in the exchange program thought of Gabriella Madison and David Hoffmann as a couple. It was their delight to examine every look or word that passed between the two in public and to dream of what passed between them in private. They wrote the script down to the last detail.

Everyone except the couple themselves. Gabriella knew that David Hoffmann did not consider her his girlfriend. Sometimes she wished it different, but his heart was not up for bid. Of that she was certain.

She couldn't take her eyes off him in class as he spoke eloquently about the Impressionists, describing the beauty and intensity of art from Delacroix and Géricault's flashing social statements to the peaceful painting of sailboats that now appeared on the projector screen.

"Of course Monet became the leading member of this expression of art, known around the world as Impressionism. The term was first used by a critic to ridicule one of his paintings called *Impression Sunrise*, part of the first Impressionist exhibition in 1874. It is just that—the *impression* of an image that Monet leaves you with. The goal is to capture the moment and reveal it with dots or streaks of color that the eye will blend into detail from a distance."

As he continued to flash slides on the screen, Gabriella jotted down the names of the paintings in her spiral notebook. *Red Boats at Argenteuil; The Artist's Garden at Giverny; Wild Poppies, Near Argenteuil.*

David spoke again. "Look at the poppies, with the artist's small son lost in the field of wildflowers. The contrast of colors, the rich variety of the landscape. Nature and human life blended together in a vibration of light. Poppies in spring. Their bright red garment that surprises and delights the eye."

Gabriella could feel his eyes on her, and she tossed her hair over her shoulder self-consciously. Hope and springtime. But fall was barely in the air, and Gabriella did not want to think beyond one day at a time.

"It's a lovely afternoon, Gabby. Why don't you come for a ride through the vineyards with me? It will certainly beat hobbling around on those crutches." David nodded toward her foot, wrapped in heavy bandages. "How much longer do you have to wear that thing?"

"Another week at least, the doctor says."

"Poor you. You will join me then?"

She could think of no good excuse to turn him down. "Why not?"

The car left the limits of Castelnau and headed north. Before them on the smaller roads lay field after field of vineyards.

"The migrant workers and starving students have finished picking the grapes now. Nothing left on those vines. But look at the colors." The sun was slipping down, and its reflection on the vines was brilliant. "See there, the bright red ones. And the yellows and oranges. It's my therapy in autumn, to drive among the vineyards and watch their colors change. The nearest thing I can find to fall in Princeton."

"Princeton? In New Jersey, right?"

"Yes, I was in school there for four years. Autumn is magnificent there. Cold and frank and bold. The maples are fiery red and crackling orange and bright yellow. Your hair would fit in perfectly."

"I can hardly imagine it. Senegal's vegetation doesn't change at all during the year. There's the rainy season and the dry season and not many trees."

"Do you miss Africa?" He changed the subject as smoothly as he had advanced the slides in the tray that morning. A simple flick of the finger.

"I miss it a lot. Sometimes more than others."

"When do you miss it the most?"

She gazed at the blue sky descending on the vines with purple and pink hues mixed in. "I guess when things get hazy where I am. When I can't see what's ahead. Then I picture myself back there, comfortable in my little niche."

David was staring at her, his eyes barely on the road. "What are you wearing around your neck?" he demanded.

"Haven't you seen it before? I guess it's usually tucked inside my blouse. Surely you recognize the Huguenot cross?"

"Yes, of course. I just didn't know you wore one."

"My mother gave it to me before I left Senegal. She got it in Montpellier. She was here, you know, after the Second World War. Dad sent her here with Jessica and Henrietta and me for a few months' break. That's when she met Mother Griolet."

"Ah, I see." His eyes were on the road, but occasionally he glanced again at the shining chain around her neck. "Do you remember Montpellier? You were how old then?"

"Five or six. No, I don't remember anything. Hardly anything."

"What made you come back?"

She fiddled with the cross, sliding it up and down its chain. "A family member offered to pay for a year of study abroad—*abroad* meaning Europe. I thought this program sounded safe, since Mother knew the town and the director. Really just circumstances and ..."

"And what?"

"Circumstances." Her tone signaled the end of her revelations. "Do you miss Africa, David?"

"And why should I miss it, Gabby?"

"Because you lived in Algeria for a year, before this war broke out."

He laughed and gave her an inquisitive look.

"Mother Griolet told me, from your résumé. I help her with the orphans now, and she was filling me in on the school and its professors."

"I see. A fine woman, Mother Griolet. No wonder you came back." He seemed a million miles away.

"Well, yes, but it was more because my mother knew her and spoke so highly of her. But we were speaking of Algeria." Gabriella gently urged him back to the subject she wanted to hear about.

"Yes, I lived there briefly. A lovely spot, before the war. Of course, I could see trouble coming fast."

"Where did you live?"

"Algiers. The capital. In the pied-noir neighborhood."

"Was everything segregated then?"

"No, not really. The pied-noirs were friends with Arab merchants and the Jews. Everyone got along pretty well."

"And are the pied-noirs now all leaving Algeria?"

"Most likely. Of course, the large majority don't believe even now that France will lose the war. They stay because they have nowhere else to go. Algeria is their home, their roots for over a hundred years."

"But wouldn't they be welcomed back to France? After all, they're French citizens."

David had been talking easily, but at her question he grew silent, brooding. Suddenly he slowed the car to a stop, pulling off the road so he could look at her directly.

"Don't you understand, Gabby?" There was anger in his voice. "Nobody wants the pied-noirs. Algeria will kill them if they stay there. France wants Algeria's oil, but the pied-noirs? As far as France is concerned, they can go to—" He started over. "There's no place for them. Just one more burdensome minority."

"But you care about them, David?"

"Hah. I've already told you. I care about my own skin. But yes, somewhere in my troubled soul I have a soft spot for minorities. I understand the Algerians who long for independence from their strict mother, France. But I have lived among the pied-noirs who only want to keep their land. They are perhaps idealistic and naive, but I understand them.

"They both have good reasons, Gabby, to fight and to want what they want. It's too bad that war is so complicated. Too bad that we can't always tell who are the good guys and who are the bad." He looked out toward the vineyards. "Like a bottle of wine—you don't know the quality of the vine until the fruit is picked and fermented and tasted. And sometimes, we would judge too quickly."

Gabriella reflected on David's words, appreciating the silence and the scenery. She focused on the vineyard in front of her. Each knotty plant was no more than four feet tall, twisted, with branches that now boasted only variegated leaves. Presently she said, "I am the Vine, ye are the branches: He that abideth in Me, and I in him, the same bringeth forth much fruit: for without Me ye can do nothing."

"That sounds rather biblical," David said lightly. "Where's it from?"

"The gospel of John. Jesus talking to His disciples." Gabriella smiled. "He was probably sitting near the vineyards with His disciples, contemplating their beauty, just as we are doing."

"Could be." He shrugged.

"Never mind. It's true what He said. No matter the minority, the position, the color of the skin. In Him the fruit is good. You know what the next verse says?" She didn't wait for his answer. "If a man abide not in Me, he is cast forth as a branch, and is withered; and men gather them, and cast them into the fire, and they are burned."

"You're getting theological, Gabby. And very narrow. Sounds like a lot of bad fruit to me."

"There is. But the good fruit doesn't depend on where you were born or your society. It just depends on God and you. He won't throw you out because of a troubled past."

"That is good news indeed. Amazing what we can learn from the vineyards."

She heard the slightly sarcastic tone in his voice and suddenly had no desire to say anything more.

David started the engine and pulled back onto the road. They drove for a long time between the tall plane trees that lined the narrow country roads like rows of soldiers saluting their advancing general. Gabriella relaxed in the beauty of the setting sun, which played its light across the canvas of the landscape. Monet would have enjoyed this ride. She was determined to enjoy it too, even seated beside this man who kept his heart locked away in some painful past.

Saturday morning Gabriella had promised to help Mother Griolet plant pansies. She arrived at the stone house at nine o'clock, exhausted after maneuvering through the cobblestone streets on her crutches.

"Are you sure you feel up to this, child?" Mother Griolet asked.

"Quite sure. It will do me good to be outside in this gorgeous weather."

"Very well then. Come along." She led her through her apartment and out the door that opened from her den into the courtyard. "I like to plant my pansies early. The middle of October is just right. Gives them time to get used to the soil before the mistral sweeps down in all its fury. Usually. M. Mistral came a bit early this year."

Mother Griolet had purchased three cardboard trays of pansies. She took out one plant and pushed the loose earth through her fingers. "I usually plant them on each side of the courtyard. One and a half trays in front of the dining hall and the other one and a half in front of the dormitory. Unless you have another idea."

"Oh, no. I'm not much of a gardener myself. You decide."

"All right then." Mother Griolet handed Gabriella a trowel and a tray of flowers, and they walked toward the dining hall. The old woman knelt on the cool soil with the agility of someone who had been kneeling for many years. She held a bunch of yellow pansies in her hands. "I love the feel of the earth on my hands. It's therapeutic."

Gabriella watched and nodded.

"And what have we here?" Mother Griolet was talking to the flowers. "My, but aren't you splendid in that bright yellow frock. A regular sunflower in disguise." She laughed and held the flowers toward Gabriella. "You see, there is a face in each flower, delicate and full of promise."

Gabriella gasped. "Why, that's just what Mother used to say! 'A face in each flower, delicate and full of promise.' We didn't plant pansies, but Mother has this art book, and it has the most wonderful still life of pansies by Fantin-Latour. That's what she used to say."

"Did she?" Mother Griolet was amused. "I'm surprised she remembered."

"What do you mean?"

"Only that many years ago, your mother knelt in this very courtyard with me and planted pansies. I suppose I told her the same thing."

"You and Mother were good friends then?"

"I guess you could say circumstances drew us together." A cloud passed across Mother Griolet's face, but then she brightened. "A lovely person. Such a woman of faith. And so smart! I believe she must have memorized half her Bible. There are few people who can find scriptures quicker than I, but your mother had me beat."

"Tell me about when we were here in Montpellier. Mother always talks fondly of getting to know you, but she never speaks directly of our time here."

"Well, there really isn't that much to tell. You were staying in the mission house over on the west side of Montpellier. Your father couldn't leave Senegal at the time, so they postponed their furlough to the States, and your mother brought you and your sisters here for three months. We met by accident." Then the old nun looked up at Gabriella and smiled. "Not by accident. It cannot have been a simple coincidence when I see you here with me, helping an old woman who won't retire. No, it was just another thread in the tapestry of God's work. She was here, and now you are here. Another instance of God weaving our lives in and out to bring about His good will."

"But how did you meet?"

"I was at an interchurch seminar. Very radical in that day, but I went. And there was your mother, sitting strong and tall in the pew beside me. She spoke easily, like you, my dear. And like a flower, our friendship bloomed so quietly and simply."

"And did you know my sisters and me too? What were we like?"

"Precious, absolutely precious. You had that curly red hair, and Jessica was a little towhead. Henrietta was just a baby. She crawled around this courtyard more than once, that little rascal. Quite a handful."

Gabriella laughed and nodded, but her eyes were wet.

"Oh my! I've made you homesick, I fear."

"It's nothing," Gabriella said, brushing away the tears. "We must have been so happy then." She did not look at Mother Griolet when she spoke. "You know, we had another sister. She was born the year after we returned from Montpellier."

"Yes, your mother wrote me about her. Ericka, *n'est-ce pas?*" She pronounced the name with difficulty, a knot catching in her throat.

"Ericka. Beautiful little Ericka. Henrietta was all mischief, but Ericka was an angelic baby. The biggest brown eyes you ever saw.

And jet-black hair. She didn't look a thing like the rest of us. Thick black hair and long eyelashes and ..." But Gabriella could not go on. She dropped the trowel and buried her face in her dirty hands and cried.

Mother Griolet knelt beside her, arms encircling the young woman's thin shoulders. "There now, Gabriella. It is too hard, too sad to remember." She pulled Gabriella close, and the girl sobbed on her breast.

"It was hard ... so awful. She was my favorite sister. My favorite sister for six years. And then she was gone. The sickness took her in four days."

"You go ahead and cry. Sometimes it is the only thing that helps. We can plant the pansies later."

11

Malika Abdel was short for her eleven years, but what she lacked in height she made up for in common sense. "Streetwise," they called her. She knew everything about what men and women did together in bed, and she knew other things that happened behind closed doors when an angry argument was followed by a slap and then a fist, and later a bruised eye. Malika had grown up fast and stood strong between her cruel father and her younger sisters.

Her father was always mad about something, and these days it was Algeria. "Someday we will go back home," he promised his girls.

Malika knew that money was one thing that appeased her father's temper, at least for a while. And she had a way to earn some. The skinny Frenchman with the thin moustache had approached her ten days ago with a simple request: make friends with the little girl who lived with the old man above the épicerie down the street.

Four hundred francs he would pay her to bring the girl to him. But Malika had not yet met her. Every day she made up an excuse to go to the shop, where she browsed for fifteen or twenty minutes, but the girl never appeared. The thin Frenchman was getting impatient.

He grabbed her arm as she left for school that morning. "You will earn nothing if you don't bring her soon. Tomorrow night there is a march to the prefecture. Bring her along, and you will have your four hundred francs."

Malika didn't normally show her fear, but she shivered as she left the school building at noon to walk home. Once again she stopped by the épicerie.

The old shopkeeper looked up from the counter. "*Bonjour, mademoiselle*. You are back again today?"

"Yes, I brought some marbles for your granddaughter."

"My granddaughter?" He looked at her suspiciously.

"Yes, the little girl who is sick. I have seen her, but she never goes to school. She is sick, your granddaughter?"

"Yes, yes, she is sick."

As if on cue, the girl came down the back stairs, coughing loudly. The old man turned toward her. "Ophélie. What are you doing downstairs?"

"I wanted a *pastille*, please."

Malika caught her eye, and the girls smiled at each other.

"Here is your cough drop. Now go back upstairs."

"Please, *monsieur*. May I give Ophélie these marbles?" Malika held out her hand and displayed the small glass balls.

"Oh! They're pretty!" Ophélie came around the corner and stared at the shining gift. "May I have them, please, M. Gady?"

She reached for the gems, and Malika took her hand. "I'll teach you to play, okay? Tomorrow afternoon, when I get back from school."

Ophélie took the marbles and placed them in her pocket, an eager look in her eyes. Malika left the store before M. Gady could refuse her offer.

David walked into the garden in the interior of the old school building where Gabriella sat, her head bent intently over a thick book. The
bright afternoon sun caught the red in her hair and made it glisten
like sparks flying from a soldering iron.

She gasped. "Oh, David! You startled me."

"I have to go to Aix this weekend on some business. Would you
like to come? We'd leave early Saturday morning and be home in
time for you to get your studies done on Sunday."

"I-I don't know. Let me think about it, please, and I'll let you
know tonight. You are coming to eat at Mme Leclerc's, aren't you?"

He was now sitting beside her, his arm brushing lightly on hers.
"I would never pass up a free meal, especially with such delightful company as Miss Thrasher and Miss Harland." He touched her
hand. "And you, of course."

Gabriella blushed, but she was careful to keep her head buried in
her anthology of English literature.

"I'm leaving on the night train for Paris right after dinner, and
I'll be there for a few days. M. Vidal has agreed to take my classes.
But please come with me to Aix on Saturday. It would give me something to look forward to while I'm away. You'll be off those crutches
by then. We can celebrate."

Gabriella's heart was thumping like a bass drum. She longed to
gently close her fingers around his strong hand, but she didn't dare.
For a brief moment she imagined his lips brushing hers. Then she
shivered. "I don't know, David."

"You needn't worry about the arrangements. You'd be staying
with a friend of mine. She's very nice and would love to meet
you."

So that was it. He was going to Aix to see a woman.

"Why in the world do you want me to come?" She had not meant to blurt the question out loud, but the damage was done.

David laughed and removed his hand from hers, the spell broken. "I for one would be bored to death if I had to spend every weekend in this silent town. It's a chance to see a little more of this great country. I guarantee you'll love it."

"I was just reading here what John Donne has to say about our all needing each other to make one big happy family. You know: 'No man is an island.' So sure, I'll go, just so you won't be alone." A hint of a smile crept upon her lips.

"I'm not sure you've interpreted Mr. Donne correctly, Gabby," said David. "Nonetheless, if he has convinced you to come along, I'm delighted. Bring some comfortable clothes. And an appropriate dress for Mass. I'm sure you wouldn't want to miss it. My friend will be glad to go along with you."

"But not you?"

"Me? I wouldn't be caught dead in a church!" Then he laughed. "Or maybe I should say that's the *only* condition in which you'd find me there."

She watched him disappear into the doors of the parsonage and shook her head. So cynical. Yet she laughed aloud, thinking about his last remark.

Gabriella turned off the hallway light, leaving the basement of the parsonage dark. The last child had slipped out the door into the courtyard, where Sister Isabelle was waiting to lead them to the refectory. They marched in single file, stealing glances back, waving and smiling. Gabriella waved too.

She stood there a moment longer, satisfied. Mother Griolet had let her start teaching the orphans, twenty-three children from four to twelve in age. Sometimes she would throw in a detail from one of David's lectures. Never too soon to introduce the children to history and culture.

She glanced at her watch. Seven o'clock. Just enough time to hobble home and get ready for dinner. *David is coming to dinner.* The thought brought a rush to her heart as she limped back through the hall toward the front stairs.

Then she heard a squeak, like a chair being pulled across the floor. What child was hiding out in the classroom? She was sure she had counted twenty-three leaving for dinner. She turned and reentered the empty classroom and flicked on the light. At first she saw nothing. But then she heard another slight noise. "Who is there?"

A young boy of about fourteen stood up behind a row of desks. He was thin and his skin dark olive. Gabriella knew at once that he was North African.

"May I help you?" she asked softly.

The boy said nothing, but stood trembling before her.

Gabriella tried to calm the fear mounting in her mind. *He's only a boy. He won't hurt you.* Still, she suspected he was Algerian, and Algerians and French were not on good terms right now, even in France.

"Do you need something?" she ventured.

He raised his eyes from the floor and stared at her sullenly. Then, quite unexpectedly, he moved toward her, reaching his hand toward her throat.

Instinctively Gabriella backed up, bumping a desk and tripping with her crutches. She scrambled to regain her balance.

The boy observed her silently. Then he reached out again and spoke. "The cross." A look of understanding was in his eyes.

"Oh," Gabriella said. "Is that all? You like my cross?" A wave of relief swept over her. This cross was going to cause her to have a heart attack someday.

"You wear the cross. Hugo?"

"Yes, the Huguenot cross."

"Hugo," he repeated again.

Gabriella stared at him blankly. "What do you want?"

He reached in his pocket and pulled out a scrap of paper, which he held out to her.

Gabriella cautiously took it. Scribbled in one corner was the crude drawing of a Huguenot cross. "Where did you get this? What is it?"

He looked at her again, silent and hopeful.

"I'm sorry," she said. "I don't understand what you want. Is it my cross?"

There was a sound in the hall, and suddenly Mother Griolet appeared in the room.

"Oh my! Hakim! ... Well, yes, Gabriella. I see you've met our new arrival." Mother Griolet looked flustered. "Hakim arrived Thursday. I'm sorry I didn't have a chance to introduce him to you over the weekend."

"That's all right. I'm afraid we surprised each other, that's all."

"Yes, I'm sure. Come along with me, Hakim. It's time for dinner. I'll see you tomorrow, Gabriella. Thank you for letting the children out."

Gabriella left the classroom and slowly climbed the steps to the ground floor as Mother Griolet turned off the light and hurried Hakim down the hallway and out into the courtyard. What could the old nun be planning to do with an Arab child at St. Joseph?

David placed a stack of neatly folded clothes into the small, hard vinyl suitcase lying open on his bed. He added several books and a map of Paris to the stack before closing the case and latching it. Then he walked across the room and leaned over the small oak desk. His eyes fell on the letter he had received in the mail two days earlier.

Algerians plan peaceful march in Paris on seventeenth. Possible information from E. Torrès. Meet him at Pont Saint-Michel, north side at 21h30.

David folded the paper and put the note inside his wallet. At last, possible information from an FLN informer. Six months of waiting might pay off tomorrow. Six months! Or was it seven years? He did not dwell on the thought.

He set the suitcase by his bed and left the room, locking the door behind him. Paris was a long way off. Meanwhile, dinner awaited at Mme Leclerc's.

Gabriella heard the doorbell ring at precisely eight o'clock. Mme Leclerc buzzed the front door open, and after a moment there was a light knock on the door.

"Entrez." Mme Leclerc invited their guest in with a wide grin on her face. *"Ooh là là,"* she added as David presented her with a bouquet of flowers. *"Merci, Monsieur Hoffmann."*

The three boarders stood obediently behind their landlady, taking in the scene. David looked stunning in his pale yellow Oxford cloth shirt, tweed pants, and leather loafers polished to a sheen.

"Mademoiselle Thrasher," he said softly, as Stephanie approached and smiled. He took her hand and kissed it lightly.

"Enchantée, Monsieur Hoffmann," she stammered.

"Et Mademoiselle Harland."

Caroline, who was wearing a tight-fitting red dress that set off her blond hair and perfect curves, came forward and lifted her eyebrows. *"Enchantée, Monsieur Hoffmann."* She offered him her hand, and he kissed it also.

Gabriella felt a tiny pang of jealousy as she noted Caroline's flirtatious ease. She felt embarrassed to meet David's eyes.

"Et Mademoiselle Madison."

Gabriella hobbled forward on her crutches and extended her hand in mock obedience.

Ignoring it completely, David bent down and held her shoulders gently. Then he softly kissed her cheeks, starting and ending with the left one. He whispered, "If I am not mistaken, it is three times on the cheeks in this part of France."

Gabriella felt light-headed and at a total loss for words. They stood there gazing at each other until Mme Leclerc cleared her throat and Gabriella stuttered, "*Oh, enchantée, Dav ... David ... Monsieur Hoffmann.*"

Yvette busied herself in her kitchen, humming contentedly. The meal was progressing fabulously, and M. Hoffmann was charming. So gracious and smooth and seductive! *Ooh là là!* She could not wait to report every detail to Monique tomorrow.

The first course, avocado halves with shrimp sauce, had been appreciated by everyone. She laughed as she brought the steaming plate of *gratin dauphinois* to the table. Americans always liked her scalloped potatoes. She went back to fetch the green beans in garlic butter and placed the dish before her guests.

One more trip to the kitchen, and she brought out the specialty of the evening: young rabbit cooked in a rich tomato sauce.

"It all looks delicious!" Stephanie exclaimed.

Mme Leclerc busied herself with serving the plates as they were passed to her. She was pleased with the picture, the blend of yellow and red and green. Such a pretty table, with her fine china and the bright colors of the food. Such a perfect evening.

She announced the names of each dish, as was her custom with her American boarders, who often wanted the recipes.

"Tonight we have *gratin dauphinois, haricots à l'ail, et fricassé de lapereau avec tomates fraîches.*" She beamed as the four young people nodded approvingly and the steam rose from their plates. *"Alors, bon appétit!"*

For several minutes the conversation stopped as everyone tasted the food that Mme Leclerc had placed before them. David, who had been talking with ease during the first course, stared at his plate with a pained expression on his face. He gingerly ate the potatoes and the green beans, as Stephanie and Caroline questioned him about one of the artists they had been studying in class.

Gabriella sensed that something was wrong, and she tried to change the subject. "The rabbit is delicious, Mme Leclerc."

"Oh yes," chimed Stephanie and Caroline.

David's silverware lay on his plate.

"M. Hoffmann, you are all right?" Mme Leclerc inquired. "The food is not good?"

David seemed to shake himself out of his thoughts. "It's superb, Mme Leclerc. Only …" He lost his composure for a moment. "I'm afraid that I can't eat the … the *lapereau*." He said the word with difficulty. "The rabbit—I'm sure it is delicious. It's just that …" Again his voice trailed off.

The girls stared at him, shocked. David Hoffmann had fallen from his pedestal. His face was red, and Gabriella noticed drips of perspiration on his forehead.

"I'm allergic," he finished lamely.

Mme Leclerc stood and nodded sympathetically. "It is nothing! If only I had known." She whisked the plate away. "I will fix you something else. It will not take long. You like chicken? *Poulet cordon bleu*, perhaps."

David wiped his face with the cloth napkin. He had recovered. "Please, no, excuse me. It's all fine. Don't bother. A nervous reaction, I'm afraid. Please, I will have some more of the delicious *gratin dauphinois* and *des haricots verts*. That will be delightful."

It took five minutes for the conversation to resume. The main course was cleared away, the rabbit forgotten. The cheese course was served, followed by a tray of fresh fruit and then Mme Leclerc's rich yet light *mousse au chocolat*. It was eleven thirty before the coffee was drunk and the table cleared.

David thanked Mme Leclerc profusely for the meal and kissed her on each cheek before he left, causing her to roll her eyes with glee as she bustled toward the kitchen.

Then he took Gabriella's arm and pulled her into the hallway. "You will come to Aix with me then?"

"Yes, David, I'll come." She wrinkled her brow. "Are you all right?"

"Yes, I'm all right. I have to go now; I have a train to catch. Good-bye, Gabby." He brushed her cheek with his hand, but he seemed distracted.

He descended the steps without looking back, leaving Gabriella to watch him go and wonder about a smooth-talking teacher who became unnerved over a dead rabbit.

Moustafa awoke to the sound of Anne-Marie's incessant coughing. He wiped the sleep from his eyes and sat up. The sole window in the room, small and barred and near the ceiling, revealed no light.

"Anne-Marie," he whispered. "There's a little water left. Take it. It will help calm the cough." He handed a bottle across to the mattress where she lay.

"Thank you," she rasped. After a long drink she said, "We're going to die here, Moustafa. I won't wait any longer."

Moustafa did not reply. She was right. They were slowly being starved to death. Might as well take the pill and be done with it.

Three and a half weeks they had spent locked in this room. Moustafa had made a mark on the wall at the same time each day, the time when a skinny hand unlocked the door and pushed in a plate of stale bread and a bottle of water.

"Anne-Marie, don't give up. We'll have our chance, and when it comes, we must be ready. As we planned, you'll say I forced you to talk and you have more information that you must give to Ali. Please."

"I'll try," she said. She lay back down and curled up like a kitten, desperate for warmth.

He reached out to touch her, but stopped himself. How he longed to hold her and love her, even in the filth of this basement. He could keep her warm. But he would not. An impossible love! A harki and a pied-noir. So he listened to her cough and watched her grow weaker by the day. And thought about the two pills that she kept in a small bottle sewn into her sleeve.

Ali lit a cigarette and stamped the match out on the cement floor. A small group of men, also smoking, sat in metal chairs before him.

"Emile has found the girl. He is a bit slow about his work, but he gets it done. We'll have the information by tomorrow night." He smiled. "Of course, we all know what an important night that will be in Paris. I am told it will be a peaceful march to the prefecture. But the French police will understand. Power to the Algerians. Freedom at last!" He paused a moment, transfixed.

"Of course, our little matter of concern will go quite unnoticed. No more harki children will escape. Nor will the pied-noirs. We will have their names, and they will pay for the sins of their fathers. Sweet red revenge! And you will bring me the proof. A coat stained with their blood!"

He had worked himself into a fury, and the men shifted nervously in their chairs.

"Leave! Go on with you. I will call for you when we have the news."

The men shuffled out into the pitch-black night. Only Rachid stayed, at Ali's command.

"What of the prisoners?"

"There is nothing to report. They are surely half-dead with hunger." Rachid eyed his leader hopefully. "Do you wish for me to talk with them?"

"You are too eager, Rachid. When Emile brings us the girl, then we'll see fear in the eyes of the Duchemin woman. She'll talk and talk. She will beg to tell us everything."

"And the harki son?"

"Moustafa is a swine. And you know what happens to swine. To the butcher! Soon. Do not worry."

12

Gabriella knocked softly on the door of Mother Griolet's office.

"Come in," came the gentle reply.

Cautiously Gabriella entered and took a chair. "I think I've gotten myself into a real mess, Mother Griolet," she began. "Could I talk to you about something ... something personal?"

The nun nodded.

"I just feel ... I feel ... how can I describe it?" She searched for the words. "I feel *unpeaceful*. That's it. As though I've made a mistake." She leaned back in the big chair and sighed. "I hate making mistakes. What do you think God thinks about our mistakes? I know He is forgiving, but ..."

"What exactly is the problem, my dear?"

"It's David—I mean M. Hoffmann." She blushed. "I'm not sure what he's up to, but I am ... involved with him, and I don't know what to do."

Mother Griolet waited patiently for an explanation.

"It's just that he's an atheist. He doesn't believe in God. Have I messed up everything?"

Mother Griolet settled back in her chair, a kind smile spreading across her wrinkled face. "Gabriella, you are very familiar with the Scriptures, *non*?" She nodded toward the large Bible on the corner of her desk.

"Yes, of course. I read my Bible."

"Then you are familiar with the stories of Abraham and Joseph and Moses and Paul and Peter and many of the other patriarchs and the saints?"

"Yes, I know about their lives." A baffled expression came over Gabriella's face.

Mother Griolet smiled. "I have always found great comfort in the fact that our Lord worked with extremely human humans. They were always bumbling around and getting themselves in the worst trouble, even when they knew better."

At this she raised her eyebrows and looked at Gabriella, who reddened and looked down.

"Fortunately for us, the Lord kept picking them back up and helping them get on with the business He had them about. I can't recall a one who was perfect. But the smart ones recognized when they had 'messed up,' as you say, and they came before God and asked forgiveness and got back on the right track. Isn't it wonderful how forgiveness works?

"We're free to sin, and for some things we'll suffer the consequences all our lives. Think of Moses missing out on the Promised Land because he struck a rock instead of speaking to it, as God commanded. And Saint Paul, how many years did it take him to convince those he'd been persecuting that he was now a believer?

"But when Christ forgives us, we're freed to start over again, in His power. And little by little we learn." She stopped for a breath, but Gabriella said nothing.

"I'm afraid I've babbled on. And perhaps I've not answered your question about M. Hoffmann."

"No. I mean yes, you have. It's true I need to get on with things. It's just that … that I think I'm in love with him." This she said so softly that Mother Griolet had to strain to hear.

"And this is a problem? To be in love?"

"Well, you know. He doesn't believe. We're so different."

"And you would be the same? Is that your wish?"

Gabriella smiled. Dear Mother Griolet, playing the devil's advocate. "You will have me spell it out, won't you, Mother Griolet?"

The old woman nodded.

"I find myself having very strong feelings for him, but I think I shouldn't because he mocks my God. I know it's dangerous to love someone who doesn't share your beliefs. But the problem is that I don't *want* to stop caring for him. And I don't know what to do."

"So you would ask me to approve what your conscience forbids? I cannot do that, Gabriella."

"No, of course not. I wouldn't ask that of you. You don't like M. Hoffmann, do you?" Her eyes begged for mercy.

"Professionally speaking, he is an extremely intelligent young man who performs his role as teacher without flaw. But you want my feeling here?" She pointed to her heart. "He scares me. There is a war going on, and people do strange things in war. Perhaps he's not involved, but there is something about him that bothers me. He's very secretive. For your own good, Gabriella, I beg you to be careful." She was quiet for a moment, searching for the right words. "I wouldn't want you to mistake something else for what you think is love. He has a certain way with the ladies, and perhaps his interest in you is—"

Gabriella was crying now. "He's using me," she blurted. "That's what you think. I'm afraid too, but I can't stay away. Will you pray for me, Mother Griolet?"

The old woman came around to the front of her desk and knelt beside Gabriella. She took the young woman's soft, creamy hands into her weathered ones. Then she looked at Gabriella with her bright green eyes that did not betray her age. "Our God is not a God of confusion. You must trust. He gives strength to do what we cannot do on our own. But, Gabriella, you must let Him do it. Even if it breaks your heart."

David made his way through the first few rooms in the Jeu de Paume museum on the Right Bank of Paris. It was crowded for a Tuesday afternoon. Entering another room, he walked toward the back wall, where there were fewer people, and then stopped suddenly, ten feet away. *Les Coquelicots.* Monet's field of poppies. He whispered, "Gabriella."

At once he saw her before him, laughing, lighting up the class-room or the courtyard or the beach. A shocking picture of hope. A lone poppy in a field of sunflowers.

He remembered how a villager in Castelnau had reproached him once when he commented on their delicate beauty. *They take over the field, you know, and the farmers hate them. Just a weed, really. A wildflower. You start with one, and it spreads like wildfire, those blasted poppies.*

Delicate beauty, that was Gabriella. Shocking with life, with an enthusiasm and charm that spread out and spilled over, infectious in its winsome spirit.

"Gabriella," he whispered again, and with one last glance at the poppies, he turned and left the museum.

David walked briskly through the Tuileries gardens that led from the Jeu de Paume to the Louvre. The bright October sky of an hour ago now grumbled menacingly above. And something grumbled even louder within his soul. It was October 17. A dark day in history. The day Louis XIV had signed the revocation of the Edict of Nantes, thus abolishing religious liberty in France. And with that quick release of ink, the blood of thousands of Protestants flowed through the caverns and mountains of the Midi. They ran and hid; they prayed and cried out to the heavens. Still the blood flowed and mingled with the mud and was forgotten. David wondered, was the cause worth the price of blood?

Yet the Huguenots had stood firm in their faith. He couldn't deny it, though he would not show Gabriella how deeply it moved him. A people who believed that their faith was worth dying for.

He listened to the wind and could almost hear its mournful warning. *Blood will flow again.* Tonight, he knew, another suppressed minority would raise their angry fists and cry, "Liberty!" But who would answer? Who in fact knew the answer for Algeria? Who could see past the passion of political parties into the soul of the people?

David shook his head as he walked through the gardens. He would observe the march, and perhaps get the information he needed to appease his conscience. But he knew there was no answer to satisfy both Algeria and France, the FLN and the OAS, the harkis and the pied-noirs. And so the blood would continue to spill onto pages not yet written, which would someday fill the history books.

Ophélie slipped out of the apartment and rushed down the stairs and out the back way. Malika waited for her in the late afternoon, her eyes glistening with excitement.

"We're going to march tonight! For independence! A march with our friends!" Malika's voice lifted and swelled with feeling, a young girl reciting her poetry into the afternoon air.

"But will you still teach me about the marbles?" Ophélie asked.

"Marbles! Ha! I'm talking about freedom. Come march with me for freedom!"

"You'll let me go with you?" Ophélie longed for excitement and the taste of the wind on her face.

Malika bent down to her height and looked her in the eyes. "Do you believe in a free Algeria?"

The young child's face clouded. What did Mama think? They had left Algeria, of that she was sure. But she couldn't remember if Algeria was good or bad. Oh well. It didn't matter. Tonight she would escape with this big girl.

"I believe what you believe! I want to be with you."

"Then I'll come back for you after dark, Ophélie. Papa says that tonight we will be part of history!"

The sky was black when Ophélie finally heard M. Gady snoring in his room. She gathered up an old sweater the old man had found for her when the weather had turned colder. Then she stopped. What if he woke? What if he looked for her and found the blue bag? Quickly she pulled it out of the pillowcase and put it around her neck, tucking it under her shirt and sweater. The cross lay safely in the bottom.

Ophélie tiptoed down the steps and let herself outside with the key M. Gady kept on a hook near the door. She pulled the door closed, locked it from the outside, and dropped the key into the blue bag.

Malika was waiting. "You're late. We must hurry."

"Is this an adventure?" Ophélie asked.

"It certainly is. You'll see. Now come on!"

Masses of Algerians crowded through the streets along the Seine. Ophélie struggled to keep up with the moving tide. Men, women, and children hurried silently along, their eyes burning bright. All was quiet. No angry, bitter words. But she could see the look of determination on their faces. "To the prefecture," they whispered in Arabic.

Ophélie searched for Malika, suddenly feeling afraid. The other girl was running ahead, laughing. She didn't hear Ophélie's cries.

By the time the crowd reached the prefecture, Ophélie felt she could walk no farther. She wished she had stayed with M. Gady. *This is bad, Mama. I want to go home.* She was crying as she ran, pushed along by the stream of Algerians. "Mama!"

Suddenly a shot rang out. Then another and another, until it sounded to Ophélie like the celebrations when the sky lit up with beautiful fire. But this wasn't a celebration. People were screaming and running.

"Malika! Help me, Malika!" Ophélie stood terrified as the crowd turned and fled down the same streets they had just come up.

Ophélie jumped as Malika grabbed her arm. "Ophélie, you must run. It's not safe." Her friend's eyes were filled with terror. "Run, Ophélie. Come with me."

The night had erupted into a nightmare. Ophélie shivered and cried, remembering the times she had run with Mama when they lived in that other country that now wanted to be free.

Mama had said they would be safe in France. But now she was gone, and Ophélie had to run. But where should she go? Which people were bad?

Another burst of popping sounded. Sharp, quick, like the beating of the drum before an important person appears. Suddenly Malika screamed and went limp, falling to the ground. Ophélie tripped over her body and fell beside her.

Malika's eyes fluttered. "Run, Ophélie, don't stay with me," she said. "I'll be okay."

Ophélie touched Malika's head. It was wet. She looked at her fingers in the light of the lampposts on the Seine. A thick, dark liquid stained her small hand. She stood up and began to run, looking over her shoulder and screaming, "Malika! Malika!"

More shots spat through the sky. Something sharp stung her leg and she fell again, screaming with pain.

"Help me! Mama! Malika! Someone help me. M. Gady!" She crawled on the wet pavement, dragging her left leg behind, until she sat in a cluster of bushes close to the large bridge they had just crossed.

She sat for a long time, sniffling back her fear as men in blue uniforms and tall hats picked up the bodies of the fallen and tossed them into the river. The men in blue, they were good, she knew. They were police. But they were shooting and beating and throwing people in the river. Only Ophélie's terror kept her from crying out. She waited and watched until the dark-skinned men with gleaming eyes and the men in blue uniforms with guns and sticks had left the bridge, yelling angry words at each other in the dark.

Near the Pont Saint-Michel, David heard the screams of Algerians as the Paris police beat, kicked, and shot at the protestors. He hung in the shadows, sickened. M. Torrès would not show up in this scene of slaughter. His plans were not the only ones to run awry.

More blood spilled. In his mind he was back in Paris in 1941. He saw the Nazi guards standing before him, the shots, the blood. "Why did you think we would be safe, Mother?" He spoke aloud, and the sound of his own voice startled him.

Once again one race's hatred for another spilled blood on the pavement of the bridge. And once again, no one came to their defense. Only the Seine, running swift and smooth, knew the count of those who were killed. The *gendarmes* threw the lifeless bodies of beaten Algerians into the river one by one and watched as they sank below her slow-moving current. And the sweet river once again closed her sad eyes and was silent.

"Mama! Mama!"

The screams of a young girl pierced the stillness of the bloody Paris night. David could not ignore them. "Where are you?" he whispered, running toward one side of the Seine as the Paris police charged off in another direction.

"Here. Please, *monsieur*, help me."

He stooped to see the crumpled form of a young girl by the light pole. Instinctively he picked her up, turning away from the bridge and the river. He ran until he reached the safety of a small square down the road from the Pont Neuf. He slipped down a side street that was now swallowed in darkness. Far away, more cries rang out and gunshots echoed. But here there were no police.

Carefully he placed the small girl on the sidewalk and bent close to inspect her wounds. Her breathing was shallow and forced, and her eyes glazed over as she stared up at him.

"M. Gady? It is you?"

"I'm a friend. Where is M. Gady?"

"Take me to M. Gady. He will help me," she rasped, frantic for breath.

"Don't worry. I won't leave you, little one." He removed his jacket and then his shirt, ripping it and tying it around the wound in her leg.

The child was murmuring incoherently. "He's near the big school. Such a pretty red-and-white awning, the little store ... yes, Mama. I know ... rue des Beaux-Arts ... yes, I can get there from our house ..." Her eyes fluttered, and she fainted.

David picked her up and held her close. "Don't die, little girl. Don't die! Not like Greta. This time I'll help."

Only the moon witnessed the tall American racing along the sidewalks of the Left Bank of Paris in search of rue des Beaux-Arts and a shop with a red-and-white awning.

David knew many cities of the world, but none better than Paris. He was not far from the École des Beaux-Arts. He hoped that this child did indeed live nearby. Moments later in the darkness, a storefront with a red-and-white awning came into view. By the streetlight he read the word *Epicerie*. As he approached the door, he stepped on broken glass. The windowpanes were gone. He did not need to ring the bell, for the wooden door stood ajar. He entered and waited in the shadows for several minutes, but he heard no noise and nothing moved. Slowly he made his way toward the back of the shop and through the doorway that led up a flight of stairs. He walked into a small room where a mattress lay on the floor. A small desk and couch were the only pieces of furniture. The desk had been overturned and every drawer emptied. The mattress and a pillow had been slit, and stuffing littered the floor.

David walked out of the room and into the hall. The door to the adjoining room was open, and David looked in, then halted abruptly.

"I am glad you can't see this," he said to the unconscious child in his arms. An old man lay slumped on the floor with a bullet hole through his head.

Emile Torrès cursed as he crossed the Seine on the Pont Saint-Michel. He had lost the girl and he had missed the informant. He knew the rules. Whatever information this man had, he could not wait around to find out. The whole night had exploded into chaos. The child was gone.

She would return to the shop if she could, he reasoned. He cursed again. But he had already searched there. The old shopkeeper had told him nothing. Terrified and shaking, he could only repeat, "The little girl didn't have the bag. Her mama said there would be a bag." And then Emile had put a bullet in his head.

Emile had torn the place apart, but the old man was right. No bag. But surely the child knew something. Emile's head would roll if Ali did not get the information. God forbid that the child lay at the bottom of the Seine with the Algerians.

He headed back toward the Left Bank and the little épicerie, where the waiting game would continue. And if he did not find the child, he knew his next step: an obituary in the paper and a changed name. He could start over. He had done it before.

David fled the épicerie immediately. One thing was obvious: the child was in danger. He carried her back through the dark streets of Paris, covering her with his jacket. He arrived at his hotel at eleven o'clock. Ignoring the puzzled look of the concierge, he carried the child up two flights of steps and unlocked the door.

Carefully he laid her on the bed. Removing his jacket and the ripped shirt, he inspected her leg. The bleeding had stopped. The bullet wound was clearly visible, having entered the child's left thigh just above the knee. He saw another small hole on the other side of her leg and shook his head in relief. The bullet had gone straight through. Perhaps he could avoid the hospital. Elevating the leg, he washed the wound with warm water. From his small suitcase he took out a white T-shirt. As he bent over the child to wrap her leg, her eyes fluttered open.

"M. Gady?" she whispered.

"M. Gady isn't here, little one. I found you by the bridge. What is your name?"

"Where is M. Gady?"

"I cannot take you to him tonight. It is not good for you to move with this wound."

Tears welled in the child's eyes. "Mama! I want my mama."

"Of course you do." David softened his tone. "Where is your mama? We'll find her tomorrow." He looked at the child's fine face. A beautiful child. Such striking features. He pushed away a memory.

"My mama is lost. The bad men took her away." Suddenly the little girl looked up at David with new fear in her eyes. "Are you bad? Do you want to kill me too?"

David smiled. "No, I'm not one of them."

Relief spread across her face. "I'm not trying to be mean, *monsieur*, but ... it's just that I can't tell who is good and who is bad anymore." She clutched the bedsheet in her small hand, wiping her eyes with a corner.

David patted her hand. "I don't know your mother or the bad men, but I'll try to help you. Perhaps you can tell me where your father lives?"

The child sniffed. "I don't have a father. It is only Mama and me. But now she is gone. You will have to ask M. Gady. He'll tell you."

"Of course. Now try to sleep. What is your name, little one?"

"Ophélie."

"And your last name?"

"My name is Ophélie. That is all." She closed her eyes, and he covered her with the bedspread. Soon she was asleep.

David sat wearily in the room's lone chair. What a fiasco. The riot, the missed contact, the police, the shootings. And now this. *I can't tell who is good and who is bad anymore*, the child had said.

"Neither can I, little Ophélie," he whispered to the sleeping girl. "Neither can I."

E. Torrès, whoever he had been, was no more. An obituary in the morning paper had announced the fact, stating cause of death unknown. David scoffed. Of course the papers would not reveal the truth. He did not know what had really happened to M. Torrès, and he was sure he would never find out. A wasted trip to Paris. And now he was stuck with a little girl whose mother was gone, who had no father, and whose sole friend was an old man who lay dead in his apartment.

The pharmacist had kindly explained what to do for the child's wound, and David had cleaned it carefully, applied ointment, and covered it with a bandage to prevent infection.

But Ophélie still refused to talk. David was only *monsieur* to her, and this he preferred. Yet he could not simply abandon her in the streets of Paris.

"I have to take you to the police," he said, exasperated. "They'll find your mother for you."

Ophélie burst into tears. "No! No! Please, *monsieur*. Not the police. They will kill me. They have already tried. Only M. Gady. He's the only one."

"Ophélie, M. Gady is dead." David said it flatly, tired, forgetting he was talking to a child.

Ophélie stared at him with wide eyes brimming again with tears. "He's dead? No ... how do you know?"

"I found him in his apartment. He ... he was shot." David held her hands. "Little Ophélie, I'm so sorry to tell you this, but you must understand. I don't know how to help you. I don't live here in Paris. Tomorrow I must leave to go home."

He tried again. "Listen, do you know why bad people would take your mother and kill M. Gady? Think hard."

Ophélie turned her eyes away. She shook her head. "No, I don't know." Suddenly she grabbed his hand. "Take me with you, *monsieur*. Please take me with you. I'm afraid to stay here."

He shook his head, bewildered. "Ophélie, I can't take you with me. I can't keep a little child." He sighed and thought of Gabriella. She would know how to talk to the girl. He was getting nowhere, and he had a train to catch in twelve hours.

13

Gabriella pulled a lightweight V-neck sweater over her starched white blouse. She looked at her reflection in the small mirror above the sink in the corner of her room. This morning she liked what she saw. Caroline's pale-blue cashmere brought out the blue of Gabriella's eyes against her creamy white skin. She patted a little blush across her freckled cheekbones and began to brush her thick hair.

The sky outside was a bright cobalt blue. It seemed to her the perfect weather for a day in Aix with David. She wanted to look mature and beautiful. She wanted him to stare at her and smile and approve. Especially when she met his "friend."

Even as she readied herself for the outing, a nagging voice played in the back of her mind. *Don't go*, it warned. She pushed the thought away as she tied back her hair with a soft-blue ribbon that matched the sweater.

She must have tried on seven of them, all cashmere, before Caroline had announced, "The blue one is perfect, Gabriella. You look smashing. He'll be all over you."

She stood back from the mirror and rose onto her tiptoes, but she couldn't see below her waist. Climbing onto the bed, she stood up and looked toward the mirror again, this time catching the reflection of her lower torso. The sweater fit nicely, enhancing her curves. Her plain navy skirt somehow took on new life beside it. She felt slim and graceful and feminine.

After sitting back on the bed, she reached for her Bible but couldn't bring herself to read it. She did not want any advice today. "I'm twenty-one, and I deserve to have fun," she said in a whisper, arguing with her subconscious.

No one answered her. She glanced in the mirror again and then left the room.

David's deux chevaux was not reliable for trips longer than fifty kilometers, he had explained as he bought two round-trip train tickets to Aix. Seated next to Gabriella on the two-hour trip, he seemed cheerful and approving, not mocking.

"You look lovely, Gabriella. You're radiant."

"Well, it was Caroline who loaned me the sweater. I mean ... I don't have anything cashmere; it's so expensive." She could feel the heat mounting in her cheeks. Why did she say these things?

"Cashmere or not, you are lovely." He touched her hand and gently pulled it to rest on his leg, stroking her fingers as he talked. "You will love Aix, Gabby. It's one of the most elegant of all French cities, with its twenty-one splashing fountains and its thermal waters, which people have flocked to for their *cure* for two thousand years.

"The old part of town is charming," he continued. "And of course we'll visit Cézanne's studio. He lived and died at a little house in the city, but he went to his studio outside of Aix every day to paint."

"I feel as though I already know this region, from all the slides you've shown us of his work."

"Yes, it's wonderful to discover the area after seeing it through Cézanne's eyes. He caught it all. The whitish blue of the mountains, the green shrubbery of Provence, the sunbathed houses with their red-tiled hats."

He took her arm in his as the train pulled into the station, and they stepped out onto the platform. As they walked into the sunlight, a gust of wind slapped against their faces.

"Yes, M. Mistral is here too." He pulled her close as she shivered and fumbled to button her dark-blue peacoat.

They walked briskly through the narrow streets to the center of town. Gabriella relaxed with his strong arm around her. She almost dared not breathe, so intensely she wished for this moment to last.

David seemed not to notice, as he excitedly pointed out a historical landmark here, a bubbling fountain there, the elegant seventeenth-century facades on the buildings.

"I'm not walking too fast for you, am I?" he questioned suddenly. "How is your ankle holding up?"

"Fine. It's fine." *As long as you keep your arm around me*, she wanted to add.

"We'll drop off our bags at my friend's house. It's right off the place de la Libération."

For a moment Gabriella tensed. She had no desire to meet his friend.

They walked toward a huge three-tiered fountain flanked by bright flowers. A roundabout encircled it, with cars dodging in and out of the four side roads that turned off like spokes on an enormous wheel.

"Right down here on boulevard de la République."

The road was wide and stately, and David strode confidently past the shops on the left side of the street.

"She lives above the *pâtisserie*. On the third floor." He stopped in front of a heavy door and pressed the bell with the name *de Saléon* written beside it. "You ring twice, pausing in between. That's our signal." He laughed, not noticing Gabriella's suddenly sour expression.

Immediately a window three floors up flew open, and a woman's head appeared. *"David! Quel plaisir! Allez! Montez."*

Gabriella squinted in the sun to see the woman's face, but she couldn't distinguish anything about her.

A loud buzzer sounded, and David pulled the door open, motioning to Gabriella to enter first. "The button is on the left, just there." He pointed to the shining orange button that Gabriella knew to be part of every French stairwell.

They climbed the winding marble staircase slowly. As they reached the third floor, a door opened and a smiling woman of about fifty-five bustled out to greet them. Her auburn hair, pulled back in an elegant chignon, was flecked slightly with gray. She was dressed in a sophisticated green tweed suit.

"Madeleine, so good to see you!" David set down the bags and warmly embraced her with kisses on each cheek. "Let me introduce you to my friend, Gabriella Madison. Gabriella, Mme de Saléon."

"Enchantée, Mademoiselle Gabriella. My, but you always pick the pretty ones." She winked at David.

Gabriella's face showed every sign of relief as she beamed back at the attractive woman. *"Enchantée, aussi."* Yes, was she ever pleased to meet her. So there was no lovely young mistress after all.

"Come in, come in, and I'll show you to your rooms. I'm sure you're anxious to be out and about Aix, but you will have a drink? Something light? The trip was easy, *non*? And the change of trains in Marseille no problem?" She threw up her hands and touched her hair. "But of course, with David there is never any problem. Such a fine young man. *Et très beau, n'est-ce pas?*" She leaned toward Gabriella, who nodded, blushing.

They sat in her salon for a few minutes, each drinking a *sirop*.

"She speaks such beautiful French, David," Mme de Saléon commented. Then, directing her gaze at Gabriella, she inquired, "Where did you study?"

"I grew up in Senegal. My schooling was in French," replied Gabriella.

Mme de Saléon nodded and talked on, making pleasant conversation. Several minutes later she shooed them out of the apartment. "To the cours Mirabeau, you two. David will tell you all about it. I'll expect you for supper at seven thirty."

By eleven thirty the biting chill of the mistral had calmed, and the sun began to warm up the cours Mirabeau. David directed Gabriella to a chair at an outdoor café on the north side of the wide, straight boulevard. Four rows of magnificent old plane trees on either side of the avenue stretched their limbs toward the center, forming a type of rustling canopy above the street and the pedestrians.

"Down there at the end of the road is a statue of *le bon roi René*, count of Provence in the middle of the fifteenth century. He's holding the famous muscat grapes in his hands. He's the one who originally thought of harvesting them for the apéritif we drink today. Very sweet and pleasant, if you don't drink too much. You should try it."

"Perhaps I shall later, at Mme de Saléon's."

"After lunch I'll take you to that spot where Cézanne painted many of his finest works. You'll be surprised."

"A view of Mont Saint-Victoire?"

"How did you know?"

"I've been reading my art books to keep up with my distinguished professor."

David let out a hearty carefree laugh she hadn't heard before. "Your distinguished professor, eh?" Leaning closer, he whispered, "And what may he offer his most illustrious pupil?"

For a moment Gabriella thought she would reach out and touch his face with her hand. He caught her look and held her gaze with his eyes, then reached his hand across the table and interlocked his fingers in hers.

"I'll have the usual," she whispered, afraid to look away, afraid that a simple blowing of the wind would destroy the magic of Aix on the cours Mirabeau.

The drinks consumed, they sat for a moment in silence. Then David stood abruptly and said, "It's time to eat."

As if on cue, she was standing too, as he fumbled for the francs and let them jangle on the table.

"I know. I'll get the bread." She laughed to think of how he was so adamant that she try every different type of bread and cheese France offered. Turning to look back at him, she said, "I remember: only *pain de seigle* for us today."

"Hurry on with you, girl." He waved to her, smiling. "They close in five minutes."

She walked along the cobblestone streets of the *vieille ville* until

she reached the boulangerie David had indicated earlier. The best
pain de seigle in town, he assured her.

The short, dark-haired man behind the counter greeted her cautiously. *"Bonjour, mademoiselle."*

"Bonjour. Un pain de seigle, s'il vous plaît." He turned quickly to
retrieve the loaf, but Gabriella stopped him. "Oh, no. Wait a minute.
I think I'd rather have the *pain de campagne*. It looks delicious."

"You are sure, *mademoiselle*?" he questioned, replacing the other
loaf.

"Yes, sure." They hadn't yet tried this kind either. She was pleased
with the thought of surprising David. She placed five francs on the
counter as the man wrapped a piece of thin tissue around the brown
loaf and taped it in place. He handed her the forty centimes of
change.

"Au revoir, mademoiselle."

"Bonne journée," she replied and trotted down the cobblestones
and back to the cours Mirabeau, where David waited with the straw
bag Mme de Saléon had filled with rice salad, pâté, cheeses, and
wine.

"Where shall we eat, David?"

"How about by the Fontaine des Quatre Dauphins? There are a
few private residences from the eighteenth century with their beautiful inner courtyards—what the French call *hôtels*—on the road that
I'd like you to see."

"Sounds perfect."

She followed him across the boulevard and onto a street behind
the Cours. Sitting down beside the fountain, Gabriella started to talk.
"I never realized that Cézanne was a contemporary of Gauguin—they

lived together and were such good friends—" But her chatter was interrupted by David's harsh demand.

"Gabriella! What have you done? This isn't pain de seigle!" He grabbed her arm and clutched it so fiercely that Gabriella gave a quick jerk back.

"For goodness' sake, David, you're hurting me! Why does it matter? I only thought it might be fun to try something different."

Immediately David relaxed his grip. "Of course, you're right. I'm sorry, Gabby." He composed himself and said softly, "Look, I know it sounds crazy, but I'd really like the pain de seigle. Could you please run back and get me a loaf?"

"But they'll be closed, David."

"Maybe not. Go."

He sounded urgent and firm, and she did not hesitate. Back across the cours Mirabeau and up the cobblestone road she ran, feeling like a rebuked child. *He is impossible, demanding,* she thought. Somewhere again in her mind she heard a piercing reminder: *Don't go!* Once again she pushed the voice away, but it kept chanting in her mind until she felt cold fear run down her back.

Something is wrong here, Gabriella. Something is wrong with this dashing young American. Get away! But she continued on. As she reached the store, the boulanger was just pulling down the corrugated siding and locking the door.

"Monsieur!" Gabriella cried loudly. "Wait! Could I please have a pain de seigle?" She slowed to a walk, out of breath.

He seemed to pay no attention, not even looking at her, but quietly he muttered, "You must go at once. Tell your friend the neighbor's bread is better. Now leave!"

Bewildered, she turned to go. What did he mean? Why was he suddenly so angry, just as David had been? And then the chanting words in her mind: *Something is wrong. Get away!*

Gabriella had never experienced a vision from heaven, but she believed God communicated in an inaudible but real voice to His chosen people. And she knew this was the voice she was hearing.

But where do I go, Lord?

The sounds of the open market and pedestrians' feet on the cobblestones suddenly seemed magnified, and she realized her heart was racing.

Then instantly David was there, walking toward her with a look of fear on his usually indifferent face. He didn't slow down as he passed her. He whispered, "Leave Aix, Gabby. I don't know you. Take the train. Go home."

His tone conveyed an urgency that struck new fear in her heart. Quickly she began brushing past the vendors in the marché, slipping beside the man selling cheese as he cried after her, "*Mademoiselle*, come try the St. Paulin!"

She limped past the butcher with the dead chickens hanging upside down from the awning above his table. She grazed the table displaying an array of pigs' hooves and weaved wildly among the fruit and vegetable stands, hearing again and again, "*Mademoiselle!*"

She never looked back, but she could feel the eyes of someone, unknown and unnoticed by the busy scene at the marché. Someone was following, and the knowledge of that had shattered David's cynical, confident air.

She reached the place de la Libération. Just five more minutes, and she'd be at the station. Gabriella did not look back to see a handsome man with hazel eyes and thick brown hair deftly stepping around the vendors in the market, following the bright flash of red hair in front of him.

David continued walking away from Gabriella, but as he turned down a small side street, he paused to watch her twist in and out through the market. Farther behind, a man followed in her steps. David groaned. She stood out like the first red poppy in a field of sunflowers.

What had he done? What should he do now?

It would be so easy to let the man suspect the girl, and he could go free. But how could he do that? Pushing aside his bitter thoughts and angry desire for revenge, he ran down the side street and mingled in the crowd of the marché, far behind the fiery blaze of Gabriella's hair and the dark-haired man who stretched out silently behind her like a long shadow in the afternoon sun.

Jean-Claude Gachon knew the red-haired girl was scared. With his small pocket camera, he clicked several pictures of her limping through the street.

You think you can get away so easily? Hop a train, and I will leave you alone? He jogged on behind her. *The train will not leave for thirty minutes, and that is plenty of time for another small accident.*

Or perhaps you will be more helpful this time. I know more than you think.

He paused at the corner of the road by the post office, watching the young woman continue her frantic flight. He heard a slight noise behind him and turned to see a bottle of wine lifted above his head. Too late, he raised his arms to protect himself. The bottle crashed down, the glass shattering on his head.

The train ride from Aix was without incident. Gabriella got off in Montpellier and walked along the place de la Comédie all afternoon, embarrassed to return to the inquisitive stares of her housemates.

When she went back to the apartment, it was dark. The girls had gone out for the evening, and Mme Leclerc discreetly prepared her a bowl of soup, asking no questions. The phone rang twice, and each time Gabriella started, hoping it was David. Surely he would check on her.

But David did not call.

The night seemed like an endless dark tunnel, offering no sleep, no soft bed of thoughts, nothing but hovering fear and a heavy heartache. Again and again she rehashed the events of the day. The enchantment of the train ride, their walk through Aix, her relief at meeting Mme de Saléon, the pure pleasure of sitting with David on the cours Mirabeau.

Then the stupid mistake with the bread. The bread! Something had been terribly wrong in Aix, and she was sure that it concerned more than a misplaced pain de seigle.

Then the terrifying wait in the train station, wondering who would appear to snatch her away like a quick burst from the mistral wind. But no one had come.

She thought of the subconscious warning that had haunted her on and off all day. *I should have listened to Mother Griolet ... and to You, Lord.*

Heavily she picked herself up off her bed, surprised to see a glimmer of sun streaking through the tiny gap in the closed shutters. Her head throbbing, she slowly pulled on her skirt and a warm wool sweater. The blue cashmere lay in a heap on the chair, reminding her of the way her day had ended.

Sunday morning. The whole weekend spoiled. Well, she would go help Mother Griolet with the orphans at the church.

She leafed through her Bible to the gospel of John and found the verse she had quoted to David on their drive through the countryside. *I am the Vine, ye are the branches ... without Me ye can do nothing.*

She closed the Bible and sat for a moment with her eyes closed. "*Nothing*, Lord. You are right. So please come along with me today."

Gabriella found Mother Griolet sitting alone in the hollow echoes of the church.

"*Ah, ma fille. Bonjour!* I was not expecting you." She reached up to kiss her softly on each cheek. Then she held her face away and stared into Gabriella's eyes. "You are not well today, my vivacious redhead. Your pretty eyes are all swollen."

"Homesick, that's all. It's nothing. Give me a job to do, and it will pass."

"Ah, that I can do, Gabriella. A new child has arrived from out of the blue, as you Americans say. Her mother is missing, presumed dead. No father. She's terrified and grieving, I'm sure of it. But that is not what you will see on her face. I cannot make her talk, so it's best that she grieves in her way. But perhaps you could take her to the beach for a walk. I'll handle the others this morning with Sister Isabelle and Sister Rosaline."

Mother Griolet rose, her long black robes silently sweeping the stone floor. Gabriella followed, wiping a tear with her sleeve and turning to focus on a new challenge. As the old woman opened the peeling wooden door to the parsonage, she turned back and whispered, "Her name is Ophélie."

The child hadn't spoken since the moment they met.

"Here we are at the beach at Carnon, Ophélie. This is where we get off." Gabriella stepped down from the bus and held out her hand for the little girl, who climbed off slowly without taking it.

They made their way off the road and down through a path leading to the beach, the little girl limping beside her. The rich scent of thyme reached out from the dunes that rose up as if protecting the beach from the noise of the road.

"I like to come here by myself, just to think," Gabriella offered, but Ophélie did not turn her head up to look or listen.

They walked in the quiet of the late morning, the chilly sea wind stinging their ears. The beach was deserted. Ophélie's long brown hair flew in wild wisps behind her, pulled by the wind. Her coat was unzipped and her nose red with cold.

"Would you like to go back? Are you too cold?"

A definite shake of the head was Ophélie's only response.

A seagull swooped down in front and cried mockingly to other birds, as yet unseen. The froth of the sea settled dangerously close to their feet. Gabriella moved away from the approaching tide, but Ophélie continued walking straight in the same direction.

"Do you mind if we sit for a moment on the rocks over there, Ophélie? I want to tie my hair back. It's such a mess in this wind."

Without waiting for a reply, Gabriella walked up the beach and sat down on a cluster of smooth rocks that were embedded far away from the reach of the tide. Ophélie followed.

Gabriella quickly untied the bright-blue scarf from around her neck, placing it between her teeth as she gathered her mass of hair into a single thick strand. As she tied the hair into place, pulling wisps out from under her collar, the lightweight chain and cross came out from under her shirt and settled on her chest, shimmering in the sun like a child blinking in the morning light.

"Much better. I should have pulled it back before we came, but I didn't think of it."

Gabriella babbled on, making conversation over nothing, but Ophélie didn't seem to hear her. The child's gaze was fixed on the shimmering cross hanging lightly around Gabriella's neck.

Slowly Ophélie reached behind her own neck and unfastened a chain, then with both hands brought it around in front of her and placed it in the folds of her skirt. She fingered it delicately.

The woman and the child stared for a long while at two identical crosses.

Ophélie whispered, "It was my mama's cross. A gift from her

papa before he was killed in the war...." She continued staring at the golden treasure in her lap. Then she straightened and turned a tear-streaked face toward Gabriella.

Gabriella gently took Ophélie's hand in hers and touched the child's cross. "And now your mama has given it to you. It's a beautiful cross, isn't it?"

"It is hope for Mama. She is missing, but I don't think she is dead."

"Yes, it is hope. Does your mama believe in the God of this cross?"

A shadow crept across Ophélie's face. "I don't think so. But Grandpapy did. Mama said he used to sing me songs about God when I was a baby. But then he died. Mama tried to sing the songs, but she would always cry. Poor Mama. She was always so sad. She didn't think I saw."

"She was sad because of her father?" Gabriella pressed cautiously for more information.

"Yes ... and because there were bad men who came for her."

"Why would bad men come after your mama, Ophélie?"

Ophélie lowered her head further so that her hair hung limply over her face. Her voice was almost inaudible. "She is not bad. My mama is not bad!" Then slowly, "But people might think she was bad because of those men. They were not nice to her."

Ophélie lifted her face toward Gabriella. Her eyes were liquid and dark and filled with a hurt too deep for a child so young.

Gabriella pulled Ophélie closer, enfolding her in her arms. "Of course she's not bad. She must be a very wonderful mother indeed to have a little girl like you."

She kissed the child softly on the forehead and held her for what seemed a long time. In her mind she had a flash of another little girl whose mother was not bad. And farther out, the peaceful Mediterranean watched the wordless embrace of the young woman and the child, and the sun danced its rays through the mingled strands of red and brown hair and dried the unseen tears that they shared.

14

Jean-Claude Gachon nursed the large bump on top of his head with a pack of ice. The headache was still there, but not as fierce as the day before. He wished the children in the streets below would not make such a racket; he wished the baby upstairs had not cried at two a.m. But these were the slums of Marseille, and he had not come here in search of luxury.

He cursed as he thought of the wine bottle crashing on his head. Ali's information had been right. Something *was* going on in Aix on October 21. Something to do with the redhead. But the girl hadn't been alone.

He held a roll of film in his hands and slid it into a thick envelope. Ali needn't worry. It was only a quick train ride from Marseille to Montpellier. He would find the redhead again. It was a simple matter of knowing where to wait. There were not so many choices after all.

He licked the flap of the envelope and sealed it tightly.

David caught Gabriella's arm as she was leaving class on Monday morning. "May I have a word with you, Miss Madison?" He waited for the other students to leave, then closed the classroom door and motioned for Gabriella to take a seat. He stood, leaning against his desk. "You made it home without trouble? I have your things. I am sorry—"

Gabriella was too angry to hear his excuse. "You're sorry, David. But not for me. You're sorry that I botched your plans. I don't know what they were, but I got in the way. You could at least have the decency to tell me what you are dragging me into."

David didn't flinch. "You're right. It won't happen again."

"And that's all you have to say? You put my life in danger, and that's it—'it won't happen again'?" She looked away, brushing her long hair over her shoulders. The late October chill made her shiver as she watched the last leaves clinging to the branches of an old gnarled plane tree. "You won't tell me what you are up to, and you pretend that it's for my safety. But there's something else."

He still said nothing in his defense, so Gabriella continued. "Does it have to do with the war?" she blurted. "Are you involved in the Algerian War?"

David laughed. "And what would I, an American, have to do with the war over there?"

"I don't know. You tell me."

His expression changed, and he leaned toward her. Suddenly she felt ill at ease, as if she had demanded that he reveal a secret she had no business knowing.

"Revenge," he replied.

"Revenge? Revenge for what?" Gabriella was incredulous.

"Revenge for a helpless little boy who watched his mother and sister die. Revenge for a Jew." He whispered with a vengeance that scared her. "This war is about minorities. Algerians who feel oppressed by the French. Pied-noirs who want to keep their land and possessions. Harkis who are faithful to France. They are all pitiful minorities.

"So I was too, in the other war. My people were killed because of our heritage. I was in a camp for a year. And I was the only child to survive."

He turned toward Gabriella, but she was sure he was not seeing her.

"I survived, but I died doing it. You cannot know! You have no right to know!" He stood abruptly and walked toward the door, then stopped.

Gabriella felt pity for him, but she was too proud to say it. "And so now you take out your hatred on others? Is that it? You are such an angry man, David."

"I deserve to be angry, Gabriella! What right do you have to accuse me, you who lived in the shelter of your mother's skirts? Don't judge me in your pious way!"

Gabriella said nothing for a moment. Then she spoke, reaching for her words, as the sun shimmered through the window.

"You think you're the only one in the world who has suffered? You think that because I call myself a Christian, life has been easy for me and my family? You think we are immune to suffering, nothing touches us? If that is what you think, you're wrong."

Her eyes were wet with tears. "I have two younger sisters, but at one time I had three. When Ericka was six, she got sick, and Father was away in the bush. Mother had some medicine, but the fever rose. Ericka needed penicillin, but we had no transportation. We'd been in this village for two years, living among the people, but they still seemed hostile and removed. Mother radioed to the closest mission station, two hundred miles away, but it would be three days before they could get to us. And so she prayed. For two days and nights she didn't sleep. She bathed Ericka and put compresses on her, but my sister only grew weaker.

"Her skin turned yellow, then blue, and she coughed up blood. And then she was gone. Mother sat beside her cold body for another day. She spent all her tears there. Then she put on her black shawl and the other traditional mourning clothes of the Senegalese. She opened her home and received the women of the village. They embraced her and wailed and held her. For, suddenly, she was like them, in her grief. We buried Ericka, Mother and I, with the people looking on. When Father returned five days later, it was all over."

David touched her sleeve, as if to touch the pain, but Gabriella's head remained bent.

"And how did you get through your pain?" he asked.

"I cried a lot, and I yelled at God. I thought I would never get over it. But the pain left, finally, and then there was something even worse. It was hate." She brushed her eyes and continued. "I was angry. Angry at my father for being away. Angry at the mission for not coming quickly enough. Angry at God for letting her die. He could have stopped it! And I was angry with myself for standing by and not being able to do anything."

David nodded, as if he understood the feeling of helplessness. "And are you still angry?"

Gabriella thought for a moment. "No, I'm not. Mother watched me grieve, and she told me and my sisters that it was okay to be mad. I could read in her eyes that she felt anger too. So senseless! In America Ericka would have had the penicillin!

"But little by little, Mother said, we had to forgive—that anger is a wound that festers and rots and turns to bitterness unless we let it go." Gabriella looked up at David. "She said forgiveness is freedom. It's not so much for those I'm angry at, as for myself. If I don't forgive, I will live forever with the hatred until it destroys me."

"And so you forgave, and everything was fine?" His voice held sarcasm.

She was suddenly afraid of his question. "I didn't say it was easy."

"You're wrong, Gabriella. You and your mother are wrong. Forgiveness is not power or strength. It's weakness. It's kneeling before the enemy and forgetting. I don't want to forget. The memory of their evil spurs me on! To forgive is to relinquish, and I will never do that. I will win my private war."

Gabriella heard the doors from the basement of the parsonage squeak open and the sound of twenty-five children spilling out into the courtyard. She jumped to her feet and quickly went to the window.

"I have to go," she said. "Good-bye, David." As she pronounced those words, she felt the distance of an ocean between them, and she rushed out of the room and into the courtyard, chilled by his icy stare and the whipping mistral.

Ophélie sat on a lower bunk in the dormitory. *"Un, deux, trois, quatre ... "* There were eight bunks. That made sixteen beds. And this bed belonged to her. The old nun called Mother Griolet had said so.

The first night, Ophélie had barely slept. She woke up three times screaming "Mama!" with the sound of gunshots in her ears. Sister Isabelle had come rushing in.

The second day was different. The woman with the long red hair had taken her to the beach. And she wore Papy's cross. Ophélie smiled to think of it. She was a pretty lady, and she smiled a lot. And she had understood that Mama was not bad.

For the first time in as long as she could remember, Ophélie felt safe. The tall man who had rescued her had disappeared, but everyone else was very friendly. Friendly with a sad, pitiful look in their eyes.

But that did not matter. The red-haired lady who wore the cross had told her that her mama was a wonderful woman to have such a good girl.

Ophélie hugged her knees to her chest and smiled again. She heard the sound of the other children's voices laughing in the court-yard. She didn't know where she was, but it was a good place to be, she was sure. A place where adults were kind and children laughed. And best of all, there was school! Today she had gone to school!

Ophélie recalled the old nun's words when she had whispered that she did not know how to read. *Ah, Ophélie! Reading! It is a gift. You're a bright child. We will have you reading in no time at all!*

Ophélie took the blue bag out from under her pillow. She could not leave it there because the Sisters changed the sheets every week. This was important for cleanliness, Mother Griolet had explained. No, they might take off the pillowcase and find the bag.

But now she had a little chest of drawers all to herself. It sat at the head of her bed. When she opened the drawers the first day, she couldn't believe what she saw. Two long-sleeved white blouses, two black wool skirts, and a bright-pink sweater in the first drawer. And more treasures in the second: five pairs of white underwear. On one pair there was even lace! And two pairs of tights. The warm wool kind. Also a robe and a warm flannel nightgown and slippers.

She liked looking in the bottom drawer the best. Inside was a pink plastic brush and comb. All her own! And two sets of pink barrettes for her hair. But the last treasure she found had made her cry with joy. A doll with black hair that reached to her waist and fancy little eyes that opened and closed when she was rocked. And wearing a pretty blue dress.

The old nun had explained that the clothes were not new, nor the brush and comb, nor the doll. Kind people gave these things to the orphanage. But Ophélie did not care. These were her treasures! Hers! She wished she could tell her mama.

It is a miracle, Mama! I have a doll of my own. And lots of little girls to play with. And, Mama, very soon I will know how to read.

Ophélie pulled the pair of blue tights out of the second drawer. Carefully she slid the blue bag down into one of the legs. Then she placed the tights back in their place, beside the white ones and the frilly panties.

I will be safe here, Mama. Don't worry. I will stay right here until you come to get me.

Mother Griolet watched the children playing in the courtyard from her chair behind the old mahogany desk. Through the closed windows, the muffled noise of their laughter rose like a faint melody, reaching into her office. Little Ophélie stepped from the dormitory into the sunlight. She stood on the edge of the grass, hesitating before she ran out to join the other children.

"This little one is a mystery to me, Lord. Oh, I know You know her well. She is one of Your precious sparrows. But, Lord, You understand that there are certain papers I must have. Certain regulations for the orphanage." She leaned back in her chair. "Yes, I know. They are warm. They are fed. They are happy. You have always provided."

Hakim stood off alone leaning against the far wall of the court-yard. He was taller than the other children, his skin darker.

"This one too, Lord. I am counting on You for the next step. I will wait. That is one thing You have taught me over the years. Your timing is best."

She reached down, pulled out the bottom desk drawer, and lifted out a faded photograph of Rebecca Madison standing beside her, with all the children. "And one more thing, Lord. Dear Gabriella. You know she wears her mother's cross. I find it a bit ironic, don't You? And confusing? But nothing is too difficult for You. You see all: the past, the present, the future. Please prepare me for the next step. That is all I need or care to know."

Settling back in the big chair, she held the old photograph in her hands for another minute. Then she closed her eyes and began a soft chant that flowed from her lips with the ease of years of repetition. Yet the emotion in her voice testified to her assurance as she prayed, "Now unto Him that is able to do exceeding abundantly above all that we ask or think, according to the power that worketh in us.

Unto Him be glory in the church by Christ Jesus throughout all ages, world without end. Amen."

Rachid waited until the middle of the night to trace his way through the maze of streets in the Casbah. At last he could make the lovely pied-noir talk. He had such an effective way with women!

Ali was angry now. Emile had let the girl get away, then he too had disappeared. But Rachid could not disappear. Ali would find him in Algiers. So he must make the woman talk. He was ready to watch Anne-Marie Duchemin squirm and scream.

He let himself into the tiny brick basement that smelled of mold and sewage. For almost a month the two hostages had been locked in this room with no facilities and no light except for the small barred windows at the top of the walls. He laughed at how easy his task would be. Bread and water and filth for a month. They would talk.

He entered the room where Moustafa and Anne-Marie lay sleeping on the two thin mattresses. He knelt beside Anne-Marie and softly brushed her hair with his fingers. She reached for his hand in her sleep, then woke with a start and screamed, sitting up quickly.

"Now my dear, why do you scream? I am only feeling your hair. It is so nice to the touch." He moved closer, pressing his body down softly on Anne-Marie's.

Moustafa awakened to the sound of Anne-Marie screaming. He scrambled to stand up, but before he could get to his feet, Rachid had his gun pointed toward him.

"Sit down, you fool. You do not know a lovely woman when you see one. We have left you here for so long together, and still you have not shown her the tenderness she deserves?" He laughed. "If you cannot show it, then I shall. I am very convincing."

"Leave her alone! She's very sick, this woman. You cannot bring her anything for her cough? It drives me crazy. She will die here, and then this place will reek even more!" Moustafa searched desperately for a way to divert Rachid. He was weak from hunger, and his head spun. "What do you want anyway, Rachid? You have not asked anything of us yet."

Rachid turned away from Anne-Marie for a moment. "It has not been necessary. You see, we have found your daughter."

Anne-Marie gasped.

"Yes, and the old shopkeeper. It's a pity the old man wasn't more helpful. But your daughter … yes! She too coughs a lot, our friend tells us."

"Where is Ophélie? You have not hurt her?"

"Do not worry so, Anne-Marie. She's a very cooperative child. She does, after all, have the information." He watched for the mother's reaction.

Anne-Marie said nothing.

"So you see, we have no need of either of you." He toyed with the gun. "Unless there is something else you wish to tell us. Something that could help Ali in his mission?"

Anne-Marie turned to Moustafa, her eyes filled with fear. He shot her an angry look.

"Yes, Rachid. I think Anne-Marie has some very vital information for Ali. It would be a pity to kill her now. I have discovered
several things she knows. As you say, it pays to be tender." He met
Rachid's eyes and smiled. "She trusts too much, this woman. Tell Ali
that she will meet with him. With all of the men together."

Rachid struck Moustafa hard across the face. "Idiot! You will
never leave here alive. You tell me now, woman, or I will kill your
tender friend." He held the gun to Moustafa's head.

Anne-Marie spoke in a cold, harsh tone. "Kill him if you wish.
He is worse than the rest of you. Get his stinking body away. But I
won't talk here. Take me to Ali."

"I can make you talk, you trash." He swerved angrily, the gun
now pointing at her.

In a flash, Moustafa grabbed him by the neck. Rachid lashed
back with his elbow, striking Moustafa full in the stomach, but the
young man held on. With one hand he gripped Rachid around the
throat and with the other he grasped for the gun, which Rachid
circled wildly above him.

"Anne-Marie!"

She had grabbed the old chair and now brought it down on
Rachid's skull. The gun went off. Moustafa fell backward with
Rachid on top of him. Again Anne-Marie brought down the chair
on Rachid's back.

With a cry Rachid pulled himself off Moustafa, waving the gun
madly about his head. "You!" he moaned, then fell at Anne-Marie's
feet.

Her hands trembling, she pulled the gun from his grip.
"Moustafa? Are you hurt?" There was panic in her voice.

Moustafa crouched beside Rachid. "Not badly. He shot himself when you hit him with the chair."

"Is he dead?"

"No. Give me the bottle."

Anne-Marie did not move.

"The bottle. The pill. Now!"

"I can't."

Moustafa was standing. Grabbing at her sleeve, he ripped the little bottle out. "Leave if you don't want to watch."

Still Anne-Marie didn't move.

Moustafa took a tiny pill and slipped it under Rachid's tongue. "Rest in peace, you coward."

He watched Anne-Marie run out into the night air and heard her gag. Instantly he was by her side, holding her as her body was racked with dry heaves. He locked the door with Rachid's keys and tucked the gun into his belt.

"Come now, Anne-Marie. Do not give up now! To life!"

15

"In the later years of his life, Coleridge was reconciled with his friend Wordsworth. After Coleridge's death, Wordsworth declared that he was 'the most wonderful man that I have ever known.'"

David's lecture comparing the literature of Coleridge and Wordsworth was ordinarily one of his favorites, but today he felt dissatisfied as the young women left his class. November was coming to a close. For the past month Gabriella had politely addressed him as M. Hoffmann in class, but otherwise she avoided him. It was his own fault. She hadn't understood what he'd tried to tell her that day in the courtyard after Aix. But the truth would only hurt her more.

So in class David kept his composure. He laughed and winked and charmed the students with his witty comments. But he never tried to touch Gabriella after the others were out of sight. Only in his mind did he reach out to the poppies and long for the laughter that haunted his dreams.

He left the classroom, briefcase in hand, walking away from the parsonage and through the town toward Mme Pons's apartment. The fruit stand outside the entrance didn't tempt him with its polished red apples and thick orange clementines. He quickly let himself into his room and closed the door, leaving his briefcase by the bed, then took a seat at the small desk. Opening his lap drawer, he brought out a stack of papers. An old photograph sat on top of the stack, and he brushed it with his hand, as if he could touch the face of the young woman who stood beside him in the picture, frozen in place, smiling out of the picture without a care in the world.

How I wish I knew where you were. You asked for my help, but I don't know where else to look.

He dropped the photograph and covered his face with his hands. Gabby's silence was not the only quiet he feared. Yesterday's paper lay on the floor. David reached down to retrieve it and reread the headline: Twenty Killed in Terrorist Attack in Algiers.

Gabriella hardly touched the delicious noon meal Mme Leclerc had prepared. Stephanie had already asked for seconds while Gabriella played with the noodles and meat in the *boeuf bourguignon*.

"Gabriella, do you think your parents will be happy to see their daughter so thin after her year in France? *Ooh là là!* You will ruin my reputation as the best cook in Castelnau."

Gabriella smiled as she set down her fork. "Now, Mme Leclerc. You know it's nothing to do with your cooking. Surely you have had other boarders who were homesick?"

"Homesick, yes. But for a whole month! You've hardly eaten a thing for all of November. It's not right!"

Stephanie laughed. "Yes, and the less you eat, the more is left over, and I always seem to find room for seconds! Imagine what *my* parents will say!"

No one said a word about David Hoffmann, but Gabriella knew what they were thinking: *She's not homesick; she's lovesick.* They were right.

Mother Griolet noticed Gabriella's quiet restlessness more than anyone. She prayed daily for the private battle the young woman fought with her God. She watched her leave the parsonage quickly after classes and return only when she was scheduled to work with the orphans. Gabriella stayed away from the American professor and clung to the children, especially Ophélie. One life to fill up the hole left by another.

Gabriella appeared in the doorway of her office, interrupting the old nun's thoughts. "*Bonjour, Mère Griolet!* I'm ready for the afternoon adventure. Is Ophélie here?"

"Yes, my child. She's thrilled to have the afternoon alone with you. She's been brushing her hair for half an hour." The nun met Gabriella's eyes. "You're a blessing to those children. And you are hope for Ophélie. You see it, *non*?"

Gabriella blushed, and Mother Griolet added quickly, "I'm not telling you these things for you to get a big head, as you Americans say. God has gifted you with the children. He has done it to help a stubborn little old lady in an orphanage. You're strong, Gabriella. Remember that." She grasped her hand and held it for a moment. "Don't be afraid. God is with you. Thank you for being with Him."

She pronounced the last phrases with great care, and Gabriella raised her eyebrows.

"I get the feeling you're trying to tell me something, Mother Griolet. But you don't dare. It's more than simple encouragement for a lovesick girl, isn't it?"

"Go on now, have your adventure. Show little Ophélie the house you lived in when you were here as a child." But as Gabriella left the office, pulling the door shut behind her, Mother Griolet added, "And be strong."

The bus ride from Castelnau through Montpellier to the west side of town took thirty-five minutes.

Ophélie chattered excitedly as Gabriella pointed out different landmarks. "I love riding on the bus! Oh, it's such fun! So big!"

Gabriella smiled at her. "We're almost there now. The next stop is ours." She glanced down at the directions Mother Griolet had scribbled for her.

At first the old nun had balked at the idea. "There's no need to go back over there. I'm not even sure the mission still owns it." But at Gabriella's insistence, she had telephoned and arranged the visit.

The bus came to a halt and the glass doors parted to release an eager little girl and her maîtresse. The air was cold as they stepped onto the sidewalk, but the wind was not blowing.

"It's just a short walk from here," Gabriella said. She searched her coat pocket and brought out a five-franc piece, which she handed to Ophélie. "A treat from me. You may buy a pastry at the first pâtisserie you find."

"Oh thank you, Gabriella!" Ophélie's eyes danced with anticipation, searching the street for a store. "May I try that boulangerie over there? Look, there are pastries in the window." She tugged on

Gabriella's coat, pulling her toward a window front filled with delicate-looking confections. "What would you choose if you were me?"

"Well, that's a good question, Ophélie. Let me see. The *éclair* is filled with cream and topped with chocolate. Or look at the *mille-feuilles*. All the thin layers of pastry with cream in between and a chocolate-vanilla-swirled icing."

"Look at that one. It looks like a person!" Ophélie pointed to two balls of pastry stacked on top of each other, like a snowman with a chocolate hat.

"Oh, that is called a *religieuse*. Can you see it, Ophélie? It's like a nun with her black scarf and robes. And inside the pastry is that same thick, delicious cream."

"That's what I want! A religieuse! Like Mother Griolet. I'm sure it will be the sweetest pastry in the whole wide world!" She hugged Gabriella tightly before she ran into the store, her long hair, braided in two pigtails, flying out behind her.

Moments later she returned to the sidewalk, beaming as she held the little religieuse in its paper doily. "This is my first pastry, Gabriella. Mama never had the money for pastries."

"She is wise, your mama. You mustn't waste money on pastries. Just this once, a special treat for a special girl on a special day. Come along now."

The mission house looked much the same as the other houses that faced the busy avenue. Its facade was sturdy, built of cement blocks and then stuccoed in the light-coral color typical of the Midi. Four pairs of heavy wooden shutters had been painted a grayish blue. They stood open, displaying the large single-pane windows that blinked back the sun's reflection.

Gabriella rang the doorbell by the street entrance. Moments later a tall, blond young woman holding a baby in her arms opened the door.

"Gabriella Madison! Welcome!" the woman said. "And this must be your little friend, Ophélie. *Bonjour!*" She reached out with her free hand and stroked the child's head.

"Oh dear. I hope we didn't wake the baby," Gabriella said.

"No, no. She had just gotten up. I'm Barbara Butler, as I told Mother Griolet when she phoned. Did you realize that our parents know one another, Gabriella? They met at a training conference years ago in the States. Your parents are in Senegal, isn't that right?"

"Yes, that's right. And yours are in the Belgian Congo, I remember. Mother didn't tell me that you would be here in Montpellier."

"We're just here briefly, on our way to the Congo ourselves. May I get you something to drink?" She smiled at Ophélie. "It looks like you've already had your *goûter* from that chocolate mustache you're wearing."

Ophélie nodded happily. "Gabriella bought me a religieuse!"

"Oh my, those are good. Well, come on up and have something to drink. Water, a sirop perhaps? We have strawberry and lemon."

Barbara led her guests through a large open room, its walls lined with books. "This is the meeting room for the students who are here to learn French and African culture—you know all about that, I suppose. Our apartment is upstairs." They walked through the room and up a winding flight of stairs.

"Have a seat in the den." Barbara welcomed them into her apartment. "I'll just put little Alice in her playpen here."

Ophélie and Gabriella stepped into the den. "I hardly remember this place at all," Gabriella called to Barbara. "Did Mother Griolet tell you I was here with my mother and sisters when I was little?"

"Oh, no! How fun to come back!" Barbara said. She returned to the den with three tall glasses of lemonade, which she placed on a coffee table. "Oh, there's the phone! Excuse me for a second."

As she strode out of the room, Ophélie took one of the glasses and moved toward the playpen.

Gabriella smiled and watched the little girl bending over the baby. Suddenly an image flashed before her, like a photograph. *A little girl with curly red hair bending down over someone. Not a baby, but a woman.*

"Mommy," Gabriella whispered.

Ophélie turned to look at her. "What did you say, Gabriella?"

Gabriella shook herself. "Nothing, dear. I was just remembering …" She closed her eyes to wipe away the picture, but it flashed before her again in the darkness. *The little redhead was looking down at her mother, whose face was bruised and bloody. She was shaking her mother frantically and crying.*

"No!" Gabriella said aloud.

Ophélie came over to her. "What is wrong, *Maîtresse*? You look scared."

Gabriella knelt down and hugged Ophélie to her chest. "It's nothing, sweetheart. I'm sorry if I frightened you. Go back and play with little Alice."

When Barbara entered the den a few minutes later, Gabriella excused herself to find the bathroom. She walked down the hall and opened a door, instinctively knowing that the bathroom was there.

She closed the door behind her and leaned over the sink. Another picture flashed in her mind. *Water was running from the spigot. Water and blood.*

"Lord! What is this?" she whispered, turning on the water. Again and again she splashed cool water on her face, washing away the memory. After a few minutes, she dried her face on a towel that hung by the sink and emerged from the bathroom. Baby Alice was giggling loudly along with Ophélie, and Barbara was enjoying the show.

"Ophélie is wonderful with babies," Barbara said as Gabriella entered the den.

Gabriella picked up her drink and patted Ophélie on the head. "Yes, we're so happy to have Ophélie with us." Her voice caught.

"Would you like to see the rest of the house?" Barbara asked.

"No, no, this is just fine. We can't stay too long."

Yet the two women sat on the couch and for nearly an hour talked of Africa as Ophélie played happily beside the baby. No other pictures flashed through Gabriella's mind, but she breathed a deep sigh when they stepped outside and waved good-bye to Barbara and Alice. Ophélie held Gabriella's hand, swinging her arms jubilantly as she matched the young woman's brisk gait.

"I had so much fun," Ophélie exclaimed. "Thank you, Gabriella. That was one of the happiest days of my life!"

Gabriella squeezed Ophélie's hand and forced a smile. "One of the happiest days of your life …"

The bell in the church chimed seven o'clock. Ophélie waited until all the other children had left the dormitory to open her middle drawer and pull out the little blue bag from inside her tights. She shook the contents out. What a wonderful day. She had ridden a big bus and eaten a yummy pastry and held hands and laughed with Gabriella.

She looked at the small photograph of her mother and herself and furrowed her brow. "I don't want you to think I have forgotten you, Mama. It's only that Gabriella is so nice. She teaches me things. And I know she likes me. I still love you the most, but when I'm with her, I sometimes forget how much I miss you."

The envelope with her name on it lay wrinkled on the bed. Ophélie removed the thin pink sheets of paper and began sounding out the words. "*D … dea … dear! Dear Ophélie. How … I lo … love … you.* Oh, see, Mama! I can read! You love me! Yes, I know it. And I will read the rest later."

She folded the letter with the other sheets of paper and then tucked the picture into the bag with them. Back into the dark-blue tights went the velvet bag. Back into the middle drawer. Ophélie stood up and pulled the cross out from under her blouse. She kissed it softly. "Mama, Gabriella talks to me about God. And His Son, Jesus. I don't think you will mind. I'm sure you would like to hear about Him too." She ran out of the room and across the courtyard to the dining hall.

Ophélie was still eating her dessert when Mother Griolet sat down beside her in the dining hall. "How was your afternoon in town?" the nun questioned.

"It was really, really fun, *Mère Griolet*. Gabriella even bought me a pastry—a religieuse—and it was as sweet as you are! And I played with the baby and rode on the biggest bus."

"I'm glad you had such a lovely time." Then an expression of concern registered on her face. "What is that you're wearing around your neck, little Ophélie?"

"My cross? It was my Papy's cross that he gave to Mama. Then Papy died." She touched the necklace, her face sad. Then she brightened. "Did you know that Gabriella has the same one? We wear the same cross! She says it was the cross of the Huguos ... the Hunots ..."

"The Huguenots."

"Yes, the Huguenots. They were brave people who lived in France a long time ago when a mean king ruled. He wouldn't let them pray to Jesus. He locked them in prisons and killed all the men. But they were very brave. And they wore this cross to show who they were!"

"I see that Gabriella has taught you a history lesson."

"History?"

"The events of the past. Well, it's a lovely cross. And what did you say your mama's name is, dear?"

"Are you going to find her for me?" Ophélie's eyes held hope.

"I hope we can find her. But not if you don't tell me her name. Surely you see now that we only want to help you?"

Ophélie considered Mother Griolet's words carefully. "I suppose it would be okay to tell you. Her name is Anne-Marie. She is the most beautiful lady in the whole world. Anne-Marie Duchemin."

"Thank you, my child. What a pretty name she has. Now at least we know who we are looking for." She patted the child's hand as she rose to leave the table. Suddenly she turned back around. "Did your mama ever tell you anything that was special about the cross? Did she tell you why she gave it to you?"

"Oh yes! She said that I should wear it so that the God of Papy would be with me. That is why!"

"And that's a good reason. A very good reason indeed."

Gabriella sat up in her bed, sweat streaming down her face. Someone knocked on the door and then opened it.

"Are you okay, Gab?" Caroline peeped in. "Boy, did you yell."

"Just a bad dream. Sorry to wake you. Thanks for checking."

Caroline shut the door, leaving Gabriella in the darkness. She switched on the lamp beside the bed.

Was it only a dream? This time it was not a single image she saw, but a whole scene playing out before her. A dark-skinned man kneeling over her mother, a little red-haired child hiding behind a door. Her mother's screams.

It couldn't be true. Not her mother.

The house was quiet. Gabriella climbed out of bed and walked over to the window. The pane was cold to her touch. She shivered, watching the shadow of the olive tree. Its leaves, still intact in winter, moved silently. She closed her eyes and saw Barbara Butler smiling at her with the baby in her arms. Then she saw Ophélie laughing. Immediately her mother took the place of Barbara in her mind, and she too was holding a baby.

Ericka. Oh no. Not Mother, not Ericka. She leaned against the pane and strained to see through the darkness. But all was perfectly black.

Ophélie woke in the middle of the night and sat straight up in bed. "Mama!" she said out loud. She smiled to think of the wonderful dream. She was walking hand in hand with Mama, laughing, running in the sand at the beach.

Then she covered her mouth with her hand. It wasn't Mama. The woman in her dream had long red hair.

16

Ali Boudani held a thick manila envelope in his hands. "At last. We have waited weeks for the slides from our friend in France. The mail is slow. Or perhaps someone else has tampered with the envelope first?" His piercing eyes glared at the five men seated around him. "You saw what happened to our brother Rachid. He went alone to have his own way. Fool! Another martyr for the cause. But he has tarnished his father's name. Dying at the hands of our prisoners!"

He handed the envelope to a rugged old man who wore a turban around his head. "Mahmud, prepare the slides."

Ali circled the room like a wolf directing his pack. "The pied-noir escaped with her harki boyfriend—but they will never leave Algeria. Perhaps they have rotted here in the Casbah, right under our noses. Do we not smell the stench? We'll find them again, and how they will howl in pain. For the honor of Rachid's name, their tortured bodies will be displayed for all to see and remember. They can't hide forever. And Ali has eyes in the back of his head."

The men nodded with a low, nervous laughter.

"The slides are ready, Mahmud?"

With a click of the switch, a picture spread across the screen. A woman with long curly red hair was walking away, her back to the camera. She wore a dark-blue peacoat.

"Go on."

Another slide appeared of the same woman, this time half-turned to face the camera.

"Jean-Claude has met this woman twice, as he waited for information. She lives in Montpellier. He has not yet found out her name, but he believes she is a student. He is quite sure she is involved in the smuggling activities." He motioned to Mahmud to advance the slides, and a close-up of the woman's head and shoulders flashed on the screen. "She wears the cross."

The men murmured as they squinted at the slide to see a small cross hanging around the red-haired woman's neck.

"Jean-Claude will find her again soon. We have lost the mother and her daughter and their harki slime. We will not lose anyone else. It's only a matter of time!"

It was barely dawn when Gabriella appeared at the parsonage. Mother Griolet opened the door slightly, peeking outside to see the unexpected caller.

"Gabriella! My dear child. What in the world ... *Entre, entre.*" She pulled Gabriella into her apartment, shutting the door as several dead leaves blew into the corridor.

Gabriella stood before her, trembling, her hair tangled and eyes swollen and red. A thick gray wool sweater covered her flannel nightgown, and her feet were bare inside a pair of thin bedroom slippers.

"Child, look at you! You'll catch your death running around dressed like that. *Mais alors!* Come back to the den!"

Mother Griolet scurried through the hallway with Gabriella

following. "Here now. Take a seat on the couch. I'll bring you a quilt and some coffee."

She stepped quickly back into her room, where she gathered up a thick quilt in her arms and smoothed her short silver hair.

She hurried back into the den and surrounded Gabriella with the quilt. "The coffee will be ready in a moment, dear. There are tissues in the bathroom if you need them."

Gabriella sat quietly on the couch, huddled like a wounded puppy.

"Here now." Mother Griolet set a small tray with two steaming bowls of coffee on a low table in front of the couch. The rich, enticing aroma of the hot drink filled the room as the church bell chimed six times. Mother Griolet pulled up an old wicker rocking chair and sat in silence beside Gabriella.

Minutes droned by, broken only by the sound of Gabriella's sniffling. She wiped her eyes with the sleeve of her sweater and curled herself up more tightly on the couch. She stared at the black coffee and the swirling steam.

Finally she spoke, her voice choked with emotion. "She was raped! Raped! Mother was raped, and you knew!" Her voice exploded with a vengeance. "You let me go to that house to remember! You have known all along." She turned, her eyes streaming with tears, to look at the older woman. "You and Mother! She sent me back here to relive her nightmare! Why did no one ever tell me?"

Gabriella sobbed uncontrollably, and her thin body shook violently under the quilt. Mother Griolet came to her side, cuddling her in her arms like a wailing baby.

"Dear Gabriella. I'm so sorry. Yes, you're right. I knew about the rape." She squeezed her lips together and closed her eyes. Tears lined her wrinkled face. "It's hard to know, sometimes, what is best told and what left unsaid."

Gabriella sat up and pulled herself away from Mother Griolet's embrace. She spoke softly into the air. "A burglar. An Arab. He surprised Mother nursing Henrietta in the den. I don't know where Jessica was, but ..." Her voice quavered. "But I hid ... I hid behind the door."

Suddenly Gabriella seemed not to be with Mother Griolet. She screamed, "No! Stop it! Stop it! Mother is yelling, she is screaming. 'Gabriella! Get help!' She is screaming, and then she is not screaming anymore. And the man ... the man picks himself up off Mother. He tucks in his shirt and zips his pants. And he leaves." She turned to face Mother Griolet.

"I saw it all. And I never said a word. I couldn't scream. I hid and watched the man ..." Her sobs increased. She stood quickly, letting the quilt fall to the floor, and ran toward the hall.

Mother Griolet listened as Gabriella heaved and sobbed in the bathroom. The nun cried and rocked herself, whispering softly, "My God, my God. Come, Lord Jesus, and comfort us now."

Sunlight streamed through the windows in Mother Griolet's den. The bell had long since chimed seven times. Mother Griolet sat beside Gabriella, praying and crying with her. Gabriella's tears had finally stopped.

Now Mother Griolet spoke. "Gabriella, your mother didn't know you saw, nor did I. A neighbor found her. She heard the baby wailing on and on and came over to see what was wrong. She called me, as she knew your mother and I were friends.

"When I got there, your mother was already at the hospital. The neighbor had Henrietta. Jessica had been playing at a friend's house. And you ..." Her eyes met Gabriella's. "You were in the garden, playing in the mud. That's where the neighbor found you. When you saw me, you hugged me. You had been crying, but we thought you were afraid because of the police. Dear child, I had no idea that you saw it all."

"Why didn't Mother ever tell me she was raped?" Gabriella said.

Mother Griolet massaged her temples and sighed. "The doctor advised against it. He said you were too young to understand. She was trying to do what was best for you."

"But ... later. She could have told me later, when I wasn't too young—not too young to know what happened. To understand that Ericka ... that Ericka ..." She could not continue.

"She would have told you, Gabriella. But things turned out differently. You were only twelve when—"

"When Ericka died. I could see she didn't look like the rest of us. But I never once thought ... I didn't remember! I had no memory of the rape until yesterday. No idea!"

"That is quite normal, dear. Such violent abuses are often hidden away until a woman is grown. Locked away in the memory." Mother Griolet paused. Then, looking out the window, she continued, "Afterward, it was too painful for your mother to speak of Ericka. She couldn't see how telling you everything would help."

"Father knew?"

"Of course. There was never any question for either of them that she would keep the baby. Gabriella, it was really this terrible circumstance that bonded your mother and me. We had only known each other a month when it happened. I helped her through the grieving process. And then, when she found out she was pregnant ...” She sighed heavily. “Such a difficult time. But you all left soon after. Back to Senegal. Of course, we corresponded.”

The nun reached for Gabriella’s hand and squeezed it. “She loved Ericka just like the rest of you, Gabriella. And she knew what a jewel that baby sister was for you. She didn’t see what good it could do to bring up the past.”

“And then Ericka got sick and died, and it didn’t matter anymore,” Gabriella said sarcastically. “And I never would have known if I hadn’t decided to come back here. That’s why Mother was worried. She was afraid I might remember. That’s why she gave me this cross!” She yanked it out from under her nightgown with such force that the chain snapped and the cross fell to the floor.

“Now, dear, calm yourself—”

“I will not be calm!” Gabriella yelled. “I can’t sweep away a nightmare ... a nightmare I never knew existed. Do you expect me to just get over it? Just like that?”

“No, no. You could never just ‘get over it.’ It will take time. Much time.” Mother Griolet reached out and touched Gabriella’s sleeve. “I will be here to walk through it with you, as I did with your mother. If you want.” She hugged Gabriella to her breast and let her cry until the young woman closed her eyes and fell asleep in the old nun’s lap.

The church bell chimed eight o’clock, and Mother Griolet quietly slipped out of the room.

By the time Mother Griolet returned to her apartment, Gabriella had gone. The quilt lay folded on the couch, and the coffee bowls were still untouched. Mother Griolet sat down, breathing heavily. She massaged a leg and then pulled it up with difficulty to let it rest on the small coffee table. "I'm afraid, Lord, that Gabriella will have a hard time with this, with forgiveness. She has that temperament, fiery like her hair. Oh, I know she deserves to be angry. Life is so unjust! Only, please, *Mon Père*, give me the strength. And the words. And the ears to hear."

Her eyes fell to the floor where the Huguenot cross still lay, the chain half hidden under the couch. Mother Griolet reached down and picked it up. She held it in the palm of her hand, fingering the dove that dangled from the end of the cross.

"You have come back to remind me, haven't you?" She spoke to the treasure in her hand. "An unconventional Catholic nun once bought you for a grieving friend. 'Come to the cross,' that nun said. 'That is the only way. There is forgiveness.' And now that same old nun must remember her words for a very scared young woman. And remember for herself." She touched the cross to her lips and closed her eyes.

"Lord Jesus, I come to Your cross today as every day. And I say, forgive me if in keeping this secret I have brought unnecessary pain on Gabriella. You know that was never my intention. I'm a stubborn old woman, but I'm trying to take up my cross daily and follow You."

The cross hung from its broken chain, swaying back and forth in Mother Griolet's hand as she prayed. A burst of sunlight invaded the room. Mother Griolet opened her eyes to see hundreds of spots of light dancing and shimmering across the wall. At first she didn't detect the source. Then she touched the cross. Immediately the bright spots of light twirled through the room, imitating and expanding the soft movement of the cross.

A sparkle returned to Mother Griolet's eyes as she watched the play of light against the shadows. "I am the Light of the World," she quoted. "He that followeth Me shall not walk in darkness, but shall have the light of life." She slipped the cross into the pocket of her robe and pulled herself off the couch.

Gabriella skipped all of her classes. She wandered restlessly through the streets of Castelnau. The two pains au chocolat that she had bought after changing her clothes at Mme Leclerc's grew stale in their paper sack. She caught a bus to Montpellier and rode all the way back to the west side of town. She walked to the mission house and stood outside across the street for two hours, numbed by the biting chill of the wind. The cold stung her eyes, but no tears flowed.

She took a stone from the sidewalk and threw it forcefully into the road. It hit the pavement, yards shy of the house. A bus stopped down the street, and she ran to jump on. For another hour the bus roamed the streets of Montpellier. Gabriella kept riding. She didn't know where she was, and she didn't care.

Suddenly she thought of David's words. *I survived, but I died doing it.* She hadn't understood him then, but now she knew what he meant. Surviving could be a living death. She closed her eyes and dozed off.

Sometime later the bus driver gently shook her awake. "*Mademoiselle*, it's the end of the line here. You must get off."

Obediently Gabriella descended from the bus. Children were shouting gleefully in a nearby school playground. Cars lined the street in the late-afternoon traffic. She stepped into the road, and an angry horn blared. She looked up to see the driver gesticulating and cursing as he swerved to miss her. She stepped back onto the sidewalk and walked until she came to another bus stop.

The comforter was pulled up around Gabriella's neck, but still she shivered in her bed. The lamp on the nightstand gave the only light in the room. Somewhere in the apartment, the telephone rang and Mme Leclerc hurried to answer. Her voice was muffled, but Gabriella knew that Mother Griolet was calling to ask about her.

The Bible on the nightstand caught her eye. Turning on her side, Gabriella let the book fall open to where a letter lay within its pages. She lifted the letter out of the Bible and unfolded the single page.

> *Dearest Gabriella,*
>
> *You are my firstborn and my delight. How proud your father and I are of you! And now it's time for you to go off on your own.*
>
> *I'm giving you this Huguenot cross. It comes from France where we lived years ago when you were only a child. Now you're returning to Castelnau, the same city that was dear to me so long ago.*
>
> *I give you this cross, which has always been for me*

a symbol of forgiveness and love. It was a gift when I was suffering. Wear it and know of my love and constant prayers for you.

We love you,

Mother

Gabriella folded the sheet of paper and wiped her eyes. She felt for the cross and remembered breaking its chain at Mother Griolet's.

I'm sorry, Mother. It will take time. To forgive, as you say. I'm so sorry that I said nothing. I was so afraid, Mother. I didn't know what to do. I was so afraid.

17

The middle of the afternoon found the streets of Algiers deserted. Fear hung on every street corner, blood stained each sidewalk. No amount of washing could erase the horror of the war.

The FLN's terrorist activities were rivaled in every way by the violent action of the OAS. Every day this military organization, determined to keep Algeria French, resorted to new methods of barbarism.

Some pied-noirs joined the camps of the OAS. Others hesitated. It was certain that de Gaulle had betrayed them. The French president was clearly pushing for an independent Algeria. Ever since the botched *putsch* of last April, the discontent French leaders had plotted and planned from their hideouts. Now it was time to act. So the daily papers announced murder after murder. Hatred bred and fermented and spread throughout the neighborhoods of Algiers.

Anne-Marie was almost too tired to care. She stared numbly out the window of the small bedroom in the slums of Bab el-Oued. This was the neighborhood of the *petits blancs*, the poorest of the Europeans in Algeria. It was also the headquarters of the OAS. Fifty thousand Europeans were crammed into the space between the Casbah and the Mediterranean. These petits blancs stood to lose everything if Algeria gained independence. They had nothing in France, and what work could they find here if the country was granted its freedom? So they joined the OAS to register their desperate cry for an *Algérie française*.

However, Anne-Marie had grown weary of political games. She knew she should feel thankful to be out of the Casbah and relatively safe. The memory of her frantic race with Moustafa through the tiny streets in the dead of night was still fresh enough to make her heart pound. Only the night had hidden the terror in their eyes from one another. Terror that the sun would rise and they would still be trapped within the arches of the Casbah, easy prey for a throat-slitting member of the FLN.

But miraculously Moustafa found his way through the labyrinth, and they had stepped from the low arches of their prison before the first streaks of light appeared in the sky. Later that morning they had slipped inside the small apartment of Marcus Cirou in Bab el-Oued.

The middle-aged pied-noir was short and lean, and his gray hair glistened with grease. He welcomed Anne-Marie; his respect for her father during the last war was immense. It was only natural, he told her, that he would shelter Captain Duchemin's daughter. He had eyed Moustafa suspiciously at first, but Anne-Marie convinced him that her companion was indeed on the pied-noirs' side. A reluctant part of the FLN when tortured, a loyal harki's son once free.

Marcus shared his humble provisions with his two unexpected guests. He even found a bottle of precious medicine for Anne-Marie's cough. But after a month there, she was still weak, her eyes dull, even when the sound of bombs reverberated through the night.

What she heard in her mind echoed louder than the bombs that exploded routinely around the neighborhood, louder than the angry shouts of the pied-noirs on the square in front of the prefecture. She heard it in the early morning and throughout the day. At night it woke her troubled sleep.

We have found your daughter. Rachid's voice repeated the simple statement incessantly in her head.

She had not wanted to kill him. She had not wanted to run. The punishment for his death and their escape had fallen on Ophélie, she was sure. She shuddered, afraid to imagine what Ali's anger could do to her daughter. Nothing mattered at all if hope for Ophélie was lost.

"Anne-Marie, please, you must eat this." Moustafa entered the bedroom with a plate of rice and beans. He sat beside her, gently stroking her back and neck. "My *habibti*," he whispered, using the Arabic term for a sweetheart. "Don't worry so. We aren't even sure that they have Ophélie. I've been back to the Casbah three times and watched these men. They haven't spoken of her. Please, you must eat."

It was the same argument he had used for the past month, but Anne-Marie wasn't convinced. She doubted that Moustafa could even convince himself.

"It's a miracle that we're alive," he continued. "Surely this is not in vain. I've reached three of the families in Algiers, and soon we'll set up another voyage for the *Capitaine*. You'll see—the children will escape. All of the children. Ophélie too!"

He shook Anne-Marie's shoulders, but she stared at him blankly.

"I'm sorry, Moustafa. I'm trying to believe. What can I think of in this room? What do I see day after day, week after week? I see the face of my daughter. I live for that face. And I fear."

He held her in a tight embrace, her head buried against his chest. Gently he took her chin in his hand and kissed her lightly on the forehead. "Live for Ophélie, my *habibti*. Live for her, of course." He looked into the depths of her sad eyes. "But live for me, too. I need you. I need you so much."

His lips brushed hers, softly, then with passion. Immediately he pulled himself away. "I have to go." He rose to his feet, touched her lips with his fingers.

Anne-Marie smiled, a weak, tired smile. "Thank you," she whispered as he left the room. She covered her mouth with her hand and cried.

Bus 11 left the cobblestone streets of Castelnau and turned into the large roundabout that connected the village to the east side of Montpellier. It veered onto avenue de la Pompignane, stopping beside a nursery that advertised a sale on chrysanthemums, two pots for forty francs. The front of the nursery was lined with hundreds of pots of the orange, yellow, and burgundy flowers, offered at a special price ever since the first of November, All Saints' Day, when the mums were bought by the dozens to adorn the tombstones of Montpellier.

Ophélie bounced happily on the bus seat, singing the old French melody they had learned in class that morning. Gabriella caught the little girl's attention. "Look there at the fountains spraying water. See all the mums they've planted?"

The bus swerved around another roundabout that encircled a small green hill topped with a replica of an ancient Roman house. Rows of chrysanthemums outlined the green grass. A fountain of water ran down from inside the Roman ruin.

"The flowers are *belle*! *Belle, belle comme toi, Gabriella!* You're so pretty." Ophélie bounced higher in her seat, laughing and hugging Gabriella as she sang. "And look, Gabriella! One of my teeth is loose." She wiggled her top front tooth back and forth. "Do you think *la petite souris* will come to the orphanage when I lose my tooth?"

"Well, of course she will. The little mouse can get in anywhere that a child has hidden her tooth under a pillow."

Gabriella looked at the child beside her, and somehow she was suddenly back in Senegal, holding Ericka on her lap, giggling with her little sister as she twisted her hair into imaginary braids. Gabriella tried to shut out the racing images. *A little girl sobbing, hiding her face in Mother Griolet's black skirts. A black-haired child lying desperately still and yellow in an African hut. A bright-eyed six-year-old raising her hand in class and beaming back at the red-haired teacher.*

She took a deep breath. "What do you like best about being six years old, Ophélie?"

The child wrinkled her nose and thought. "Hmm. I like learning how to read. *Oui!* That is best." Again she bounced up and down, up and down, pigtails swishing back and forth behind her. "*Non!*" she cried joyfully. "That is not the best thing about being six! Not even reading. The best thing about being six years old is meeting you!" Impetuously she grabbed Gabriella around the neck and kissed her cheeks.

The bus stopped abruptly, and Gabriella and Ophélie held each other tightly, bracing themselves against the sudden motion. They both burst out in laughter.

"You're glad then, Ophélie, that you're six?"

"Oh yes. Very glad."

The bus pulled to a stop across the street from the Montpellier train station, beside a park where another fountain spewed and children climbed on jungle gyms and slides.

"Time to get off, *ma chérie*."

"May I play in the park, Bribri?" Ophélie pleaded, using the name she had adopted for her friend.

"Yes, go ahead for a moment."

Gabriella followed Ophélie, who dashed through the park toward a swing set. Higher and higher she pushed herself, pumping her legs vigorously against the wind.

"Look at me! Look how high I can go, Bribri. Look!"

Gabriella waved from the bench where she sat. "Live, Ophélie," she whispered to herself. "And laugh and love. That is what you should be doing at six years old."

Gabriella and Ophélie walked up the street from the bus stop to where it opened onto place de la Comédie. Hundreds of people mingled around the outdoor cafés, huddling together in the brisk chill of the afternoon. Ophélie skipped along, swinging Gabriella's hand with hers.

"Look! Another fountain." She giggled. "With three naked ladies standing in the middle." She squinted in the sun as she turned toward her maîtresse. "Isn't that funny? Naked ladies in the fountain."

"That's a statue of the Three Graces. They represent beauty. You'll study about them one day. Come along now. We must find the jeweler somewhere behind la Comédie."

They twisted through the narrow streets of the *centre ville*, Ophélie straining like a dog on a leash to peek inside a toy store, a boulangerie, and a store lined with rows of children's shoes. They came upon a man drawing a picture of the Virgin and Child with bright-pastel chalks on the sidewalk. Ophélie planted her feet and refused to budge.

"*Ooh là, regarde ça!*" she chirped, tugging on Gabriella's hand. "Have you ever seen such a pretty picture? And on the sidewalk. That is too bad. It will wash away when it rains."

"The artist wants you to give him some money." Gabriella handed Ophélie a franc. "It's people like you who make him happy. See? Go put this in his hat over there."

Cautiously Ophélie tiptoed over to where the man's hat lay overturned with a few francs and centimes sparkling like real treasure inside. He looked up and smiled at Ophélie. "*Merci, jeune fille,*" he murmured before returning to his work.

A vendor was selling *châtaignes* at his stall a few feet away. The smell of the roasting chestnuts enticed Ophélie. "Oh, Bribri! May we please buy a *cornet* of those? Oh, please?" She jumped up and down with excitement.

"Ophélie, come on with you. I won't have any money to pay the jeweler if we stop and buy everything we see. Just observe. And on our way home you may pick one treat. Only one. *D'accord?*"

"Oh yes. Thank you." She planted a kiss on Gabriella's cheek.

At four o'clock Jean-Claude Gachon stepped off the train and walked out into the sunlight of Montpellier. He strode across the street and up the wide avenue that was flanked on both sides by waiting pedestrians and stationary buses. When he arrived at place de la Comédie, he found a chair at a café that gave him a good view of the open square.

"*Un pastis*," he mumbled to the waiter, unfolding a newspaper and settling back to read it. If one had to waste his days, this was not a bad way to do it. Hundreds of students milled around the center of town, gossiping and laughing as they walked. At this time of day, la Comédie belonged to them.

He had spent the month there, watching for a red-haired woman to appear. Each day he sat for two hours at a café, observing the gathering of youth that played out like a movie before him. Then he strolled along the Esplanade and through the old part of town to place de Peyrou, an immense park with an ancient water tower at the end, a hexagonal building standing majestic over the pond at its feet. Long arches of an ancient aqueduct spread out behind the park, running through the city as a silent witness to days gone by. But the red-haired woman hadn't appeared.

Today Jean-Claude was restless and impatient. He decided he wouldn't leave the café until long after dark. He needed news to send to Ali. He needed a little bit of luck.

M. Edouard Auguste was one of the best-known goldsmiths in Montpellier, Mother Griolet said. She also said that he was an encyclopedia of information if Gabriella wished to question him about the Huguenots.

M. Auguste spoke with the thick accent of the Midi. His eyes were deep blue and lively, and he had the dignified air of a true gentleman, tall and proper. A silk scarf was tied smartly around his neck. His gray flannel suit matched his hair and mustache.

"*Oui, oui, mademoiselle,*" he said, nodding in response to Gabriella's inquiry about the origins of the cross. "The Huguenot cross strongly resembles the Medal of the Order of the Holy Spirit that was created by Henri III in the sixteenth century. It was used as a military decoration to distinguish excellent French warriors in the cavalry. But of course Protestants were forbidden to receive it, despite their military prowess. The Huguenot version has the dove hanging from the lower branch with its wings spread and head pointing down. It's likely that this dove symbolized the Holy Spirit. Also four fleurs-de-lis were embedded between the branches of the cross and rays of sunlight chiseled in as though the Holy Spirit were sending out His power."

Gabriella was fascinated by the jeweler's knowledge. "And now? It's very popular?"

"*Oh, oui, mademoiselle.* Very popular, of course, among Protestants. Yours is especially beautiful. Eighteen-carat gold, and see how the cross has been chiseled on both sides. A very nice one."

"Mother Griolet said she bought it here, many years ago."

The goldsmith nodded politely. "Yes, Mother Griolet." He furrowed his brow. Then he slapped the counter with his hand. "Of course! I remember now. Yes, it was a bit strange at the time—a Catholic nun buying a Huguenot cross." He shrugged. "Of course, people can do what they want." He looked curiously at Gabriella. "And how do you happen to have this cross?"

"My mother gave it to me. I only recently found out that she had received it as a gift from Mother Griolet." Involuntarily Gabriella shivered. "I'm afraid we must be going now. Thank you for your help."

"My pleasure, *mademoiselle*. Your chain will be ready Friday. Shall I keep the cross with it?"

"Yes, that will be fine. *Merci.*"

"Je vous en prie. Bonne journée."

Ophélie turned from the counter, looking relieved, and took Gabriella's hand. "I thought we would never go," she confided. "And I'm starving."

"Of course you are. *Allons-y.* You may pick whatever you want."

By five thirty the Comédie was a mass of cars and pedestrians, mingled into a slow-moving stream between the grand buildings that outlined the square. From their perch atop the fountain the Three Graces looked down upon the chaotic scene with the peace and calm befitting the seductive symbols of love.

Jean-Claude had camped on the steps by the statue along with several students, and from this vantage point he could see most of the moving human traffic. He was watching a striking young woman with bright-pink lipstick and a very short skirt. Then he saw it. A flash of red hair farther across the square. *Red hair. Lots of it. Moving toward the avenue that led to the train station.* He hopped down from the statue and made his way across the Comédie, increasing his gait as he went. Soon he was trotting quickly through the crowd, eyes riveted on the red-haired woman a hundred yards away.

The crowd thinned as it fanned off from the Comédie. Jean-Claude caught a full view of the woman. Yes! He laughed out loud and fumbled for the camera in his leather bag. The zoom lens on, he inspected the woman and clicked a picture. Running, he clicked another and knocked into an elderly woman who was pulling a wheeled cart behind her.

"*Pardon!*" Jean-Claude called back, sidestepping another woman. He stopped to focus and cursed happily. A small child was with the red-haired girl. A small child whom he knew quite well. Two more pictures as the little girl turned around and pointed toward a man playing the clarinet. Jean-Claude caught both of their faces in the shot.

The camera went back in his leather case. Jean-Claude jogged closer to the pair, then slowed to a walk. Coming up behind them, he touched the woman on the sleeve. "Excuse me, *mademoiselle.*"

She glanced back but continued walking. "Whatever you're selling, I'm not interested," she said.

This time he grabbed her arm and held it tight. Still his voice was calm. "*Mademoiselle.* We have met before, *non?*"

She stopped to look at him, her face suspicious. Then she recognized him. "Oh, yes, you're right. Aigues-Mortes, right?"

"Precisely. How very nice to see you again. I see you have recovered from your fall."

The woman blushed. "Yes, I'm fine now. What brings you to Montpellier?"

"Business. And you, *mademoiselle*?"

"Me? Oh, I live nearby."

Jean-Claude had pretended not to see the child. Now he glanced at her and exclaimed, "*Non!* Can it be? Ophélie? Ophélie Duchemin? Do you remember me?"

He picked up the startled child in his arms and kissed her on the cheek. "My, you have gotten big! Why, the last time I saw you was a year ago in Algeria. Imagine finding you here in France."

He put Ophélie back down, and she cowered close to the woman.

"Ophélie? Do you know this man?" The woman bent down to the child's level.

Ophélie nodded, a smile playing on her lips. Her big eyes gazed up at Jean-Claude. "Yes, Gabriella." Then she whispered, "He was my mama's friend."

Jean-Claude cleared his throat. "Excuse me, *mademoiselle*. Allow me to introduce myself. I'm Jean-Claude Gachon. I don't believe I know your name."

"It's Gabriella!" Ophélie volunteered happily.

Jean-Claude patted the child's head and smiled. The woman frowned at Ophélie, but Jean-Claude didn't show that he noticed. He continued, "Gabriella? May I call you by your name?"

"If you wish," she said flatly.

"Yes, may I offer you a drink? The last time I offered, you said you were with a friend. But do join me today. It would be an honor to have a drink with two such lovely young ladies."

"I'm afraid we have a bus to catch."

"Please, Gabriella, please!" Ophélie begged. "Maybe he knows about Mama! Please let us talk with M. Jean-Claude."

Gabriella nodded uncomfortably. "Well, all right. But just for a moment."

Jean-Claude led them to a table at the edge of the Comédie. He quickly ordered them three glasses of sirop, which arrived in tall glasses with thin, bright straws.

His manner was smooth, polished, even kind as he addressed the child. "Little Ophélie, whatever brings you to Montpellier? Is your mother here? It was quite a shame that we lost contact." He directed his gaze at Gabriella. "Do you know Anne-Marie? I mean, you must. A very dear friend of mine."

"Mama went away," Ophélie stated. "Do you know where she is, M. Jean-Claude? It was some bad men that took her." She started to cry.

Jean-Claude looked shocked. "Took her? What do you mean?" He held Ophélie's hands in his. "What men took her? Did you know them?"

"I ... I think so. It's hard to remember. I didn't really see them." She wiped her eyes. "Please, won't you help me find Mama?"

Gabriella squirmed in her chair. "Ophélie, chérie. This man doesn't have any idea—"

"I would be most glad to help you," Jean-Claude interrupted. "I will do anything I can. But you must tell me where you live, so I may reach you, little one."

"I live at the church!" Ophélie blurted out.

"Ophélie, please! Let me talk to the man ... to Jean-Claude," Gabriella scolded.

He sat back in his chair and ran his fingers through his thick brown hair. "Excuse me, Mlle Gabriella. I didn't mean to intrude.

It's just such a shock to see Ophélie here. I had lost touch, you know, what with the war going on in Algeria. I don't mean to invade your privacy. It's only that if I could help in any way, I would be more than happy to do so."

He removed a pen and piece of paper from his shirt pocket and quickly scribbled a number. "I live in Marseille, but I travel a bit. Give me a call. Perhaps I could have your number. In case something turns up?"

Again Gabriella hesitated. "It's just that we don't have a private line. It might be hard to get through …"

"But, Bribri! There's a phone in the office. I've seen it."

Gabriella glared at Ophélie. "Yes, dear, there is, but I don't know the number. Listen, *monsieur*, I'll call you back next week. Will that be all right?"

"That will be fine. Just fine," Jean-Claude said. "Why don't we say next Tuesday, a week from today? That will be the fifth of December, I believe."

"Yes, that sounds okay. Now I'm afraid we really must be going. Thank you for the drinks." She stood up and reached out her hand, which he took and squeezed.

"The pleasure was all mine, I assure you. May I accompany you home?" He had picked up Ophélie again and was tickling her neck.

"No, that isn't necessary. But thank you all the same."

He took out a ten-franc piece and handed it to Ophélie. "Here, my child. Go buy yourself a pastry. From *Tonton Jean-Claude*."

"Oh, merci!" Ophélie laughed and hugged his neck.

"And I hope we will have the chance to see each other again too," he said softly to Gabriella.

He watched the woman and child walk to the bus stop far down the road. He didn't move from the café but pulled his binoculars out of his bag. "Bus 11," he murmured when Gabriella and Ophélie climbed aboard. "Bus 11 leads to the east side of town. And little Ophélie lives at a church. That shouldn't be hard to find. Not hard at all."

18

David didn't leave the classroom after he finished his lecture on the morning of December 4. Instead he stared aimlessly out the window from the second story into the courtyard. The orphans were at recess. Some were playing tag, squealing as they chased one another around the garden.

Several children wandered alone on the outskirts of the game. The Arab boy was one of these. He was too old for the orphanage, too tall, his skin too dark. Everything about him called attention to the fact that he didn't even fit in among the misfits.

In sharp contrast, the little girl David had stumbled upon in Paris seemed to feel right at home. It made him smile to watch her dash about the courtyard in pursuit of a playmate. He liked to watch her from his window, although he was careful that she never saw him. He preferred that she think the benevolent stranger in Paris had disappeared as quickly as he had come. The child had found a kind of home, and that was something positive to think about.

But the rest of his work left him numb. He no longer looked forward to class as he had for the past year and a half. At first the classroom had given him the challenge of impressing and puzzling the young ladies. Of baiting them in an innocent game of cat and mouse. He had felt satisfaction in knowing he held a certain power of presence over his class.

That need for power had waned during the fall with Gabriella's arrival. She answered his deep-felt need to dig deeper into the human soul. It had been a pleasant detour for David, taking his mind off the weighty matters of war. A companion and an unwitting accomplice. But now he dared not try to gain back the friendship that had budded. He was sure he could win her over, if he tried. Perhaps it was his pride that kept him away from Miss Gabriella Madison.

But David knew that his silence came from much more than that. It came from respect. He cared for her. He cared that she was safe, that no other man would chase her through some crowded marché. It wasn't love, that wasn't the feeling. Respect, perhaps friendship, but certainly not love. He could not afford to feel love again. There was enough trouble for him still from the first time.

Gabriella stood in the hallway just outside David's open door for a full five minutes. His back was to her, and he was looking out the window. When he finally turned around to retrieve his briefcase from his desk, she reluctantly knocked.

He looked up, startled; and seeing Gabriella, he frowned. "Yes?"

She felt her heartbeat accelerate and almost turned to go. There he stood, ever confident and cynical, while she trembled before him. "May I come in?"

"Of course," he said curtly.

"You aren't going to make this easy for me, are you?" she accused.

"I don't know what *this* is, Miss Madison."

She felt as if a wall stood between them. Taking a deep breath, she began, "I came to say I'm sorry."

"To ask forgiveness, is that it?" His tone was cutting. "If I remember correctly, that was the subject of our last conversation."

"I knew I shouldn't have bothered. Never mind." She turned to leave.

"Wait! Gabby, please." He came around his desk and touched her sleeve. "Please, wait."

They regarded each other in silence. David cleared his throat and motioned to a chair. "Please. Sit down."

Gabriella obeyed. She didn't take her eyes off him.

He ran his fingers through his short dark hair. "I don't know what to say." He rubbed his eyes with his hands. "Untrue. There are many things I could say, but it would just be a game. You're not here for that." He grasped the rim of the desk and raised his eyebrows quizzically. "Why are you here, Gabby?"

"I will tell you on one condition," she answered.

"What is that?"

"That you listen, really listen, before you say a word."

He grinned, an almost boyish, sheepish grin. A dimple that she had never seen before appeared in his left cheek. "Agreed."

Suddenly Gabriella longed to hug him. He actually looked vulnerable. Not a posture typical of David Hoffmann.

She sighed and began talking. "You probably have not wanted an explanation for my aloofness of the past month, but certain recent circumstances have convinced me that you deserve one." She twisted her hands together nervously. "I've heard it said that there is a fine line between love and hate. Something like that. I suppose I decided that it was much safer to hate you than ... than the alternative." Her face was flushed.

"I'm sorry that I got so mad over what you said about forgiveness and revenge. You have every right to believe whatever you want to believe. It's true that I hoped to convince you otherwise, but that was only because ..." She struggled for the words. "That was only because I felt a compassion for you, a caring."

He wrinkled his brow, his dark eyes intense, but he didn't speak.

Gabriella continued. "It was ridiculous of me to think that you cared for me too. I mean, beyond a casual friendship. I'm sorry that I've made things awkward between us." She closed her eyes for a moment, trying to regain her composure as her heart thumped loudly in her ears.

He looked as if he would like to hop down from the desk and come to her, so she hurried on. "One other thing. I'm almost through." She blinked back tears. "You were right. There is a death of the soul that makes life a living hell. A memory that is bitter and haunting. And perhaps it takes a very long time to forgive. Perhaps the pain will swallow me up whole until there is nothing left to forgive. Perhaps that's what you meant. I didn't understand then. But now ..." She stopped and buried her face in her hands, shaking her head. "Stupid girl," she whispered. "I promised myself I wouldn't cry. I'll go now. That's all I had to say." She fumbled with her purse, found a tissue, and turned to go.

But David was at her side, pulling her toward him, his strong arms holding her against his chest. Neither breathed nor moved, but it seemed to Gabriella that everything was racing madly. His hand was stroking her hair, carefully, cautiously.

Gabriella didn't dare to look up. "Please, David, don't ... don't care too much. I didn't come here for this. I can't."

He stepped back, his hands resting lightly on her shoulders. "I'm sorry. You're right. There is too much that separates us, Gabby." He breathed heavily. "But there is something that has broken you, my friend." He pronounced the last word with caution. "Let me walk with you to Mme Leclerc's. I promise I'll listen."

Gabriella nodded as he wiped a tear from her cheek.

They passed Mme Leclerc's apartment, walking through the center of Castelnau and out into the countryside beyond the village. The frost of the morning dissipated under the sun's warm regard as Gabriella related her memory of the rape, her nightmares, her anger with Mother Griolet. David interrupted occasionally to ask a question, but otherwise he was quiet.

"I can't understand why Mother didn't tell me before I came. It was as if she knew I would find out, but she didn't want to be the one to reveal it. It's so unlike her. I've never known her to be afraid to confront the truth."

"But you said that neither she nor Mother Griolet knew you had witnessed the rape," David interjected. "Perhaps she wasn't worried that you would remember; perhaps it was only so painful for her to know you were returning to this place."

"Perhaps," Gabriella said thoughtfully. "But Mother Griolet? She sent me to the mission house with her blessing."

"You would have preferred her to sit you down and tell you about the rape, about the pregnancy and Ericka? I don't know if she felt it was her place."

"Oh, David, maybe you're right. I don't know. All I know is that something is dead in me. In a different way from when Ericka died. And every night I hear a voice in my head that says, 'It's your fault! Why didn't you scream, little girl?' I know it's not God's voice accusing. Excuse me—I realize you don't believe. But God is not the accuser. It's another who accuses." Her voice was barely audible. "And then everything gets confused. I should have screamed. Then there would have been no rape. But that means no Ericka. No pain and no joy. And I'm so angry!"

"Have you written your mother?"

"I've tried several times, but I always sound accusing and harsh. And what good will it do her to know I'm dying in my soul? She'll only worry."

"I suppose she would want to pray for you," he said softly.

Gabriella stopped walking and stared at him in disbelief.

"I'm only trying to see as you see. Perhaps it would be of some comfort to your mother if she felt she could pray for you. Isn't prayer supposed to bring comfort? A conversation with the Almighty?"

"Something like that, yes. I don't feel like talking about it anymore. I'm too tired." She rubbed her forehead, feeling suddenly drained. How ironic that David was ready to talk about prayer and she had no energy for it. She changed the subject. "There is something that has been bothering me ever since you came to eat at Mme Leclerc's. The rabbit. You aren't really allergic, are you?"

David grimaced. "A very bad memory from the past. I don't wish to talk of it now." He glanced over at Gabriella and took her hand. "Someday, perhaps."

"Won't you tell me anything about yourself, David? Why you can't forgive? What wakes you in the middle of the night?"

"I have already told you, Gabby. It's too painful to rehash all the details. It's pointless. I'm a half Jew, and I lost my mother and sister in the camps. I was the guilty little boy who stood by and said nothing."

"But what could a little boy say? You're not guilty!" Gabriella was adamant.

"Then neither are you, my dear. Neither are you."

It was noon by the time they returned to Castelnau.

David left her at the door leading up to Mme Leclerc's apartment. "May I dare ask you for something, Gabby?"

"Yes, ask."

"Come with me to Les Baux on Saturday. As my friend. It's beautiful there. It will get you away from the memories."

"Oh, David. I can't." She smiled as he looked at her questioningly. "I promised someone I wouldn't run after danger anymore."

"And I am danger? Surely not. There's business there, but no danger. Please?" His dark eyes were soft, like a puppy's, hopeful for play.

Gabriella said nothing. She closed her eyes.

"What are you doing?" David asked suspiciously.

"I'm praying," she retorted. "I'm sure it sounds silly to you, but I'm praying for the strength to say no. Can't you understand?"

He took her hands. "No, I don't understand, Gabby. I only know that I've missed you. Our talks. Your wit. Does your God forbid friendship? What would be the intrigue of a life spent only with people who think just as you do? Please, please don't tell me your religion forbids friendship. Don't tell me you're afraid to be with someone who makes you think."

In her mind she heard the word *friendship*. It was, after all, only a friendship. *Ye are the light of the world*, she heard. *Ye are the salt of the earth.*

"Oh, why must you confuse everything? Of course my God does not forbid friendship with … with, um … atheists."

David laughed. "You pronounce the word as if I'm some sort of despicable enemy!" He bent down to look her in the eye. "I'm your friend. Only your friend."

"Good-bye, David," she said with appreciation in her voice. "Thank you for listening to me." She turned her key in the lock and pushed open the heavy door. Without looking back, she added, "I'll go on Saturday."

"Thank you too, Gabby," he called after her. "You have a lot of courage. You're going to be okay."

Ophélie huddled on the bottom bunk at rest time. Anne-Sophie was asleep next to her, snuggling contentedly with her teddy bear. Above her, Marine whispered to Lorène on the next bunk. Most of the other girls slept. But rest time was Ophélie's time alone. And what a wonderful time it was, now that she could read. Every day she pulled out Mama's letter. It had taken her three weeks to get through the first page, sounding out the words in a whisper. Then she would reread each sentence again and again until she had practically memorized it.

Once in a while she could not figure out a word, no matter how hard she tried. Then she would copy it carefully in her *cahier de lecture* to show to Gabriella the next day. One word at a time, and Bribri had never seemed suspicious.

Finally today she was on the last page. Page one was all about how much Mama loved her and how she never wanted to leave Ophélie. And something about the war and helping other mommies and children. And M. Gady. Ophélie had cried when she read that part.

The second page was about the cross of Papy and how when she wore it, she would be safe. Ophélie had not taken off the cross since she had read that page last week. Now she turned to the third page and, with difficulty, began sounding out each letter as Mother Griolet had taught her.

I m ... mu ... st, I must tell you one m ... more t ... th ... thing. I h ... have never talk ... talked to you of your fa ... fat ... father. Ophélie gasped. *Father!* That was the word, she was sure. Somehow, she had never imagined that she had a father.

She wanted to read faster now, before the bell rang and ended rest time. *I don't know w ... whe ... where he is, but, Ophélie, he is a good man.* She frowned.

He does not know he has a dau ... daugh ... She struggled with the word for several minutes. "Daughter!" she said aloud.

Marine peered down from the top bunk and giggled. "You're talking to yourself, Ophélie."

Ophélie said nothing, waiting for Marine to start whispering again with Lorène.

I c ... cou ... could not tell him. Please forgive your mama. But he is a good man who h ... hel ... helped me w ... whe ... when we were bot ... both very young and living in Algeria. Algeria! Where they used to live.

Per ... perhaps some ... someday you will be able to f ... find him. The shrill clanging of the bell startled Ophélie. She pushed the letter under her pillow as the other little girls scurried off their bunks and out the door. One more look! Just one more look!

She pulled the letter out and quickly found her place at the bottom of page three. She wouldn't have time to finish it all. But maybe one more line. *He is an Ame … Amer …* She threw down the paper in frustration. Another word she could not read! Sister Rosaline would be coming at any minute to look for her. Just one more line. She skipped the big word and continued reading. *Very han … hand …* She skipped that word too. *and smart. His name is Da … Dav … David.* David! Like the shepherd boy in the Bible. She had read the story in class yesterday. The boy who killed the giant. Her papa had the same name!

She stared at the letter again. Another word came after David, but it was long and complicated too. *Ho … Hoff …*

"Coucou, Ophélie!" It was Sister Rosaline's high-pitched voice. "Come on now. Time for afternoon class!"

Silently Ophélie stuffed the letter into the tights and closed the middle drawer. She jumped off the bed and bounded into the court-yard, screeching to a halt behind little Christophe, who was pulling Anne-Sophie's pigtails and giggling.

A father, she thought all through the afternoon. *A father named David.* She felt happy with the knowledge. A secret from her mother. But how in the world would she find him? She could not even find her mother, and she knew just what Mama looked like. How could she find her father, who for the moment was only a name written on a pink piece of paper in Mama's hand?

Afternoon class was over for the orphans. They filed outside into the chilly December afternoon. The sky was already growing dark. Gabriella waited for Mother Griolet to come back through the hall.

"Can we talk for a moment?" she asked the nun.

"Of course, my dear. Do you wish to come to my office?"

"Yes, yes ... that will be fine." They walked to the ground floor without talking. Gabriella disliked the awkward distance she felt.

Mother Griolet unlocked the office door and motioned for Gabriella to enter. When they both were seated, Gabriella fiddled with her hair, twirling it absently around her fingers. She didn't know how to start.

"Well, I'm sure you realize why I've come to see you," she said finally. "It's my conscience. Today is my day to say I'm sorry. I'm not very good at it, but"—she sat up in the chair—"I need to apologize for my anger the other day. I'm sure you didn't wish to see me hurt. I'm sorry that I accused you."

"*Merci, ma fille.* I know it's not easy. And your anger is normal," Mother Griolet reassured her.

"Mother Griolet, have you ever felt like you were dying inside?"

"Yes. I have known that pain before."

"And how did you find the courage to forgive? I have already forgiven once for what happened to Ericka. Now it seems I must back up and start over ... only it's even more painful. Somehow it feels like it's my fault. In my head I know that's wrong. But I feel responsible."

"It is often that way. Gabriella, I don't mean to sound like a distant doctor who has all the answers. It's simply that I deal often with children who have been abused—physically, psychologically, emotionally. The grieving period can be long. You must be patient with yourself."

"And in the meantime? What do I do in the meantime?"

"You keep living. And talking out your feelings. Actually your outrage last week was very good. A necessary step. I prayed you wouldn't feel embarrassed to come back. It's too hard to carry your anger alone."

"Do you think we can forgive *anything*, Mother Griolet? The worst offenses? Do you think it's possible?"

"Forgiveness is not just for the offender," the nun stated, compassion in her eyes. "You're a victim, and until you forgive, you will always be a victim, locked in your hurt and bitterness. Forgiveness frees." She paused for a moment. "How big is your God, Gabriella? Mine turns tragedy into triumph. A rape, and a precious daughter born."

"But she died!" Gabriella protested. "Why must Mother grieve twice for her? You said Mother died in her heart when Ericka was conceived. But then she looked past the awful pain and found love. Why did she have to die a second time? It wasn't fair!"

She held the cross in her hand. Just yesterday she had returned to M. Auguste's shop to retrieve it with its chain. She thought of Mother Griolet's words. *An intricate weaving of lives.* A Huguenot cross that a Catholic nun had given a Protestant mother to help her forgive an unknown Arab. A daughter born, only to be yanked away too soon. Gabriella closed her eyes. The story tormented her. How could a simple cross bring peace to such a tangled mess?

Her eyes still closed, Gabriella saw the image of Ophélie smiling before her. She whispered, "And now this same cross has brought another six-year-old into my life." She opened her eyes and looked at the nun, who seemed to be in prayer. "Tragedy to triumph, is that what you said, Mother Griolet? Your God can bring triumph out of tragedy, *n'est-ce pas?*"

Mother Griolet lifted her head and nodded slowly.

Gabriella stood up. "He is my God too. I have something to do now. I will try to keep living, as you have said. There are others I must keep living for."

The phone booth stood at the back of the small square in Castelnau where an olive tree rose from within the stones of the street. The small fountain beside it sprayed water into its moonlit pool, occasionally sending its mist toward the glass booth when a gust of wind caught the water. Gabriella closed the sliding door behind her and felt in her pocket for the paper and franc piece. She squinted in the dark to read the number and slowly lifted the receiver from its hook, then dialed.

It rang once, twice, a third time. She was about to replace the earpiece in relief when a man's voice answered.

"Allô? Oui, est-ce que c'est Jean-Claude?" Her voice shook.

"Oui, c'est Jean-Claude."

"Jean-Claude, this is the woman you met in Montpellier. Gabriella? I'm sorry to bother you, but I promised Ophélie that I would call to see if you have any news."

"I am glad you called, *mademoiselle*. I do indeed have some news."

"Yes? Do you know where Anne-Marie is?"

"Why don't we meet, and I will tell you what I have learned?"

Gabriella hesitated.

"Perhaps this Saturday on the Comédie? I'm sure little Ophélie is eager for information about her mother."

She felt annoyed at his persistence, afraid he was more interested in pursuing her than helping Ophélie. Why couldn't he just give her the information over the phone?

"No, that isn't possible. I'm going to be in Les Baux-de-Provence on Saturday. But I'll call you on Sunday." She quickly thanked him, said au revoir, and hung up before he could reply.

Gabriella left the phone booth with an uneasy feeling. He seemed nice enough. Perhaps it wouldn't be so bad to go out with a green-eyed Frenchman. For Ophélie. But halfway back to Mme Leclerc's house, it was not the young Frenchman she was thinking of, but David Hoffmann and their brief embrace that morning.

19

"I'm glad you decided to come with me, Gabby."

"I only agreed because you promised no more secrets, David. You're sure there's nothing to tell me?"

"*Au contraire*, there's so much to tell you! We're driving through a scene from Van Gogh or Cézanne or Gauguin. This is where they painted, throughout this rich region of Provence. There is nothing else like it anywhere on earth, Gabby." He reached over and squeezed her hand.

"David Hoffmann, you're so hard to resist! A walking history book, the king of culture. Tell me then, please. Tell me about this magical land of Provence. I only hope your faithful little *bagnole* will get us there." She lovingly patted the car's ripped upholstery.

"You can't get to Les Baux by train. But it's only a hundred kilometers from Montpellier, and we've already come eighty. We'll make it. But I'm afraid we'll have a bit of wind up on the mountain. December isn't the ideal time to see Les Baux, but ..."

"But you have business in town." Gabriella said with a mocking tone.

He laughed. "Yes, something like that."

The sun was bright on the road, but as they drove, Gabriella watched the wind whipping through the fields, checked only by rows of tall, pointed cypress trees outlining the fields, leaning at a forty-five degree angle to the ground.

David noticed Gabriella staring at them. "Those trees are there precisely to protect the fields from the wind. Even on a calm day, they remain perpetually bent in adoration to the mistral.

"Here, we're coming closer. See the small chain of miniature mountains in the distance? They're called the Alpilles, the little Alps. This entire region used to be marshes, from Arles to the Alpilles, until one of your Protestants, a M. Van Eys from Amsterdam, figured out how to drain them and turn them into cornfields. Unfortunately he had to rush back home for safety when the Edict of Nantes was revoked. Now let me see, what have I told you about Les Baux?"

Gabriella knitted her brow and reflected. "I think you said there are now only ruins of the village and castle. It was built into the mountain, right?"

"Yes, into the southern side of the Alpilles. There used to be over four thousand inhabitants in the city. Now you have at best three hundred, most of whom gain their livelihood from the tourist industry."

The road separated into a V, and David took the left branch, following the signs indicating Les Baux-de-Provence. "We'll park down in the valley and hike up to the town."

"From back here you can't even tell there's a city up there," Gabriella commented as they approached the valley and stared up at the massive piece of granite before them.

"That way, they were protected against their enemies. A good strategy. It worked, too, for years. Les Baux was often in rebellion against the king of France and lodged many a Huguenot during the sixteenth century. In 1632 Cardinal Richelieu put an end to Les Baux as it had been. The castle and ramparts were destroyed." David pulled his car into the dirt driveway of an old farmhouse and parked in the grass.

"We'll get out here," he said, coming to her side of the car and opening the door. He offered Gabriella his hand.

"How noble." Gabriella laughed, taking his hand and stepping out.

They walked along a small paved road, enclosed on either side by the old stone walls of the farmyard. As the wall ended, David took her arm, and they slipped into what looked to be a private garden.

"Oh, it's beautiful," remarked Gabriella, looking around at the perfectly groomed boxwood hedges. She crossed the garden to explore a small stone pavilion flanked by two giant cypress trees. "What is this?"

"This is the Renaissance pavilion of Queen Jeanne, wife of the roi René. It was called the Temple of Love by the *fibrigues* poets of the last century." He raised his eyebrows invitingly, pulled her toward him, and softly kissed her cheek. With an exaggerated French accent, he said, "It's too bad that we are just friends, *ma chérie.*"

Gabriella laughed and pushed him away, her cheeks red.

"*Allons-y!* We have many other points of interest to see today," he said, and led her out of the garden and down the road.

They walked in silence for at least ten minutes, winding behind farmhouses and a few elegant hotels that offered food and rooms to the wealthiest tourists. The road took a sudden turn, and the large stones that had seemed far above them were suddenly at their level.

"This, Gabriella, is the Val d'Enfer."

"The Valley of Hell ... hmm. An interesting name." As she looked around, she exclaimed, "And I see why. Look at those huge rocks! And that one there. Why, you'd think they were gigantic skulls."

He smiled. "Exactly."

As they walked and climbed higher through the rocks, looking down on the large pieces of granite, Gabriella had the eerie impression that three or four cruel giants had been laid to rest in the valley.

"We need to be getting up to the city. Don't want the boulangerie to close before we get there. I know a shortcut we can take."

He found an overgrown path that cut through trees and vegetation, rocky and steep. Gabriella wished she had worn more comfortable walking shoes. Her low-heeled beige pumps slipped as she climbed over the stones.

David caught her easily and held his arm around her waist as they continued climbing. "Raymond de Turenne, the viscount of Les Baux who lived here in the fourteenth century, was a real colorful character. Apparently the way old Raymond got his kicks was to leave his mountain refuge with his band of warriors and ravage the countryside, kidnapping whomever he wished. He'd take his prisoners up to the castle and demand a ransom. Of course some of the peasants had no one to pay ransom for them. So Raymond led them to a window in the dungeon that gave a splendid view of the valley below and *oop là*! He pushed them over the side. As they fell to their grisly death, he laughed until he cried."

"David! That's awful! Are you sure it's true?"

"Quite true. When we get to the top, I'll show you the very spot."

"I'm not sure I care to see it, thanks all the same."

Out of breath from the steep ascent, they arrived by a little side street that led directly to the back entrance to the city. "The south side of the city has been restored, and merchants sell their wares to the tourists in the summer. There are only a few shops open in the winter. But if we climb higher, we can get into the ruins of the castle and the dungeon."

By now the wind was biting, and Gabriella tucked her hands inside the pockets of her peacoat. She was only half listening. "Hold on a minute, won't you?" she called after him. "I'm freezing. Let me just warm up inside this store." Before he could protest, she disappeared behind the open door of a boutique.

Immediately she was greeted by a young gypsy-looking woman with thick black hair that fell in curls around her shoulders. She wore a white lace blouse with a full skirt made from a Provençal print.

"I may help you, yes?" She sang each word, adding another syllable to the end.

"*Merci*. I'm just looking." Gabriella was surrounded by Provençal material, bold, bright patterns in reds, yellows, and blues. The store was perfumed with the scent of dried lavender mingled with sachets marked *herbes de provence*. Large bars of soap were arranged by color in wooden crates.

Along the back wall of the boutique stood a large assortment of clay figures in different sizes. "These are the *santons* of Provence, *n'est-ce pas?*" Gabriella inquired.

The shopkeeper smiled broadly. "Yees, dey are all originals, handcrafted in dis region. You will see dey are marked wif de stamp of de artisan."

Gabriella had heard much about the small clay figures that were created by Provençal craftsmen to depict the people of Provence, each bringing his or her gift to the *crèche* of the baby Jesus. One shelf held a full nativity scene, complete with the holy family, a donkey, lamb, camel, and dozens of Provençal villagers bringing their trades to the Christ child.

Gabriella reached to touch the brightly painted clay figures. Some were only a few inches high. The larger ones stood a foot in height and wore real Provençal fabric: an old woman dressed in bright yellow and red with a bunch of lavender in her hands, a graying shepherd with cloak and staff and a lamb around his neck, a baker with his sack of long loaves of bread in one hand and his white hat falling to the side, his mustache powdered with flour.

Ah, he is perfect! Without further thought Gabriella took the clay figure from the shelf and placed it on the counter. "Could you wrap this, please?" she whispered, not wanting David to suddenly appear in the store and discover the treasure she had found for his Christmas gift. Eighty francs was expensive. But the urge to buy it for David was stronger than her practical reasoning.

My professor who loves the French bread but always makes me buy it. Ah, David ... I pray that you, too, will someday come to the crèche of our Lord Jesus and lay the loaves of your heart before Him. She was still imagining the scene when the gypsy woman handed her the well-wrapped box and the change from her purchase.

David had taken a seat farther up the road and waited for Gabriella with a scowl on his face, his nose red from the cold.

"I couldn't resist one small purchase," she said with a wink.

"Shopping!" he said. "Well, we must hurry. The store will close soon. I'm almost positive there's a boulangerie around the corner."

"That's fine, but could you put my package in your knapsack first?" Gabriella asked.

Grudgingly he obliged her. But around the corner they found only another brightly colored store window advertising Provençal prints and pottery. David cursed under his breath.

Gabriella continued up the street and turned onto the next side street. "Look, David," she called, "there's a boulangerie right here."

"Ah! Good, you found it." Relief spread across his handsome face. "Be a love and get me a pain de seigle, not too dark, mind you." He rummaged in his pocket for a five-franc piece and gave it to her.

Gabriella, red hair shimmering in the high noon sun, narrowed her clear blue eyes. "Me get the bread? Not on your life. Not after Aix. *You* get whatever kind of bread you want, David Hoffmann."

He shrugged his shoulders and slipped into the store.

Jean-Claude Gachon pulled his gray plaid wool scarf over his mouth and crept back into a corner of the narrow side street, as a lean man with powerful shoulders entered the boulangerie just within his view. He raised his eyebrows in surprise.

Jean-Claude waited as the young man came back out with a short, rounded loaf, which he placed in a small knapsack before rejoining his lovely red-haired companion. The couple continued up the tiny road. The man stood a good half foot taller than the woman, his hair thick and black. Jean-Claude studied him carefully, snapping a photo of the two together.

So, M. Hoffmann, you are here after all. Of course it would be you.

Anne-Marie's old lover. Yes, Jean-Claude remembered her confession when he had questioned her about the picture he had found of David Hoffmann two years ago. Jean-Claude frowned. M. Hoffmann might prove more difficult to deal with than Mlle Gabriella.

He followed them up the uneven street to where it was blocked by an iron barrier. An arrow on a sign indicated that tickets to visit the ruins of the castle and dungeon could be purchased in the building to the right. Five minutes after Gabriella and M. Hoffmann entered the building, they left by another door and continued their ascent toward an open plain. Jean-Claude stepped up to the window to buy his ticket.

He glanced briefly at a miniature reproduction of Les Baux-de-Provence as it would have appeared in the Middle Ages. He was not very interested in the history of the city, but he wasted time reading and studying maps and panels until at last he stepped out of the ancient stone refuge into the open air. A strong gust of the mistral's power greeted him. He leaned into the wind, climbing the hill until it opened before him onto a vast plateau. In the distance he saw the young couple huddling together as they pushed against the force of the wind. They didn't suspect a thing.

Gabriella clung to David's arm, her head bent down to protect it from the cold gale. Their progress was slow. The ruins of the castle spread out before them, still hewn into the sides of the mountain. David headed them into a small cove of the first in a series of large rocks. There the stones protected them from the rushing wind.

"I hope you aren't planning on picnicking up here," Gabriella yelled over the wind's whistle.

David's face broke into a wide smile. "What could be better? To face our fate against the elements." Seeing that she remained unconvinced, he added, "We'll just have a look around. Then I'll take you back into the village for a piping hot bowl of *soupe au pistou*. It will stick to your bones and warm you up. But come along now. Be brave, my fair princess!"

Gabriella screwed up her nose and retorted, "As long as you're not Raymond de Turenne, I will follow you anywhere."

He led her to the side of the mountain. Before them the plains below spread out for miles in every direction. "There in the distance is Mont Saint-Victoire, the farthest peak you can see. And over there, the Camargue, and even farther out, on a very clear day, you can see Aigues-Mortes. You can understand how, at the time, the Baux family could control all the traffic on the roads from Aix to Arles. That was the ancient Roman Way, called Aurelia."

The Alpilles dotted the horizon, while directly below them lay dozens of fields outlined by the tall cypress trees. "If I weren't so cold, I'd love to stay here all day," Gabriella commented. "As it is, let's see these ruins and get back to warmth."

"Gabriella! I'm surprised at you. Where's your sense of adventure?" He grabbed her shoulders and rubbed his hands vigorously up and down the sleeves of her coat for a few seconds. Then he took her hand and led her along the plateau. It was fifty feet wide, with either side walled in with the castle ruins. They stepped over a low wall of stones into the facade of what had been a large square room. Ducking their heads, they made their way through a doorway and down a short flight of stone steps into the skeleton of another room. Gabriella grabbed on to the stones as a gust of wind pushed her backward.

"The mistral must be nearly a hundred kilometers an hour," David calculated, but his eyes shone with pleasure, as if he would challenge the wind and conquer it.

Gabriella shivered beside him. "How can you be enjoying this? We're nuts to be out here. There's not a single soul up here besides us."

"Patience, Gabby. We'll just go to the end and climb up to the dungeon ruins. I don't want you to miss the view."

They pressed on, up narrow steps and down others, following the jagged outline of the fallen castle. At the farthest end of the ruins, David pointed to a steep set of steps that led up to what had been the second story of the dungeon. A wrought-iron guardrail had been placed beside the steps for the tourists. Cautiously Gabriella mounted the steps, with David close behind. She clung to the rail for support against the force of the wind and flattened herself against the wall. They came around the corner, where they could see the outer wall of the dungeon built into the mountain.

"Look below!" David shouted through the screaming wind. "This is where Raymond did his deed."

Gabriella peered down, barely daring to look. But indeed the wall ended abruptly, and all that was left was a deep abyss.

"Horrible!" she yelled back. "Let's leave."

Jean-Claude watched the progress of the two young people like a hawk contemplating its prey. He stayed forty feet behind them, hidden within the ruins. As they rounded the corner of the dungeon, slipping out of sight, he gleefully scaled to the top of the cliff and perched ten feet above them. He waited for Gabriella to peer over the ledge and laughed. "You're perhaps with me in this little game, David Hoffmann, *non*?" The position was perfect. Eyes blazing, he rubbed his hands together in a frenzy, as if he himself were the ghost of Raymond de Turenne come back to haunt the castle.

He would hardly have to push the rock. The wind would do the work. He kicked his foot against a loose stone the size of a soccer ball and moved closer to the couple, the large stone now in his hands.

Gabriella stood to the right of David, clutching the rail as she peered into the valley. She let go momentarily. Jean-Claude stepped out of hiding and with a grunt threw the stone forcefully at her feet. It hit her hard and bounced off into the ravine. Jean-Claude waited to hear the woman's chilling scream above the mistral's fury. Then he raced to the top of the dungeon wall and hid in its shelter, laughing till tears ran down his face.

Gabriella had just turned to retrace her steps when she felt a large rock hit her hard in the shin. She screamed as she stumbled. David lurched toward her outstretched hand, but she had fallen through the railing, past his grasp.

"David!" she shrieked, grabbing the jagged stones of a narrow ledge leading to the precipice. Dust blew into her eyes as she hung awkwardly on the ledge. Heart pounding, she managed to pull her chest onto the rock. Her feet dangled in the air. One shoe came off and fell into nothingness, swept by the wind into Raymond's territory.

It was no use to cry out. Who else would hear? David was bending down from above, reaching toward her. She thought of the strength in his hands. Yet he had nothing to grab on to himself. Before them the whole valley stretched like an opened mouth, ready to swallow them whole. David was on his stomach, reaching, leaning across the pale-yellow boulder. He wedged one foot in between a split in the rock. It was all there was to hold him in place.

Gabriella watched his hand. The wind blew as if it were in a battle with David for her life. It pushed against her with the brute power it had gained running across the plain. She felt her hands sweating in the freezing air, slipping from the jagged rock. Her eyes met David's, and for that moment she read his thoughts louder than the howling wind. *Hold on!*

With a heave he pulled her up, against the craggy, pointed rocks that ripped deep into her coat and legs. She fell onto the narrow ledge and lay breathless beside him. The roaring wind stung her eyes, bringing tears and drying them in the same effort. She was planted on the ledge in fear, not daring to move. David's arms gripped her tightly, pulling her against him, so that his back sheltered her from the wind.

"Can you get up, Gabby?"

She felt his hot breath against the back of her neck as he spoke in gasps.

"I'll hold you. Only a few feet and you'll have the railing. Can you grab it now?"

He loosened his grasp on her and she slid through his arms, forcing her body over the short distance to grab hold of the railing above her. Her head swam. She felt dizzy with fear.

David had raised himself from the ledge, gently pushing her up to safety. As she sat, clinging to the railing, he pulled himself back up beside her. They inched their way around the corner of the castle and rested their backs against the wall. The mistral buffeted them in its fury, but they did not move. Nor did they see a lone figure running across the plateau, swept along by the wind like a dust ball in a ghost town.

The way back was much easier as the wind pushed them along, back across the plateau. David held Gabriella in his arms. She didn't protest. He felt her body shiver against him, felt the low sobs that racked her fragile frame. Her coat was torn and her stockings full of runs. Blood held them against her legs. He looked at her stockinged left foot and felt a shudder rip through his soul. Somewhere at the bottom of the ravine, where the bones of less-fortunate victims once rested, lay a woman's low-heeled tan pump.

It didn't make sense. He had glimpsed the rock that hit her before it fell over the mountain. Even the bitter wind could not dislodge such a rock. It had come from nowhere. It was as if some-thing, someone had pushed it. But the place was desolate except for them.

He let himself out the iron gate that led back into the village. Two hundred yards down the cobblestone road he set Gabriella down on a curb.

"Here, we're at the restaurant. Do you want to go in?"

She looked up at him with her chapped, tear-stained face. Her hair was a mass of red tangles.

"We can go on to the car if you'd rather. I only thought you might wish a place to wash up."

She nodded slowly. "Yes, let's go in."

They entered the small restaurant, which smelled of thick soups and strong cheeses. Its empty tables were covered with bright-blue Provençal print, and warmth hung in the air. A young, stocky woman with short brown hair greeted them with a smile. Then she noticed Gabriella's disarray. "*Mademoiselle* is hurt?" she asked.

"An accident, yes," David whispered. "Could you show her to the *toilettes, s'il vous plaît?* And would you have a towel or cloth she could use to wash up?"

"*Bien sûr,*" the woman replied, taking Gabriella by the arm. "You may come into my apartment. It's here, just behind the restaurant."

David watched Gabriella limp along beside the woman and disappear behind a bright-red curtain. He ran his hands through his hair. He removed the knapsack from his back, but his shoulders still sagged under some unseen weight. He thought back to Aix and the young man he had knocked out as he followed Gabby. David hadn't found any identification on him. Just a camera.

But today he had been sure no one was around. He had been so careful. For ten minutes his eyes stared blankly at the menu as his mind wandered.

Gabriella came back through the curtains. Her face was washed and her hair brushed. She wore slippers on her feet and carried her coat and shoe in her arms. "*Merci. Merci, mille fois,*" she said, smiling at the young woman who accompanied her to the table.

"Shall I bring you two bowls of la soupe au pistou? It is delicious—potatoes and vegetables and cheese."

David and Gabriella nodded simultaneously, and something in that small gesture made them both laugh. As the waitress left their table, they looked at each other.

David took her hands. "Gabby, I'm so sorry. Forgive me, will you? I never dreamed ... It was foolish of me to take you up there in this wind."

"I must admit, we had quite an adventure. Enough to last me awhile!" She thought for a moment, then said, "Enough to cover last week's nightmares over with the fear of today."

"Are you sure you're all right?"

"One lost shoe, a pair of ruined hose, and numerous scrapes and bruises. Nothing very exciting, really, to show for what I've been through."

"The lost shoe is the proof," he said, smiling, but immediately his face clouded. "Gabby, it's time I explained a few things to you. Do you want to know? You're not afraid?"

"I *have* to know, David. Surely whatever this secret business of yours is can't be more dangerous than the little accident I just had."

"Yes, you're right. But I can't tell you here." He covered her hand with his.

The young woman brought them two earthen bowls of thick, steaming soup, and they ate in silence.

David and Gabriella rode back toward Montpellier with the wind whistling outside the car. David kept glancing in the rearview mirror. No one was following them.

He cleared his throat awkwardly. "Gabby, I'm not quite sure how to start. I ... I'm afraid that somehow what happened today wasn't an accident."

"I knew you were thinking that."

"I was sure you suspected the same. Every time we've gone somewhere, there's been trouble. In Aigues-Mortes you sprained your ankle, in Aix there was the man following you, and now ..."

"But, David! That's crazy. Aigues-Mortes was just an accident. I was clumsy, and then Jean-Claude helped me—" She looked up at David, sudden recognition in her eyes. "Jean-Claude! He knew I was coming here today. I didn't see what harm it would do ... He knew!"

"Hold on, Gabby. Just who is Jean-Claude?"

"He's the man I met in the Tower of Constance at Aigues-Mortes. I ran into him again in Montpellier the other day with Ophélie—the new orphan. I think I told you about her?"

David nodded.

"He used to know her mother, and he said he could help us find her, and I was supposed to call him back. When I did, he wanted to meet today, but I told him I couldn't because I would be in Les Baux."

David was wrinkling his brow, thinking. "You told him you were coming here?"

Gabriella blushed. "Yes. I did. I know I talk too much."

"Never mind that now. Tell me what this Jean-Claude looks like."

"He's maybe five foot ten, thick brownish hair. Quite handsome, really. And green eyes. I ... I notice eyes. Their color, I mean." Her face reddened again.

"He's the man who followed you at Aix too."

"What? How do you know that?"

"Because I knocked him over the head with a wine bottle."

"You what?"

"Believe me, it was to protect you. I didn't see what good it would do to tell you afterwards."

"David, you think Jean-Claude is trying to hurt me? That he was somehow here today? But why in the world?"

"I think he is indeed after you. But he should be after me. It's a case of mistaken identity." David sighed deeply and turned his piercing eyes on Gabriella. "I can't tell you everything, Gabby. It's a long story. A story of war and innocent victims. You don't need to know all the details. But it was the bread, as you have guessed, that got you into trouble in Aix." He reached behind him and placed the knapsack in Gabriella's lap. "Go ahead. Take out the bread."

She did so hesitantly.

"Break it in two and pull out the center part."

Gabriella obeyed. As she broke the loaf, a small piece of paper wrapped in plastic fell into her hands. Gabriella stared at him, bewildered.

"It is *this* that I find in the bread. My instructions. Do you understand?"

She nodded, trembling. "I see … I see."

He reached for her hand. "Gabby, please. Hear me out."

"You're frightening me, David. Perhaps I shouldn't know. You mean when I went to get the bread, this man was watching me? And you knew it?"

"No, of course I didn't know. I'm afraid someone has talked. It's too complicated to explain it all now. But you deserve to know, because I'm sure you're in danger. It's my fault, and I'm sorry."

"David, my heart is still racing from the fall. And now what do I do? Walk back out into the wind and wait for some sadist to kill me? Now I'll be looking over my shoulder until I leave France."

"No, Gabby. No. You'll be safe in Castelnau. The next time he'll come after me. I'll make sure of it."

She didn't reply but placed the plastic-covered paper on the dashboard.

"You must say nothing about this, Gabby. Can I trust you?"

Her eyes were sad, void of any blue sparkle. "Who would I tell, David? Who in the world would I tell?"

20

Ali sat in his room, impatient and brooding. He had no time to finish his little work with the FLN on his back, sure of victory in the near future. He too wanted victory for Algeria. But first he wanted revenge.

His office in the Casbah was a tiny cubicle with a single window overlooking a polluted alley. Lined across his desk were old framed photographs: In one he was a child, standing beside a man in military uniform and a young woman with long, thick black hair. In others he was older, posed with first one, then two, and eventually six other siblings. The young mother smiled in each picture, seemingly pleased with her growing family.

Finally there was a larger framed photograph of Ali as a young man in military dress, standing tall and proud beside the older man he so closely resembled. Ali let his eyes fall on this picture and smiled briefly. "Father," he whispered.

He stood up and walked to the cement block wall, running his fingers over the cool stones. Taped to a dingy whitewashed wall was a yellowed newspaper clipping with a picture of a group of soldiers. Ali's father stood in the back row, looking confident. Around his head a bright-blue circle had been drawn. A dozen other men's heads were circled in red, and several of these circles had a red X drawn through the middle. The caption below the photograph read:

PARIS, FRANCE. *The Scout Platoon of the Thirteenth Battalion of the North African Army has made a name*

for itself in several major battles of 1943. This platoon,
made up primarily of Algerians and pied-noirs, has
been decorated for its bravery. The platoon is led by
Lieut. Mohammed Boudani under battalion leader
Capt. Maxime Duchemin.

Ali spat. "Captain Duchemin! You traitor. I'll find your daughter
and granddaughter, and then I can draw the line through your family. No one will remember them. My father will be avenged."

Another clipping was taped next to the picture of the soldiers,
and one paragraph underlined:

In what has been called one of the ironic tragedies
of this war, French forces, on the brink of victory,
raided a German campsite in the middle of the night
April 5. Thirty-seven men of the Scout Platoon of
the Thirteenth Battalion of the North African Army,
made up primarily of pied-noirs and Algerians,
inflicted heavy casualties on the German battalion.
The platoon suffered only one casualty: the body of
Lieut. Mohammed Boudani was found hanging
from the rafters of a dilapidated barn, with evidence
of extreme torture.

Beside the newspaper clipping Ali had posted a piece of paper
with numbers from 1 to 37. He had written names by the first
twenty-two spaces. Four of these, including his father's, were crossed
out with the words *died in war* written beside them. A red line was

drawn through the names of eleven others: men who, along with their families, had been killed to avenge his father's death.

Ali would find the names of the rest. And make them suffer.

Anne-Marie unfolded a crumpled sheet of paper. "It's no use, Moustafa. I can't remember everyone. You have warned these families?" She pointed to a half-dozen names scratched on the paper.

"They are warned, the ones who are in Algiers. The *Capitaine* will sail to Marseille tomorrow night with four children. Ali will not murder any more innocent young ones."

Anne-Marie rubbed her forehead and sighed. "It's all my fault. Oh how I hate this life. It's as if I reached out a gun and shot them myself."

Moustafa took her hand, squeezing it tightly. "You were forced to talk! No one judges you! Certainly not I. We're here now because I too was weak. Every night I wonder if the other children escaped to France or if they were found because I talked. Bachir—is he safe in France? And Hakim?" He closed his eyes briefly, remembering Ali's cruel laughter as Moustafa had writhed in pain. "I'm only glad I didn't know more. Only dates and cities." He stroked her face. "And where you were. It's my fault that you're here. I'm so sorry."

Anne-Marie placed a finger over his lips and shook her head. "Don't, Moustafa ... don't think of it now. You couldn't help it."

His eyes flashed. "If I let them, these thoughts will smother me in hopelessness. But we must not give in to self-pity. You have forgiven me, Anne-Marie, for my weakness?"

"Of course, Moustafa. You know I have." Her eyes were liquid and sad as she answered him. "But can I forgive myself? For the families I betrayed to Jean-Claude? For my own daughter, who is living another nightmare because of me?"

He grabbed Anne-Marie's shoulders, his voice a passionate whisper. "We're in a war of madness, and we're dealing with a madman. Don't live in guilt. We can help." He looked at her lovingly. "Do you wish to leave now, Anne-Marie? There's room on the boat for you."

She shook her head. "No, I'll stay with you here. If they have brought Ophélie to Ali, she's somewhere in this town. We'll keep searching."

She reached out for his hand, and he pulled her against his chest.

"Moustafa," she whispered, coughing. "How can Ali believe that our fathers left his father to die? It was a casualty of war. He is pure evil."

Moustafa waited a moment to speak. "Anne-Marie, my love. I've been thinking how it grows more dangerous daily for all the children trapped in this war. We have to keep using this operation, even after Ophélie and the others Ali seeks are safe. Algeria is going to explode in a final clash of power and blood. Marcus tells me what the OAS plots. I have to stay and help. Tell me you'll stay too."

She was still holding on to him. "Moustafa, our love too is madness. There's no place in the world for a harki and a pied-noir who are in love."

"Then stay with me here, Anne-Marie. For now no one says a thing. For now we're alone in the eye of the storm. Stay with me here." He cradled her face in his hands. "You are so beautiful, my love."

He kissed her carefully, as if to bring a spark of life back into her eyes. He kissed her again and again, until she answered back hungrily. Until for a moment they forgot how impossible indeed was their love.

Gabriella left her room as the doorbell to Mme Leclerc's apartment sounded. She pulled on her coat and looped a green scarf around her neck.

"A date on Sunday night?" Caroline teased, stepping out of her room. "Don't stay out too late, Gab. Remember there's school tomorrow."

"Don't worry," Gabriella replied, forcing a smile.

Mme Leclerc had opened the door and was chatting politely with David.

The smile still plastered on her face, Gabriella kissed the landlady softly on the cheek. "I won't be late. But don't wait up. I have my key."

"*Ooh là là, ma chérie!* I will long since be asleep. You just have fun." She winked at her boarder.

David took Gabriella's arm and escorted her out the door. "I'll take good care of her, Mme Leclerc," he said.

They walked casually down the steps and out into the deserted street. The moon was full. The air smelled of smoke as all around town the black vapor wisped and twirled out of chimneys.

Gabriella could see her breath. "Where shall we go?"

"Do you have the phone number?"

She reached into her pocket and withdrew a piece of paper.

"Good." He looked over at her. "Are you okay?"

"Scared stiff," she replied.

David put his arm around her shoulders and gave her a playful hug. "You'll do great, my dear."

She broke away from him, walking ahead. "I get the feeling this is all a little game to you, David. Cat and mouse, is that it? I'm not laughing, I hope you notice. I'm not a spy. My training is in literature and art, you may recall. I've studied under a very distinguished professor."

He caught up to her, grabbing her arm and pulling her around to face him. "Listen to me, Gabby. You have every right to be angry. But what's done is done. You said Jean-Claude expects your call. This is our chance. Shake him up a little. It's the only way to get the heat off you and onto me."

Gabriella looked at the ground. "David, for all we know, he thinks I'm lying dead at the bottom of Les Baux. Why prove to him that I'm alive and well? Besides ..." She turned her blue eyes up toward his. "I don't want you to take the heat either."

"You're too sweet, Gabby. Don't worry about me. I guarantee you he won't just wait around thinking you're dead. He'll be up to something. This is our chance."

The phone booth was hidden behind a row of small shops. Gabriella stepped inside, and David followed. He towered over her as she dialed the number with a quivering hand. She listened for a ring and cleared her throat. On the third ring, a voice answered.

"Allô?"

"*Allô?* Jean-Claude, this is Gabriella." There was a long pause before he responded.

"*Bonsoir, Mademoiselle Gabriella.* How nice to hear from you."

"I'm just calling to let you know that we've had good news about Ophélie's mom. Thank you for your help, but I think they'll be back together soon." She let her words soak in.

"Really? That is good news indeed. I'm very happy for you. Could we perhaps see each other? I'd like to take you to dinner."

"Well, thank you for the offer, but actually I'm already seeing someone. It was nice meeting you anyway, and again, thank you for trying to help. *Au revoir.*"

She hung up the receiver and fell into David's arms, eyes shining. "I did it! I think he believed me!"

He hugged her lightly, then let her go and stepped out of the booth. "That was great, Gabby. Let's celebrate. Can I get you a coffee?"

Gabriella hesitated. "A coffee," she teased. "I'm sure that is not how you normally celebrate."

David laughed loudly. "I won't touch that with a ten-foot pole, Miss Madison. No comment." He brushed his fingers through her hair and said, "There's only one café open on Sunday night anyway. We'd better at least make an appearance to keep the town gossips happy."

They entered the café, which was empty except for the barman and two older men huddled at the bar. David chose a table in the back of the small room. He ordered a coffee for himself.

"*Un chocolat, s'il vous plaît,*" Gabriella told the waiter. ·

A soft love song played in the background, its melody drowned out occasionally by a burst of laughter from the men at the bar. The café smelled of smoke and strong liquor.

David reached out to touch Gabriella's hand. "So tell me, favorite student, what's going on inside that red head of yours?"

She blushed and gave him a quick smile, then pulled her hand away from his. "Too much is going on in my head."

"Tell me."

She closed her eyes, afraid to meet his gaze. "I feel trapped, David." She glanced up at him. The music in the background grew louder, and a man's voice crooned, "Love is the sweetest thing, what else on earth could ever bring, such happiness to ev'rything ..."

David didn't move or speak.

"I'm afraid, David. Mother Griolet said the best way to get past the hurt and anger is to keep living. And to be honest about what I'm feeling. So I tried. But now ... now I'm trapped not only in my mind. Now I'm trapped in some awful little war game of yours. I don't want to know what it is, and yet I wonder ... I wonder who you are." She fumbled with a white cloth napkin. "I wonder what you're doing." Her eyes met his. "And I don't know what I'll do when I find out."

The waiter placed the hot drinks on the table. Steam rose and twisted enticingly between them as they held each other's gaze.

Finally David broke the silence. He lifted his hand to touch the cross around her neck. "The Huguenot cross, Gabby. Such a strange cross."

Again she felt his power over her and drew back. "That's what everyone says," she whispered. The haunting music stopped, and

Gabriella shook herself out of her lethargy. "It was this cross that interested Jean-Claude at first, in Aigues-Mortes. At least that's what he said."

David smiled. "Of course. That makes perfect sense."

"What do you mean?"

He unbuttoned a little pocket inside his blazer and pulled out a piece of paper. "You didn't want to see it yesterday. But this is what was in the bread." He held it carefully in his hand for Gabriella to inspect. In the center of the paper were written the words *jeudi 21 16h30sncf.* In the top left-hand corner was scribbled the picture of a Huguenot cross.

Gabriella touched her cross as another love song floated across the café. She glanced briefly at David, then down at the paper. "I see," she mumbled. "I see."

Moustafa waited until midnight to start back through the slums of Bab el-Oued and pass under the arches that led into the Casbah. His heart raced as he walked briskly through the labyrinth of streets. After a month of nighttime wanderings, he was beginning to feel at home in the Casbah. The thought made him shudder. At home in the neighborhood that plotted his extinction and that of all French loyalists.

Since Rachid's death, Moustafa had observed Ali's frantic gait, like that of a captured stallion. He was not as careful as before. The room that had been Moustafa's prison with Anne-Marie was now used for Ali's weekly midnight meetings with the few trusted men needed to carry out his plot.

Moustafa perched himself on the roof of the adjoining building, concealed in the pitch of night, and peered through the small window. The men were there, as they were every Sunday night.

Ali was pacing the floor, talking in hushed tones. The men nodded and focused their attention on the screen at the front of the room. Straining to hear through the open window, Moustafa watched as a picture of a woman with long red hair appeared on the screen.

"We have received more slides from Jean-Claude. You remember this lovely woman that he has bumped into several times. He has found her again. A student in Montpellier." Another slide flashed before them, a crowded square with the back of the red-haired woman to the camera. Another slide showed her closer up. "Notice the small girl at her side!" Ali cried triumphantly. "None other than Ophélie Duchemin."

Only the murmurs of approval from the men in the room covered Moustafa's gasp.

Ali was crooning on. "Jean-Claude met them in Montpellier. The child of course remembered him as a dear friend of her mother's. She didn't know of Jean-Claude's way of convincing Anne-Marie to talk." He laughed cruelly. "The child begged this woman, Gabriella she is called, to have drinks with Jean-Claude to see if he could help them find her mother.

"Of course, Jean-Claude was happy to comply. This Gabriella has contacted him once, and Jean-Claude has planned to meet her not far from Marseille. In fact, I believe the appointment was for yesterday. We are confident that this woman, Gabriella, is behind the operation. She is the one they call Hugo. We will get rid of her and take the child. The rest of the information will come quickly. In the meantime, there are still three pied-noir families here in Algiers who must be done away with. On with you now."

Moustafa scrambled up the roof and hid himself behind the arch of the two adjoining buildings. Six men filed out of the basement and slipped silently down the streets of the Casbah. He waited for fifteen minutes before springing to the ground like a cat and tracing his way back through the night to the apartment of Marcus Cirou.

The nightmare woke her with a start. Anne-Marie's nightshirt was covered with sweat as she sat straight up in bed, breathing heavily. It was only a dream, a vivid picture of another haunted night. She had seen him before her, laughing as he reached out to her with the red-hot iron.

The hazel eyes she had thought so warm and inviting during their last night's passion now gleamed with a wild power. Somewhere Ophélie cried out for her mother.

"I don't know anything else. What can I know? I was his daughter, not his officer."

Enraged, Jean-Claude touched the hot iron to her right arm. Her screams filled the night. Twice more he burned her, laughing as he watched her writhe with pain. Then he grabbed her long hair and jerked back her neck. "You will find the list of names, Anne-Marie. Thirty-seven names.

You will find them before next Friday when I come back. The next time, it will be your daughter screaming."

Anne-Marie looked at the black skies. Moustafa wasn't back yet. She switched on a lamp that sat on the floor by her mattress and picked up the crumpled piece of paper that lay beside it. Rubbing the sleep from her eyes, she studied the page. At the top she had written in capital letters SCOUT PLATOON OF THE THIRTEENTH BATTALION. Underneath she had printed the name of her father and the words *murdered along with his wife by Ali*. Beneath that were many other names followed either by *killed in battle* or *murdered by Ali Boudani*, with details about the members of each soldier's family.

She closed her eyes and tried to picture the list she had copied so carefully and placed in the blue bag so many months ago. But she could not remember another name.

The door to the room opened then, and Anne-Marie saw Moustafa bathed in the light of the moon, standing before her. His eyes glowed as he rushed to her and picked her up in his arms.

"It was all lies, Anne-Marie! Ali does not have Ophélie. She's in the south of France with a young woman. Jean-Claude has seen her, but she's not with him."

Anne-Marie pulled herself out of Moustafa's embrace. "You are sure?" She touched her forehead, suddenly feeling dizzy.

Moustafa caught her again, swinging her around. "Yes, I am sure! I saw the slides of her with this woman. A woman named Gabriella who wears a Huguenot cross. They say she is Hugo. Unbelievable! Do you know her?"

"No, I've never heard of her. She is Hugo? She has Ophélie? And how do we know that she won't harm her?"

"In their voices, I could tell. They know Ophélie is safe with this woman."

Anne-Marie wrung her hands together. "If this woman is working for us, then she will help. She'll protect Ophélie."

"Yes, of course. Now sleep, dear one. Go to sleep. I'll join you later." Moustafa slipped out of the room.

Anne-Marie lay awake for a long time, staring into the blackness of the room. "If this woman is Hugo," she whispered to herself, "then where are you, David Hoffmann? Are you there too? And do you know that Ophélie is your child? Do you even care?"

Her eyes were closed, but she was still wide awake when Moustafa entered the room and lay down on the mattress beside her.

Gabriella could not sleep. She flipped through her Bible, reading underlined passages aloud to herself. "I will not fail thee, nor forsake thee ... the Lord shall preserve thy going out and thy coming in from this time forth, and even for evermore ... I am the Vine, ye are the branches: He that abideth in Me, and I in him, the same bringeth forth much fruit: for without Me ye can do nothing." She spoke the words with emotion, as if she could pull God out of the black book and into the room with her.

"You have promised to be here, Father." Her voice was a faint whisper, a feeble but fervent cry. "I'm so confused. So scared." Sobs escaped as she spoke to the air. "Lord, I didn't mean to get into this. It's too much for me. Please. Show me what to do.

"And forgive me, Lord, for loving a man who is not Yours. He's pulling me along with him, and now I can't get away." She buried her face in her pillow and cried, a low soul-wrenching cry. "Oh, God, who is he? Who is David Hoffmann?"

It was the middle of the night as Ophélie tossed in her bed. Her mind was racing. Somewhere Mama called out for her. She ran toward her mother, when suddenly her mother's voice turned into piercing screams. Ophélie tried to open the door, but it was locked. The screams quieted, and the door opened. Jean-Claude stood in the doorway, his eyes bright. Ophélie screamed and woke herself up.

"Mama! Mama! He isn't your friend after all. Now I remember. He isn't your friend."

Ophélie cradled her pillow in her arms. She heard the wind rattling the windows and stared at the shadows that flickered across the wall. She thought about her mother for a long time, picturing her thin, beautiful face and sad eyes. Then Ophélie closed her eyes and thought about her father. In her mind there was only a black void. She saw nothing.

"Papa," she whispered. "David Hoffmann. Who are you?" She turned over and went back to sleep.

21

Monique paused in the narrow street to rest, breathing heavily. The seven-kilo turkey she had just purchased weighed down her straw basket. In the daytime, the Christmas lights that had been attached across the road were not blinking, but everywhere the air spoke of Christmas.

"Monique! There you are. *Coucou!*"

Yvette caught up with her friend. Her cheeks were rosy red. "Let me help you with that turkey. *Ooh là!*"

Together the two women walked across the busy square to Monique's apartment and carried the turkey up the flight of stairs and into the kitchen. Then Yvette hurried back down the steps to retrieve her basket of fruits and vegetables from the marché.

"Do we have everything now for the meal? It's only two days away." Monique's eyes sparkled.

"And such a feast we will have!"

They had decided to celebrate the midnight Christmas Eve meal together, with their boarders, since it seemed that two of them were a couple again.

"Let's see. We have the *foie gras*. We have the *pâté*, and the *saumon fumé*, and the olives for the *entrée*. We have the turkey and chestnuts, and you're making the *gratin dauphinois*. The green beans I will get tomorrow."

"And I will make the *bûche de Noël* on the twenty-fourth. The girls will love it. Americans are always enamored with the Christmas log for dessert. Perfect!"

They looked at each other and burst into happy giggles, like two schoolgirls sharing a secret. "A midnight meal for Christmas," said Yvette. "And I believe Gabriella has a gift for your M. Hoffmann. *Ooh là!*"

"I'm sure M. Hoffmann will find something for his young lady too. A great surprise, no doubt."

Mother Griolet closed her grammar book and smiled at the twenty-five children seated before her. "*Mes enfants*, school is over for the holidays. No work for ten days."

The children broke into a loud cheer, laughing as they put their books into the wooden desks.

Mother Griolet spoke again. "Attention! Children! We will have a special Christmas meal in the cafeteria on Christmas Eve. And you will all bring one shoe up to my den to leave by the tree, *n'est-ce pas?*"

Most of the children nodded eagerly, but Mother Griolet saw the perplexed look on Ophélie's face. "We have two children who were not with us last year—Hakim and Ophélie." She smiled at the tall, dark-skinned boy who brooded in the back row. "It is our Christmas tradition at St. Joseph for each child to leave a shoe under my tree for Père Noël. Yes, old as I am, Father Christmas still comes to see me every year! And oh my! Such goodies he leaves for all the children."

"It's true!" piped up little Christophe. "He brings the goodies while we're eating our Christmas meal. Then we come and sing around the tree. We stay up very late on Christmas Eve!"

"*Oh, oui, oui!* Last year every girl got a different dolly. Every one of us," volunteered Anne-Sophie.

Gabriella entered the classroom then, and the children erupted once more into excited chatter. Mother Griolet clapped her hands together.

"*Les enfants!* Please, calm down. I have one more announcement. Today we shall be receiving four new children—one boy and three girls. Isn't that a nice Christmas present?"

The children nodded.

"I expect you to welcome them warmly, just as you always do. Now Gabriella has asked me if she could bring you a present today, something for each of you."

Smiling broadly, Gabriella came to the front of the class. "Who can tell me what is so important about Christmas?" she questioned.

Several little hands flew into the air.

"André?"

The shy six-year-old stood up and grinned nervously. He looked down at the floor. "It's … when … when baby Jesus was born." He sat down quickly, his face red.

"Exactly! Thank you, André," Gabriella said. "So here are your gifts. No use grabbing; they are all the same. So you can read for yourselves about the greatest story in the world." She hefted a large basket onto Mother Griolet's desk.

As she called out the children's names one by one, they filed forward to receive their gifts. Mother Griolet smiled as she watched them tear open the bright, shiny paper and proudly hold up their books for the others to see. Children's New Testaments.

Gabriella was learning the secret: to get past her pain, she must give to others who hurt. As the children clustered around Gabriella, Mother Griolet quietly slipped out of the room. She climbed the steps to the ground floor, entered her apartment, and went into her office. She walked around her desk and stood at the window, staring out into the empty courtyard.

"Four more children, Lord. I don't know them, but You do. And I'm sure You will provide everything we need to take care of them. I think I'm ready ... but only in Your strength."

She watched the pansies in the courtyard below, their petals fluttering in the winter wind. "Delicate and strong," she murmured. "Even in the coldest months they keep their smiling faces. Blown by Your Spirit, O Father, may I do the same."

Gabriella met Mother Griolet in her den. Her face was radiant. "It's so much fun to be with the children. I feel as though they need me, even if my life is a mess."

"I understand how you feel, my child," replied the old nun. "It is rewarding work." She paused awkwardly. "May I ask you to do me a favor?"

"Yes, of course. What is it?"

"I was hoping that you could go into Montpellier this afternoon to meet the new children. M. Vidal had offered, but he is unable to get away."

"The children are coming by train?"

"Yes, it's a long story. They are refugees from the war."

"From Algeria?"

"Yes. They need shelter here in France." She smiled weakly. "This is a bit of a secret, my dear. If you would not talk about it, I would be most grateful. And if you don't wish to go, I will find someone else."

"No, it isn't that. Of course I'll go. Tell me where to meet these children, and I'll go."

Ophélie jumped at the chance to ride the bus into town with Gabriella. As they pulled into the train station, she clasped her teacher's hand tightly.

"Thank you, Bribri! For the bus ride and the beautiful Bible with pictures!"

Gabriella patted the child's hand as they descended the steps from the bus. "Let's see now. Mother Griolet said the train will arrive at four thirty." She searched the large board that announced the arriving trains. "There it is. It will be at quay number 2 in just a few minutes."

People were milling about the station, stringy-haired students with knapsacks, somber men in business suits. Gabriella watched Ophélie's exuberance.

Suddenly the child's face clouded. "Bribri," she said. "I had a dream. I remembered something scary."

They had arrived at the quay as the train slowly approached.

"I don't think M. Jean-Claude is good. I think he was one time Mama's friend, but then he turned bad and made her scream."

Gabriella put her arm around the child. They shivered together as the train screeched to a halt before them. "Oh, Ophélie. I'm so sorry. But don't you worry. He doesn't know where we live. We'll never see him again."

Four silent, wide-eyed children followed Gabriella and Ophélie out of the train station. They carried nothing with them; their clothes were filthy and their eyes hungry. Two were Arabs, Gabriella was sure. The other two looked French.

"We'll ride the bus to the church," she told them as they waited for bus 11. "Mother Griolet will have a nice supper waiting for you."

The children remained silent. The youngest, who was about five, began to cry. Her sister put an arm around her. The bus approached.

"This is it, children. Let's climb on."

Reluctantly the children obeyed.

"Have you seen Gabriella, Mother Griolet?" David asked as he met the nun in the stairwell of the parsonage.

"Oh, hello, M. Hoffmann," the old nun replied. "Yes, I believe she took Ophélie into town this afternoon."

"I see." David frowned. "You're sure?"

Mother Griolet nodded.

"Thank you. Thank you very much."

David hurried out of the parsonage, grumbling to himself. "To town! I told her to lie low. Whatever is she doing in town? Today of all days! Unless ..." He cursed angrily and trotted down the street to where his deux chevaux awaited him at the curb.

Jean-Claude had followed the children from the port in Marseille. Again Ali's information had been right. Four scraggly kids. Kids whom Ali wanted dead. Jean-Claude had jumped on the train to Montpellier. Now he scowled as he watched the woman, Gabriella, herd her little flock onto bus 11. He ran toward the bus as the doors closed and the bus veered into the busy street.

"Taxi! Taxi!" he called.

A young man puffing on a cigarette pulled up in an old BMW taxi, and Jean-Claude hopped in.

"Where to, *monsieur*?"

"Please, if you could follow that bus? I was to meet some friends at the station, but I just missed them." He flashed a quick smile as the taxi driver took off in pursuit of bus 11.

Ophélie screamed as the bus doors closed. Gabriella, who was busy comforting the refugees, turned.

"What in the world, Ophélie? What's the matter?"

"It's him! I saw him. M. Jean-Claude. He's following us. He's trying to get us."

"Ophélie! Are you sure? Perhaps you're just imagining it because you're afraid."

But Ophélie was adamant. "I'm sure, Bribri." She began to cry, and other passengers looked questioningly at the child.

Gabriella, heart pounding, led Ophélie to a seat. Then she cautiously looked out the window at the back of the bus. She could see a taxi following them, but she couldn't make out the person sitting in the back.

Through each intersection, the taxi kept close. At each stop as people got on and off, Gabriella watched the taxi until she was sure that Jean-Claude Gachon sat in the backseat.

At any moment she expected him to jump out of the taxi and onto the bus, a pistol in hand, ready to shoot them all. She sat, frozen with fear, until the bus passed the Castelnau stop. She couldn't let him know where they lived. They would stay put for now, she decided, until she could think of what to do.

"Children," she said, trying to sound cheery. "Children, I must go up front and ask the bus driver directions. Please just sit tight." She caught Ophélie's eyes. The child sat perfectly still, eyes wide with fear.

Gabriella made her way to the front of the bus. "Please, *monsieur*," she began, trembling. "I have a ... a problem. Someone is following me and my children. In the taxi. He must not find us. Could you please change your route?"

The bus driver, gruff and stocky, glared at her. "What are you saying, *mademoiselle*? I can't outrun a taxi. I'm sorry."

"No, of course not," she agreed.

"If you're going to stay on the bus to go back through town, it'll cost you each another ticket."

"Yes, of course … of course." She brought a handful of change from her purse to pay the driver.

He looked at her and then at the change and said, "Never mind."

"*Merci, monsieur,*" Gabriella stammered as she swayed with the turning bus and found her seat again.

Jean-Claude grew impatient as the bus wound slowly in and out of town like a giant centipede. Still they didn't get off. "The woman saw me," he muttered to himself.

He fought to control his urge to leave the taxi and jump on the bus. But he had explicit instructions from Ali, admonishing him for the accident at Les Baux. *See to it that you draw no more attention to yourself,* the scrawled letter had read. *Just find out where these children are being housed and how this Gabriella and M. Hoffmann receive information. Later you will get the list from Ophélie Duchemin. Be patient. She must still believe you're a friend of her mother's. Slow down!*

Jean-Claude didn't like to slow down. He was an athletic man, trained for action. But he knew how to wait. He could wait all night if he needed to, until the red-haired woman thought the coast was clear and led him straight to where Ophélie Duchemin was hiding.

When David arrived at the train station, it was well past five. A quick search of the building revealed no one. Angrily he pushed his deux chevaux into gear and drove back toward Castelnau. He was sure Mother Griolet had sent her to pick up the orphans. A terrible mistake if anyone was watching for a woman with red hair.

He slowed down, passing a bus 11 as he drove to the east side of Montpellier. He scanned the faces in the near-empty bus. No Gabriella.

As he headed into Castelnau, another bus 11 was leaving the village, going back toward Montpellier. He glanced at it, saw a shock of red hair, then the bus was gone. Quickly he turned the deux chevaux into a side street and backed around. If indeed it was Gabriella, why was she going back to town? He caught sight of the bus again, fifty meters in front of his car. David pulled up closer to the bus, behind an old BMW taxi—and saw why Gabriella had not gotten off in Castelnau.

By six o'clock Gabriella had not returned with the children, and Mother Griolet was struggling to suppress the panic rising inside her. Twice she had called the station to make sure the train from Marseille had not been delayed. Twice she had been assured that it had arrived on schedule. She could not imagine what had happened. She waited and prayed.

Now she walked through the girls' dormitory for the third time, making sure the three beds were made up for the new children. Sister Rosaline had made sure that the small chest of drawers for each new child was filled with the appropriate clothes.

Preoccupied with thoughts of Gabriella, Mother Griolet opened a drawer. The long-sleeved blouses and wool skirts were there, the panties and tights, the barrettes and brush and comb. And the doll. Sister Rosaline loved to prepare the drawers for the new orphans. The clothes always smelled sweet and fresh, even if they were used. The doll had on a bright new dress, crocheted by Sister Rosaline herself. Even as Mother Griolet contemplated her fellow worker, Sister Rosaline came in the room.

"There you are, *Mère Griolet*," she exclaimed happily. "Have the children not arrived yet?"

"No, I'm afraid not, Sister Rosaline."

"Don't you worry now," the Sister said. "Gabriella will have them here in no time. Anyway, I have a few more things to find. I'm afraid there aren't enough tights." She scratched her head as she hurried to the last bunk and opened a drawer. "Could I take a pair from one of the other girls? Half of them don't wear them anyway. That little Ophélie, for instance. She only wears her white tights. I wash them three times a week."

Mother Griolet was hardly paying attention. "Well, then go ahead and take her other pair if you wish. I'll explain it to her later. I'm sure she won't mind."

Sister Rosaline scurried to Ophélie's bed and opened the second drawer in her small bureau. She grabbed the blue tights and closed the drawer. "Now what in the world has the child put inside these?"

she fretted. She wiggled her broad hand down the leg of the tights and pulled out a small blue velvet bag. "A child's treasure, no doubt. No wonder she never puts these on."

Mother Griolet came out of her reverie with a frown. "Could I see that bag?" she asked.

"Why of course," Sister Rosaline answered, smiling as she handed her the sack.

Mother Griolet took the velvet bag into her hands. "Just leave the tights here, Sister Rosaline, and I'll take care of them."

"Thank you, Mother." Sister Rosaline patted her lightly on the back before leaving the room. "And don't you worry about the children. I'm sure they'll be here any minute."

Mother Griolet didn't like to snoop in the personal belongings of others, not even the smallest of the children. She held the blue bag in her hands for a moment, considering what to do. Then she looked at her watch again. Six thirty. Whatever could be keeping them?

She pulled open the little bag, letting the contents fall onto a bed. There was a tiny photograph of Ophélie next to a lovely dark-haired woman with large, sad eyes. Two small pink envelopes, wrinkled and folded, were the only other contents. *M. Gady* was written on the outside of one; its seal had not been broken. She carefully opened it and removed several pieces of stationery. The first two pages were a personal letter to the man, M. Gady. The last two pages contained a list of names, apparently soldiers. Their family members' names were written beside them, then their addresses. And by some names were the words *murdered* or *killed in war*. Mother Griolet gaped at the list. Then she read the letter.

Dear M. Gady,

I send you my daughter, my treasure. I know you will care for her as we have arranged. If you have this letter, it's because I have been forced to flee, for Ophélie's safety. You now have the only complete list of the Scout Platoon of the Thirteenth Battalion—the list Ali wants. I have marked the families whose names he already knows with a red X.

Hugo awaits your news. Moustafa has already arranged for trips through October. Send these names to the following addresses. Hugo will answer you with further instructions as soon as you contact him. Assume that I can no longer help. I will do my best to get back to you soon. Until then, keep close contact with Hugo. Tell him that you have another child who must come to him. He must not know she is my own.

Please, please take care of Ophélie. She is my life.

Thank you for all your help.

Anne-Marie Duchemin

Four addresses were written underneath Anne-Marie's signature, with arrows drawn back to the names of different children on the list. There was another address, a post-office box, beside the name *Hugo*.

Mother Griolet shook her head and sighed, setting the papers on the bunk. It was unbelievable. Little Ophélie's mother was somehow connected to Operation Hugo! How could it be?

Slowly she picked up the other envelope, which had already been opened. *Ophélie* was written across its front. The old woman took out three thin pieces of stationery. So this was why the child had been so eager to learn to read. She read the letter silently to herself:

> *Dear Ophélie,*
>
> *How I love you, my dear. You must always know that I'm with you, even if you can't see me now. I never wanted for us to be apart. But for now, my love, it's necessary.*
>
> *There is a war in Algeria, you know. When we lived there, I made friends with people whom I thought were kind. But they turned out to be mean and only wanted to hurt innocent people. So we had to leave Algeria to get away from them.*

Amazingly the letter talked about Algeria and rescuing orphans and the Huguenot cross! Mother Griolet crossed herself and read on:

> *I must tell you one more thing. I have never talked to you of your father. I don't know where he is, and he doesn't know he has a daughter. I couldn't tell him. But he is a good man who helped me when we were both very young and living in Algeria. Perhaps someday you will be able to find him. He is an American, very handsome and smart. His name is David Hoffmann.*
>
> *Mama was very foolish and young when she loved him, but I know he would take care of you. He would be proud to have a daughter like you.*

I must go now, my love. Someday I will see you
again. I'm holding you tight in the arms of my soul.
Be brave, little Ophélie. You are special. The God of
Papy be with you.
I love you,
Mama

Mother Griolet put down the letter, tears trickling down her lined face. Forgotten were the orphans and the hour. All she saw was a beautiful child with a secret she could not share.

She shook her head again and again. David Hoffmann, Ophélie's father? It was impossible. It was crazy. And he didn't know. Or perhaps he knew and said nothing because he feared for the child's safety. Who in the world was this David Hoffmann?

Mother Griolet sighed heavily. An unexpected piece of a puzzle she never meant to put together lay in her hands. "I'm being pulled deeper into this secret, Lord. I'm not sure whom to trust. But I trust You." She returned the letters to the blue bag, slipped the bag into the leg of the tights, and placed them back in Ophélie's drawer. "Keep your treasures, little girl. For a while longer, you keep them." Mother Griolet walked back to her apartment to wait.

David parked his car on the side of the street just in front of the bus stop. He quickly mingled with the other pedestrians awaiting bus 11, hunching down to hide himself from view. A moment later the bus pulled into the stop and he got on.

"Gabby!" he called out, fumbling in his pocket for change, but the bus driver just shook his head.

"If you're with the young woman, there's no charge."

In spite of the circumstances, David laughed. "*Merci, monsieur.* It's very kind of you."

"Don't mention it—I haven't had an adventure like this in a long time."

David walked to the back of the bus where Gabriella, Ophélie, and four other children sat, looking fearful.

Gabriella gasped. "How did you get here? How did you find us?"

"A bit of luck, Gabby. How long have you been riding around town on this bus?" He sounded amused.

"Over an hour, maybe two. Have you seen who is following us?"

"Oh yes. Our old friend is running up quite a bill in that taxi."

"I was petrified he would come on the bus and shoot us all," she whispered. "But I didn't know what else to do, so I talked to the bus driver and he let us stay on. At no charge!"

"You've done just fine, Gabby. Except I thought I told you to lie low for a while."

"Mother Griolet asked me to pick up some children arriving at the train station today. Refugees from Algeria." She eyed him suspiciously. "You knew about that, didn't you? That was what the instructions meant on the paper you found in the bread."

"Yes, you have guessed."

"You're helping save children? That's your secret? At St. Joseph. Hakim? And Ophélie?"

David raised his eyebrows. "I'm afraid it's rather complicated. And Mother Griolet has no idea of my involvement. She must not know, Gabby." His tone was stern.

"But why not?" Gabriella was incredulous.

"To protect her. The less she knows, the safer she is."

"But after today, the children will surely say something to her."

"I'm sure with your lively imagination, you can make up a good excuse for my sudden appearance." He winked at her.

Gabriella felt a flood of relief. "This is what you do, David Hoffmann? This is your secret ... saving children." She squeezed his hand tightly. "It's a wonderful secret. This secret, David, I can live with. And I'll help you."

He shook his head. "I'm glad you approve, my dear, but for right now you're in a bit of hot water. A crazy man is on your trail. So listen to what I'm going to do. It will be simple. It's all a question of timing."

Nearing the place de la Comédie, bus 11 pulled into its stop in front of the train station. Jean-Claude saw Gabriella descend the steps with the children.

"*Arretez!*" Jean-Claude commanded as he thrust a wad of bills into the surprised driver's hand and leaped from the taxi. Instantly a tall man blocked his way. As Jean-Claude tried to step around him, he felt a crashing blow to his chin. The last thing Jean-Claude remembered was people all around shouting, "A doctor. Get a doctor!"

David left Jean-Claude on the sidewalk, surrounded by a group of curious pedestrians, and raced toward the Comédie. When he was a safe distance away, he stopped and turned around. From this perspective, he watched Gabriella climb back on the same waiting bus, five children trailing obediently behind her. A moment later the bus took off down the road toward the east side of town. Jean-Claude still lay on the sidewalk, surrounded by curious pedestrians.

David shook his head. That was a little too close for comfort. He lost himself in the backstreets of the centre ville and didn't head back to Castelnau until well after dark.

22

December 24 in Algiers came and went like every other day during that long fall of 1961: filled with fear. The streets were empty of people by dusk. Somewhere a plastic bomb exploded in the Casbah as the OAS unloaded its fury. The graves of innocent victims littered the countryside, but the terrorists on both sides paid little heed.

An old man with a turban around his head knocked softly on the door on the second floor of an apartment building in Bab el-Oued. The middle-aged woman who opened the door eyed him suspiciously.

"A letter for you and your children, from Moustafa," he urged as the woman took an envelope from him. "Something about leaving Algiers. Instructions from Hugo."

A spark of relief lit up the woman's eyes. "Thank you, sir. Thank you," she said, closing the door behind her.

The man in the turban walked away, pausing only long enough to hear the woman calling, "François, Emilie, *venez ici*! We have news!"

He was almost to the steps when he heard the explosion. Gazing back at the apartment, he saw smoke escaping from under the door. He nodded slowly and murmured, "Merry Christmas to you from Ali."

The Christmas Eve meal ended at midnight. Monique and Yvette glowed with pleasure as the young people crowded around the long dining-room table at Monique's house. Stephanie and Caroline were chatting about how much they had eaten. They begged Yvette for her recipe for the bûche de Noël. Gabriella and David were in deep discussion about a French poet. The conversation around the table had been lively all night, Yvette thought with satisfaction. Much better than the fiasco with the rabbit two months ago.

Candles flickered by the window. She could tell that the students didn't want to leave the party just yet. Stephanie was terribly homesick, and Caroline seemed bored with classes out.

"Girls, will you go to Mass tomorrow?" the older woman inquired.

"I doubt it," Caroline replied casually. "I'm going to sleep late. Then I'm getting together with a few other girls for the afternoon."

"And you, Gabriella. What are your plans?" Yvette asked.

Gabriella looked around, her face red with embarrassment. "I … I don't know. I mean, I haven't made plans. Church of course—"

David took her hand in his and interrupted. "I'm afraid Mlle Madison will be quite busy all day." He lifted an eyebrow and winked at Gabriella. "*N'est-ce pas*, my dear?"

Yvette clapped her hands together. "Marvelous! Busy on Christmas, even so far away from your family. That is just right. I don't want my girls to feel homesick."

She bustled into the kitchen to meet Monique, who was clearing off plates and humming to herself. "Did you hear what M. Hoffmann said, Monique? Mlle Madison is going to be quite busy all day tomorrow. *Ooh là!*"

"Our Christmas meal has been a wonderful success, Yvette. We can leave in the morning *tranquilles* to see our families. Our boarders will be having a delightful time of their own." The two widows giggled for a long time before they composed themselves and joined the young people in the salon.

It was almost two a.m. when the little party broke up. Yvette started back to her apartment with Caroline, Stephanie, and Gabriella.

David caught Gabriella's hand before she left. Yvette pretended not to notice but nonetheless slowed down enough to hear their whispered conversation.

"I'll pick you up at ten, Gabby. We can go to church together, and then you can come here for lunch. Mme Pons is leaving me all the leftovers."

"You really mean it?" Gabriella furrowed her brow. "You want to go to church with me?"

"Of course. It's Christmas."

The Eglise Réformée, one of two Protestant churches in Montpellier, was tucked behind the place de la Comédie on a small side street.

"Thank you for coming with me," Gabriella whispered as the worship service ended. "I need to stop at Mme Leclerc's for a moment. Do you mind?"

"Not at all." They walked to where the deux chevaux waited patiently behind the large open square. David drove through the deserted streets back to Castelnau and stopped in front of Mme Leclerc's apartment.

Gabriella left him in the dark stairwell as she rushed up the stairs and into the apartment. In her room she retrieved two brightly wrapped packages.

"What have you got there?" David questioned, amused, as she joined him on the stairs.

Suddenly Gabriella felt foolish. "Nothing much. Just a gift for Christmas."

"I thought everyone exchanged gifts last night, at Mother Griolet's."

"Oh, yes, that was for the children and the students, but ... but ... you weren't there."

He put his long arm around her shoulder and held her close as they walked back to the deux chevaux. "You're sweet, Gabby. Too sweet."

Mme Pons's apartment was dark and empty, and at once Gabriella felt awkward. David turned on the light in the salon and took her coat.

"May I get you something to drink, Mlle Madison?" he teased. "A *pastis* perhaps, or a *muscat*? For Christmas."

"I'll try a muscat. You said it's really good."

"That's right, you never got to taste it in Aix. And would you like to hear a little Christmas music from the good ole USA?"

"You have some?" she asked, delighted.

He brought their drinks and sat across from her, raising his glass. "A toast to us, Gabby. Friends." He tipped his glass against hers.

"Friends," she murmured.

He disappeared into his room, emerging moments later with a record album in its folder. He held it out for her to inspect: *50 Favorite Christmas Songs*.

"This is great. Where did you find it?"

"I have connections," he said with a wink. He placed the record on the phonograph and put the needle down. "Rudolph the Red-Nosed Reindeer" began to play.

"Would you like to open your presents now?" she asked. She handed him a rectangular box.

He raised his eyebrows as he took it from her. "You shouldn't have gotten me anything."

"It's nothing. It's just … symbolic."

"Symbolic of what?"

"Just open it," she said, laughing.

Carefully he unwrapped the gift, laying the wrapping paper on the floor. In the background Bing Crosby serenaded them with "White Christmas." David opened the box and reached inside, withdrawing the statue of the baker.

"A santon!" He laughed heartily, obviously pleased. "A boulanger!" He raised it in his hands and admired the clay figurine. "It's perfect. Thank you, Gabby."

"I found it at Les Baux, before all the problems. He reminded me of you. A lover of French bread!" Her eyes were shining with excitement. "I couldn't resist it, and now … well, now that I know what you're up to, it seems even more perfect." Her left foot was jiggling nervously.

"Gabby." He brushed her face. "I have never known anyone so thoughtful."

"I'm glad you like it." She glanced down at the other package that lay at her feet. "There's something else, too."

"Another! This is my richest Christmas yet."

"You're teasing."

"Well, let's just say that my father and I have never really celebrated the holiday."

He ripped off the paper from the second present, uncovering a thick black leather-bound book. "A Bible?" he said, sounding confused. He ran his fingers over the new leather. "It's a very handsome volume, but Gabby—"

"I know you don't read it," she interrupted quickly. "But I just thought it might remind you of me someday ... of our friendship."

"Yes, indeed it will." He was quiet for a moment. "I *have* read it, you know. Parts of it I know by heart. There's some very beautiful literature in the Bible. And some pretty far-fetched stuff, too, you have to admit."

She didn't reply.

"I'm sorry, Gabby. I don't want to spoil your holiday. I know it's an important day for you, the real significance. Thank you for the Bible. And I'll read it again. Just for you. How's that?" He patted her hand.

"That would be really nice," she answered. "Start with the Gospels, why don't you? Perhaps you're not as familiar with the New Testament?"

"Why do you say that?"

"You're Jewish, aren't you?"

"Half-Jewish. Jewish enough to be put in a camp but not enough to follow the teachings. Not without a mother ..."

"I'm sorry to bring it up."

"Don't be, Gabby. You seem to be finding out a lot of other things about me." David suddenly seemed eager to talk. "You might as well know. My mother was a devout Jew, a God-fearing woman. I remember her praying by my bed at night, singing to me from the Psalms. But when you're only six and you watch your mother die, something happens.

"After the camp, I couldn't find anything to bring back the joy in life. And I was only a little boy! My father and I lived a tense, miserable existence, hating the sight of each other because it reminded us of the family we once were."

He leaned forward, holding his head in his hands. "By the time I was ten, I was sure there could be no God. I've never been able to see as you see. To believe. The hate is too strong. And, Gabby, I'm afraid to forgive."

She looked at him and felt pity. "Why are you afraid, David?" she asked quietly.

"Why? Because I don't want to be reconciled with my past. I want to flee it, and yet somehow I keep finding it staring me right in the face." He stood and walked over to a window.

"I wish I knew what to say to you, David, but I don't. Only that in walking on through the pain, not avoiding it, there is a certain freedom over your past. At least, that's what I'm finding."

"Your freedom is found within the confines of your religion, Gabby. I don't want that kind of confinement." There was no anger in his voice, no accusation.

"I understand why you think religion is confining, but I'm not really talking about a religion, you know. I'm talking about a Person. My faith centers around a Person."

The music swelled, and the choir finished with its last phrase: *Christ the Savior is bo-orn; Chri-ist the Savior is born.*

The record turned silently round and round. David walked over to the phonograph and flipped the disk over to the other side.

"Excuse me for a minute," he said as he slipped out of the room.

Gabriella walked around the den. It still smelled of the delicacies from the previous night. She felt a quick pang of homesickness and a sudden desire to be alone.

Then David reappeared, grinning sheepishly, the same vulnerable boyish grin she had seen once before. "I have something for you too."

Gabriella could not hide her surprise or pleasure. "You do?"

He smirked. "You're not the only one who likes symbolism, remember." He handed her a thin square package.

Unwrapping it, she found a gold-framed print of Monet's painting of the poppies. A card with her name on it was taped to the glass.

"Should I open this now?" she asked haltingly.

"Yes, why don't you." His voice was soft, tender, his eyes filled with quiet admiration.

She took the card from its envelope and read David's script.

> *A wildflower, bright and red*
> *Exuberance that softly spread*
> *To capture fields of dreams and hearts*
> *A silent splendor stops and starts*
> *And I found pleasure in the touch*
> *and smell of such*

a wild and happy
crimson-coated poppy.

            —*David*

Gabriella's eyes brimmed with tears. She bit her lip, then looked up at him, a smile on her face. "It's beautiful. The print and the poem. Thank you. I … I don't know what to say."

He was smiling too. "Funny how sometimes it is through pictures and poems that we express what we can't say." The record played on softly as the young man and woman gazed silently at each other.

They had eaten the leftovers and listened to the record three times. The afternoon was waning. David took Gabriella's hand and led her to the couch. He put his arm lightly around her shoulder.

"Somehow it seems that we are more than friends," Gabriella whispered, leaning against his shoulder.

"Am I making you uncomfortable?"

"No, not exactly. Only confused."

He rested his head on the back of the couch. "You're wondering if our attraction is not merely platonic, but romantic? Why I don't kiss you? How we can share so intimately and yet leave out the physical? And you're fighting with yourself, because you don't want to want what you want."

Gabriella blushed. "Something like that, yes."

"And do you want to be my girlfriend?"

She didn't know what to say to his blunt question.

"Gabby, I want to explain something to you. I think you'll understand. I have enjoyed the presence of many women. I'm sure you're not shocked. Brief encounters to bandage a deeper hurt. But I have rarely found a soul mate. Someone who looks deeper and feels. Someone who makes me question and care." He stroked her hair.

"And then you came along, a welcome surprise for this cynic. A safe bet, an unwitting accomplice to my secret mission. I found you delightful. And off-limits. The friendship was possible, but our moral and spiritual outlook differed so …" He played with her hair. "An angel and a devil."

She squirmed away from him, feeling suddenly naked, vulnerable.

"I wouldn't mind a romantic fling, Gabby, if that was what you were after. But I know better. You want a meeting of souls, a sharing that encompasses the whole being. And I can't give you my whole being. I don't own it yet." He rubbed his forehead with his hand. "Perhaps you won't believe me, but the fact is that I respect you too much to pull you into an affair that would leave you heartbroken and guilty. After all, I'm not wooing you away from another man. It's a jealous God who demands your total devotion. I can't fight that, Gabby. I will not."

He moved closer to her again and gently put his hand under her chin and lifted her head so their eyes met. Hers were brimming with tears.

"Dear Gabby, you don't want me. Ours is an impossible love. Please don't cry. Forgive me for speaking so bluntly." He offered her a white handkerchief.

She blew her nose loudly and dabbed her eyes. "You're right, David. You've seen my heart and my questions. But it doesn't seem fair. Aren't you afraid that you'll go through the rest of your life and always wonder, if only we had given it a chance?"

He grinned, turning up one side of his mouth. "Sure, I'll wonder. I'll think about you in ten years and hope you aren't married to a boring old pastor who preaches hellfire and brimstone but puts you to sleep in bed." He raised his eyebrows mischievously, and Gabriella laughed.

"So I'm doomed," she stated. "I can't be a disobedient child even if I want to. You, my tempter, will protect my purity." Her eyes were sparkling again.

"Innocent and chaste, I used to picture you. But I'm afraid I've at least destroyed the first stereotype. You're in the thick of things with me now."

"Yes," Gabriella said, happy to change the subject. "I want to know more about this secret mission of yours. Why are you helping to bring kids out of Algeria?" Before he could answer, she continued, "And don't give me that bit about revenge and minorities. Maybe it's true. But there has to be a deeper reason. Something has made you feel strongly enough about this war that you're here in lowly Castelnau, smuggling orphans into France."

He sighed, shifting his lanky frame to another position on the couch, so that they were facing each other, no longer touching hands. "You really want to know?"

The way he regarded her made Gabriella's heart skip a beat. If she was merely David's friend, he could care about another.

"Yes, of course I want to know."

"Mother Griolet told you that I once lived in Algeria."

She nodded.

"I made friends during that year, 1953, just before the war started. Then in late 1959, one of those friends wrote me about a desperate need to get children who are in danger out of Algeria. I had just graduated from Princeton and had some time on my hands, so I decided to see how I could help."

"You must have cared a lot about this friend to come here," Gabriella said.

David smiled. "Yes, I suppose I did. At one time. But that was a long time ago. And now ... now I'm involved in this operation and I find it ... compelling."

"And the cross?" Gabriella had removed her cross from under her blouse and now held it in her palm.

"The cross is the symbol of our operation. Nothing religious. It was a reminder of the past. It seemed to fit. Quite a coincidence that you wear the same one."

"Yes, a coincidence, David. A simple coincidence."

The sun was peeping behind the red tiles of the houses facing the apartment. "I should take you back, *non*? I have a few things to do, and perhaps you will be seeing Mlles Thrasher and Harland?"

"Yes, I suppose I should get back."

He helped her with her coat and they left the apartment, walking out into the dusk of Christmas Day. The streets were empty. Gabriella thought of a hundred things she wanted to say, but she could not bring herself to say any of them. *Don't leave me alone tonight. I want to stay with you. Just a while longer.*

He stopped at the entrance to Mme Leclerc's apartment. "Listen,

Gabby. I'll be leaving for about ten days. Until school starts. Please remember what I've said. Lie low. Jean-Claude won't come here. You'll be okay?"

"I'll be okay. I have four new orphans to look after." She didn't meet his eyes, for hers were filling with tears. "Thank you for a lovely day, David. The lunch, the print. The poem. I won't forget this Christmas, David Hoffmann." She stood on tiptoe and kissed him softly on the cheek.

"Nor will I, Mlle Madison," he whispered. "Nor will I."

The Christmas record played softly in the background as David packed his suitcase. He hummed along with "Silent Night," reliving the afternoon. Gabby knew too much now, but there was nothing to be changed. Ten days on the road. He hoped that Jean-Claude Gachon would decide to stay away from Montpellier, but nothing was certain. Quickly he scribbled a note on a scrap of paper. Before placing it in an envelope, he sketched a rough drawing of the Huguenot cross in the top left-hand corner.

The santon standing on the chipped desk caught his eye, and he shook his head. *You've explained things to her clearly. She agrees. Get her out of your mind.*

The black leather Bible sat beside the santon. David leafed through its thin gold-lined pages. The words were in French. He closed it, then opened it again. Gabriella's handwriting adorned the inside cover, and he paused to read the inscription.

Dear David,

    Wise professor! Shakespeare memorized it, John Donne preached on it, Victor Hugo quoted it. Throughout the centuries God has drawn man to His Word to read and be transformed. You who can so eloquently transmit the deeper meaning of works written by mere mortals, tarry a moment on these immortal pages. May you find here, as I have, the Bread of Life for your hungry soul. If not, at least you will have dared to seek an answer to its heavy questions.

    Thank you for being my friend.

    Gabriella

    December 25, 1961

Underneath her note she had written a verse: *For every one that asketh receiveth; and he that seeketh findeth; and to him that knocketh it shall be opened. Luke 11:10.* A Huguenot cross was sketched underneath the verse.

David remembered his promise to her and put the book into his suitcase. He left his room and stretched out on the couch, listening to the familiar melodies of Christmas carols, the tinkle of a bell, the soothing violins, the triumphant trumpet. *O come let us adore Him, Chri-ist the Lord.* The record ended, again turning silently on its table. David didn't move to stop it. He fell asleep, still hearing the refrain of the last carol in his mind.

23

The plane trees in Castelnau that offered shade in the heat of summer had been trimmed far back so that they appeared like men with no forearms, thrusting their knobby appendages toward the magnificent blue sky. Early January shone bright and full of promise, Gabriella reflected as she hurried through town. The ten days without David had passed swiftly, taken up with the children and their games and cares.

She had agreed to sleep in Sister Rosaline's quarters by the dormitory while the nun went on a spiritual retreat. Ophélie had especially taken advantage of the extra hours with her Bribri. Gabriella smiled to herself, thinking of the child. What was it that Mother Griolet had said? Tragedy to triumph?

Sometimes when the six-year-old lay curled on Gabriella's temporary bed, the young woman would smell the child's clean hair and remember Ericka cuddling up beside her in Senegal, squeaky clean after her bath in the iron tub behind their hut. Then it would take an extreme effort to pull herself back to the present and into the life of the bright-eyed girl lying at her feet. And every time Ophélie shared a story or a new discovery, Gabriella would think, *So this is what comes after six.* The thought haunted her when she was alone, an aching, joyous hurt.

At night, alone on her cot in Sister Rosaline's room, Gabriella often felt a crushing weight of sadness. But when she awoke the next morning, the heaviness would be gone, replaced by a chorus of happy children. Hearing their voices, Gabriella believed she could go on.

The four new orphans began to shed their masks of fear, warming up to the merry laughter of the other children. Mireille and Julie, five and eight, told Gabriella of the terrible night their mother was beaten to death in their apartment. The girls had escaped out a window and fled to a cousin's house. Elima was thirteen, shy, reserved, and distrustful, a beautiful Arab girl. Gabriella didn't know her story. Youssef, the twelve-year-old Arab boy, had formed an immediate friendship with Hakim. They laughed and played and planned together.

But Mother Griolet seemed distant and disturbed. Gabriella approached her this morning with care.

"Mother Griolet," she began softly, as she met the nun in the basement hall by the classrooms.

"Yes, my dear, what may I do for you?"

"It is only that you seem … concerned. I know you have such responsibilities, but you're not yourself these past days, and I'm wondering if it is something I have done."

The little woman's face broke into a smile. "For goodness' sake, no. No, Gabriella. Here, come into my apartment."

Gabriella followed Mother Griolet into her den.

"*Au contraire*, I don't know what I'd do without you! I suppose I'm feeling my way through a new adventure. There are quite a few concerns, with these children from Algeria. You see, for now it's quite clandestine … and no one knows how long this war will go on or how many more children will come." She paused for breath. "But I'm forgetting who is in charge. There's a verse from the Psalms I learned years ago, during the other war. It jumped out at me, and I grabbed it and used it for all it was worth." She chuckled. "'Lord, my heart is not haughty, nor mine eyes lofty: neither do I exercise myself in great matters, or in things too high for me.' I keep reminding the Lord of this verse."

Gabriella had taken a seat on the sofa. "I think you're amazing. Look at all you've done for these children and so many others. And yet you just keep going, without taking any credit. You're my heroine, Mother Griolet. I hope you don't mind. I want to be like you someday."

"*Ooh là*, Gabriella. Watch out now! You may see me as a role model if you wish, but don't put your hope and glory in simple humans. I'm sure to disappoint you." She winked at Gabriella. "Glory is a dangerous thing, linked with that enemy, pride. No, sweet child, give the glory to God. He is the only one who deserves it." She turned toward the door. "Lunchtime in ten minutes. I must call the children."

Gabriella rose to leave too, with a feeling of fresh anticipation. Today David would be coming home.

Pierre Cabrol arrived at work at three o'clock in the morning, just as he had done for the past thirty-five years. He flicked on the light in the boulangerie and pulled a stained white apron over his head, tying it around his trim waist. Thirty-five years of baking bread had not gone to his middle, he was proud to say.

Pierre relished the early black hours before dawn alone in his kitchen, preparing the dough, letting it rise, smelling the first whiff of cooked bread as it baked in the ovens. He enjoyed creating the pastries, their creams and the chocolate fillings. He especially liked the special orders for parties and weddings.

Even in the World War when flour was so scarce, he had kept the store open, handing out loaves to the famished villagers who came by. But his favorite memory was not of handing out bread to starving people. It was even better, more delicious, like the first bite of a brioche fresh from the oven. It was that memory that held him this black morning, as he rolled the dough and felt it seep slowly up through the openings between his fingers.

He wasn't young anymore, but he remembered the knives he'd hidden in the bread. Baked them right into the dough, and off they went! Remembered the papers and the names of those imprisoned. And now once again he was playing a game of hide-and-seck.

He reached into the pocket of his heavy gray trousers and pulled out a small piece of paper. He had received it yesterday in the delivery from Marseille, hidden in a bag of flour. A piece of paper that he now rolled into a thin cylinder and placed in a tube of plastic.

"And *oop là*, in she goes!" he sang as he embedded the plastic tubing into the middle of the dough in one of the pains de seigle. On this loaf he added no fancy cuts that baked up into crisp little ridges. It was a simple omission. No one ever noticed. But he knew. And he would be ready when the right person came into the store, asking for a pain de seigle.

Jean-Louis Vidal passed up the café-bar on his way through town. Tomorrow classes resumed. His thin lips were pressed together as he toddled along the cobblestones, turning down a side street and into a boulangerie. The aroma of fresh bread hung thick and succulent around him.

"*Bonjour, Jean-Louis*," called out the aging baker from behind the counter. "*Alors, quoi de neuf?*"

"Nothing much today, Pierre," the broad-bellied professor answered back. "Only thought I might be tasting a bit of your bread. That's all. Pain de seigle, if you don't mind."

The baker's mouth opened into a delighted bellow. "Pain de seigle, Jean-Louis. *Mais bien sûr!* I have one just for you." He handed over a hot loaf with a wink. The store was empty.

"Just like in the old days, *n'est-ce pas, mon ami*? I've not seen so much fun in almost twenty years. Though I was a lot sprier then. We both were, as I recall."

The two men laughed, and Jean-Louis paid for his bread. "Keep the change," he said, still smiling.

The afternoon sun shone through the windows of Mother Griolet's office. She didn't notice the flirting rays as she tapped her foot nervously under her desk. A note lay before her with a Huguenot cross drawn in the corner. She had received it ten days ago and reread it now.

> *Someone is seeking information about the new orphan Ophélie. Potentially dangerous for the operation. Watch the child carefully. Don't let her leave the premises. Answer no questions.*
> *Hugo*

Mother Griolet had worried over the note all week, unable to forget the letters she and Sister Rosaline had found concealed in Ophélie's tights. This child was an important link with what was happening in Algeria. She was sure the list of names was not a simple coincidence.

But how could she protect Ophélie? Thankfully M. Hoffmann had been gone for the past ten days. Mother Griolet feared him the most. But surely he wouldn't betray his own child! Or did he even know she was his daughter? The letter said Ophélie's mother had never told him. And Ophélie seemed to have no idea that her father was nearby either. Mother Griolet sat in the office, perplexed. She needed to confront the child with the facts.

She walked quickly to the girls' dormitory and found Ophélie's dresser. Opening the second drawer, she retrieved the pair of blue tights and pulled the velvet bag out. The two small envelopes appeared to have been untouched.

Mother Griolet took out the letter to M. Gady. Carefully she copied every word into her small spiral notebook. Then she took the other pieces of paper and began copying the names and addresses listed there. Her hand was shaking as she wrote.

Dear Lord, forgive me if this qualifies me for a spy. The thought made her laugh. *A seventy-two-year-old nun spying on a six-year-old orphan. Your sense of humor, Father, indeed. But the child will not be bothered. She will continue in some state of blissful ignorance. This, I think, is best.*

The bell rang, announcing the end of classes. Mother Griolet slipped the envelopes back into the velvet bag, then tucked the bag far down into the leg of the blue tights and placed them neatly in the second drawer. She reviewed her work. Not bad for an old nun. She walked briskly out of the dormitory as the children burst out through the basement doors into the courtyard.

There were thirty-two churches in Montpellier, and Jean-Claude had visited twenty-three of them. At first he had limited himself to those on the east side of the city, but when that search turned up empty, he decided to include all of the churches, Catholic and Protestant. But so far he had found none that housed children.

Three days recuperating from a concussion had been a waste of time, he contemplated angrily, furious at the thought of the man who had struck him. He was sure it was that cursed David Hoffmann.

Now it was January 10, and he needed to get news to Ali. He came to the parish of St. Pierre on the quai de Verdançon. A kind-looking priest opened the door to his knock and straightened his clerical collar. *"Oui, monsieur?"*

Jean-Claude cleared his throat and spoke with the same gentle, flowing words he had used when talking to twenty-three other priests. *"Bonjour, mon Père."* He inclined his head. "I'm looking for a pied-noir orphan." He produced a picture of Ophélie. "Her mother was killed in the war, and I'm her uncle. The child has been lost, but the last word we received was that she was living in a church in Montpellier. I have visited most of the parishes now, with no success. I'm desperate for news. Would you perhaps know of this child?"

The priest shook his head, rubbing his chin as he thought. *"Non,* I'm sorry. We don't house children." Then he smiled. "Ah, but perhaps you have not tried the communities around Montpellier. Have you been to Castelnau? There's an orphanage there. It's been run for years by an old renegade nun." He stopped himself, looking embarrassed. "Forgive me. I mean, a kindly Sister has run the orphanage for years. Perhaps she would have some information."

Jean-Claude kept calm. "That's a good idea. Castelnau, did you say?"

The priest nodded.

"And what is the name of this church … the orphanage, if I may ask."

"St. Joseph. It is called the Church of St. Joseph."

"Merci. Merci beaucoup," Jean-Claude said.

"De rien," the priest called out, as Jean-Claude skipped down the stone steps. "God be with you."

Jean-Louis Vidal finished his afternoon history class on January 11 and watched the girls file out of the room. He liked to observe the legs of Mlle Caroline when she wore her skirt high above her knees. Not such a bad profession, this teaching of American girls. Even if it was difficult to get inspired after two weeks of vacation. Ah, but the legs of Mlle Caroline could at least make his heart beat faster!

Jean-Louis removed his worn leather coat from the back of the chair, retrieved his battered briefcase and papers, then closed the classroom door and locked it. His disheveled appearance contrasted with the neat Ivy League attire of M. Hoffmann, he knew, but it didn't matter. Why throw away a coat if it still kept him warm? Why indeed, when there was no money to buy another.

He paused as he came to the ground floor and knocked lightly on the door to Mother Griolet's apartment. After a moment the nun opened the door.

"*Ooh là!* M. Vidal, it's you. Good. Come in, please."

They stepped into her office, and Jean-Louis pulled the door closed. "Jeanette," he said softly. "Are you well?" His red eyes were tender. "You look tired, *mon amie.*"

"Oh, Jean-Louis. I *am* tired. I have told the Lord I will not worry, but there seems much to worry about. A daily battle in the mind." She sighed. "I have something for you. You will know how to get it where it needs to go, I'm sure."

"Of course. And I have something for you too." They exchanged papers silently, briefly touching fingers. "Jeanette?"

"Yes?"

Jean-Louis cleared his throat. "You're doing a good job." He said it quickly, feeling a flush come to his cheeks.

"Thank you, Jean-Louis." She looked grateful. "You're sure we are not too old for this now?"

"Jeanette Griolet," he scolded playfully. "Was it not you who told me that the Lord takes care of His own? That He gives strength to the weary? Dear woman, you will not stop now?"

"Of course not, Jean-Louis. As long as the sun shines and the rains fall, O Lord, I will follow You."

They caught each other's gaze and broke out in laughter, like carefree children.

"Your eyes are still as bright as they were in the other war, Jeanette. Don't tell me that you're tired of this. I know you love it."

"You're right, old man," she teased, a twinkle reappearing in her eyes. "Now off with you. We both have work to do."

Jean-Louis left her office, shaking his head as Mother Griolet called after him, "Go easy on the pastis this afternoon, will you?"

Jean-Claude took bus 11 from the center of town to Castelnau. He chuckled to himself. After six weeks of hunting, surely this was it. The Church of St. Joseph must be where Ophélie Duchemin was living.

The town was small, its main road cobbled. The bus let him off in the middle of the village, across the street from a small square where a fountain sprayed. People were milling about in the late morning. Jean-Claude stopped a pedestrian and asked for directions to the church.

The woman nodded and pointed to her right. "It's just down the street there. You can't miss it."

He turned a corner, and the stone church came into view. It was small, with a wrought-iron spire and bell on top of the steeple. The side door was unlocked, and he stepped down into the cold, deserted chapel. His shoes echoed on the stones. "*Allô?*" he said softly, but no one replied.

Leaving the chapel, he walked around the side to where another building joined the church. He knocked loudly on the door. No answer. He knocked again, banging his fist on the large wooden door. From within he heard a woman's voice calling, "*J'arrive.* Just a moment."

"Take your time," Jean-Claude muttered to himself. "I'm in no hurry now."

Mother Griolet opened the parsonage door, panting for breath. "Excuse me," she huffed, greeting the young man who stood before her. "I'm sorry to make you wait. What may I do for you?"

The man looked about thirty. He was muscular and handsome, with thick brown hair and a disarming smile. Mother Griolet was sure she had never seen him before.

"*Bonjour, Soeur,*" he began, his voice soft and respectful. "I'm searching for my niece, a pied-noir orphan whose parents were killed in the war. Most recently we have heard that the child is being housed in a church in Montpellier. A priest in the city told me of your orphanage, and I have come hoping you will be able to help me. The child's name is Ophélie Duchemin." He pulled out a photograph from his shirt pocket and handed it to Mother Griolet.

The old nun had placed her hand on the door to steady her balance. A cold chill ran through her. *Compose yourself, Jeannette*, she rebuked herself silently, keeping the smile on her face. *Lord Jesus, help me. You have promised to give the words in the appropriate time.*

She cleared her throat as she stared at the picture of Ophélie. "I'm sorry, but we are a very small orphanage. We only have room for thirty children. Most have been with us for several years. It is difficult to place them." She lowered her voice to a whisper. "The priest perhaps told you?"

The young man leaned forward to catch every word, eager anticipation on his face. "No, he only said it was an orphanage."

"Ah, yes ..." Mother Griolet paused and gazed up at the billowing clouds. "Sometimes they don't like to mention it. The children are handicapped. You understand?" She tapped her head with her fingers. "Nothing inside. Poor ones." Then she feigned a surprised look. "Oh dear, I have been rude. Is this child ... handicapped?"

For a moment he stared at her stupefied. "Handicapped? Ophélie? No, no, of course not."

Mother Griolet shook her head slowly. "Well, I'm afraid she will never be sent here then. We are, shall I say, selective. I would invite you in, sir, but I'm afraid the corridors smell rather bad. I was just cleaning up an accident."

The man looked horrified. "Yes, how terrible for you."

"It is so sad, so sad. But, *monsieur*, excuse me ... I do not know your name."

"It is ... I'm called Philippe," he replied nervously.

"Well, M. Philippe, there is another orphanage in a town farther out, past Assas. St. Bauzille-de-Montmel. You have heard of it?"

"No, no, never." His eyes had narrowed. "And can you get to it by bus?"

"By bus?" Mother Griolet paused. *"Oui!"* She brightened. "Yes, the same bus that brought you here. Number 11, is it?"

He nodded.

"Yes, well, take it till you get to Teyran. There you must change. I'm not sure of the number, but the driver can tell you."

The young man shifted his weight on the steps, his hands fidgeting in his pockets.

Perhaps he has a gun, she thought. *He will shoot me right here and barge in and have a look for himself. And he will find the child.*

But after a moment he slowly turned away. *"Merci,"* he said. "St. Bauzille-de-Montmel, you said."

"Yes, exactly. Good luck, M. Philippe. God be with you."

She waited until he was out of sight back in the village before she closed the door. Slowly she made her way to her office and sank into the large leather chair. Her hands were trembling uncontrollably, and she could hear the beating of her heart. She rested her head in her shaking hands. "Lord, he will be back. I know it. And what will I tell him then?"

24

If ever there was a confused time and place on earth, Anne-Marie was sure it was Algiers in January 1962. A tangled web of terrorism and counterterrorism, espionage and counterespionage threatened to trip up every citizen, Arab, pied-noir, French soldier, and mercenary. While President de Gaulle worked on compromise with the FLN, three separate branches of the French secret service prowled about, seeking to stop the OAS's brutality. Everyone belonged to some clandestine movement. Anne-Marie reminded herself that she too had belonged to several. But protecting children from a vengeful Ali Boudani was not recognized by anyone else.

She slipped out of Marcus Cirou's apartment late in the afternoon of January 18. The real terror in Algiers occurred between dark and dawn when most of the bombings by the FLN, OAS, and now the new secret police took place. She needed to deliver information to two more families. For now they were the last ones Ali knew about.

Anne-Marie traced her way along the narrow streets. Every wall sported a painted slogan. *OAS* was painted one night, only to be covered the next morning with the French secret service initials, *MCP*. She walked past a shopkeeper who was sweeping out his store from the debris of a predawn bombing.

She found a dingy apartment building called La Fillette. Clothes hung from every balcony, refusing to dry in the cold, humid air. She entered the stairwell, which was littered with beer cans and cigarette butts. The stench of urine filled the air.

On the third floor, she searched for apartment 36. She waited to make sure no one was following her on the steps. Then she knocked lightly on the door.

"Who is there?" a woman's voice called out.

"It's Anne-Marie Duchemin."

The door opened a crack, and a gray-haired woman peeped out. "Come in," she whispered.

Anne-Marie stepped into the apartment, which smelled of couscous cooking on the stove. She greeted the older woman and quickly gave her the news: "On January 25 at eleven thirty I'll pick up your grandchildren in the alleyway behind your building and take them to the dock. But that's a week away, and it's not safe for you to stay here, because Ali Boudani has your address. You heard about the bombing last week where the woman and children were killed?"

The grandmother nodded, her eyes showing fear and fatigue.

"Is there anywhere you can hide until the twenty-fifth?"

The woman thought. "Yes, we can go to my cousin's home outside the city."

"Very good. Be careful and have the children back on the twenty-fifth. Don't worry."

"Thank you, child. Thank you." The aging woman glanced to the sky and crossed herself. "God be with us. God spare us."

"Yes, it's as you say." Anne-Marie closed the door behind her, tiptoed down the stairs, and stepped back out into the streets of Algiers, heading back to meet Moustafa. Together they would warn one last family.

"Tomorrow we will discuss how the themes used by artists and writers of the late nineteenth century are linked," David said, concluding his lecture. "And on Friday we'll visit the Musée Fabre in Montpellier. There are many great works in the museum, most notably those of Frédéric Bazille, a contemporary of Monet. And please don't forget that your papers on André Gide are also due Friday."

Several girls groaned at the reminder.

"That is all. You're dismissed, *mesdemoiselles*."

He closed his briefcase. When the other students had left, he joined Gabriella, who was staring out the window. They watched the children playing in the courtyard, their high-pitched squeals reaching up to the classroom.

"Your Frenchman came to St. Joseph," David said flatly.

Gabriella gasped and looked up at him. "Jean-Claude? When? Did he speak to anyone? Why didn't you tell me before now?"

He ignored her questions. "I saw him from a second-story window, talking to Mother Griolet. I don't know what she said to send him away, but I'm sure he was looking for you and the child. And I've no doubt he will be back. You must be ready."

"What do you mean?" Gabriella's voice was agitated.

"Never answer the door to the parsonage. Watch your step, and Ophélie's. And find a place to hide with the child, in case he shows up. Neither of you must be seen. We will be receiving more orphans next week. He cannot know, or the whole plan will backfire. You must help me, Gabby." Fatigue showed on his face.

"I've said I will help. But you're worried about something else, David. What is it? What's wrong?"

"Everything, Gabby. Everything and nothing. 'The world is too much with us; late and soon.'"

Gabriella smiled. "Does quoting Wordsworth help you relax?"

"Perhaps," he answered absently. "Perhaps it's like reading the Scriptures for you." He brushed a wisp of hair away from his eyes. "Will you come with me for a drink? Just here in town."

"Of course." She beamed up at him.

Dear Gabby, he thought as they left the room. *What shall I tell you?*

They trotted through the town to the old café-bar. Several older men were seated at the tables, enjoying a late-morning apéritif.

"Excuse the ambience," David whispered. He led Gabriella to the same table where they had sat after the phone call to Jean-Claude in early December. The music was louder, the laughter more raucous, and a chilly gust of wind swept through the room each time the door was opened. Gabriella huddled over the table.

"May I take your coat?" he asked.

"No thanks. I'm freezing."

He ordered two hot chocolates and waited for them to appear before speaking. "Gabby, I've received some more information about the work. It will take me a while to sort it out with my contacts in Algeria. It's been so long, you see, since I've actually heard from them. But when it's all worked out, St. Joseph may be flooded with kids. And Mother Griolet will need someone to help her get the children and deliver messages. I need you to be that person."

Gabriella sighed as he took her hand. "David, you know I want to help. I have no choice, really."

"I may be gone for a while. I'm convinced there will be more peace talks going on between de Gaulle and the FLN to try to settle this Algerian question. Things will start happening fast, Gabby. And we must be ready for something bigger than we bargained for."

"And if Jean-Claude finds us in the meantime? What will we do then?"

"Contact me. I'll leave an address and check in every few days. But, Gabby, he *must* not find you. He works for an Algerian, high in the FLN. A man with a grudge from another war. This man seeks to wipe out whole families through cold-blooded, premeditated murder.

"But I have a feeling that when Algeria is independent, it will all break up. If we can hold on a few more weeks, a couple of months, this danger will be over—and another, different one will come."

Gabriella's eyes glistened. "War and danger and secrets and spies. I never expected this from little Castelnau." She gave him a wry look. "I never expected cruel memories of my past either. But I'll try to help. Tell me what to do, and I'll try."

He stroked her fingers. "You're beautiful and brave, my Gabby. You will tell me the inner strength comes from your God. I don't know if it's from God or simply from an amazing woman's drive, but I know you will do it."

"And Mother Griolet? Won't she grow suspicious if you go away again?"

David chuckled. "My dear, she is already very suspicious. She dislikes me. But M. Vidal will take my classes. She won't protest."

"When will you go?"

"Next week. Sometime after the twenty-fifth."

They finished drinking their hot chocolate; then David scooted his chair back and stretched out his long legs under the round wooden table. He folded his arms across his chest and smiled as he stared at Gabriella.

"Have you ever been in love, Gabby?" he asked suddenly.

Months ago she wouldn't have dared to answer his question, afraid of a snide remark. She could feel the heat of embarrassment on her face. *What I really want to say, dear David, is that I'm in love with you.* But she could not.

The long silence was broken by her one-word reply. "Once."

David didn't question her further, but in his eyes she read his hunger for a few details, so she continued.

"I was fifteen; he was seventeen. His name was Dimby. A brave, strong, kind boy. We grew up side by side, like sister and brother. We didn't mean to fall in love. I learned African customs from his sisters. I spent many hours at his home. His family was the first in the whole region to accept our God.

"Dimby thought about deep things. We could talk and laugh and ... and suddenly we were in love," she finished quietly, unable to explain the depth of emotion that had passed between them.

"You mean you were in love with an African? He was black?" David asked incredulously.

"Correct on both counts." A slightly defensive edge crept into Gabriella's voice.

"And what did your parents say? Surely they forbade it! A white missionary kid from the States in love with a black man from a tribal village in Africa." His voice was full of wonder.

"No, they didn't forbid me to love him. My parents also liked Dimby very much. Perhaps they were strange, but I don't think they saw black and white when they looked at people. They saw hearts and souls and hurts. They didn't discourage me, but they knew that our love wouldn't ... wouldn't work."

"What do you mean?"

"Dimby was promised to a young girl in a nearby village. The fathers had arranged it years ago. To break this tradition would create distrust and hatred towards us as missionaries."

"Surely Dimby realized this. Why did he pursue you? How did you do it?" His question was unfocused, but she understood his meaning.

"We cried and whispered our love. He brought me a wreath of African lilies—a sign of commitment in his tribe. He held them out for me to smell, and the sweet scent curled up between us. Then we burned the flowers and scattered the ashes, as is their custom when someone very cherished dies. We never touched, never kissed, never held each other in an embrace, but in our hearts we knew. We had loved. He left that night, and soon after was married to his promised bride. He lived in a hut a half mile from my home, but I never saw him again. His tribe was known for its discipline. For honor and respect, they would never go against family."

"But he loved you! And he wasn't really one of them anymore. You said he was a convert."

"There are things we can't understand but we must accept. I didn't think it was wrong that he left. It had not been wrong to love him, but it was not wrong to lose him."

"And your mother. What did she say to you?"

"She said, 'I will lift up mine eyes unto the hills, from whence cometh my help. My help cometh from the Lord, which made heaven and earth.' And she hugged me. I cried for a long, long time, and she held me. Then she said, 'Gabriella, someday you'll see, our God does not make mistakes.'"

David reached over and tenderly took her hand. "I'm sorry, truly."

She didn't meet his searching, compassionate gaze. Instead she asked, "And you, David, have you ever been in love?"

Still holding on to her hand, he replied, "I don't know." His voice was soft but tormented.

"Is it so hard to know whether one is in love?"

His eyes caught hers in a moment of recognition. The eyes that were so often dark and brooding now carried a spark of something. What was it, Gabriella wondered. Then she knew. Like the faraway gleam of a lighthouse promising safety to the weary, wind-tossed vessel, his eyes carried the light of hope. Just a flicker, but nonetheless, hope.

In that moment he took her other hand, squeezing them both softly in his, and whispered, "Perhaps, my dear Gabby, it's not so hard at all to know when one is in love."

Ali Boudani didn't notice the stench of rotting fruit that seeped in the window of his apartment as he read the paper on the morning of January 20. He was quite pleased with the headlines. In Paris two days earlier, the OAS had set off numerous explosions and killed none of their intended victims. In Algiers, however, two of the prime men with the OAS had been assassinated from within their own ranks. Surely the brutality of this desperate operation would benefit the FLN, as the French were divided among themselves. Surely de Gaulle would give in to the FLN's demands before long, and a free Algeria would result.

He stood up from his dilapidated desk and reread the names listed on the wall. Mme Sentier and her children had perished soon after her husband's neck was slit. That was good. Another harki family dead. But two remained in Algiers. Mahmud had more information about Mme el Gharbi, whose husband had been murdered last week. The family was in hiding, but Mahmud had news. They would be the next target, Ali decided. Tomorrow night if possible. Then there would be only Mme Bousquet and her grandchildren.

Ali contemplated this as he picked up a slide he had recently received from Jean-Claude. He held it to the light. The elusive David Hoffmann. It was good to know he was back in France. So it had been him all along. Of course! How foolish of them not to have guessed this sooner. Ali closed his eyes and saw the young man as a strapping teenager.

"This is Ali Boudani," Anne-Marie said. "His father was in my father's division in the war. An excellent soldier." She turned her cherubic adolescent face toward Ali. "David's father is here in Algiers working in the American embassy. I'm showing him around the city."

The encounter had lasted only a few minutes, but now Ali recalled it vividly. Anne-Marie had paid time and again for her foolishness. She would pay again. And so would David Hoffmann.

A young Arab boy entered Ali's room after knocking lightly on the door.

"Hello, Hussein, my boy. Do you have news for me?"

"Yessir, Ali. Good news!" The boy grinned, his eyes shining with excitement.

"Let me hear it then," Ali growled.

"I've seen the woman you search for. She went into La Fillette apartments in Bab el-Oued. She talked to an old woman. I was quiet as a mouse. She didn't see me. She said the children must be at the docks by midnight on January 25."

Ali patted the boy's thin shoulders. "You have done well, Hussein." He dropped a few shiny coins into the boy's dirty hands. "And did you see where this woman lives? Did you follow her to her house?"

The young boy's face fell. "No. I tried to follow, but a tall man met her. He had a gun with him and I was afraid. I followed as far as rue Tripoli, then I lost them."

"That is good enough for now. Out with you, Hussein. Keep looking, my son. Keep looking."

The boy nodded and dashed out of the room. Ali sat back in his chair, lit a cigarette, and took a slow drag. "Midnight on the twenty-fifth at the docks. We will be waiting."

It was late afternoon on January 22 when Mother Griolet climbed the steps from the basement and opened the door to her apartment. She was glad for a moment of silence, for her mind was racing. More children were set to arrive in five days. She unfolded the note that Jean-Louis had handed her ten days ago. He would meet the children as they arrived by boat in Marseille. She sighed as she thought through the logistics of lodging five more children. The dormitories had exactly five free beds left. One in the girls' and four in the boys'.

A smile erased the worried expression on her face. Hadn't Jean-Louis said there would be one girl and four boys coming? The Lord always provided just what was needed at the right time. She sank onto the brown couch in her small den and slowly bent to unlace her shoes. She propped up her swollen feet on the coffee table.

She could not forget the handsome young man at her door last week asking for information about Ophélie. Nor could she forget the letter from Ophélie's mother with her revelation about David Hoffmann.

Something else bothered her about M. Hoffmann. It was only a faint memory, but as she dwelt on it, she felt a sharp panic rising within her. Quickly she went to an old file cabinet in the back corner of the office and pulled out the bottom drawer. She leafed through some files and found several dated 1943. She pulled them out, cursorily perusing the contents. Her eyes fell on one short paragraph. She read it over twice, then sighed heavily. Slowly she replaced each file.

"Whom can I talk to about these things, Lord? Whom shall I trust?" She thought of her old friend Jean-Louis, with his bloodshot eyes and ruddy cheeks. Did he remember as well? But it was not Jean-Louis who needed to know.

Then she thought of Gabriella. "She is young and strong, Lord. But she is already dealing with a lot of pain from her past. And she loves David Hoffmann. In spite of herself, she loves him." She closed her eyes and didn't move from the couch for half an hour. When she rose again to her feet, she felt confident. "I will talk to her, Lord. I will tell her the secrets she does not know about two people she loves very much."

Ophélie grabbed Gabriella's hand as they left the schoolroom following afternoon classes. "When can we go to ride the train, Bribri? When will we take the bus again to town?"

Gabriella hugged the child tightly and, kneeling down, looked her in the eyes. "We cannot leave the church for a while, Ophélie. We don't want to meet M. Jean-Claude again, you know."

Ophélie shook her head and frowned. "But I have only ridden a train once, Bribri. It was so much fun, when that nice man brought me here from another place."

"You mean when you came to St. Joseph?" Gabriella asked.

"Yes, I came with that nice *maître*. He never talks to me, but I've seen him at the school."

"You mean M. Hoffmann?" Gabriella asked, surprised. "M. Hoffmann brought you to St. Joseph?"

Ophélie's face went pale. "I … I don't know his name." Her eyes were wide. "He is the tall man who likes you."

Gabriella laughed. "Yes, M. Hoffmann and I are friends."

Ophélie felt as if she might cry.

"What is it, sweetie?" Gabriella was still kneeling beside her. "Is something wrong?"

"No, nothing. I don't think." Ophélie furrowed her brow. "What did you say his name is?"

"His name? It's David Hoffmann."

Ophélie let out a low cry and broke away from Gabriella's grasp. She ran through the courtyard and toward the dormitory with Gabriella following after, calling out to her. When they reached the dormitory, Ophélie turned on her heels and gazed up at Gabriella. Tears welled up in her eyes. "Please, Bribri. I want to be alone."

"You're sure, Ophélie? I can't help you? I'm sorry if I upset you."

"It's okay," she replied and ran to her bunk. She waited until she saw Gabriella walk back across the courtyard, stopping to play with Christophe and Anne-Sophie. Then Ophélie opened her second drawer and brought out the dark-blue wool tights. She reached inside the leg and found the blue bag and pulled it out. Carefully she unfolded her mother's pink pages on the bed. She stared down at the words on page three. *He is an American, very handsome and smart. His name is David Hoffmann.*

Ophélie began to tremble. "Oh, Mama. I don't understand. If that man is my father, why doesn't he talk to me? Why does he pretend I'm an orphan? Why didn't he tell me who he was? Maybe he doesn't love me. Maybe he is very mad that I'm his little girl." She cried softly into her pillow as the other children giggled and played outside her window. When the bell sounded for dinner, Ophélie stuffed the letter and the blue bag into the tights. Her stomach was in knots as she replaced them in her drawer. "Papa?" she whispered. "Please come to me, Papa. Please love me."

She remembered something Gabriella had taught her. Dropping to her knees, she folded her hands across her bed and closed her eyes. "Dear God ... Bribri says that You love little children. That You listen when they talk to You. Please make my papa like me."

She could not think of what else to say. Then she added, "And please take care of Mama. And someday, God, can we all be together? As a family. Someday, please?"

She wiped her eyes with the sleeve of her navy sweater and left the dormitory, pulling her coat around her shoulders. It was dark outside as she walked the short distance to the dining hall. Ophélie was not sure if the butterflies dancing in her stomach were from excitement or from fear. But at least now when she thought of her father, she had a picture in her mind. Now she could see a tall, kind man cradling an injured child by the bridge in a city that had erupted into madness.

25

Following morning classes on January 25, Gabriella sat in Mother Griolet's office trying to push a gnawing question from her mind. Ophélie was upset about something that had to do with David. What was it? If only she could have asked him, but he had left town last night.

The old nun bustled in after her and took her chair. "Thank you, dear, for sparing me a few minutes of your time. How are you today? *Ça va?*"

"*Oh, oui. Ça va.* Everything is all right, I guess."

"You're not too overworked? I'm afraid I'm asking a lot of you these days."

Gabriella shrugged her shoulders. "It's good for me, Mother Griolet. I like to think too much. To analyze and run ahead of the Lord and plan my own endings." She blushed. "So you see, it's good for you to keep me busy."

Mother Griolet folded her hands on the desk and regarded Gabriella kindly. "My dear, I'm afraid I have something else to talk to you about." She cleared her throat. "I know that you have a great affection for Ophélie ..."

Gabriella nodded.

"... and for M. Hoffmann also."

Gabriella shot her a surprised look. "Yes ... I've told you about my feelings for him before."

"Yes, yes, you have." She straightened a stack of papers on her desk. "I don't really know how to begin.... Recently I came across some very puzzling and astounding information. I feel it's best to share this with you."

Gabriella scooted toward the edge of her chair. Mother Griolet's usually serene face was outlined with worry. The wind outside knocked on the heavy wooden shutters, begging to come into the warm office. Again Mother Griolet cleared her throat.

"Perhaps if you would come with me, I could explain things better." The old nun rose slowly to her feet, hesitating before she came around her desk and left the office.

Gabriella followed obediently through the hall and den, out into the courtyard, across the sparse lawn, and into the girls' dormitory. The room seemed silent and somber without the chatter of little girls. Mother Griolet went to Ophélie's bed and opened a drawer in the chest.

"We found this quite by accident when Sister Rosaline was preparing for the latest arrival of orphans." She produced a pair of tights and slipped her wrinkled hand down one leg. "I don't suppose you have seen this before?" She held up a blue velvet bag.

Gabriella shook her head.

"There were several surprising items in this bag. But I think this letter from Ophélie's mother will interest you most." She handed Gabriella three thin sheets of pink paper.

Gabriella met her eyes with a questioning look. "I ... I have the feeling that I'm about to find out some more bad news, Mother Griolet."

"It's not bad news, my dear. But quite unexpected. And important for you to know."

Gabriella sat down lightly on Ophélie's bed, bending her head so as not to bump it on the top bunk. Mother Griolet stood beside her.

Silently Gabriella perused the letter, her eyes brimming with tears as she read about a mother's love for her child.

"This is why Ophélie wanted to learn to read so desperately. Look ... here are the words she could not understand. She asked me about them." She glanced up at Mother Griolet.

"Yes, Gabriella. Read on."

There was not a sound in the room except the gentle rustling of paper as Gabriella turned from the second to the third pink page of paper. Suddenly she let out a sharp cry. "No! No! It can't be!" She dropped the pages and stood up too quickly, bumping her head on the bunk.

"Ouch!" she moaned and fell back across the bed, sobbing.

"Gabriella ..." Mother Griolet touched her shoulders, but Gabriella pushed her hand away.

"It's nothing. I'm all right." She turned her distraught face to the nun. "At least, my head is all right. But my heart ... It can't be! How could David be Ophélie's father? He has no idea."

Immediately she remembered Ophélie's reaction when she had mentioned David's name. So this was the reason.

"Poor little Ophélie. She has no one she trusts. She has been betrayed too often." Gabriella picked up the last page of the letter and stared at it again. "Thank you for showing this to me, Mother Griolet. It was the right thing to do, I assure you."

"I'm afraid it may be hard on you, dear."

"I'm finding that there are many hard things in life. I have a lot to learn." She forced a smile. "Give me a few days to digest this and I'll be fine."

Mother Griolet reached up and placed her worn hands on Gabriella's freckled face, then kissed her softly on each cheek. *"Que*

Dieu soit avec toi, ma chérie." She patted her lightly on the back. "Go on home and have some lunch."

"Yes. That's a good idea, Mother Griolet. *A bientôt.*"

It took every ounce of strength Gabriella could muster to walk through town with her head held high. Somehow she felt sick and betrayed. She argued with herself all the way to Mme Leclerc's apartment. What was David up to? What cruel game was he playing? Mostly she felt a burning jealousy of Anne-Marie Duchemin. Years ago David had loved her, and they conceived Ophélie. But perhaps he truly didn't know he had a daughter.

"But you came to France for her mother," she whispered as she climbed the steps, not bothering to press the orange button in the stairwell. "You're here because you love Anne-Marie. You want to help her."

Again the sick, angry emotions choked her. Gabriella went into her room and let her book bag fall to the floor with a thud. She leaned back across her bed and stared at the ceiling, noticing the uneven plaster. Water stains from an old leak showed through the paint. In the corner a spiderweb hung, forgotten, covered with dust.

She reached in her mind to try to untangle her thoughts. Everything was running together in her head, like a mass of dusty webs.

I hate you, David. I hate this mess you have pulled me into. I hate caring about you. Oh, God, if only I could rip out this heart and replace it. Then I could smile for a family reunited.

She closed her eyes and imagined David embracing Ophélie, and a beautiful young woman running to hold them both. David turned and let his head fall back in ecstasy. He kissed her as they laughed and wept while Ophélie shouted, "Mama!"

"Oh, God, this is how the story should end. It's only right." She clenched her fists. "But I will be honest with You, because there is no one else I can tell. It isn't fair. It seems as if You dropped these people in my life for me to love, for me to somehow bring together. And now You will rip them away. They aren't mine. I know it! I hate myself for caring so much. But I do care. I need them!" She hit her fist on the bed.

"You're asking too much this time, God." Suddenly another thought came to her. Perhaps Anne-Marie was dead. Gabriella felt a twinge of twisted hope, followed immediately by guilt. *How can I even think that? How could I wish Ophélie's mother dead? Oh, Gabriella, you are really mixed up.*

Anne-Marie watched the orange ball of fire slowly descend across the horizon. The clock on the wall in Marcus Cirou's kitchen showed five thirty. In five hours she would leave for the tiny alleyway at the edge of Bab el-Oued and wait for the children's arrival. She bit her lip anxiously. Moustafa would be coming soon.

She didn't know how to break the news that she was leaving with the children on the boat. She had wrestled with the idea all through the night. It had to be so. There on the other side of the Mediterranean she would find Ophélie.

She knew Moustafa wouldn't protest. He would nod and agree. But leaving Algeria now meant that she wouldn't come back. She felt sick to her stomach to think of Moustafa left behind, alone without her. But the longing to see Ophélie, to hold her, to know she was safe … the mother love was stronger. Anne-Marie could not imagine life without Moustafa near her, but Ophélie deserved her mother. Right now she could not have both of them. She wondered if it would ever be possible.

She thought of another she might meet in France. Somewhere, she was sure, there was a brilliant young American who had once loved an adolescent pied-noir. She shivered to think of meeting David again. The man who had given up a career in the States to help her launch a desperate mission. What would she see in his eyes?

The kitchen door opened, and Moustafa walked inside. He was thin and haggard, his curly black hair tousled by the wind. "It seems everything is working as planned," he said, grinning wearily at Anne-Marie. "This is good."

"Moustafa," Anne-Marie said. She came to his side and put her arms around his neck. "Moustafa, I must tell you something."

His brow wrinkled as he held her close. "What is it, my *habibti*?"

She saw in his eyes that he knew, even before she spoke the words. "I'm going with them tonight. I have to see Ophélie." She held his unshaven face in her hands, tracing his three-day-old beard with her fingers. "Come with me, Moustafa. We can make a life there. We'll have rescued all of the families that Ali knows about. We've done our best. Please."

"Do not beg me, Anne-Marie. I have already deserted my people once."

"But you're not deserting. You're helping. You have saved lives. I'm sure there will be work to do in France. David will know—" As she pronounced David's name, she stopped short. Moustafa released her. "I'm sorry. But you know, Moustafa, that he is somewhere helping."

"Of course I know. We set it up this way two years ago. It's only that I'm afraid of losing you to the father of your child."

"Then come with me, Moustafa! David Hoffmann is not the man I love. It is you. Please come with me tonight."

He held her again and kissed her softly, ran his fingers through her thick hair, and sighed. "You will go tonight, Anne-Marie. You are right to go."

A light-skinned young Arab man slipped out of the Casbah at nine p.m. He was well built, muscular, with close-cropped black hair. In his right arm he carried a machine gun.

Ali's instructions had been explicit. Midnight on the docks. Children boarding a boat. Get there at least two hours ahead. There are many docks, so watch well and wait. And kill. Ali wanted nothing left. Nothing but bloodstains for the mourners, if they dared turn out to mourn in this city of creeping death.

No one roamed the streets of Algiers at this hour. No one except men on a mission, like himself. He was not afraid. He had killed before. The FLN called him their little terrorist. He was good. With bombs, plastiques, and especially a machine gun.

By the time he reached the port, the moon was high. The sound of the sea lapping against the body of the boats lulled his racing heart. The smell of fish hung pungent in the air. Nothing moved. The young Arab crouched beside a long sailboat and waited.

In a narrow alley of Bab el-Oued, huddling behind heaping barrels of trash, three children clung to their Arab mother. It had started to drizzle. Another woman, a pied-noir, drew a dingy raincoat over her graying hair and held on to two of her grandchildren.

Anne-Marie whispered, "It's time."

Silently the buxom Arab mother pulled three small boys to her breast and wept. The pied-noir woman crossed herself and kissed a young girl on the forehead and then embraced the smaller brother. Anne-Marie took the women's hands and squeezed them. She read the fear in their eyes.

For a moment she thought it was unfair that she should leave with these women's children. She remembered her last sight of Ophélie, running through the streets of Paris. She prayed a silent prayer to an unknown god and left the two women weeping and clinging to each other.

Moustafa crept out of Marcus Cirou's apartment at eleven o'clock. He had to have one last glimpse of Anne-Marie. Her kisses were still fresh on his lips; he could still smell the fragrance of her hair and soft olive skin. She had cried for two hours before leaving to meet the children. He wouldn't let her see him, but he must have one last look. He must know that she was safe with the children.

He made his way through the empty streets of Bab el-Oued until he came out onto the wide boulevard in front of the sea. All was black. He hid himself behind several fishing tugs and waited.

A light breeze blew in the frigid air as the children crawled along the dock on their bellies. The boards creaked under the movement of the tide. Anne-Marie's heart raced. She crouched in the shadow of a yacht, watching the five children slithering ahead of her like a procession of snakes. Cautiously they made their way to the small sailboat that floated unobtrusively between several larger vessels. One by one they crawled toward the outstretched shadow of a man aboard the *Capitaine*. As Anne-Marie observed their progress, she glanced behind her to make sure no one else was there. It had become a habit. But no one had followed them.

Suddenly, from behind a tug, a man sprang out onto the dock across from her, pointing a heavy machine gun in the direction of the crawling children. Anne-Marie jumped to her feet and screamed, throwing her weight into the man and knocking him off balance. With a curse, the young man swung the gun at her head. It crashed on her skull, the force of the blow sending her into the sea. She hit the ice-cold water, still conscious, but sunk down, deeper down. She heard the ricochet of bullets popping through the water as she scrambled helplessly to pull herself up for air. Her legs stung with pain. All was dark.

She bumped her head against the hull of a ship and swam, panicked, to the side, desperate for air. Her legs felt like dead weight, dragging her down. She fought to maintain consciousness, grabbing frantically for something, anything. A ladder! Under the dock she pulled herself up the rungs of a mussel-covered ladder until her head was above water. She tried to control her gasping lungs as she intertwined her arms between two rungs, wedging herself against them. In the water below, her legs dangled with no feeling at all, and then she fainted.

It all happened so fast that Moustafa hadn't had time to think. *React!* his senses told him as Anne-Marie fell in the water. The shadowed man turned his gun to the waters and sprayed the surface with bullets. He rose to aim again at the children, and Moustafa drew the gun he always carried inside his belt. Rachid's gun. He fired once, then twice as the man cried out and turned. Another shot rang out. The machine gun spat a round of bullets into the air, and the man fell with a crash and lay silent.

In the distance Moustafa watched panicked children diving into the boat as it cast off from shore without a sound. He threw himself into the water where Anne-Marie had fallen. "Anne-Marie!

Anne-Marie!" he cried in a hoarse whisper. "It's me! It's Moustafa." A thick dread stabbed at his heart in the icy black waters. He swam around boats, underneath them, and back to the docks. When he resurfaced, panting, he listened. A dripping somewhere. He swam toward the faint noise. Anne-Marie's arms were pinned through the bars of a ladder. She hung there in shock.

Carefully he pulled her limp body to him and lifted her rung by rung up the ladder. Two feet, four feet, six … until her upper torso collapsed on the dock. Moustafa shimmied up beside her. He pulled off his sopping coat and wrapped it around her. Then he left her side and ran to where the young Arab man lay lifeless on the dock. Quickly Moustafa dragged the body to the edge of the pier and shoved it into the water. Picking up Anne-Marie, he carried her across the dock, stopping only to retrieve the machine gun that sat beside a puddle of wet blood.

Jean-Louis gulped down a last pastis as he waited for a sailboat to dock in the port of Marseille. A foghorn sounded, and a light drizzle fell outside. The café-bar was crowded and smoky. He glanced at his watch. It was seven a.m. on January 27. The boat should be here by now. He pulled his casquette over his head and left the bar, an umbrella in his hand.

"It is likely that you will not be alone," David had warned him last week. Now Jean-Louis watched out of the corner of his eye for a handsome brown-haired Frenchman, tall and muscular.

The docks were quiet. Boat after boat floated peacefully in its place in the morning mist. "The *Capitaine*," David had said. "Black with white trim." Every boat looked black in the predawn light.

For thirty minutes the round-bellied history professor strolled along the docks nonchalantly. In the distance a boat crept silently into harbor. Jean-Louis watched its approach. Squinting, he could make out the name *Capitaine* on the side.

Anne-Marie breathed shallowly in Marcus Cirou's bedroom. Her legs were wrapped in thick gauze, and a large bandage covered her head. Her eyes were closed. Moustafa held her hand as he sat beside the bed, stroking her fingers.

Every few minutes her eyelids would flutter and almost open. She moaned softly. "Ophélie."

She opened her eyes and stared at Moustafa. Sad brown eyes. He touched her face.

"He came … from … nowhere," Anne-Marie whispered feebly.

"Shh, my *habibti*. Save your strength. You're safe now."

She closed her eyes. "I'm sorry, Moustafa. I don't know … I don't know about … the children.…" She began to cry.

"Don't worry about the children, Anne-Marie. They all got to the boat. It's okay."

"Okay.… Yes." She smiled weakly, squeezed his hand, then fell back asleep.

Moustafa bent over her and kissed her forehead. "I'm so sorry that you are still here, my beautiful one. But I will care for you. We will survive."

26

Mother Griolet leaned on her desk as she looked out at the thirty-four children seated before her in the basement classroom. Their eyes were riveted on her. Soft-brown eyes in pale-white faces. Black eyes surrounded by dark-olive skin. French eyes, pied-noir eyes, Arab eyes.

"*Bonjour, mes enfants*," she began. "Today we are happy to welcome the five new children who arrived at St. Joseph on Saturday. Most of you have already met them, but I would like to introduce them to you again."

She came around the desk and walked to the first row. Smiling down at a little girl, she said, "This is Rachel and her little brother, Guy. Welcome to St. Joseph."

The children stared up at her with fearful eyes, and Mother Griolet felt a pang of pity for them. She tried to imagine the scene Jean-Louis had described, the details he had heard from Jacques, the captain of the boat. The children had barely escaped death when a man opened fire on them while they were boarding. The assailant had thrown the young woman who was accompanying the children into the sea, and then, miraculously, another man had shot the attacker down as the children scrambled on board.

The terror was still in the children's eyes when they arrived at St. Joseph, so Mother Griolet had ordered three days of rest and games and good food. No classes for the new children until Thursday.

"And these are the three brothers who have come to us, Yacin, Hamid, and Amar," she continued. "We are very happy to have you here with us."

The other children clapped their hands loudly, enthusiastically, giggling together.

"*Les enfants!*" Mother Griolet reproached them. "Please calm down. There are times to have fun and times to be serious. I have told you this before. And you remember our little play of last week? One day you will perform it for real. You must be ready. Remember? We thank God for our healthy bodies. What would we be like if it were not so?"

Immediately twenty-nine children went limp on their desks, while the new children stared at them wide-eyed. Christophe and André slapped clumsily at each other. Anne-Sophie stood up with her eyes closed and felt about her desk, bumping into another chair. Hakim moaned softly in the corner, crouching on the floor. Lorène and Marine rolled their eyes and shook their heads. Ophélie ran to the back of the room and hid in a broom closet.

"Children, please behave," Mother Griolet said sternly. They acted as if they didn't hear her. "Children!" She raised her voice, but still the children ignored her. Then quietly she whispered, "Thank God for our healthy bodies."

Finally the children returned to their desks, sat straight and attentive, and were silent.

"Very good, children. Excellent. Now please get out your math books." As they took out their workbooks, Mother Griolet muttered under her breath, "I think we are ready now, Lord."

The open market bustled with people in the old part of Aix-en-Provence. Mme de Saléon busied herself squeezing avocados, picking through endives, apples, and lettuce.

"*Coucou!* David," she called, waving a thick bunch of radishes his way. "What do you think? These will be heavenly for lunch, *n'est-ce pas?*"

David looked up from where he had been examining green and black olives. "Of course, Madeleine, they'll be delicious with some soft butter. And a good glass of rouge." He winked at her. "Will you excuse me for a moment? I'm going to fetch the bread. I'll meet you at the apartment."

"*Impeccable, mon ami,*" Mme de Saléon agreed.

David wound his way through the twisting, narrow cobblestone streets of Aix until he came to the small street directly behind the cours Mirabeau. Quickly he found the boulangerie and entered. A line of customers waited in front of him. The boulanger saw him enter and lifted his eyebrows, still talking merrily with a pretty young woman who was paying for her purchase.

When the store was empty of other customers, the baker smiled at David. "*Alors, mon pote*, what's up with you?"

"A baguette and a gros pain will do me fine today, Gilbert. I suppose that is no trouble?"

"No trouble at all," replied the baker. The store remained deserted except for the two men.

"And your friend, the redhead?" Gilbert asked quietly.

David shook his head. "My friend the redhead, poor woman. She has her hands full."

"Nice woman," Gilbert commented, raising his eyebrows. "You should keep her out of trouble, *mon pote*. Take care of your women. I have a nice little place in the mountains with a chimney and a double bed. You work too much, M. David."

David laughed heartily as a stooped woman with a straw basket teeming with fruits and vegetables puffed her way into the boulangerie.

"Thanks for the advice, Gilbert. I might take you up on it someday." He picked up the two loaves of bread and his change and departed.

Mme de Saléon brought a plateful of radishes to her elegantly set table and sat down across from David. "So tell me, my friend. How are you? The last time we talked you had just sent your girlfriend off unexpectedly to Montpellier." She looked at David with tender gray eyes.

David shifted his weight in his chair and began buttering a radish. "I'm doing pretty well, Madeleine. But there are some problems back in Montpellier. How much longer do you give the war? Another month? Six?"

Mme de Saléon's eyes sparkled. "We never tried to guess in the other war, David. We just kept doing what there was to do each day."

"I know. Each man has his part to play. Keep quiet, and the others will be safe. I know."

"Do you have the 'information' you need?"

"We had brought all that we could ... until now. Now I have some more work ahead. A lot more."

"When will you go back to Montpellier then?"

"Two days, maybe three. I still have a visit to make in Aigues-Mortes."

"And your girl, Gabriella, she enjoys this line of work too?"

David chuckled. "If you asked her, she would say she has no choice. She's got the guts and the brains for it, but she's so blasted religious. She looks at life in a strange way, Madeleine."

"Religious!" Madeleine clapped her hands together enthusiastically. "Why, that is just fine. Religion has its place, you know. Look at your orphanage in Castelnau." She prodded him playfully. "If it weren't for religion, where would you keep your 'information'?"

"True, but Gabriella is more than devout. She really believes a God up there is directing her life. It makes her untouchable!" He wiped his mouth and laid down his napkin on the table.

"Untouchable, and so all the more desirable. Is that your problem?"

David's eyes flashed. "Maybe. Or maybe it's that I know it just can't work. I've seen firsthand what happened to a woman who loved God and fell in love with a man who did not."

Mme de Saléon's face clouded. "David … you exaggerate."

He raised his voice. "No, Madeleine! I don't. Mother's love for Father was passionate and pure. And he abandoned her. He abandoned us."

"David! It isn't true. Why must you insist on this? Do you forget that I was there? I wouldn't be sitting here now if your mother had not stayed in Paris. Yes, there was a risk involved. But your mother and father were in agreement. And she had an American passport.

He had no idea it would turn out—" She paused, a mist in her eyes. She continued softly. "He had no idea that she, that you all, would be taken."

David said nothing, his dark eyes brooding. He bit into a buttered radish. "Anyway, it's of no use. Gabriella loves another. I've never been very lucky at fighting with the gods." He smiled wryly.

Madeleine shrugged, stood up, and hurried off to the kitchen for the main course.

Gabriella let out a loud sigh as M. Vidal concluded his lecture on Gustave Flaubert. Stephanie had been right. Two classes a day with the alcoholic history prof was unbearable. Gabriella wished David would come back. She wanted to rush into his arms and cry and tell him that she loved him. But she didn't let herself dwell on that image.

She knew what she would have to do when he returned. She had rehearsed her lines for the past ten days. She would act casual and a little removed. Then she would say, "I need to tell you something. Ophélie Duchemin is your child. You know, the little orphan you brought here on the train? Your daughter!" While he looked on, amazed, she would produce Ophélie's letter from her mother.

Gabriella had reached the basement, lost in her thoughts. She didn't feel a desire to be with the orphans right now, but Mother Griolet was counting on her more and more. The new children were terrified of everything. Mother Griolet looked tired and almost feeble lately. And to make matters worse, several children had broken out with chicken pox.

Gabriella wanted to help. But every time she saw Ophélie, she felt a prick of pain in her heart. *I need to tell you, too, dear little friend. I need you to know that I know.* But Gabriella had not felt strong enough to be able to hug Ophélie and act thrilled with the news that David Hoffmann was her father.

She walked into the classroom, poised and seemingly carefree. Mother Griolet was just finishing up the reading lesson. From above, the doorbell sounded loudly.

Gabriella whispered to her, "You get the door and then rest a bit. I'll watch them until lunch. Go on."

The nun gave Gabriella a grateful nod and exited into the hall, patting Gabriella on the shoulder as she left the room.

"Children!" Gabriella shouted, for they had erupted into chatter. "Listen, please! You have a few minutes till recess. I'd like a drawing of the sea and every kind of thing you can think of that you find in the sea."

Several children grimaced, protesting. Jérémie shook his head vehemently. His face was still covered with scabs from his recent bout with chicken pox. Anne-Sophie and André looked much the same.

"Children, please," Gabriella added crossly. "Get to work."

She stepped out into the hall and listened. She could hear Mother Griolet talking excitedly, her voice agitated. "Yes, I understand, M. Philippe. You're desperate for the child, but as I told you before, she's not here. I'm afraid I can do nothing for you."

Gabriella could make out Jean-Claude's voice laughing, threatening.

"Yes, of course you may look around." Mother Griolet was talking quickly, loudly. "Of course. Follow me."

At once Gabriella raced back into the classroom. Trying to sound composed, she whispered, "Children! It's time for the play to begin. Wad up your papers! Quickly. Thank God for our healthy bodies. What would it be like if it were not so?"

The children, delighted, began crumpling up their papers, tossing them into the air, grunting and yelling as they played. Gabriella grabbed Ophélie's hand and motioned to the Arab children to follow her down the hall to the large storage closet at the end. She rattled the key and unlocked the door, pulling Ophélie and the other children in after her. With the same key, she locked the door from the inside.

"It's going to be fine, children," Gabriella whispered. "We mustn't make a sound."

She led them to the back of the closet, where they squatted behind boxes of cleaning supplies and old brooms. In the darkness Gabriella listened for Mother Griolet's voice, but all she could hear was a low moan coming from Ophélie.

"Mama. I want my mama."

She put her arms around the child, and they waited.

Mother Griolet's hands were trembling as she opened the door to the basement classroom. She sent up a silent prayer of thanksgiving at the sight before her. Some of the children were babbling, throwing wads of paper at each other, while a few crouched in the corner, drooling. M. Philippe stood beside her, observing the scene.

"Children! Children! Please be quiet. We have a guest."

This only caused the children to increase their wild behavior.

Mother Griolet, looking harried, turned to M. Philippe. "I'm sorry, it's hard to control them."

"I can control them if I have to," he said, striding into the classroom.

Mother Griolet cleared her throat. "M. Philippe, excuse me, but I must warn you that several of the children have chicken pox. It's quite contagious. I'm sure you have had it?"

He wheeled around angrily. "Never mind. I'm not afraid." He turned and glared at the children with scabby faces.

"No, of course not. It's only, as I'm sure you realize, that it's quite dangerous for adult males to catch the disease." She lowered her eyes. "You know what I mean?"

"What?" He cursed impatiently while he scanned the room. Then understanding flashed across his face. He reddened and turned to the nun. "Go on then. Show me around this place."

"As you wish," she replied calmly. "You will excuse me. I must call one of the Sisters to stay with the children. Here, step out into the courtyard with me." She rushed him past the storage closet and into the frosty February air.

"*Coucou!* Sister Rosaline! Sister Isabelle!" After a brief wait Sister Rosaline appeared, her cheeks flushed.

"Yes, Mother Griolet?" she questioned, eyeing M. Philippe with suspicion.

"Sister Rosaline, could you please watch the children for me? This nice young man would like to have a look around the facilities. I'm afraid the children are a bit wild today."

Sister Rosaline nodded and let herself in the basement door.

"Now if you'll follow me, I'll show you the dormitories."

He caught Mother Griolet roughly by the shoulders. "I'll look around myself," he spat. "I want to check things out real well."

Mother Griolet followed him into the dormitories, calling to him calmly, "As you wish, *monsieur*. But I assure you, we don't have your niece here with us."

She sat down on a bunk bed in the boys' dormitory and watched the frenzied man at work, looking under beds, in closets, in restrooms. All the time, Mother Griolet kept repeating silently to herself, *I will lift up mine eyes unto the hills, from whence cometh my help.... The Lord shall preserve thee from all evil.*

The Frenchman never stopped his search long enough to see how violently Mother Griolet's hands were shaking in her lap.

Jean-Claude Gachon searched through every room of the church and orphanage of St. Joseph. An hour passed, and still the children played loudly in the courtyard and threw food in the dining hall as Jean-Claude looked on in disgust. "Nuts. Real nuts," he muttered angrily. But no little Ophélie Duchemin and no redhead named Gabriella.

He felt a slow rage building inside as the wind whipped and banged the shutters of the school building. He walked into the basement from the garden with the nun following behind. Jean-Claude turned to his left and pointed to another door. "What's in here?"

"Supplies," the nun answered. "Have a look if you wish."

He tried the door, but it was locked.

"Oh, I'm sorry. I keep it locked because of the children. You never know what these little savages might get into. Just hold on a minute, and I'll fetch the key."

"Forget it," he said impatiently. Jean-Claude was angry that he could not frighten the old woman. She must be nutty too, he deduced, as she answered each of his questions with quiet composure. But she was getting tired, he could tell. If he could keep her talking for a while longer, perhaps she would reveal something.

"I'm sorry to have disturbed you, Sister. You have been most kind to show me around. I'm afraid I will have to keep looking. Please give my best to M. Hoffmann when you see him." He let the phrase dangle before her like bait for a fish.

The nun looked at him, perplexed. "Excuse me, but I don't know a M. Hoffmann. Are you quite sure you're all right, M. Philippe?"

"Yes, I'm just fine. I'll be going now."

"As you wish, sir." They walked up the stairs to the ground level together, and the nun opened the door for Jean-Claude.

Once again he looked around furtively. "*Au revoir*," he mumbled over his shoulder. He walked briskly to the center of town, cursing to himself. "A house of nuts. A real house of nuts."

"Dear God," Mother Griolet cried, collapsing against the heavy wooden door. "He's gone. Thank You, dear God. Forgive me, Lord, if You disapprove of our little scheme. Somehow it seems that You do not."

Slowly she descended the stairs into the basement and hobbled along the hall to the end. She knocked softly on the door to the storage closet. "Gabriella? You can come out. God has given us healthy bodies."

A shuffling noise came from inside the closet as someone fumbled with a key. Then the door swung open, and seven children escaped into the hall. Gabriella exited last, looking exhausted. She fell into Mother Griolet's arms, and they embraced each other tightly.

"I was sure he would come in," Gabriella confessed.

"It was the Lord who put the idea in my head: act as if you would be happy to show him the closet. I don't know how that man could not see that everything about me was shaking."

"Oh yes you do," said Gabriella, with a tired smile on her face. She glanced upward.

"You're right. Our God can blind the eyes of the enemy."

The children still huddled around the two women, not moving.

"Come, children," Gabriella prompted. "The game is over. Let's go get some lunch. I'm starving."

The Arab children eagerly ran after her to the dining hall. Ophélie stayed nearby Mother Griolet.

"What is it, Ophélie? You're afraid, is that it?"

Ophélie nodded.

Mother Griolet hugged her to her breast. "There is nothing to be afraid of anymore. Everything is all right."

"I want my mama," the child replied. "I'm asking Jesus to please give me back my mama … and my papa, soon." She stared at Mother Griolet with hopeful eyes.

The old nun patted the child's head. "This is a good prayer, little Ophélie. This is good."

David left Aigues-Mortes on February 7, following the beach road in the direction of Montpellier. Within an hour he would arrive back at St. Joseph. He was glad to be heading there after two weeks of traveling. He watched the wind play through the marshes, dividing them like a comb parting hair.

He was anxious to see Gabriella. Suddenly he turned his car onto a dirt road leading toward the sea. He parked it in the dry shrubs and got out. He walked in the direction of the beach, kicking the sand with his black loafers. He pulled his leather jacket together and buttoned it. Two weeks of information made his head feel clogged and thick. He had visited contacts in Marseille, in Aix, in Aigues-Mortes. He had written letters to Algeria. Now he waited for a response.

As he inhaled the sea air, he stretched out his long arms, swinging them in large circles to the side of his body. A few lonely gulls cawed at him, reprimanding the tall stranger who had interrupted their peaceful habitation.

He walked out to the sea and took off his shoes and socks, leaving them in the sand. He rolled his tweed pants above his shins and splashed his feet in the freezing water.

"Feel it, David. Feel something," he said softly to himself. Then again, this time yelling, "Feel something!"

He welcomed the frothy sea rushing over his feet. It stung him at first, but after a few minutes his feet grew numb. He left the water and lay down on the beach, letting the fine, dusty sand sweep over him. Lying on his back, he raised his arms to the sky.

"Gabriella claims that You're up there, God. Prove it then! Open up Your heavens and drench me with rain. Still I won't believe. Life is not ordered by a god. It is coincidence and fate. I have read some of Your book, as I promised. Your Gospels that promise life and peace and forgiveness." He rolled over onto his stomach and began writing with his finger in the sand.

"You don't seem to understand," David argued to the deserted beach. "I'm not going to *forgive*!" He spat out the word like a rotten piece of fruit. "Dear Gabby, I will never forgive them. And so, I suppose, I shall never be forgiven."

Closing his eyes, he imagined Anne-Marie coming toward him, laughing, an adolescent shimmering with beauty. She had needed him then, all those years ago. She had seen the war coming, as her father predicted, but she wouldn't leave with David! And so he sent her a hundred unanswered letters from America. And then, out of the blue, she needed him again. She knew he would come to help.

David wiped his hand across the sand, then absently began drawing in it with his finger. He thought of Mother Griolet, her green eyes twinkling as she spoke to the American girls. Then he thought of Gabriella.

He pulled out a folded piece of paper from his leather jacket. He studied the list of scribbled names and addresses that he'd received a month ago, a list he had copied and sent across the ocean to Anne-Marie. "Answer me soon, Anne-Marie. Someone please answer."

He rose to his knees and brushed the sand from his coat and hair. Standing, he looked down at what he had drawn in the sand. A cloud passed overhead, obscuring the image momentarily. Then the bright sun broke through and illuminated a crude sketch of the Huguenot cross.

"Someone please answer," David repeated and walked back toward his car.

27

On the tenth of February David and Gabriella entered the crowded café in the beach town of Palavas, fifteen minutes from Castelnau, unnoticed by the men and women engrossed in lighthearted conversation. The last color, an orangey-pink hue, was leaving the Mediterranean sky. The café smelled of coffee and whiskey mixed with the stench of sweat and cigarette smoke. Spoons clanked against saucers as waiters yelled orders across the counter.

One waiter hurried them to a round metal table that tilted to and fro as they shifted weight. With a swish of his rag, he wiped away a puddle of beer with several flies hovering above it. "What will it be?" he asked impatiently.

"A Coke," Gabriella stammered.

David, completely collected, ordered a pastis.

"So, my beautiful Gabby, how have you been? Tell me about the adventures of the past two weeks at St. Joseph." He was all smiles.

She wondered if, after all, they would only make small talk. David seemed cool, removed from any sign of emotion. She couldn't meet his eyes as she held her hands together on the table to keep them from shaking. The waiter approached with their drinks.

David looked up, as if sensing her pain. Silently he slipped his strong hand over her trembling ones.

I have to tell him.

With a deep breath, she squeezed his hand and met his gaze. "Jean-Claude came back," she said, biting her lip.

"When?"

"Two days ago." She closed her eyes as if to blot out the memory. "I suppose it would have seemed comical if we hadn't been so completely terrified. You would have been proud of the kids." She told him the whole story.

David shook his head, looking amazed.

"It was a miracle that we weren't found, David! It was so frightening. The Arab children are still terrified, especially the ones who just arrived. Did you hear about their trip?"

Again David shook his head.

"Something awful happened at the port in Algiers. A man started shooting at the children as they were getting on the boat. Then a woman who was with the children tried to stop the man, and he pushed her into the sea and shot her. Another man shot the first guy, and the children escaped. The stuff a spy novel is made of, yes?"

"The stuff of war," David muttered.

Gabriella took a long sip of her drink. She tossed her hair over her shoulders and pulled it into one thick strand; then she released it, letting it tumble across her shoulders again. "Ophélie is scared too."

"Hmm." David nodded, but he seemed lost in other thoughts.

Gabriella cleared her throat. *Now you must tell him.* The room swirled about her, the noise of the waiters' shouts amplified. Beads of perspiration broke out on her forehead. "David?"

"Yes?"

"David, could we go outside for a bit? I ... I'm not feeling too well."

"Of course." He got up quickly and came to her side. "What's the matter?"

"Nothing that a little fresh air won't help."

He left the change for the drinks on the table and followed Gabriella out of the café.

They walked for ten minutes in silence. The beach air was cold and pure. Gabriella thrust her hands in her jacket pockets. She stared at the sand as she walked, almost dragging her feet. David took his long strides in slow motion, not passing hers, but he didn't speak.

Gabriella stopped abruptly, turned to face him, and took his hands. "I have to tell you something, David. And I don't know how." Her eyes brimmed with tears. "I need you to help me with this one."

He raised his eyebrows, perplexed. "Sure, Gabby. I'm all ears."

She didn't speak. Gently he touched her chin with his hand and looked into her eyes. She bit her lip to try to control her tears.

"This is so wrong. I shouldn't … be … crying. It's … I think … I think you will find … that it is good news." She wiped her eyes with her fingers. "Okay." She sniffed. "I'm going to try again. But I can't look at you."

They started walking.

"Mother Griolet found some information in Ophélie's drawer, some papers from her mother. One was a letter." Another pause. "In the letter, she told Ophélie about the father the child had never met." Gabriella reached out and took David's hand. "Ophélie's mother's name is Anne-Marie Duchemin and …" She stopped and looked up at him. "Her father's name is David Hoffmann."

A hundred expressions washed over David's face as Gabriella regarded him with teary eyes. "Me?" he whispered in amazement. "What? Me? Ophélie's father?" He ran his hands through his hair. He stood transfixed, watching the waves lap onto the shore.

Gabriella wanted him to deny it, to wonder how it was possible, to ask to see the letter. But he didn't. He slowly shook his head, and as if she were not even there, he said, "Of course. That's why you never answered my letters. And why so suddenly you asked me for help. Ophélie ... my daughter."

Gabriella backed away from him, feeling unfit to share this private moment of revelation. She was an intruder in this story. Nothing but a bumbling intruder. She watched David. Still he stood straight, composed, a tall tower. Silent and strong. She knew he was reliving something from his past, and she was jealous of his memories.

Couldn't he see that this was stabbing her? But why should he see? Trying to reason made her head throb. She felt dirty, ugly.

If only you could see how deeply I care for you, for Ophélie. If only you could see how afraid I am that you won't need me anymore. I'm sorry I can't smile for you, David. It's wrong of me, I know.

He left the water's edge and came to her side. "Dear Gabby. Thank you for telling me. As you can imagine, this is quite a shock. It's unbelievable that my daughter has been with me. I have watched her play day after day. And I never knew."

"It was you who brought her to St. Joseph, she said."

"Yes, I found her in Paris on that crazy—" He stopped midsentence. "Ophélie said? She knows I'm her father?"

"She just recently found out. She learned her father's name from Anne-Marie's letter, once she had learned how to sound out the letters ... but she didn't know *your* name. And when I mentioned it in conversation, she went white. Then Mother Griolet showed me the letter, which she had only discovered a short time ago, and we realized that Ophélie had been trying to read it all these months."

"And she never said a thing?"

"No. Even now she has no idea that Mother Griolet and I know." She hesitated. "And now you."

"But I must see her! I must tell her. What will I say?" He paced on the beach.

"We'll figure out a way to tell her. Don't worry."

"Gabby, it's such strange, good news. I have never thought of myself as a father. Never felt the least bit interested. But now ... suddenly I am."

"She's very worried about her mother," Gabriella broke in.

"Yes, I'm sure she is. For Anne-Marie. I'm worried too." He looked at her sympathetically, his cynical eyes caring.

He started to speak, so she quickly said, "And I hope you find her."

For a moment his gaze was quizzical, pained, even confused. She could say no more. The courage to speak had drained her. She relaxed her fierce grip on his hand and let the breeze run through her hair.

But David didn't relax his hold on her. With his black eyes intent on Gabriella's face, he whispered, "Dear Gabby, don't you know that I have already found the one I'm looking for?"

David Hoffmann had wanted to be many things during his twenty-four years of life. A professor, a writer, a poet, a spy, a diplomat, an explorer. But he had never wanted to be a father. The word connoted all that he despised in humanity: anger, abandonment, prejudice, betrayal. Yet as he lay on his bed in Mme Pons's apartment and thought of being a father to Ophélie, he felt a sudden warmth.

How will I learn to be your father? he wondered. *Who will teach me the lessons I haven't learned? I never saw Anne-Marie's round belly. I never held you as an infant or knew when you took your first steps. I don't even know what I missed. So how will I learn to love you … the way a good father should?*

A phrase flashed in his mind. *Like as a father pitieth his children* … Somewhere in the Bible Gabriella had given him, he had read that verse. He remembered laughing at the idea that a father would have compassion on his children. But now he wanted to read more.

He picked up the large leather book and flipped through its pages. He was sure he had not read it in the Gospels. The Psalms! Last week he had read through the Psalms. Some he knew by heart from his childhood. And this one was there in the webs of his memory. He came to Psalm 103 and began to read:

> *Bless the Lord, O my soul: and all that is within me,*
> *bless His holy name…. Like as a father pitieth his*
> *children, so the Lord pitieth them that fear Him.*

He finished the psalm and closed the book. He had a daughter now. Perhaps the God of Gabriella would teach him how to be a father.

David turned out the light in his room and watched the crescent moon cupping a piece of the sky in its hand. He saw the beautiful face of Ophélie in his mind. He laughed at the irony as he relived the night of October 17 with the wounded child. He had found her by the bridge where he was to meet Emile Torrès. He recalled the note he had received those months ago. Torrès had information for him. *Was it you, Ophélie, he had for me? And by a wild providence, we are here together.*

He rubbed his eyes with his long, thin fingers and sighed. *I don't know where you are, Anne-Marie. But Ophélie is safe with me. I'll keep her safe for you, until you come back. I promise. I will be her father. I'm ready now.*

The sliver of a moon cradled a lone star in the black Algerian night. Anne-Marie's breathing came in gasps. Her eyes were glazed. A wet rag lay on her forehead as Moustafa desperately tried to bring down her raging fever. He cursed himself for not having taken her to the hospital. But hospitals were not safe in Algiers. A whole ward of pied-noirs had been murdered in one a few months ago. Equally gruesome stories were reported weekly.

But now he feared he had been wrong to try to care for her himself. Both legs had become infected from the bullet wounds. A thick yellow pus oozed from below her right knee. She didn't speak coherently.

Marcus Cirou came into the room, wringing his hands and begging Moustafa to take her to the hospital. "She is dying here," he said. "She can't do worse there."

They drove through the night to the Santa Maria, a Catholic

hospital on the outskirts of Bab el-Oued. The French nurses greeted Moustafa with a suspicious air. "Let me take care of this," Marcus ordered. "You can't help her now."

Moustafa waited outside in the cold night air, stamping his feet and cursing the moon. He tried to think of something besides Anne-Marie's gaunt, pale face.

The list of names had appeared miraculously in the mail last week. This was good news. He supposed that Ophélie had given the list to the redhead, and she had mailed it to him. Now the operation could continue.

But Anne-Marie had seemed indifferent to the long-sought-after list. She had only cried out feebly for Ophélie, staring blankly into space. Then she had gotten the fever and the infection. Moustafa had no stomach to continue his work if Anne-Marie died.

"Live!" he cried out to the moon.

He was not sure how much time passed before he felt Marcus's hand on his shoulder. He wheeled around to face him, fearful to read the verdict in his eyes.

"She is stabilized. They said we got her here in time. Just in time." They walked to the car in silence.

Normally the aging history professor and the dashing young American teacher didn't meet for drinks on a Sunday afternoon. But this afternoon they sat like old friends sipping pastis while the mistral howled outside.

"He's still in Marseille, I'm sure," Jean-Louis commented. "He didn't bother us at the port as you had feared, when I picked up the children. But when he came calling at St. Joseph last Wednesday, I followed him back home." A smile crept across his face.

"Good job, Jean-Louis! And what did you find?"

"Here is his address, right in the middle of the slums. No surprise. He's got a screw loose, that man. At first glance he appears perfectly normal, but there's something not right about him." He lowered his voice. "I'd be getting rid of that one as soon as I could, if I were you. I'm glad I can leave the dirty work to someone younger."

"Thanks." David scowled.

"You should not waste any time, David. I'm not sure what he would have done if he had found Mlle Madison and the children. He might be capable of just about anything."

"I'll be leaving again then. Tomorrow morning," David agreed reluctantly. He thought of Ophélie. "What did Jacques tell you about the *Capitaine* incident?"

"Pretty messy. Apparently the woman who was with them was shot and pushed into the water. Someone else killed Ali's boy, and the children got away. Jacques didn't waste any time waiting around to see what happened, you understand. He took off with the kids."

"I'll make the rounds again. Aix, Aigues-Mortes, and Les Baux. You talk to Pierre. I'll be back as soon as I have news." David scratched his head. "You don't mind handling my class again, *mon pote?*"

"No problem for me, David. It's just your girls. They can't seem to stay awake for me." Jean-Louis chuckled.

"Women." David rolled his eyes. "Listen, I was just thinking ... second-quarter exams are scheduled for the first full week in March?"

"*Oui, bien sûr*," Jean-Louis confirmed.

"Then you can start a review for them, of both quarters. I'll leave all my notes. I hope I won't be gone long."

The two men nodded, touched glasses, and parted ways.

David knocked lightly on the door to the parsonage. After a moment's wait, a voice asked from within, "Who is it?"

"It's M. Hoffmann."

The door opened slowly. The nun looked surprised to see him. "M. Hoffmann? How may I help you? You don't look well."

"Mother Griolet, I'm sorry to bother you at this time of night. I must talk to you."

"Yes?" Her expression was worried, reserved. "Come in." She showed him into the office and offered him a chair.

"I know you are not fond of me, and for that I'm truly sorry. You are … you are a fine woman." He hesitated. "I admire your work with the orphans." He looked at her straight in the eyes. "And with the pied-noir and harki children."

Mother Griolet raised her eyebrows. "Exactly why did you come to see me tonight, M. Hoffmann?"

"Because it's time that you know. Things are becoming more confused, and I think it best that you understand … in case anything happens to me."

"What do you mean?" She sounded alarmed and almost angry.

"I mean, Mother Griolet, that I am Hugo." He met her eyes again, and they were filled with shock. "I'm sorry to announce it to you in such a way. For a long time I thought you were safer not knowing. But now there are so many other things to consider, and the war will soon be over. There will be more refugees, many more."

Mother Griolet was sitting forward now, eyes dancing. "You, David Hoffmann, are Hugo? You are behind this operation?"

"Yes."

For a moment she looked bewildered. Then her face broke into a wide smile, and she clapped her hands together. "It's impossible! I mean, excuse me, but I would never have guessed. Amazing." She shook her head in disbelief. "Why, this is wonderful news!" Impulsively she came around her desk and kissed him on both cheeks.

David's face turned crimson. "I'm glad that you find it so good. I was afraid you would be concerned ... about the future of the operation."

"Oh yes, of course I'm concerned about the future and the dear pied-noir and harki children. But the wonderful news is that I was wrong about *you*, M. Hoffmann! I was sure you were working against us. And then when I found out about Ophélie—" She stopped short. "But perhaps you do not know?"

"Yes, I know. Gabby told me yesterday. It was this that made me realize I must have you on my side. For Ophélie's sake. My daughter's." He pronounced the word with an air of wonder. "Forgive me, Mother Griolet. It's all so new and strange. I had no idea I was a father."

They smiled at each other.

"It's ironic, you know. The whole idea of the Huguenot cross came from her mother, Anne-Marie. She wore the cross, a gift from her father, who was Protestant. I met Captain Duchemin years ago in Algeria. He was a respected and much-decorated pied-noir from World War II."

"Did you know that Ophélie now wears her grandfather's cross?"

"Really?" David exclaimed. "No, I have not been close enough to her to notice … yet." He paused, looked away, and then continued. "I also met the captain's beautiful daughter. We were rebellious adolescents, but she gave me hope for the first time in years. I left Algeria for my studies in Princeton, and we lost contact. The letters I sent her were never answered." David stopped himself and apologized. "I'm sorry to bore you with my past."

Mother Griolet shook her head. "*Au contraire!* Please go on."

"Then, out of the blue, Anne-Marie wrote me, a desperate sort of letter. It was December of 1959. She said that a madman named Ali, who was with the FLN, had a personal vendetta to eliminate all the soldiers with whom his father served in World War II, and their families. He blamed his father's platoon for leaving his father, the lieutenant, to be murdered by the Nazis. And he blamed Anne-Marie's father, the battalion captain, for setting up the raid that cost his father his life."

Mother Griolet waited, intent on every word.

"Anne-Marie's parents were killed in a bombing in Algiers in 1958. Afterwards, she was tricked into disclosing the names of some of the men in the platoon. Ali then began systematically eliminating them, disguised of course in the realm of terrorism and a war that kills at random.

"That is when Anne-Marie begged my help to get these families out of Algeria—especially the children. And so I devised this little operation. The cross, I remembered, was the jewelry of a persecuted

minority. I am from a persecuted minority too." He cleared his throat
and didn't try to hide the pain in his eyes.

"Yes, I have not forgotten after all these years," Mother Griolet said.

David read compassion on the old nun's face.

"It came back to me not long ago. You were here with us for a
few months, *n'est-ce pas*? A Jewish orphan?"

"Yes, I was."

For a moment neither could speak. When David broke the
silence, it was with a hoarse whisper.

"You gave me life, Mother Griolet, in this orphanage. I didn't
remember it was you, but the only happy memory of my childhood
after my mother was taken from me is of a warm, smiling woman in
black rocking me in her arms." He swallowed hard.

"There were so many orphans here at that time. I had completely
forgotten your name," Mother Griolet said. "I only realized last week
that you had been here. Then I was really confused." She winked.
"But now I'm beginning to understand."

David rubbed his forehead with his hand. "I did a bit of research
after receiving Anne-Marie's letter and found that St. Joseph was still
here. I figured this part of France would be a good contact point.
And I was sure there would still be some members of the Resistance
around who would help me."

Mother Griolet's eyes twinkled. "Dear Jean-Louis. So you're the
one who got him back into this!"

David nodded. "Jean-Louis and several others. I hoped in the
process to find Anne-Marie. I haven't heard from her directly now
for months. I don't know where she is, or if she is even still alive. And
now things have changed. I have a daughter ..." He looked away,

past Mother Griolet, out the window. "And I'm in love with another … with a Raphaelite angel who also wears a Huguenot cross."

He took a deep breath and composed himself. "It's good news, Mother Griolet, but there is also great danger for Ophélie and Gabby. It's my fault. This Ali is determined to have his revenge. You have already met one of his assistants, Jean-Claude Gachon."

Mother Griolet nodded. "Yes, he calls himself Philippe. I'm afraid I may have been unwise. I didn't know how to keep him away. Thank the Lord I received a note—from you, perhaps?—warning me of him."

"Yes. You have done well. Gabriella told me about the incident. The man is determined, so I must become more visible—so he will chase me instead." Now David regarded Mother Griolet, pleading with his eyes. "I need you to watch over my daughter … and Gabby. You'll have to keep them hidden with the harki children until I know that it's safe. Until I can convince Ali and his friends that they have no use for them."

"You will sign your own death warrant then."

"I hope not, dear Mother Griolet. I have made a mistake in letting the suspicion fall on innocent shoulders. I can't let it continue. You will help?"

"Yes, I will help. But be careful, David. And God be with you."

The afternoon sun was low in the sky, but Ali didn't turn on the light as he entered his basement apartment. Yesterday's paper still lay across the desk, with the date visible: Tuesday, February 13.

Ali smiled as he read of the eight victims who had been killed as anti-OAS demonstrators clashed with police in a metro station in Paris. Today hundreds of thousands of working-class Parisians had gone to mourn them, the largest turnout of the public since the Liberation. The French were killing the French. This was good.

But Ali was most pleased by the news his turbanned friend Mahmud had brought him earlier that day. Mme Jacqueline Bousquet was buried Thursday after her apartment burned to the ground. No other bodies were found.

"Fool woman!" Ali snarled. "You didn't think you would join your grandchildren in France." He spat on the floor, then glanced at the list of names on the wall. He drew an X through the name of M. et Mme Guy Bousquet. Then he scribbled beside their names: *grandchildren escaped to France.*

Ali had received no word from his young terrorist. He knew what that meant. Somewhere amid the boats in the port, a body sank down to touch the bottom of the sea. And somewhere in the south of France, five children were free. Their freedom angered him more than the news of the French slayings brought him pleasure.

He had heard from Jean-Claude, the bumbling idiot. He'd lost the child and the red-haired woman, and David Hoffmann as well. But it was only a matter of time. *Algérie indépendante! Death to pied-noirs, death to harkis, death to you, M. Hoffmann.* It was only a matter of time.

28

Gabriella stopped to admire a large chocolate heart in the window of the pâtisserie across the street from Mme Leclerc's apartment. It sat, rich and inviting, on a bright-red doily that sparkled and shimmered as the afternoon sun caught its reflection in the window. February 14. The day for lovers. The holiday was unknown in Senegal, yet every year her parents had celebrated. Gabriella remembered helping her mother confect some elaborate chocolate heart to present to her father by the light of a candle after she and her sisters had been shooed out of the hut.

But there would be no valentine from the self-assured American teacher. He was off on another adventure, leaving her once again to straighten out the details of his life.

She caught a glimpse of herself in the window of the pâtisserie. She was pale and thin, tucked inside her peacoat. Her eyes stared back at her with an emptiness that angered her. Her eyes had always been her favorite feature. Not the unruly hair that everyone either hated or loved, but her eyes. She liked their bright-blue color. But today they looked dull.

For only a moment she imagined what it would be like to get a valentine from David. How many times had she reread the poem he had penned for her? How many times had she stared at the print of the poppies that hung on the wall of her room and wondered? And that last little phrase he had spoken to her, as he held her hand in the crowded little café. *Dear Gabby, don't you know that I have already found the one I'm looking for?*

What did it mean? *Please, please tell me, David.* She was afraid to guess. He loved her. Was that it? *He loves me. He can't say the words, but he wants me to know.*

And yet his silent response after that brief awakening brought waves of doubt to her mind. At first they lapped gently at her feet like the lazy tide of the Mediterranean. But gradually the doubts rose and swelled in magnitude, crashing into every part of her thoughts and destroying her concentration.

Exams were still two weeks away. Surely he would return for exams. Until then, she was left to play the childish game of "He loves me—he loves me not" as she silently picked off the petals of her memories of the past six months.

She turned away from the store and dragged her feet along the cobblestones, ignoring the barking of a small gray poodle that pulled furiously on its leash beside the heels of its owner. She didn't want to reach the church too quickly. There was no bounce to her step as she descended the staircase into the basement and walked down the hall and out into the courtyard where the children ran and played.

Ophélie squealed with delight as she caught up with André, tagged him, and turned to flee in the other direction. "You're it!" she called after him, laughing.

Waiting until the little girl had stopped running and stood watching the other children, Gabriella approached her. "Ophélie," she said.

"Bribri!" exclaimed Ophélie. "I didn't see you. Come play with us!"

Gabriella smiled. "Actually I was wondering if I might borrow you for a moment. Do you think the others can get along without you?"

Ophélie giggled. "Of course." She grabbed her teacher's hand, and together they entered the girls' dormitory.

Gabriella sat down on Ophélie's bed and motioned for the child to join her. Then, carefully, she opened the second drawer of Ophélie's chest and removed a dark-blue pair of tights.

Ophélie watched Gabriella wide-eyed. She let out a small whimper of protest as Gabriella reached into the tights and pulled out a little blue velvet bag.

"How did you find it?" Ophélie whispered.

"Quite by accident," Gabriella assured her with a hug. "You are very smart, Ophélie. It was a very clever hiding place. Sister Rosaline found it when she was preparing for the new orphans. It was Mother Griolet who read the letters and showed them to me."

Ophélie stretched out on the bed, away from Gabriella, and buried her head in her arms.

Gabriella pretended not to notice. "I was so surprised to learn that M. Hoffmann is your father. I could hardly believe it! But you know who was even more surprised than I was?"

Ophélie shook her head but didn't look around.

"M. Hoffmann! I … I told him a few days ago, and well, he was just speechless." Gabriella stretched out on her stomach beside Ophélie. She laid her head on the bed and caught Ophélie's eye. "He was overwhelmed. And very, very happy."

A hint of a smile curled onto Ophélie's lips. Then at once she frowned again. "Then why doesn't he come to see me?"

"Oh, he will! It's only that he has had to go away for a few days. But when he gets back, we'll have a party. A celebration."

The child rolled over onto her back, letting her long brown hair trail over the side of the bed. Gabriella imitated the child's move, sweeping her curly mane behind her. She met Ophélie's eyes, and they giggled.

"Bribri, why did my father not know about me? Why was Mama afraid to tell him that he was my papa?"

Gabriella grimaced, searching for the right words. "That's a good question. I can't say for sure. But your mama was very young when you were born. And your papa was living far away in America. He was going to school. I think she didn't want to make him come back to Algeria. She knew he would want to see you, but somehow she thought that it wouldn't be fair."

Ophélie furrowed her brow. "But wouldn't he want to be with my mama and me? Why did he leave her in the first place?"

"I don't know, sweetheart. Someday your mama will tell you. All I know is that both your mama and your papa love you very much. And your papa does want to see you now."

"He saved me once, you know, Bribri. He told me to tell no one about it, but since you know he's my father, and since he likes you so much, I'm sure he wouldn't mind." She was staring at the wooden slats on the top bunk. "It was when we lived in another city. Paris. And I went with Malika to march for freedom. That's what she told me. Only it wasn't like that at all. The police shot people, and everyone was running and screaming. And Malika fell, and then something hurt my leg. I was so scared.

"And then this nice man picked me up and took me to his room and helped me get better." Ophélie's words were tumbling out faster than she could talk. "I begged him not to take me to the police because they were killing people. And I couldn't go to see M. Gady anymore because ... because he was ... dead." She scrunched up her nose and looked at Gabriella with sorrowful eyes.

"So M. Hoffmann, I mean, my papa, brought me on a train and left me, and another man came and got me. You know, the fat man with the red eyes who comes to St. Joseph. And then ... and then I met Mother Griolet, and then you had the same cross."

Gabriella placed her arm around Ophélie and squeezed her tight. "That's a very remarkable story. Your papa saved you, and he didn't even know that you were his daughter."

"And now he must love me even more, right?"

"You're right. Yes, you're right."

Ophélie said nothing for a moment. Then she asked, "What will happen to me, Bribri, if my father marries you?"

Gabriella laughed. "M. Hoffmann is not going to marry me, Ophélie."

"Oh," she said quietly. "But he likes you."

"Yes, but we are only friends."

"Then will he marry my mama? Will she come back, and will he marry her?"

Gabriella's voice caught. "Would you like for that to happen, Ophélie?"

"Oh yes! Then I'd have a mama and a papa together. I'd like that very much!"

"Yes, that would be very good for you, Ophélie."

Gabriella turned onto her side, propping herself up on one

elbow. The Huguenot cross slipped out from her blouse and dangled in the air from her neck.

"It's such a beautiful cross, Bribri," said Ophélie, pulling her own cross out and holding it in her small hand. "Mama was right. She said that I would be safe if I wore this cross. Soon everything is going to be just right."

She leaned over and kissed Gabriella on the cheek. Gabriella brushed Ophélie's hair with her fingers and smiled through the mist in her eyes.

"You're a wonderful little girl, Ophélie. A very brave, wonderful little girl." She replaced the velvet bag and the tights in the drawer.

Hands intertwined, the two walked back out into the sunshine together.

The slums of Marseille sat, squalid and run-down, in the heart of the city by the Vieux Port. Cement apartment buildings rose into the sky. The view of the Mediterranean was no compensation for the stench in the corridors, David reflected, as he climbed to the fourth floor of a dingy gray building. He sat down on the steps of the top floor and waited.

Doors slammed, dogs barked, babies screamed. Occasionally he could make out the sounds of a fight in the street below. The repugnant smells of urine and trash mingled and clashed. David rubbed his eyes, which were red from lack of sleep. Two days of waiting, and Jean-Claude had still not shown up at his apartment.

David had decided his next step: he would give Jean-Claude the list of names—a false list, of course—for a steep price and a threat and a guarantee that he was the head of this operation and that Gabby and Ophélie had nothing to do with it. Somehow he would convince the madman. Somehow. If only Jean-Claude would show.

Forty-eight hours without sleep. David headed back to his own dingy hotel room for the night. Surely tomorrow he would find Jean-Claude.

Jean-Claude returned to Marseille in the middle of the night. As he entered the stairwell of his apartment building, a young woman dressed in a tight, low-cut black dress greeted him.

"Ooh là là, monsieur." She smiled, revealing a row of cracked teeth. Her strong perfume drifted up to entice Jean-Claude. "A stranger has been hanging around these parts looking for you. I've seen him waiting near your apartment. Do you care to know more, *monsieur?"*

"Of course," Jean-Claude replied. He pulled the woman behind the steps, wrapping his arms around her waist. "Tell me everything."

"You will pay?" She raised her eyebrows.

Jean-Claude removed a wad of bills from his leather sack and held them before her. "I will pay for everything you give me, lovely lady. Everything."

She took the money and led him through an alleyway and across the street. "A tall young man, very handsome, with black hair, has been here two days now, watching your building. He has only just left." Her eyes shone brightly. "Do you know this man?"

Jean-Claude threw back his head and laughed. "*Oh, oui! Oui*, I know this man. Where is he now?"

The woman shrugged. "I'm sure I can find him for you, for a price."

"Good. We'll look for him later. Right now I need a place to spend the night. I won't be going back to my apartment, you understand." He touched her ear and played with the earring.

"I understand perfectly, *monsieur*. Follow me."

Moustafa held the thin sheets of paper in his hand, reading carefully over the list of thirty-seven names and addresses. They were all there. And twenty-two families had been taken care of, one way or another, he thought grimly.

The rest needed to be contacted. He felt confident the pied-noir families would leave anyway, as soon as the war ended. They would flee to France and find shelter from Ali. They need only be warned.

But the harki families. He felt sick as he thought of his father, thrown out on the street like a piece of trash, his throat slit from ear to ear. Five harki families still needed to escape before the war ended. But what would they find in France? Only angry stares and hatred.

His thoughts turned to Anne-Marie. He would not let David Hoffmann have her. Not yet. Not until he lay dead like his father in some forgotten street of Algiers. *Until then, David Hoffmann, we will work together, but in our hearts, we will be enemies. It must be so.*

Jean-Claude was not coming back to his apartment in Marseille, of that David was sure. But he was still in town. David had paid handsomely to get the information from the pretty little prostitute who hung around the neighborhood beside the Vieux Port. She promised, for more money, to lead him to Jean-Claude's new hideout, once she discovered it.

David's hotel room was cramped and filthy. An orange bedspread, torn and stained, covered a rotting mattress. He spread out his briefcase on the bed, took out a piece of stationery, and began writing.

> *My daughter. You must think your papa doesn't care about you. But it's not true. It's only that you're not safe until I find this bad man. Then I will come to you.*

He wrote a little more, then twirled the pencil in his hand. How should he sign the note? *Sincerely, Your father?* No. That was terrible. *Your loving father?* Still too formal. He thought back to the letters from his father. Cold, distant, unfeeling.

What had he always wanted to hear? He knew it before the pen touched the paper. He wrote the words slowly, carefully, as if he were climbing into the pen and spilling himself out onto the sheet. He held up the letter to read it and smiled when he came to the signature. *I love you, Ophélie. Papa.*

The pansies in the courtyard tossed their heads impatiently in the wind, their petals folding in and out like coy maidens, reluctant to reveal their velvet faces. Gabriella studied the flowers from the basement doorway. The yellow and white pansies had flourished in the winter months, yet several of the dark-purple and amber flowers had died out.

"What makes some of them stronger than the others?" she questioned Mother Griolet, who had joined her. "You bought them at the same nursery, and we planted them at the same time."

"It's like that every year, Gabriella. The yellow and white pansies have what it takes to withstand the winter."

Gabriella pulled a withered flower from the dirt and held out the roots and dried petals for Mother Griolet to observe. "This one didn't make it." She let the dead flower fall to the ground and gently took hold of Mother Griolet's arm. "And I don't know if I'll make it either. I'm being eaten by jealousy, Mother Griolet," she said. "I'm jealous that David loved Anne-Marie at one time. That he fathered her child. I know it's far in the past, but I'm so jealous."

The old nun sighed. "My dear child, I think you could use a good cup of hot chocolate. Come along."

When the two women were settled in Mother Griolet's den, cups of hot chocolate in hand, Gabriella continued.

"I'm … I'm jealous because he has every right to love her again. And he won't love me because I'm too … too something. Religious, maybe. Or naive. And I know it's for the best, I suppose, but it makes me furious, and now it just seems like God is punishing me for ever loving David Hoffmann." Her words were gaining momentum, nearly rushing ahead of her thoughts.

"But really, I didn't *mean* to care about him, and he's the one who dragged me into this whole thing. And now he's going to take Ophélie away from me—though of course she's not even mine to keep. I just want to leave this whole mess."

Mother Griolet leaned back on her worn couch and propped one leg on the coffee table. "It's sounds as though you're more angry than jealous. Angry at a lot of people. Maybe even God. Am I right?"

Gabriella fidgeted with her hair. "Probably," she answered sulkily.

"Why do you think God is punishing you, Gabriella?"

"I don't know. Some sort of discipline because in my mind I'm straying from the straight and narrow."

"Do you think God is more interested in our circumstances or in what we learn from them?" the nun prodded.

Gabriella didn't answer. She couldn't think of anything worthwhile to say and wondered why she felt such a need to reveal her thoughts to this old woman. But Mother Griolet didn't seem to mind her silence.

"Years ago I loved a man."

Gabriella perked up, startled at this revelation.

"He was a fine man. I met him here in Castelnau. I considered leaving my calling for him."

She had closed her eyes, and Gabriella watched them flicker underneath the wrinkled skin. Suddenly the nun seemed very old and fragile. Gabriella almost spoke, to stop Mother Griolet from sharing something Gabriella had no right to hear. But when she opened her mouth, no sound came out.

Mother Griolet seemed not to notice; her eyes were still closed. "But then the first war came along, and he left. Four months later I received word of his death. But you know, Gabriella, I never thought God was punishing me for some sin of loving a man. Nor did I think He caused this man's death so that I wouldn't leave my calling. God is bigger than our simplistic or most complicated reasoning. I could not box Him in."

She paused, then said, "I learned many things, though. How much it hurts to love and how deep a soul can ache with missing another. How unfair life can be. I learned how to grieve, and I found God was there in a much deeper way than I'd ever known before. Of course I was angry and crushed. It was part of the grieving. But I'm not sorry for these painful lessons. I use them every day of my life."

The old woman rubbed her eyes softly and opened them to look at Gabriella with her usual compassionate gaze. "You will be all right, my child," she said. "You'll see."

David stood alone on the beach near Marseille. The dark sky was interrupted occasionally with brief flashes of lightning in the distance, and he realized that if he were a painter, this scene would be paradise. A tranquil tide touched his feet, but farther out in the Mediterranean tiny whitecaps rose and fell, dotting the sea like the stars above in the black sky.

"It's beautiful," he said. Beautiful and vast and eternal.

Like You, God of Gabriella. I don't believe in You. I don't believe an ultimate being of good exists. There is too much misery around. But Gabby does. If You were a man, I know I could win. I have always won. I can charm with intellect.

But, God of Gabriella, I don't know how to fight against You! In her mind, You're bigger and better than any man. You understand the questions we're afraid to ask. And she believes You love and forgive.

He kicked at the sand and cursed. Forgiveness! Who would talk about that impossible word if they knew! Could he forgive his mother's and sister's murderers? Could he forgive his proud and guilty father?

No, God of Gabriella, I cannot. And can I forgive You? God of the Jews, who watched silently as they were slaughtered by the millions? I will not forgive You, God! You will never be my God.

He raised his clenched fists to the quiet sky as the water gently brushed his feet and the lightning flittered around. God wasn't here. He couldn't be. For if He was, then Gabby was right, and all David had done in life was a hopeless waste....

He lowered his arms until they hung loosely by his side and slowly loosened his fingers. He stared at the living painting before him. The breeze felt unexpectedly chilly on his face, and he realized that it was because of his own tears mixing with the night air. He had not cried in many years, but he remembered all too well the last time he had.

They had stood still in the frozen camp of Dachau, awaiting roll call in the frost of an early December morning in 1943. His mother was in front and his little sister, Greta, behind him. Suddenly a rabbit appeared from behind the barracks, scampering in front of them toward safety. An officer laughed, raised his gun, and fired. The little beast burst into fragments before the weary onlookers. Greta cried out "No!" in the innocent voice of a three-year-old and began running toward the lifeless rabbit. "You shot the bunny! You shot the bunny!"

And then in a flash, his mother was running after her, crying, "Come back, dear, quickly! It does not matter." But it was too late. Far away from the tower, a shot rang out, and Greta fell. His mother screamed in horror and ran to grab her fallen daughter.

"Leave her there!" an officer shouted.

But Mother didn't hear. Didn't move.

"Leave her there!" The only sound in the quiet of that tragic dawn was Mother's sobbing. Then one more shot. And all was still again.

David's tears ran down his cheeks. Greta had run, his mother had run, but he had stood still in his place, dying in his own silence.

Roll call continued, and then this hopeless mass of humankind turned their dull eyes down and walked back to the barracks. Past the remains of the rabbit and the small body of Greta and the bleeding body of Mother. Only David stared as he walked by, and he whispered, "Good-bye, Greta. Good-bye, Mother. Good-bye, life."

That night, sandwiched on his bunk between other women and children, he could not stop the tears from flowing. He sobbed into the filth of the torn blanket for hours. And when he could cry no more, he lay awake with the eyes of an old man on the face of a child and said, "I am alone."

Weak and spent, David stood motionless on the shore, his shoulders slumped. For two hours he had wrestled with the God of Gabriella and the nightmare of his past. How could the two be reconciled?

Forgiveness. It had worked for her. Could it work for him?

God couldn't exist. But Gabby was real. And to be with her was to taste eternity. She brought hope. To love her, he must love God. And yet that would never work, Gabby said. It had to be from the heart. What heart?

But God must exist....

David placed a hand on his throbbing head.

I give up, God of Gabriella. You're too strong for me, and now I have no more strength tonight. Forgive me, God of Gabriella, for hating. For wanting revenge. If You exist, then take me if You want me. Take me, as Gabby says, and see what You can do. I'm tired of being alone.

Suddenly he was on his knees, barely noticing the wet sand beneath him, until, reaching down, he scraped the damp earth into his hand and held it up toward the flashing heavens. *Here I am, God, with nothing to offer but a hardened heart and a handful of sand. Here, God of Gabriella. Take it, and be my God too.*

29

The bedroom in Marcus Cirou's apartment was dark, the shutters drawn to keep out any sunlight. Anne-Marie dozed fitfully, her frame but a skeleton under the sheets. The effort of reaching for a glass of water beside the bed exhausted her.

She needed the care of nurses, but she refused to return to the hospital. Three weeks there had nearly killed her, she explained weakly to Moustafa. It was not a safe place. She could not go back.

Moustafa gently wiped her forehead with a cool rag. "I'll bring you some soup, my *habibti*," he whispered.

"Yes, soup will be good."

When he came back into the room, Anne-Marie turned her haggard face to him. "What's the news today?"

"More of the same. Rumors that the cease-fire will come soon. Dear one," he said, "I must get you to France. You'll get stronger as soon as you see Ophélie. Please, drink this soup." He lifted her head off the pillow and slowly brought the spoon to her mouth.

"Thank you," she rasped. "Yes, if I could only get to France. Will you take me to the *Capitaine*, Moustafa? Will you come with me?"

He stood up and walked to the window, staring at the peeling paint on the inside of the shutters. "You know I can't leave yet, Anne-Marie. But I will get you there safely." He came back to the bed and sat down beside her. "You must concentrate on getting stronger. I will do the rest." He stroked her hair.

Anne-Marie forced a feeble smile on her face. "The doctor said I would walk again. The bullets were taken out. I can't understand why it's taking so long to heal."

"We nearly lost you twice, you know. It takes time. In another week you'll be walking. It will be March then. And you will spend springtime in France, Anne-Marie. With Ophélie."

It had started as chicken pox. All the children got chicken pox in February, Mother Griolet reassured Gabriella. It was the same every year. But Gabriella didn't feel peaceful. For five days Ophélie's fever had raged at 104. The other children were now healthy and strong, but Ophélie was confined to Sister Rosaline's room on a cot. Gabriella took turns with the Sisters sponging her, holding a cool rag on her head, trying to relieve the itching. The child was covered with scabs, and some had become infected. The doctor ordered antibiotics. Still the fever hung on.

"Why doesn't Papa come? If only he would come to see me, I know I would get better." At times Ophélie called out, delirious, "Papa! Mama! Come now!"

Gabriella didn't know why David had not come back. His absence of a week had slipped into more than two. She fought to control her anger. Didn't he care about his daughter?

She closed the door to Sister Rosaline's room and walked down the corridor toward the girls' dormitory. Coming to Ophélie's bed, she fell heavily to her knees and prayed. *Oh, Lord. She must get better. The doctor says there is nothing to do but wait and try to get the fever*

down. Even he doesn't know why the medicine isn't working. But You do,
Lord. What does she need?

Suddenly she saw her mother, exhausted and red-eyed at the
bedside of little Ericka. Gabriella could almost smell the stench of
death again and see the yellow tint of Ericka's skin.

Oh, God, please. Daddy never made it back to see Ericka alive.
Please, Holy God, may it not be so for David. Bring him home to meet
his daughter. And let her live to know her papa.

Sister Isabelle startled Gabriella, touching her on the shoulder
as she prayed. "Excuse me, Mlle Madison. But something has just
arrived in the mail for Ophélie."

Quickly Gabriella got off her knees and stood, taking the envelope from Sister Isabelle. She recognized the handwriting.

"Thank you, Sister Isabelle. Perhaps this will be just what little
Ophélie needs."

Sister Isabelle grinned and, looking heavenward, whispered,
"Yes, maybe it is just what the Doctor ordered."

As the nun left the dormitory, Gabriella opened the envelope and
read the page-long note. It revealed a tender side of David Hoffmann
and sent a tingle through her too deep to describe. It couldn't have
been easy for him to write. His hand was clear and measured, as if
he were writing slowly, instead of the hurried script he used on the
blackboard in class. These words had mattered to him.

She walked back to Sister Rosaline's room and peered in the
door. Ophélie's eyes were closed. "Ophélie? Sweetheart? May I come
in? I have a surprise for you."

Ophélie turned her head weakly toward Gabriella. "*Oui*. Come
in, Bribri."

Gabriella gently sat on the end of the cot. "A letter has just come for you in the mail. It's from your papa."

With extreme effort Ophélie raised her head off the pillow. "Really?" she asked, a wisp of eagerness in her faint voice. "My papa wrote me?"

"Yes, dear. See? Shall I read it to you?"

"*Oui, oui*, Bribri. Please read it." She let her head fall back on the pillow and listened.

Gabriella reached the last line, inwardly refusing to yield to the tears she felt welling up inside. "I love you, Ophélie. Papa."

She watched as Ophélie fingered the cross around her neck, a fragile smile on the little girl's lips.

"You were right, Bribri. Papa does love me. He said so. I'll get better now. Your God will protect me, and I will be all well when Papa comes back."

Rosie Lecharde was not beautiful or rich. But she was smart. She had grown up on the streets of Marseille, and she was not afraid of anyone. She laughed at the slimy little men who pawed her body in raunchy hotel rooms. She always got an extra tip before they left—it was easy to take a few bills from a wallet.

And Rosie knew that the handsome young Frenchman could bring her more money. He was hungry for many things, this man. And she could give him everything he needed. Ten days with him had already provided her with more money than she had seen in a year.

She preferred the lanky American gentleman with the black eyes. But he was not as hungry. She wondered how to lure him along. Careful and smart, he was. But maybe desperate.

The streets behind the hotel were silent. She pulled her tattered shawl around her shoulders. At least she would sleep well tonight. Jean-Claude was a madman, but at least he kept her warm. She pranced into the lobby, her high heels clicking on the crackled linoleum.

"Room 32," she said, winking at the desk clerk.

"He's waiting for you," the young man mumbled.

Rosie pinched her cheeks and rubbed her hands up and down her arms. Jean-Claude wouldn't like to see that she was cold. She spread a thick coat of bright-pink lipstick across her lips, checking her work in the mirror of her compact. She slipped it back into her purse and knocked on the door.

"Come in," Jean-Claude crooned. He sat in the room's lone chair smoking a cigarette, a half dozen empty bottles of cheap red table wine at his feet. "Well?" he growled.

"I found your tall friend all right. He says he has the information you want. He'll bring it to you. You say when, and he'll be there."

Jean-Claude nodded approvingly. He stood up and stumbled over to Rosie, a gleam in his eyes. "Very good, my little tramp." He slapped her hard across the face.

Rosie cried out as she fell across the bed. Jean-Claude leaned down over her, looking worried.

"Are you hurt?" He slurred his words. "I didn't mean to hurt you, little Rosie. *Au contraire, ma petite pute.* We have every reason to celebrate tonight, *n'est-ce pas?*"

He pressed his body down on top of hers. Rosie closed her eyes, trying to ignore his putrid breath as he fumbled with the buttons on her blouse.

"Every reason to celebrate," he said again.

Rosie didn't struggle. She let the drunken Frenchman paw while she thought of money and freedom. Rosie Lecharde was smart.

David didn't look any different to himself as he shaved in the bathroom of his one-star hotel room in the slums of Marseille. The same long, thin face with deep-set black eyes and thick eyebrows stared back at him. But something felt different to him as the razor slid smoothly through the white foam on his face.

"Hope," he said suddenly and laughed. Yes, that was it. Today there was hope. Never before had he awakened with the excitement that he had felt during the past week. Ever since the night on the beach. Hope.

He shook his head. It almost sounded, well, fabricated. Shallow. That would be his response to anyone who tried to explain what he was feeling. That had been his response to Gabriella. But he could not deny the deep sense of hope he now carried.

He grinned at the mirror. He wished he could tell Gabriella. He wished he could see the expression on her face when he said, "I've done it."

But he couldn't return to Montpellier and Castelnau. Not yet.

He rinsed his face and dabbed it with a towel. The sun was

peeping in between the slats in the rotting wooden shutters. David pushed them open, welcoming the cold air on his freshly shaven face. He returned to his bed and spread out the briefcase on it. Jean-Louis would be waiting. Tomorrow was the first of March, and exams were only four days away.

He had explained to Jean-Louis where to find last year's exam in his desk at Mme Pons's, in case he didn't have time to write another. That would be the simplest way.

He pictured Gabby waiting for him, coming to class each day. He recalled her last words to him, two and a half weeks ago. "I hope you find her." He wondered if she remembered his response. Had she understood? Couldn't she see? He *had* already found the one he was looking for, his Raphaelite angel.

And now, with hope, with some new, naked faith, he longed to run to her and say it. "I love you, wild red-haired angel! Don't you see? Don't you understand? Be mine!"

Gabriella deserved a love letter, he mused, running his hand over his now smooth face. *She* needed hope! So far his only response to her had been silence. Thick, tense, smothering silence. The spark had not been fanned to flame. With silence the heat would ebb and die, and ashes, like those of the sweet African lily, would be the only memory of another unwise romance.

But now there was hope! "Dear Gabriella," he whispered. How could he tell her? Slowly he took up his fountain pen and began to prepare questions for the exam. Suddenly his pen flowed more quickly, and he smiled as an idea burst forth and shimmered with hope. He nodded. *Yes, my angel. You'll understand this, darling. It will be perfectly clear.*

"There must be another woman," Yvette concluded, as she sipped her coffee in Monique's kitchen. "He's gone too often, this M. Hoffmann, to really care for Gabriella. Poor child. You can read it all in her eyes. The love, the hope, the fear that after all there is someone else."

Monique nodded broadly as she lifted a cup to her lips and sipped the dark coffee. "You can read Gabriella's face, but M. Hoffmann's is a dark puzzle. He seems to like her, but off he tramps to another town. I'm surprised Mother Griolet stands for it. He's supposed to be teaching."

By the time the coffee cups were empty, Mme Pons and Mme Leclerc were no longer sure that David Hoffmann was worthy of the fair Gabriella.

Monique changed the subject. "Thank heavens February is out of the way. You think the sun is going to warm up at the end of January and then, whoosh, in blows the frost of February."

Yvette agreed. "And it's soups, soups, soups. The girls are tired of soups, but what do I say? We start our meals with soup until February leaves us *tranquilles*. It's very difficult, you know, to feed these American girls. It's the same each year. One will nibble and another will gorge."

"I suppose Gabriella still does not eat well?" Monique inquired.

"She picks at the food. She is losing hope, poor child. And not a thing I can say. Poor foolish child."

Hussein looked no more than ten years old, when in fact he was fourteen. He wished for the fuzz his friends had underneath their noses. He wished for a sudden growth spurt. He wished that the young Arab girls would lift their eyebrows and flirt with him as they did with others.

But at least he had something to do in Algiers. At least Ali paid him a few coins for his eyes. At least no one had turned a gun on him and shot him in the middle of the day, in the middle of the street. That was something to be thankful for indeed.

His mother wrung her hands together and worried when he left the apartment each day. "Don't you understand, Hussein? They kill anyone. What is a boy to the OAS? Just another empty can to be knocked down. Please, Hussein, be careful."

It was true. Yesterday he had walked by a café at noon. It was sunny, and people were out, happy to think of spring coming. The patrons sat and smoked and sipped their cognacs and whiskeys. Then a shot came from somewhere around the corner, and Hussein saw a young man groan and fall to the ground, slipping out of his chair like a stuffed dummy. Right there at the table in the café. A newspaper was placed on his face. An ambulance eventually hauled off his body. Later the firemen hosed off the bloodstains. And still the people ate and pretended that nothing had happened. Pretended that their lives were not falling apart.

Thirty or more murders a day. Innocent civilians. Arab and pied-noir. But Hussein had work to do, and it helped him ignore the tight knot in his stomach as he walked through the neighborhood of Bab el-Oued, flashing a picture of a lovely pied-noir woman and a young Arab man with curly hair at shop owners along the street.

He had seen the woman one time. Surely, surely, she would step out into the sun someday and lead him to her apartment. The rest would be up to Ali. And Hussein would have more change jingling in his pocket.

Ali smoked and spat, smoked and spat. The February negotiations for cease-fire had failed. But rumor from the top of the FLN was that they wouldn't fail in March. The mail was no longer delivered in Algiers. The OAS had slaughtered five postmen. Life was shutting down.

Ali thrust his cigarette stub on the floor and crushed it with his shoe. *So we will crush you, slimy French. You think we are afraid of your terrorism. Who, after all, did you learn it from?* He chuckled softly. It was useless for France to try to hold on to Algeria.

The last news from the nutty Jean-Claude had sounded promising. A sleazy little prostitute was keeping Jean-Claude warm and well-informed about M. Hoffmann. That was fine.

His last instructions to Jean-Claude had been very clear: *Don't eliminate M. Hoffmann. Not until he has led you to the child and the woman and you have the names. Then you may do whatever you please with the whole lot. And do it quickly.*

Meanwhile, through the littered back alleys of Bab el-Oued, hiding behind overflowing trash cans, stepping on slimy orange peels, listening in cafés where students congregated, was a small, smart Arab boy. Ali liked to imagine Hussein at work.

"Someday you will be like me, Hussein," he had told the boy. "You will be powerful if you develop sharp eyes and a quick mind."

Ali Boudani was not a man to give up hope in his cause. Not for Algeria. Certainly not. Victory was sweet. It hung on the tip of his tongue. And he would not give up hope for revenge. *For revenge,* thought Ali, *is sweeter still.*

30

Rosie Lecharde wore sunglasses for her meeting with David Hoffmann. There was no use in showing him the ugly bruise around her eye. She had a feeling he might somehow care, and she didn't want David Hoffmann to care. She only wanted him to talk. Five hundred francs Jean-Claude had given her, with five hundred more if she could bring M. Hoffmann to him.

A shaft of sunlight peeked through the billowing clouds. Rosie clicked her heels and wiggled her hips as if it were any other day in the world. She wished that she could go with the smart American. Jean-Claude was beginning to frighten her.

Don't think of it, Rosie. Don't even think.

She turned onto the Canebière, the main street in Marseille, busy, loud, full. He had said to meet him where the cours Saint-Louis joined the Canebière, where the whole world sat and watched. The black-skinned sailors and blond-haired cadets, the buxom, white-teethed women from Martinique, the tourists in bold, hot colors waiting for the next trip to the Château d'If.

As if on cue, M. Hoffmann stepped out of the shadows. He grabbed her arm and yanked her back into a hidden street while the rest of the world teemed by, jostling and hurrying to and from the great port.

Rosie gasped as he swung her around.

"Is he with you? Where have you left him, little lady?" He shook her hard, and Rosie was surprised by the strength in the American's arms and the anger in his black eyes.

"I-I'm alone," she stammered.

He shook her again and laughed. "You lie well!" She thought he would strike her, as Jean-Claude had done, but suddenly his grip relaxed. "So?"

Rosie straightened up and looked him in the eye, feeling stronger behind her sunglasses. "So!" she spat. "It won't do you any good to bully me, M. Hoffmann. I only do as I am told."

"And who is telling you, Rosie?" he snarled. His grip tightened again. The terrible strength in his hands!

But she didn't shirk at the pain. "Whoever pays most is who tells me what to do, M. Hoffmann. And right now, you are not the one." She wiggled up close to him, pressing her curves against his hard chest. "I'm very friendly with those who pay, don't worry. All is fair."

The tall American pushed her away, a disgusted look on his face. "You're lying, Rosie dear." He pulled out a brown envelope, thick with French bills. "Will this do?"

Quickly she counted nine, ten, eleven, twelve hundred francs. She smiled up at him, her wide lips parting. "This is adequate. Yes, adequate."

"So?"

"So he stays at the Hotel Poseidon," she said. "A real trash heap near the Vieux Port. It's not hard to find." She eyed him through her sunglasses. "Room 32. I told him you'd have the information for him tomorrow night. He'll be waiting for you. Eleven thirty." She smiled again, batting her lashes out of habit, though he could not see them under the glasses. "But in the meantime ... since you have been so generous ... I have a few hours to spare, if you wish?"

He laughed outright, deep and angry, so that Rosie backed away from him. "No thanks, Rosie. I haven't got time for such an offer."

He softened his tone. "Get yourself a good meal, and stay away from Jean-Claude for a day." He reached over and pulled off her glasses, then gently touched the ugly bruise around her eye.

Rosie stared at him defiantly, then took back her glasses and put them on. "I will be going then, M. Hoffmann. Tomorrow night."

She wheeled around and left him standing in the shadows as she stepped back onto the Canebière, where the whole world watched and shrugged.

Moustafa's hand trembled as he held the pen above a blank piece of paper. *M. Hoffmann*, he scribbled.

> *I must stay in Algeria for now. While there is hope. But Anne-Marie has been badly hurt. She is dying here. I can't send her alone with the orphans. Come get her, M. Hoffmann.*

He put the pen down. David Hoffmann was used to getting his notes, Moustafa reflected. He only hoped the American still cared enough about his old lover to respond quickly. Suddenly he knew what to say, even if it broke Anne-Marie's confidence.

> *Anne-Marie has a daughter, Ophélie. I'm sure she is there with you. If only Anne-Marie could see her child, I know she would get well.*

He hesitated, then carefully penned the address of a store two streets away in Bab el-Oued.

> *Come to this address. Someone will know where*
> *we are. Come soon, please, if you wish for her to see her*
> *daughter again. It is the only hope.*

He signed the note, rolled it carefully into a cylinder, and taped it shut. Then he wrapped a pile of old newspapers around it.

Hope. What a strange little word. He hoped that David Hoffmann cared enough to save Anne-Marie. But he also hoped that M. Hoffmann didn't care enough to take her away from him forever. It was a risk Moustafa had to take. Otherwise there would be no Anne-Marie left to love at all.

The store had absolutely nothing to draw attention to it, huddled on the corner of rue Michel and rue Estanov in Bab el-Oued. Moustafa paused outside to touch a potato and finger several onions, picking off their flaking skins.

The broad-shouldered pied-noir who ran the market gave him a wide smile as he entered the store. "Yes? What do you have?"

"Another bit of news to go, Luc," Moustafa said, lowering his voice. He nodded to the newspapers in his hands. "Is it possible? The mail has stopped."

Luc let out a soft chuckle. "*Oui.* Do you blame them, when the postmen are murdered one by one? But never mind. The boats are still leaving port. Our boat. Your cargo is still going?"

Moustafa nodded. "Yes. And this. It is urgent. It must go directly, with the cargo."

"This is not a problem," Luc insisted as Moustafa handed him the bundle of old papers. He stuffed a fish inside the newspapers and smiled. "Don't worry so. It will leave tomorrow night. Have I ever been late for you yet?"

Moustafa tossed a handful of change on the counter and nodded. The young shopkeeper placed the papers in a small box behind him. Moustafa watched the street from the shop window. He didn't like to be out in the day. Someone could see. Someone had seen before.

But today no one was about. Hanging in the shadows of the yellowed buildings, he slipped out onto the sidewalks stained with dog urine and bird droppings and even, Moustafa thought sadly, yes, even the blood of humans.

Hussein crouched in the alleyway between two larger streets of Bab el-Oued. Here he had seen the woman disappear with the Arab the last time. That was almost six weeks ago, and he had not seen them since. But he hung out in the alleyway nonetheless, at least an hour a day. There was always the possibility.

He crept in the shadows toward rue Estanov. The sun was blinking down on the smelly road, but it had not peeped into the alley. Someone walked by. Hussein's heart skipped a beat as he peered around the corner. Yes! There, on the other side of the street, in the shadows of the sidewalk. Walking briskly. A young Arab man with tightly curled black hair.

Hussein didn't need to look again at the photograph Ali had given him. It was the same man.

Hussein stepped into the street cautiously, blinking in the sunlight. Not a sound, he reprimanded himself, as his shoe scuffed on the pavement. The young man, walking so swiftly ahead, didn't turn around. Hussein started to cross the street to the side with the shadows, but he was afraid. Calmly he tiptoed, yes, tiptoed fifty feet behind the young man. Now he was turning up another street and disappearing from view.

In a flash Hussein was safely in the shadows of the sidewalk of rue Estanov. He ran hard to the corner and peered around, but no one was there.

Impossible. His eyes scanned the street. No movement, no sound. No one. He whispered an oath, then regretted it. The man must be nearby. He was perhaps the one spying now.

Hussein kicked at the pavement and turned his head down. He milled in the streets for several minutes. He walked up rue Cambriole. Nothing. Hussein decided that he could wait too. He could outwait the Arab. He slipped into another alleyway with a view of rue Cambriole. The sun blinked and flickered, but Hussein stood perfectly still.

It was a whim, and David was not used to acting on whims. But he could not get the thought of her out of his mind. Today Gabriella would sit down in class and take the exam. She would wonder why he was not there, and then she would read the first question. He smiled at the thought. He wanted to be there to see, to hold her, to at last say, "Yes!"

Only that one word, and then he would race back to Marseille. Then he would sneak through the putrid backstreets of the Vieux Port and to the room of Jean-Claude Gachon. Then … he didn't think any further. *What then, God? What then?* He started to curse, stopped himself, and smiled. Gabriella.

It was barely dawn. Two hours on the train, two hours in Castelnau, two hours back to Marseille. It was all the time in the world. He grabbed his jacket and briefcase and locked the door behind him.

St. Charles station was only a ten-minute walk away, and the first train left for Montpellier at seven fifteen.

When David Hoffmann stepped into the street in the predawn gray, Rosie Lecharde laughed out loud. She shivered, standing up and shaking the crumbs of a croissant from her shawl. *I did right to be here early*, she congratulated herself. The long hours yesterday, hiding and following him to his hotel, would pay off today. M. Hoffmann was in a hurry to get somewhere.

The streets were vacant and calm, and even the noises at the Old Port were dulled in the early morn. The Canebière lay long and wide, like a silent river, its cafés closed, its banks and shops locked behind a jail of bars. David Hoffmann darted across the street. The stream of cars was thin and fast. Rosie followed.

Five minutes later the train station, massive and glimmering as the first streaks of sun touched its dome, came into view, perched high on a hill. A long row of steps led up to the station. Rosie hurriedly climbed them, pausing only as David Hoffmann entered the doors and walked toward a *guichet*. He waited impatiently behind a wild-looking student at the only open window. The train station had long since awakened, and the lobby was brimming with well-dressed businessmen waiting behind their copies of *Le Monde*. A train screeched on the quay.

Rosie watched, breathless, as he purchased a ticket and moved quickly toward quay number 3. Where was he going? She glanced at the large tumbling billboard as it rattled forth, changing trains and destinations. *Avignon 6:43; Aix-en-Provence 7:05; Nîmes 7:15.* Nîmes! Then on to Montpellier. Yes, that must be it! He lived in Montpellier. Jean-Claude had said so.

Rosie raced to the guichet and panted, "My friend, the tall dark-haired man. He was just here? Did he buy one or two tickets for Nîmes?"

The woman, without looking up, replied, "One."

"Ah dear! Then give me another. To Montpellier."

"Fifty-two francs, please. Train leaves at quay number 3 at 7:15."

The thrill of a race enchanted Rosie as she ran down the steps and halted abruptly before walking onto the quay. David Hoffmann was just disappearing into the third car. She waited five long minutes before she stepped quickly onto the quay and walked in the opposite direction, letting herself into the next-to-last car. When the train groaned and bellowed and screeched its way forward at 7:15, Rosie Lecharde was sure the American didn't suspect a thing.

Gabriella climbed the steps to the second floor of the parsonage with a fleeting hope that David would be there to smile back at her, to hand out the exams—anything, just so she at least would know he was still alive. But when she walked into his classroom, M. Vidal sat in the chair, pudgy and morose behind the desk.

The hope fell in her breast as she took her seat, her mind racing. She couldn't decide if she was angry or worried or disappointed. Or all of the above.

The bells in the tower chimed nine o'clock as Stephanie slipped into the desk beside her. She rolled her eyes at Gabriella and mouthed the words, "Did you study?"

Gabriella shook her head. "Not much."

It was true. She had tried to study, but all she could hear with every page she turned in her spiral notebook was *Don't you know, dear Gabby? Don't you know?*

John Donne preached it. Shakespeare scribbled it across the page in iambic pentameter. Monet splashed it onto a blank canvas, and suddenly it was vivid with color. *Don't you know?*

But she didn't know.

"Excuse me, class." M. Vidal stood up, clearing his throat. His face was pure apology. "M. Hoffmann has asked me to give out the exam and remind you that you have two hours to complete it. He urges you to use your time wisely. There are twenty identifications of quotes, then one poem to analyze. Afterwards I will be showing slides for identification. And there are two essay questions. He wants you to reserve the last forty-five minutes for these. You may begin as soon as you get the exam."

He handed Gabriella five pages stapled neatly in the top-left corner. Five pages written in David's bold script. Her heart raced. His hand! But he was not here.

She picked up her pen and wrote her name across the top of the first page. She read the directions for the first exercise: identify the quote, by work and author.

She glanced at the first quotation. *Sole judge of Truth, in endless Error hurl'd: the glory, jest, and riddle of the world!*

She almost spoke aloud: *Why, it's from Alexander Pope's "Essay on Man"!* She heard herself pronounce the words, months and lifetimes ago, the first time she had looked into David Hoffmann's eyes. "I didn't know you then," she whispered to herself as she wrote in the information.

The next quote was Donne. "Meditation XVII." Familiar. The one from which "for whom the bell tolls" comes. But David had chosen the last sentence of the meditation to quote. How odd.

> *But this bell that tells me of his affliction digs out*
> *and applies that gold to me, if by this consideration*
> *of another's danger I take my own into contemplation*
> *and so secure myself by making my recourse to my God,*
> *who is our only security.*

Strange that he would cite that, she thought. And she remembered that second day of class when he had challenged her to speak on Donne, and she had met him square on. *She* was the one who had quoted the end of the meditation! Gabriella felt her cheeks burning.

But none of the other girls seemed to notice. There were a few groans and one flat-out protest of "This is impossible" from Stephanie, of course, and a few girls laughed. But no one said what Gabriella felt: *He wrote this exam for me.*

There was a quote from Milton's *Paradise Lost.* But such a quote!

> *Henceforth I learn that to obey is best*
> *And love with fear the only God, to walk*
> *As in his presence ever to observe*
> *His providence and on him sole depend.*

How could the others not see, she wondered, as she continued the exam? It could not be coincidence that she could take the first nine quotes and read them almost as a thesis and argument for faith.

He was clever, that David! And she found herself laughing quietly. Then she stared at the tenth quote, and her heart skipped.

> *The Lord shall preserve me from all evil; He shall*
> *preserve my soul. The Lord shall preserve my going out*
> *and my coming in from this time forth, and even for*
> *evermore.*

Psalm 121! But he had misquoted it, replacing *thee* and *thy* with the first-person pronoun. Why in the world? ... And then it came to her, drifting up as if out of a dream. *You will wait a very long time if you hope to hear me claim it as my own prayer....*

He had been mocking her during their first visit to the place de la Comédie. And yet here in the exam, David was doing just what he said he would never do. He had changed the pronouns so she would know, without a doubt, it was his prayer.

David Hoffmann believed. Somewhere between the café of two weeks ago and the classroom of this morning, David had believed. She felt a tear sting her eye and swept it away.

The next quote came from an early poem of Shakespeare:

> *O mistress mine! where are you roaming?*
> *O stay and hear! your true love's coming,*
> *That can sing both high and low.*
> *Trip no further, pretty sweeting;*
> *Journeys end in lovers meeting.*

She blushed, her head hot with sweat. Now what was he saying? Journeys end in lovers meeting? No, she was reading too much into it. It was just a poem they studied in class ... not a declaration of David's love for her.

She focused on the next quote, trying to forget the last one. It was Coleridge's love poem to Sara, who would later become his wife. Gabriella gave a little gasp as she read the lines that David had chosen:

> *But thy more serious eye a mild reproof*

Darts, O beloved Woman! nor such thoughts
Dim and unhallow'd dost thou not reject
And biddest me walk humbly with my God.
Meek Daughter in the family of Christ!

Shaking her head in amazement, she recalled how David had teased her with this poem, claiming that she would wish him to write such a thing to her. And now, in a sense, he had.

And then a quote by D. H. Lawrence.

The pain of loving you
Is almost more than I can bear.

So simple, so direct. She felt dizzy and confused. Surely he was not saying this to *her*. What were the other girls thinking? But none of them looked embarrassed or anything other than frustrated with a difficult exam.

He told her with Wordsworth and Keats and T. S. Eliot, and then he switched to prose and French and said it again with Hugo and Flaubert. *I love you.*

She tried not to cry as she scribbled out a response to the poem she was analyzing. But it was Matthew Arnold's "Dover Beach," which always made her cry. And David knew it.

Finally M. Vidal's slow, placid voice broke into her thoughts as he announced the time for identification of slides. He turned off the lights, and Gabriella felt safe despite her wet face. She was still writing about "Dover Beach" when the first slide came onto the screen. As she glanced up at the slide, she felt a piercing pang of deep, pure joy. The poets would understand it. For there on the screen was Monet's *Wild Poppies, Near Argenteuil*. There was not a shadow of doubt now.

Gabriella wrote furiously, freely, happily. She barely noticed the other girls standing, turning in their exams, and leaving the classroom. How could they be done already? There was so much more to say. By the time the two hours were up, she was the only student left in the room. M. Vidal cleared his throat apologetically.

"Mlle Madison ... I'm afraid time is up."

She flashed him a smile. "Yes, sorry. I'm almost done." She buried her head in her paper again. Five minutes later she came out of her dreams as she heard, "Mlle Madison."

It took her a moment to react. Only a moment to realize that it had not been M. Vidal's voice she heard. She gasped and looked up. David stood in the doorway of the classroom with the strangest expression on his face.

He moved toward her quickly, whispering, "Mlle Madison. It's time."

Head swirling, Gabriella only saw that the room was empty except for her and the very real presence of David. She dropped her pen and gaped at him, rising awkwardly. "David," she murmured.

He was beside her then, picking her up in his strong arms, swinging her around, squeezing her tightly, tightly as he laughed. "Gabby, my dear Gabby!"

And then he put her down, holding her against his chest. She heard his heart thumping, thumping. He gently reached down, cradling her chin in his hand and lifting her face up to meet his eyes. "Gabby. Gabby, do you understand? Do you know?"

She nodded, feeling her eyes fill with tears. Her voice caught, and she could not speak.

He leaned toward her, and the simple gesture seemed to take moments or hours, before at last his lips reached hers. They touched hers softly, and she shivered with pleasure.

He lifted his head and smiled. Then he reached down once more, pulling her against him and kissing her again. Softly, convincingly. She folded her arms around his neck. Kissing, laughing. It was something, a blossoming, a deep, luxurious feeling that she had waited, it seemed, all of her life to know.

Later Gabriella could not remember how long they had stood and held each other and kissed in the middle of the classroom on the second floor of the parsonage at St. Joseph. She could only remember the desperate desire to keep David there forever and not step out into the hallway, where life must resume.

But presently he took her hand and entwined his long fingers with hers. He placed his other hand on top of hers and patted it. "This is how we should be, Gabby. We are right for each other after all."

It was a statement, and she knew he meant it. Yet she read something else in his eyes. Before he pronounced the next word, she heard it. *But* ... That terrible little word with the strength to change a destiny.

And then he spoke, confirming her fears. "But, Gabby, I can't stay. Not yet. I came on a whim. Because I had to ... I had to see you."

Gabriella felt her legs wobble.

"I have to go back. I have found Jea—"

Immediately Gabriella put a finger to his lips. "No. Don't say that name. Don't bring it here, to destroy ... this. You and me."

"Of course," whispered David, kissing her again. He held her face in his hands and peered at her. "Dear, dear, beautiful Gabby. Can it be?"

Gabriella smiled. "I think it can." She rested her head on his chest for only a moment. But then her mind started racing, full of questions. "David?"

"Mmm?"

"How did it happen? How did you come to believe?"

He sighed deeply. "You, my angel, could explain it much better than I. It's a mystery, and yet it's suddenly so clear. I read a lot, as you said. The Gospels. The Epistles. The Psalms. And I argued a lot with your God." He was playing with Gabriella's hair, watching the red strands, thick and curly between his fingers.

"In the end it came to the cross. And forgiveness." He chuckled as he touched the gold chain around Gabriella's neck. "How very ironic, *n'est-ce pas*? It had been here all along to remind me of Someone who suffered a whole lot more than I had. The very hardest thing: forgiveness."

They stood at the doorway of the classroom, his head resting on hers, locked in a sweet embrace. She didn't move but asked, "And the rest? How did you know the *other* part?"

He chuckled softly again. "The other part, as you say, Gabby, was wonderfully easy. It was just admitting it that was hard." He held her away from him and looked her full in the face. His eyes were deep, shining, sincere. "I have always known that I love you, Gabby. For the longest time, I have known."

When he leaned down to kiss her again, she met him eagerly, and once more, time ran by unnoticed.

The classroom was dark, and David turned the key to lock the door.

"Do you have my exam?"

"Yes, of course," he said, patting his briefcase.

"It was a bit embarrassing, David. I was sure the other girls must have caught on. But apparently not."

David laughed. "The others could not decipher a code if it were spelled out for them. But you needn't have worried. Except for the slides, their exam was completely different from yours." He was grinning, proud of himself.

"Why ... how in the world?"

"M. Vidal simply used the exam from last year ... and I sent him a different one for you."

"Well, aren't you clever," Gabriella teased. "And now M. Vidal knows all about our love, I suppose."

David let his head fall back and roared with laughter. "My dear Gabby, you would be surprised at what M. Vidal knows!"

Gabriella wrinkled her nose in feigned disgust but didn't question him further.

They stood poised for a long minute at the top of the stairs. Then he led her down the steps until they stood outside the parsonage. "And Ophélie? May I see her quickly?"

Gabriella hesitated. "David ... she's been very sick."

"Sick?"

"Yes, but she's much better now. Your letter was just what she needed. But ... but if you're only going to pop in and out today, I think that would be unwise. She might become even more upset. You understand?"

"Yes ... I suppose." He looked lost in thought. "Listen, Gabby. Listen carefully. I want you to meet me at the Pont du Gard with Ophélie." He talked swiftly, before she had a chance to protest. "Today is the sixth. Will she be strong enough to come on the twelfth? That's almost a week."

"I-I don't know," Gabriella stammered.

"No, don't worry. By the twelfth all will be finished in Marseille. It will give me time to check back in Aix and Aigues-Mortes. Take the train to Nîmes. Then the bus from Nîmes to the Pont du Gard. Bring a picnic, and we'll go to the little beach area beside the river. It will be perfect. No one will be there at this time of year."

Gabriella was not convinced. "Can't you just come back here, David?"

"No, not yet. That would be unwise. But I must see her. The Pont du Gard on the twelfth." He was whispering excitedly now. "I'll meet you at the bus stop."

"But, David ... you're making me afraid." She was suddenly clutching his coat as he turned to go. "Please. Please stay here with me."

He smiled and caught her up in his arms, pulling her behind the corner of the church, out of view. He kissed her forcefully, passionately. "Don't worry. I'll get word to you if I need to. Only pray for me, sweet Gabby. Don't worry. Only pray." He gave her one last kiss and was off.

Gabriella touched her lips as she walked back through the parsonage, dazed. Little explosions of joy were dancing through what must be her heart, and she found herself breathing deeply, deeply to regain her breath.

David Hoffmann loved God. And David Hoffmann loved her. It was some strange miracle, blowing in from above to warm her in every part of her being.

Gabriella smiled and, turning her eyes upward, whispered, "Thank You. And please, God, keep him safe."

Rosie Lecharde stepped out of the small side door to the chapel. Such a convenient place to hide! So much news to hear! She was in no hurry to catch the train back to Marseille. She laughed aloud as she watched David Hoffmann rushing along the cobblestones, out of Castelnau.

He could hurry home to meet Jean-Claude if he so desired. Rosie was going to take the bus in town to the Comédie. Her wallet was full, and she could sip *verveine* all day at a little café. Perhaps later in the afternoon she could find some interesting work in Montpellier. No rush. She would take the midnight train to Marseille. She had all the time in the world to get back to Jean-Claude and tell him who would be visiting the Pont du Gard on March 12.

31

Eleven thirty at night in the slums of Marseille was a lively time. All around, David could hear taunting shouts and fistfights and gunshots. Rosie Lecharde had been right. It wasn't hard to find the Hotel Poseidon. It sat in the heart of the city, next to the Vieux Port.

There was absolutely nothing in David that wanted to go into room 32 and face a lunatic. Rosie's information had come too easily. Twelve hundred francs was too little.

Or perhaps he was simply scared. Lately it mattered a great deal that he was alive. Someone cared. Two people cared about him very much. Not for what he could get them. Not as a leader of a cause. They cared about him. They needed him. And, he admitted to himself, he needed them.

He shook himself back to the present. This was no time to feel distracted. No time to listen to his heart. He would offer Jean-Claude the false list for a price and, once the madman had paid him, give him the key to a post-office box where he'd stashed it. Surely it would work.

David shivered, suddenly unsure of his plan. What if Jean-Claude turned on him and blew his brains out? David had no weapon. How would he defend himself? He couldn't trust a madman, could he?

He didn't go inside the hotel but hung in the shadows beside the overturned garbage bin with its rotting fruit and broken bottles. Above him the windows from the rooms on the north side of the hotel looked out into the filthy alleyway. Thirty minutes passed.

Music blared from a nearby bar that welcomed its clients with a bright flashing neon sign. A cat rubbed against David's leg, causing him to jump. The cat leaped onto the garbage bin and disappeared. But no one came out of the hotel.

What should he do? He couldn't afford to lose track of Jean-Claude again. In two days he was due in Aix, and soon afterward at the Pont du Gard. He slouched down and leaned against the garbage can, ignoring the reeking smells. One o'clock came and went. David remembered seeing the hand approaching two before he drifted off.

David awoke with a start. He heard a muffled cry coming from a window above him. It was still dark outside, but the bar across the street was closed and its neon sign turned off. He couldn't read his watch. Another sharp cry from above, and then a woman's voice. "I don't know why he hasn't come. I promise. Please.… It's good information … please!"

David flinched at the sound of a scream, followed by a gunshot.

He cursed, ran into the hotel, and crouched in the lobby. No madman emerged from down the hall. He found room 32 and hesitated only a moment before pushing against the door. It was locked. He rammed it with his shoulder, then kicked it hard with his foot, and it swung inward.

Rosie Lecharde lay on the floor with a bullet through her head. He felt in vain for her pulse. The window was open. David ran to it and looked down the back alley. He jumped through the window and landed amid the rubbish on the ground below, then cautiously searched up and down the alley. Soon he heard sirens. He ran through the alleyway and out onto a deserted thoroughfare. Jean-Claude was nowhere in sight. And David was sure he wouldn't be coming back to room 32.

He walked slowly toward his hotel. Rosie was dead because he didn't show. The bullet would have surely been his. And Jean-Claude was roaming the streets again, like a raving mad hyena.

"Oh, God, I don't know what to do," he whispered, climbing the winding wooden staircase that groaned loudly with each step. He collapsed on the ripped orange bedspread in his room and slept.

The orphans were singing grace before the evening meal. The faint melody caught Gabriella's attention as she wandered down the hall of the parsonage basement. Drifting as if in a trance out into the courtyard, she found herself humming along softly with the children. *"Pour ce repas, pour toute joie, nous te louons, Seigneur."*

Oh yes. As the blessing said, she had so much to be thankful for. She sat in Mother Griolet's wicker chair and studied the sky. It was not yet completely dark, and streaks of crimson and periwinkle blue sat for one last moment poised behind the church's bell tower. The air was almost balmy in sharp contrast with the cold of last week.

"Rain is coming. A big storm," Sister Isabelle had told her earlier, pointing to the sky. "You can smell it in the air."

For Gabriella, it was the smell of spring. Renewal. New birth. Hope. No more storms. She knew she was grinning foolishly as she thought of David. He was a romantic after all. Her heart began to

race just as it had when she first understood what he was saying
to her through the exam. Then his voice behind her. She, startled,
standing awkwardly to greet him. And then in his arms. And the
kiss....

It was better than the movies. So much better, because it was
actually happening, it *had happened*, to her. No doubt, no daydream.
Three days ago he had kissed her and told her that he loved her. And
in only three more days they would be together again. The short week
in between was like a brief intermission, a moment to step outside and
collect her thoughts and be sure of her lines before rushing back in for
the final act. She was glad to have this time to think and remember.

It had been only seven months since she left Dakar. It could have
been seven years. She laughed. Maybe seven lifetimes, and she, like a
cat, was entitled to two more. Nothing had been what she expected.
Absolutely nothing. Except ...

Yes. You, Lord, have been the same yesterday, today, and tomorrow.
Your love has not failed me. You have not left me alone, even when I was
sure there was nothing left to hope for.

She heard the children's laughter from inside the dining hall, but
she saw only Ericka before her, spinning around, delighted with her
big sister's attention. Ericka had known what joy was. The thought
suddenly brought with it an overwhelming peace to Gabriella. In
Ericka's short life, she had known joy. Conceived by hate and brought
forth in sorrow, she had still known joy.

Mother Griolet was right. Life was not fair. But there was hope.
And what had David said? Forgiveness? He had said the word! She
laughed out loud. He had found forgiveness from above, and he had
also forgiven.

Gabriella dropped to her knees in front of the wicker chair, the cool, damp earth soaking through her stockings. She touched the cross around her neck. "Lord Jesus," she whispered. "Forgive me for hating because I could not make sense of so many things." She paused, thinking of Ericka and then of Ophélie. "I forgive them. The one who did it to Mother. The ones who didn't come. Daddy for being away. I forgive Mother for not telling me about the rape and Mother Griolet …" She was sobbing now, but as she cried, she felt a physical sensation. Someone was pulling a weight, like a huge, overstuffed knapsack, off her.

She rose from the ground, light-headed, free. It was another step in the process of grieving that Mother Griolet had described. There would be others, she knew. But Gabriella didn't want to think ahead tonight. She just wanted to be. *To abide*, she thought, and images of the vineyards bright with color as she and David had driven by them in the late fall settled in her mind.

She heard a slight rustling behind her and turned around. Mother Griolet was approaching her, silhouetted against the light coming from the dining hall.

"Hello, child," she said. "I didn't know you were still here. Aren't you eating at Mme Leclerc's?"

"Oh, yes, yes, I am. I was just enjoying the evening … and thinking of some things you said to me."

"Things I said?" Mother Griolet laughed, surprised.

"Yes. Thinking of forgiveness and … and what comes after." Gabriella locked arms with Mother Griolet, and they began to stroll around the courtyard.

Gabriella talked excitedly about what was bubbling inside her, and the old nun listened thoughtfully. Then before she could stop herself, Gabriella told her about David.

"He believes, Mother Griolet. David believes."

The nun pursed her lips. "He believes? What do you mean?"

"He believes in God. In Christ. In forgiveness."

Mother Griolet gave a cry of delight. *"Ce n'est pas possible! Dieu merci."* She clasped her hands together. "M. Hoffmann is full of surprises lately. Wonderful surprises. He is quite a different character from what I suspected." Then she frowned suddenly. "And how do you know this? Is he back?"

Gabriella blushed. "Not exactly. Well, he came back, briefly." She nibbled her fingernail as Mother Griolet raised her eyebrows.

"Briefly?"

"Yes, very briefly. He came back to tell me ... to tell me about ... about believing. And ..." She stopped, flustered.

"He came back to make sure you and Ophélie were well. Something like that?" Mother Griolet volunteered with a gleam in her eye.

"Yes, something like that." They walked for a few minutes in silence. Gabriella cleared her throat. She began again, "Mother Griolet?"

"Oui, ma chérie?"

"You said you were in love once."

"That is so."

"Do you mind ... I mean, excuse me for asking, but ..."

"Gabriella, child. Don't be afraid to love. If this is right for you, you will know it. I have thought wrongly of M. Hoffmann for many reasons. I think you know what I mean?"

"Yes. He has told you then?"

"He has told me about his part with the orphans. Amazing. I have seen the tender side of this man. But, Gabriella, you must decide. It's between you and him ... and your God." She pressed her fingers softly around Gabriella's arm.

"I know. I've been so confused, but you're right." She smiled. "I think I know."

Mother Griolet nodded. "I believe you know quite a lot. You have been helping M. Hoffmann, and now he wants you and Ophélie to stay put."

"Yes, and what about M. Vidal? David said he knows something too."

Mother Griolet smiled. "Dear Jean-Louis." She looked at Gabriella. "M. Vidal has been a friend of mine for a very long time. You see, it was his brother whom I loved."

"Really?"

"Yes. And Jean-Louis was a great comfort to me after his death. He gave me something else to do. He was the one involved in the Resistance. He started the whole thing with the Jewish orphans. I could never have done it without him."

Gabriella gave a low whistle. "Well, I would have never thought of him." She reddened. "I mean ... I mean, he is so ..."

"Yes," the nun chuckled. "He is definitely inconspicuous. So you see, we have been friends for a long time. And now he helps us again. M. Hoffmann and he are very careful."

"I'm sorry about M. Vidal's brother. I'm very sorry for you."

The nun's green eyes clouded for a moment. "God has filled up my life in so many ways. I live with sadness at times. But not regret.

There has been too much else. Our God, remember, is in the business of bringing good out of bad. Never forget it."

"I won't," Gabriella assured her. "I have learned it myself." The wind picked up as the bells chimed eight o'clock. "Oh my. I'm late for dinner."

"Hurry on with you then, *ma fille*. Go on."

Gabriella hugged the old nun quickly and left the courtyard running.

The scabs were gone and the fever, too, finally. Ophélie looked at her face in the mirror. A few shallow pockmarks lined her forehead. She wrinkled her brow. "I look ugly. Papa will think I am so ugly."

Gabriella came to her side and brushed back Ophélie's thick, tousled hair with her fingers. "Nonsense! You're beautiful. You're only a little pale from being inside for so long. The doctor has said you can sit in the courtyard for a while. In two days you will be feeling stronger. Then we'll see your papa. And he'll be so pleased."

Ophélie turned her face toward Gabriella. "Do you really think he'll be glad to see me?"

Gabriella shook her head. "No, not glad." She winked at Ophélie. "He will be absolutely delighted."

Ophélie hugged Gabriella. "What shall I bring him? What would Papa like? I must have something to give him."

Gabriella didn't reply immediately, and Ophélie began reciting possible gifts. "A piece of candy maybe? Does he like candy? Or a picture? Yes, I could draw him a picture."

"A picture is a wonderful idea. Color it and sign your name, and he will be the proudest papa in the world."

Ophélie was laughing now. "Bribri, I'm going right now to get my colored pencils and paper from my desk!" She dashed out of the dormitory and danced into the courtyard. She held her arms high above her head, twirling around in circles. Soon she felt dizzy and collapsed into Gabriella's arms, giggling.

"Ophélie, sweetheart! Calm down. You must not overdo it on your first day up."

"But, Bribri," the child panted, "I'm just so happy. I'm all better, and I'm going to see my papa very soon. I have to dance; I can't help it!"

David sipped a coffee on the cours Mirabeau in Aix-en-Provence. A storm was brewing, and the first drop of rain landed neatly on the scrap of paper in his hand. His face was emotionless as he stared at the latest messages that Gilbert's bread had revealed. There was the usual one about the children. This time nine of them would be arriving in Marseille on the eighteenth. Nine children. David felt thankful to know that someone had gotten the real list he had sent to Algiers. The remaining harki and pied-noir children threatened by Ali would be rescued. But the other note that lay before him brought different news.

"Not now," he said to himself, shaking his head. "Oh, Anne-Marie, not now." He fingered an old photo that lay before him on the round café table. "You know I have never been able to turn you down, beautiful woman."

He sighed heavily, letting the coffee cup rattle in the saucer as he set it down. He was, after all, relieved that Anne-Marie was alive. This was good news. For Ophélie. For the operation, too. For him. Yes, of course he was glad. He had come because of her in the first place. It's just that it was such an inconvenient time to go to Algiers.

He laughed at his own thought. Yes, just a tad bit "inconvenient," with the war and cease-fire imminent. But of course he would go. He left a handful of change on the table and rose to leave the café.

The rain fell freely now. He walked halfway across the Cours and stood at the base of the smiling statue of Roi René holding his muscat grapes. "Gabriella," he murmured.

Then, angrily, David crossed the broad avenue and walked behind the Cours, into the small side streets of Aix. He kicked at the curb, cursing to himself.

Suddenly the voice of Gabriella floated up to him. *I cannot prove that prayers are answered or that God is above if you do not want to believe it. But that isn't my business.... I dare you to ask Him to prove Himself to you.*

"And what am I supposed to pray anyway?" he begged cynically to the cobblestones. "You figure this one out, God of Gabriella. Figure it out, if You will."

He stopped outside a child's clothing store. A bright-pink stuffed pony was in the window front. Impulsively he stepped inside the store and purchased it. The saleswoman wrapped it in bright-pink paper and put a pink bow on top. He paid for the gift and left the store.

"You see, God," he continued his argument, "I'm in love with this woman. You know her well. And I have discovered I'm the father of Ophélie. A precious child. And now her mother needs me to rescue her from the jaws of a wild Arab. And so I will go to the mother of my child, and perhaps I will find that ... that this is what You want. A reunion. A family.

"But then what will happen to Gabby, God? Excuse me for saying it, but it does not quite seem fair...." He laughed at himself, talking to the wind and the rain. "It is, if You remember, this woman that I love." He laughed again, a skeptical, hard laugh. "Well, there You have it, God. A rather unorthodox prayer as I stroll through the backstreets of Aix. I hope it will do."

The French would say it was raining ropes, Gabriella reflected as she watched the torrential downpour. Cold, damp, and gray. The winds gusted outside her window. She snuggled into her comforter, bringing her knees to her chest and wrapping her arms around them. She relished the sound of the rain pelting against the window and the olive tree twisting and blowing in the storm. A flash flood, the radio in Mme Leclerc's kitchen announced as she and the girls crowded around it after lunch.

But Gabriella felt warm and safe. Monet's print of the field of poppies hung on the wall in front of her. She stared at it and then closed her eyes.

Tomorrow, surely, the skies would clear. Then she would bundle up Ophélie, gather up the picnic basket of goodies, and take bus 11 to the train station. The train to Nîmes, then the bus to the Pont du Gard.

She had never seen the imposing Roman aqueduct, but she imagined it rising out of the trees, and David Hoffmann standing in the middle of the bridge, waving slowly like a Roman warrior, beckoning to his family to join him in another adventure.

32

With great difficulty David put the note from Moustafa Dramchini out of his mind as he drove to the Pont du Gard to meet Gabriella and Ophélie. A frown crossed his face when he thought of Jean-Claude Gachon, a lunatic murderer, still on the loose. But David had made sure that no one was following him. This would be a private reunion, far away from the crazy business of the Algerian War.

A bright-pink package sat beside him in the front seat of his deux chevaux. He felt a sudden nervous twinge at the thought of seeing Ophélie. His daughter. What if she didn't like him? He reminded himself that, although he had developed quite a reputation with young women, he had no reputation at all with little girls.

But Gabby would be there. Gabby would know what to do if things got awkward.

Today he would walk across the Pont du Gard hand in hand with "his women." He laughed approvingly. Then he frowned. Only for today.

Afterward, somehow, he would tell them about Anne-Marie. Ophélie would let him go again, to find her mother. But Gabby. He shook his head. She would let him go, but …

All at once he was following signs to the Pont du Gard and pulling his car into the parking lot two kilometers away. There were no other cars. He stepped out into the nippy March air. The sky was still overcast.

His hands were sweaty at the thought of a bus approaching. He held the pink package under one arm and stuffed his hands in his pockets.

Five minutes passed, but to David it seemed more like five days. He rehearsed what he would do. Ophélie would be holding Gabriella's hand. Yes, of course. Hiding behind her, shyly. That was only to be expected. Children were usually shy around adults they didn't know.

Then what would he do? Ah yes. He would walk forward and shake the child's hand and then offer her the package. Maybe a kiss on the forehead.

No, no, no! It was all wrong. That was what his father had done after every trip when they were apart. Always a bright package and shake of the hand and a quick kiss on the forehead. So cold and mechanical.

A bus loomed ahead of him, coming from nowhere. He stepped back to let it pass and park. Yes, they were there! A little girl's nose was flattened against the window. Her eyes were bright, and she was smiling. My, but she looked like her mother. How had he not seen it before?

The bus stopped, and he walked briskly toward it. Ophélie scrambled off and broke into a run. David opened up his arms, dropping the package, to receive her embrace. He bent down and she was in his arms, laughing and hugging him tightly around the neck.

"Papa! Oh, Papa!" she cried.

It surprised him how quickly the tears came. How naturally he picked her up and kissed her. "Ophélie," he whispered, his voice choked with emotion. "Little Ophélie. You are such a beautiful girl. My daughter."

He held her at arm's length and stared as she stared back until they both burst into laughter. "Oh," he said quickly, as if coming out of a dream. "I brought you something." He reached behind him and retrieved the fallen package. "I didn't know what to get you. I mean, it's such a gift, such a wonderful gift just to have you and I ..."

Ophélie laughed, a carefree, childish laugh. "Oh, Papa. I didn't know what to bring you either. I only hoped that you would be happy to see me."

He squeezed her again. "Oh, I am, my child. I am."

From over Ophélie's shoulder he looked up and saw Gabriella for the first time, standing with a picnic hamper in her hands. Her red hair was swept back from her face in a French braid. Her blue eyes twinkled. He wiped his eyes and motioned for her to join them, and she walked up behind Ophélie, smiling broadly. David pulled her close and kissed her.

Ophélie ripped open the bright paper. "A pony!" she exclaimed. "A pretty pink pony." She turned to David and threw her arms around his neck again. "Oh, thank you, Papa! Thank you. How did you know?"

Without waiting for his reply, she pulled a sealed envelope out from the picnic hamper and handed it to him. He held it softly, almost reverently. *Papa* was written across the front in Ophélie's childish script. She had drawn large red hearts all around the word. He felt the tears coming again.

Carefully he unsealed the envelope and took out a piece of paper. Unfolding it, he smiled. Six brightly colored ponies were running across a green field. The sky above was dark gray, but in the top right-hand corner a bright yellow sun spilled out its rays.

The ponies ran toward it, a pink pony in the lead. In between the ponies and the gray strip of sky Ophélie had written *I love you, Papa. Ophélie.*

"It's an extraordinary picture, Ophélie! Thank you!" He caught her in his arms again. "Please explain it to me."

Eagerly she pointed to the drawing. "The ponies are all of us. I'm the pink one. I'm leading us to Jesus. He's in the sky, in the sun. And the red pony is Gabriella, because she has such long, pretty red hair. And then after her comes Mother Griolet. She's the gray pony there, see? And you are the black one. You're catching up with us and running to the sun. And the beautiful white pony with the black mane and tail is Mama. She is far behind, but she's coming with the brown pony. That's Moustafa." Ophélie looked into David's eyes. "How did you know to get me the pink pony?"

David glanced at Gabriella, who was blinking back tears. He wiped his eyes again. Before, he would have said coincidence. Now, he took his child's soft, smooth hands, enfolding them in his own. "Inspiration," he whispered, and Ophélie seemed to understand.

David replaced the drawing in its envelope, sliding it back into the picnic hamper. Arm in arm the three walked leisurely toward the Pont du Gard.

As they rounded the corner, an enormous three-tiered aqueduct spread across the river before them. David sighed. "There it is." He admired again the elegant posture of the ancient bridge that gracefully arced its way across the tempestuous waters.

"It's absolutely magnificent," Gabriella said.

David lifted Ophélie onto his shoulders for a better view. "It's the tallest of all known Roman bridge-aqueducts, you know. A hundred and sixty feet high. The bottom two tiers have extremely wide arches—fifty to eighty feet. Surprising, even for the Romans. And the upper tier has thirty-five smaller arches, you see. The top is covered with huge flagstones that are twelve feet wide. Although it's forbidden, many a tourist searching for a thrill has walked on the top."

"No thanks," quipped Gabby. "I had my thrill in Raymond's territory in Les Baux."

"*Oh, non, Papa!* I would never want to walk up there! Never." Ophélie had one arm around David's neck and held her stuffed pink pony with her other arm.

"I understand, *ma chérie*. Don't worry. It is, however, quite an impressive view."

Gabriella gasped. "Do you mean to say you've been on top? You've walked across on a stone slab one hundred and sixty feet up with only the sky to catch you if you fell?"

David grinned. "Surely you aren't surprised, my Gabby. But not just the sky. The Gardon River welcomes you below. It's usually very peaceful and not too deep. But you see how high the waters are now, and violent from the flash flood yesterday. Never fear, though. The Pont du Gard has withstood many a flood. Ingenious the way it was built. Some of those stones weigh over six tons. Imagine!"

"It's beautiful, Papa. And so big! One must feel very tiny to walk on it."

"Ah, you will see how it feels, *ma petite puce*. We'll walk across the bottom tier. There's no danger there. And then you can climb to the top and walk through the actual aqueduct, where the water ran."

Both Gabriella and Ophélie looked at him suspiciously.

"Again, perfectly safe—you're completely enclosed," David assured them. He smiled and continued, "But we can't picnic down on the beach as I'd hoped. With the flood, it's totally covered. But there are many other spots in the woods. Come along."

It was well after one o'clock when they reached the base of the huge bridge. The overcast skies cleared, showing patches of blue interspersed between the frothy gray clouds.

"We may see the sun after all, girls," called David. He stepped onto the bottom tier of the bridge, motioning for Gabriella and Ophélie to follow. It was twenty feet wide, and on one side a road had been built. They walked across in silence, Ophélie clutching David's right hand and Gabriella walking beside him on the left.

"We're about sixty feet up here. Amazing that this thing has withstood two thousand years of use." He ran his fingers over the stones of one of the arches that rose up to form part of the second tier.

Gabriella walked near the edge of the bridge. "It's still dangerous, David. Anyone could just plunge right over, even here. There are no guardrails."

David laughed and pulled her back toward him, hugging her and kissing her softly on the forehead. "You and your vivid imagination, Gabby. Don't look down. Look out. Can't you just imagine the Romans walking across the waters on this masterpiece?"

Ophélie interrupted. "*Papa, j'ai faim*. Please, may we eat?"

There was not another soul about. "Is there any reason we shouldn't spread our blanket out here?" David inquired.

Gabriella shrugged. "Sounds okay to me." She spread out Mme Leclerc's plaid woolen afghan beside an arch. They leaned against the huge stones to rest their backs, and she pulled out sandwiches and cheeses and yogurts and salads from the basket.

"A real feast—I'm sure Mme Pons helped plan it," David said, chuckling. He eyed the wine bottle tucked into the straw basket. "What have you told those dear women anyway, Gabby?"

Gabriella smiled. "Nothing. I only said Ophélie and I were going to a picnic, and we might meet someone else. Can I help it if they are always planning and scheming?"

Ophélie leaned back against her father, cuddling the stuffed pony, and sighed. "I'm so happy to be here with you, Papa. And with you, Bribri. I can't ever remember being quite so happy in my whole life."

"I know just what you mean," replied Gabriella, beaming.

David stretched out his long legs and pulled Ophélie onto his lap. He tickled her lightly, and her childish laughter echoed out over the noise of the busy river. She squirmed, but he held her tight. "You can't get away from me, girl. Not up here, you can't."

He held her still, and Gabriella watched him soften. The child and the father. Ophélie resembled the picture she had seen of Anne-Marie, it was true, but she saw something of David there too. The way she tilted her head, the dark eyes that sparkled and flashed.

Looking at the two snuggled happily by the enormous arch, Gabriella felt a rush of emotion. It was so simple, after all. Just the three of them, together. As if all the centuries were standing still, frozen in a gentle smile on the Pont du Gard at this precise moment. A father and child on an ancient bridge. And a woman, she thought, a woman who loved them both.

Gabriella was never sure afterward what had been the order of events in that wild moment. David had suggested that Gabriella ask a blessing for the food, which had pleased and surprised her. Then Ophélie had leaned forward out of David's lap to hold Gabriella's hand. Likewise, David had reached out to hold her other hand. The instant his hand touched hers, a gunshot fired from far off. At first Gabriella had looked toward the woods to see. It was a second's reflex. But when she glanced back around, Ophélie's eyes were wide, and a sickly expression covered her face. They both screamed. David lay collapsed by the arch, his hand clutching his shoulder. Fresh blood seeped through his fingers.

"David!" Gabriella screamed. "David!"

He groaned, "Get down. Flat on your stomach."

Another shot rang out, and a bullet ricocheted off the stone arch as they lay flat on the cold stones.

David rasped, "Gabby, crawl back across when I tell you. Crawl, and you'll find a path leading up to the top tier, over in the brush. Follow it. Climb the steps and hide there inside the aqueduct. Don't look at me like that. Do it! Ophélie, stay with Gabby. When I count to three." He took a breath. "One, two, *three*."

David rose to his knees and forced himself forward in the opposite direction. Gabriella saw him out of the corner of her eye as she pulled Ophélie along beside her.

"Dear God, oh, dear God!" She heard another shot and another, but she didn't dare look back. The end of the bridge was forty yards away. They ran, crouching, until they reached the relative safety of the thick underbrush. Gabriella pulled Ophélie up beside her, climbing the embankment and scrambling over the rocks and loose stones. Ophélie dropped her pony and cried out as it bounced down the slope.

"Come on, sweetie. We'll get it later. We must hurry."

She saw Ophélie's strength fading, her face ashen with fear. It took only a few moments to reach the ancient stone steps leading to the aqueduct. She pushed Ophélie in front of her as they climbed the narrow circular stair that suddenly plunged them into darkness. Quietly they huddled in the narrow conduit. It was barely two feet wide and six feet high.

Only then did Ophélie speak. "Bribri," she said between sobs. "Papa's shot. He's bleeding. Will he die?"

Gabriella shook her head. "No, no, of course not. He'll be fine. We must wait here. He'll come get us. He'll tell us what to do."

Her voice sounded surprisingly calm, she noticed. But inside, pure panic was rising. David was shot. It was a nasty hit. And somewhere, somehow, a madman with a rifle was waiting to shoot again.

Dear Lord, she prayed silently, *You alone can see. Oh, God. Protect us. Protect all three of us. And give me wisdom to know what to do.*

She sat with Ophélie for a moment. "Do you feel strong enough to walk, Ophélie?"

The child nodded.

"Then come. We'll follow the aqueduct through the tunnel."

They inched their way forward in the dark. Every thirty feet or so an opening in the slats above let in a shaft of light. It was all the hope they had.

David was beginning to feel light-headed as the blood seeped from the wound in his shoulder. It could have been worse, he reasoned. It could have been his heart. He had reached the other side of the bridge and sat panting. Four bullets had missed. That was good. It had to be Jean-Claude. Jean-Claude, the sniper, was baiting him. Even now he was doubtless heading for the bridge to finish his work.

Head spinning, David fought to keep conscious. Gabby and Ophélie. When Jean-Claude didn't find them on the bottom tier, he would surely search inside the old aqueduct. They would be easy prey.

Forcing himself through the thick foliage, David climbed up toward the second tier. There was no path on this side to help him, and he slid as he climbed. Another fifty feet and he would reach the end of the third tier, which spilled over onto land by a wide stone-walled walkway. Back across the walkway he knew he could enter the aqueduct.

He paused, listening for the sound of twigs breaking. Nothing. But Jean-Claude would not be far behind. David fell onto the stone

walkway and lay there for only a moment. Then he got to his feet
and stumbled inside the dark aqueduct. He ducked his head to enter,
for it sloped down, allowing less than six feet of height. He heard the
sound of footsteps inside the hollow chamber and stopped.

God, he thought. *God of Gabriella. I don't know what to pray. Life.
Please, life. For us.* His heart jumped erratically. More footsteps. Far
away, he heard Ophélie gasp.

"Someone is there," she whispered.

"It's Papa," David said with difficulty. "I'm here. Wait. I'll come
to you."

The steps were running now. They met near the center of the
aqueduct, and Gabriella caught him in her arms. "David! David, are
you all right?"

He winced with pain, ignoring her question. "Gabby. He'll
come here. But ... but I don't know from which way. When he does,
take Ophélie the opposite way. He'll follow me." He nodded upward,
toward a hole between the slabs.

Gabriella gasped. "On top? You can't ... you're hurt!"

"Gabby, dear." He managed to smile at her as the light flickered across her face. "Gabby. This is very serious. Go to the buses.
Have the police come. You'll be safe with them." He felt his head
swimming.

"David!" Her voice startled him back to consciousness.

He turned around. Jean-Claude Gachon stood outside the aqueduct forty feet away, laughing.

"Run now," David whispered and watched as the woman and
child turned and fled down the narrow dark corridor they had just
come up.

The rifle was slung over Jean-Claude's shoulder. *A madman*, thought David. *I am dealing with a madman.* A thought resounded in his mind, as if heaven itself were screaming down to him: *Then make him mad.*

With a groan he hoisted himself up through the hole in the slate, using his good arm for support. He called back to Jean-Claude. "You're not afraid of heights I hope."

The Frenchman laughed, a piercing, evil laugh. "Of course not." He too heaved himself onto the roof from outside the aqueduct, and suddenly the two men stood facing one another on the twelve-foot ledge atop the Pont du Gard.

Don't look down, David told himself, as Jean-Claude eased his muscular frame toward him. *Keep him moving so he doesn't have time to aim.*

"You're hurt!" Jean-Claude howled, delight in his voice. "Blood! I can see it."

The height was dizzying. David crouched. Jean-Claude inched forward, a wild gleam in his eyes. The river, running high, tumbled past so far, far below. *Jump!* David thought. From his position in the center of the bridge, the river was directly below. Surely the water was high enough to break the fall. But then with a sick feeling he saw that the lower tier of the bridge jutted out beyond the top one. One would have to jump out awfully far to avoid hitting it.

Jean-Claude inched closer and drew his rifle. He stood twenty feet away from David. "You're a pitiful sitting duck. A helpless hare."

Helpless hare! The words stung David's mind. Not another helpless rabbit to be blown to bits by an enemy rifle. Adrenalin pumped through his body. He moved toward Jean-Claude.

The Frenchman stepped backward, laughing.

"You have been smart, Jean-Claude," David said. "How did you find us?"

"You fool! Rosie followed you to your stinking orphanage. And now you will lie in your own blood even as she does."

David made a quick movement again, from his crouched position, like a lion waiting to pounce.

Jean-Claude stepped back again, laughing. "I'm not afraid of a maimed cat, you filth. I will blast you in a breath."

One more move backward, David thought, and Jean-Claude would back into a hole in the slate and lose his balance. He moved forward again and yelled, "You are nothing, Jean-Claude. Nothing! Just a simple pawn for Ali. He'll use you, then throw you away."

Enraged, Jean-Claude lifted the rifle. In that instant David jumped toward him. The Frenchman stepped back into the hole in the slate, teetering precariously as he fought to regain his balance. He dropped the rifle as he grabbed for thin air. The rifle floated, momentarily suspended in time, until it hit the bridge below with a hollow thud.

For a brief second Jean-Claude seemed to lose his concentration as he followed the path of the rifle with his eyes. He fell to his knees, grasping the two-foot ledge to the left of the opening in the slate. David lunged at him, and the two men struggled on the narrow ledge.

Jean-Claude grabbed for David's shirt, but the movement caused him to lose his balance. "Fool," he screeched as he slipped; then terror replaced the mad gleam in his eyes.

The man clutched hopelessly at David's shirt as he dropped a few more inches, and David felt his weight pulling him down and over the edge. David grabbed on to the ledge with one arm, and a searing pain shot through his other shoulder.

"Help me!" Jean-Claude cried, but already his body was hanging perilously off the top of the bridge, and his grip on David's shirt was slipping. David struggled to pull his weight away from the edge.

Jean-Claude cursed. "I'll take you with me," he said, and with a last grunt he yanked David in his clutch before his fingers lost their grip and he fell, tumbling far, far down.

David saw it in a flash, out of the corner of his eye. The man's body struck the first tier of the bridge a hundred feet below.

David fought to pull himself back up on the ledge. It was no use. Now his legs hung out into the free air. He clung to the ledge of slate with his good arm, but he couldn't hold on much longer.

Two thoughts flashed through his mind: *I have too much to live for now, God.* And then: *Kick out with your feet. Kick off from the stones!*

With all the strength of a man who had suddenly been given another chance to live, David forced his feet against the hard rock and shoved himself off the bridge with such force that he propelled his body out, far out. It seemed an agony of hours as he fell, struggling against the sky to straighten his torso before he hit the river and sank beneath its roiling waters.

33

Victory was in the air. Ali could taste it. Somewhere, huddled in dark rooms in Évian, France, the FLN met with de Gaulle's men at yet another attempt to resolve the fate of Algeria. The talks had dragged on now for a week. But Ali was confident of the outcome.

It was all he had hoped for, all his father had promised, and for a brief moment the sweet taste of a free Algeria made him forget his personal vendetta. But only briefly. He fingered a page from the *Midi Libre*, southern France's daily paper. It had arrived by boat that morning along with the news of the Évian peace talks.

Ali took a long draw on his cigarette and then ground the butt in an overflowing ashtray. A caption caught his eye: DESPERATE DIVE TO DEATH.

The body of Jean-Claude Gachon, 31, was found on the first tier of the massive 2,000-year-old Pont du Gard yesterday afternoon. Witnesses said Gachon had shot at them as they picnicked on the ancient aqueduct. Gachon and an American, David Hoffmann, apparently climbed to the top of the aqueduct, where Gachon lost his balance and fell 100 feet below to his death.

Hoffmann, who also fell from the top, landed in the Gardon River. Police attribute his survival to the fact that the waters were swollen after Sunday's flash flood. Despite a bullet wound in his left shoulder, Hoffmann managed to swim to shore and was taken to the hospital in Anduze.

The reason for Gachon's attempt on the lives of the picnickers is not yet clear.

Ali wadded up the newspaper and threw it on the floor, cursing loudly. "Fool! Bumbling idiot!"

Rachid and Jean-Claude, two of his most promising men, dead. And now Ali had no information whatsoever, except that the three he wanted dead were still alive. He spat on the floor.

Hussein, who had brought him the paper, hovered beside him, a scowl on his young face.

"And what news do you have for me?" Ali questioned.

The boy straightened and spoke in his deepest voice. "No one has come from that street, sir. I have watched and watched. But sometime they will. They have to. Give me another chance."

"Then go!"

The boy shuffled out of the grungy room.

Ali glanced at the newspaper clippings on the wall. His little mission was not complete. But the war would be over soon, and then there would be cause to celebrate. Then he would crush the pied-noirs and their filthy harkis like the butt of a cigarette. And the three he sought would be swallowed up as well. It would all work out in the end.

Ophélie's pink stuffed pony smelled of perfume. Mother Griolet had scrubbed off the mud from when it had fallen out of her arms at the Pont du Gard, and now it looked like new.

"A bath for the pony," Mother Griolet had said with a chuckle.

They had all laughed that night. Nervous, worried laughter. Papa was alive. Ophélie closed her eyes and saw him falling down, down until he was swallowed up in the angry river. She remembered Gabriella screaming. From their perch it had been impossible to tell who had fallen first. Only later, when the police had found Jean-Claude's body on the bridge, had they dared to hope.

Three days had come and gone. Today she could see Papa.

She stood outside the heavy, whitewashed hospital door and cuddled her pony in her arms. Then she lifted a small hand and knocked lightly.

"*Entrez,*" a low voice answered.

Ophélie peeped her head inside. Her father lay engulfed in white sheets. His face was covered with bruises, black and yellow. His left shoulder was bandaged awkwardly.

"Come on in, sweetie. Don't be afraid. Papa is going to be fine." His voice sounded weak and sad.

She inched near his bed. "I brought you the picture, Papa. I thought it would make you happy to have it on your wall."

He placed his good hand on her shoulder and smiled. "That will help me feel much better. Pull up a chair, Ophélie."

She dragged a metal-framed chair up to the bed. Still holding the pony, she handed the drawing to him.

"You know everything is okay now, don't you?" he asked softly.

She nodded hesitantly.

Papa continued, "The bad man is gone. He will not come again, dear. We are all safe."

"What is the matter then, Papa? Why do your eyes look so sad?"

He smiled, and she saw the faintest little dimple appear in his cheek. "You understand too much. I'm sad because I have to leave again soon. But don't worry. Not for long."

Ophélie turned her head down. She didn't want to read anything else in his eyes. Papa was right. She did understand too much. But he was whispering now.

"I'm going to get your mama. Moustafa has written to tell me where she is."

Ophélie's eyes grew round. "Mama? You will find her for me?"

"Yes, Ophélie. I'm going to get her. To make sure she comes back to us safely. So you must be brave for a little while longer. And you must help Gabby. It will be very hard for her to let me go."

Ophélie frowned. "Because she loves you."

"Yes."

"And you love her too. Right, Papa?" She peeked at him timidly.

"Yes, Ophélie. Yes, I love her."

"And Mama? Did you love my mama?"

He cleared his throat, and she thought he looked sad again. "Yes, Ophélie. I loved your mama. A long time ago. And then I had to go away. I wrote to her, but she didn't write back. She didn't want me to know about you."

"Why not?" She stuck her lip out in a pout.

"I think because she knew I would come back to Algeria if I knew about you. And she knew that I was supposed to be doing other things."

Ophélie wrinkled her brow. "I don't understand." She spoke defensively, irritated at adults who always complicated things.

"No, I'm sure it seems ridiculous to you, dear. You must simply believe me when I say your mama was doing what she thought was right. She loves you so much." He squeezed her hand. "And I love you too."

That was good. That was what she longed to hear him say. But she still had one more question. "Will you ever love Mama again?"

His eyes looked very sad now, and she was sorry she had asked. He pulled her head onto his chest and held her tight. When he spoke, his voice was muffled. "I don't know, Ophélie. I just don't know."

Ophélie thought hard. What could she say to make Papa feel better? Suddenly she knew. She took out the cross from under her blouse and touched it to his finger. "Mama gave this to me. She said it would protect me. And Bribri says it too. If we believe in God's Son, He will protect us. You'll see, Papa. It will be okay."

David fingered the cross gently as it hung around his daughter's neck. "It's beautiful, Ophélie. And you're right. God will protect me."

The room was austere and white. David's coarse black hair contrasted starkly with the starched white pillow. A small clay pot filled with primroses sat in the window, their petals bright red with a splash of yellow in the middle. The clouds outside the window billowed, puffy and white. A beam of sun shone through the glass and blinded Gabriella for a moment. She watched David, arm bandaged, face bruised.

"The doctor said it's more than a miracle you survived," she said.

David chuckled. "Thanks to the flash flood. I can't say I'd like to repeat the act." He studied her face. "Maybe it was a miracle. Your God ... *our* God saw fit to answer my prayer. I have a lot to live for now." He reached over and patted her arm. "Don't look so worried. I'm okay. We're all okay."

A knock came on the door, and Mother Griolet inched her head inside.

"Come in, come in," David invited. "Have a seat." He motioned to the free chair.

"Praise God, you're recovering," the nun exclaimed, and placed her hand on his. She kissed him on each cheek, laughing. "It's not my custom to greet young teachers in such a manner, but this is a special occasion. Dear M. Hoffmann." She shook her head from side to side, patting his hand.

"Please call me David."

"Well ... *bien sûr*. David. How glad we are to see you in one piece. How much longer will they keep you here?"

"Just till tomorrow. I've got to get out. There is still much to be done."

"Yes, we're receiving nine children on the seventeenth. Imagine." She looked heavenward.

"How many more will come after that, David? Do you have any idea?" Gabriella asked.

"I think this is the last of those at risk from Ali," he stated. "But when the war ends ..." He shrugged.

"And just who is this Ali?" Gabriella blurted out. "Could you please explain it to me from the beginning?"

David turned toward the two women. "You have both heard bits and pieces. It's not a pretty story, but I'll tell you. You're ready to hear?"

Gabriella whispered a faint yes, and Mother Griolet nodded.

"In 1936, the French government in Algeria voted against granting equal rights for Algerian war veterans. Lieutenant Mohammed Boudani was enraged. He had fought well in World War I. His son Ali was likewise furious with the ruling. He was twenty-one and a soldier loyal to his father, who had always been his hero. They were both in Hitler's war. The anger in their souls against this racism mounted as they fought beside the privileged pied-noirs, but they remained loyal to France. And Ali's father promised his son that someday Algerians would know equality.

"But in 1945, Lieutenant Boudani was captured, tortured, and killed in a raid. When the details of his death became clear, Ali was delirious with rage. His father, the leader of this platoon, was the only man to be captured. And that platoon belonged to the battalion under Anne-Marie's father, Captain Maxime Duchemin."

"But how do you know all this?" Gabriella interrupted. "Do you know Ali?"

"I met him in 1953, when I was with Anne-Marie. But she was the one who learned all the details later. Ali moved into hiding in the fifties. He became a leader in the FLN, determined to create a free Algeria. Still, the image of his dead father tortured him.

"Then a small incident brought things to a head. In the spring of 1958, he saw Captain Duchemin at a political rally for the North African Army. He was possessed by some twisted desire to avenge his father's death."

"But Anne-Marie's father didn't kill him!" Gabriella protested. "He wasn't even in the platoon, right? He was much higher up. Wasn't it the German army that was responsible? The SS?"

David nodded. "Yes, but Ali could not get past the image of a sacrificial lamb. He was convinced that Captain Duchemin sent his father in to be killed and that the members of his platoon abandoned him. Of course it isn't true, but …" He shrugged. "He determined to avenge his father's death, and he began in May of '58 by slaughtering Maxime Duchemin and his wife. Ali is an intelligent and methodical man, and he organized a group of six men to gather information about his father's platoon. Documents were hard to come by. He targeted Anne-Marie, the captain's only child. She was twenty-one at the time and known to be politically involved in the war, for the pied-noirs."

David closed his eyes and remembered Anne-Marie's hysterical voice across the miles, crackling through the phone wires. He didn't want to dwell on that part.

He continued speaking in a sterile, removed tone, like a doctor reporting a cancer. "In December, Ali and some of these men abducted and raped Anne-Marie."

Gabriella gave a soft moan and shook her head. For a moment David's eyes met hers.

"Ali's a sick man. After that, he sent a dashing young Frenchman to 'rescue' her—Jean-Claude Gachon. For several months Anne-Marie felt safe with him. Of course she had no idea of his link with Ali. Jean-Claude convinced her that Ali wanted to harm other families of the men in one of her father's platoons in World War II. So at his suggestion she began looking for the names of these families and gave him several.

"But Anne-Marie is not dumb. Gradually she wondered what was happening and found out that two harki families whom she had identified had been murdered, and she grew scared."

David rubbed his eyes and lifted a glass of water to his lips, wincing with pain at the movement. "That is when she wrote to me at Princeton. I hadn't heard from her since I'd left Algeria in 1954, though I'd written her letter after letter. I had finally given up, hoping her silence was merely indifference and not an omen of the war." He set the glass down. "Now I know she was afraid to answer. Afraid to tell me about Ophélie.

"Anyway, in December of 1959, she wrote and then called me and begged me to help these children who were going to be systematically murdered. She knew—well, she hoped—I would be able to come to France ... because of my past...."

He let the phrase dangle, and Mother Griolet shot him a sympathetic look, with a question in her eyes.

"Mother Griolet, would you explain that part please?" He rested his head back on the pillow and closed his eyes. As Mother Griolet picked up his tale, David drifted off.

"In 1944, when David was just a boy, he came to our orphanage, alone. It took several months before his father located him. The man was sick with worry."

David heard the words and opened his eyes. "My father? Sick with worry?" He laughed.

"David! Of course he was. He stood before me and wept. He kept repeating, 'It was all my fault.' He was heartbroken, David. Crushed."

"He was not! He couldn't stand the sight of me. He, he ... left us in Paris with American passports. And then the SS came, and my father was nowhere to be found." David's voice had changed. He spoke loudly, angrily.

"David, please stay calm." Gabriella touched his hand, then held it tightly.

He sighed. "That's another story altogether. It's something I will resolve in time, if God wills." But still he was lost in the nun's words. *He stood before me and wept.* David had never once seen his father shed a tear.

Mother Griolet was talking softly. "You see, Gabriella, when David sent in his references and wanted this job immediately, well, I was delighted. I needed a teacher, and it was obvious he was brilliant, even though he had just finished college and had never taught before. I never connected him with the child who had come to St. Joseph until recently." She winked. "Perhaps if I had, I wouldn't have disliked him so much."

"It was better for a while that you disliked me. That you didn't suspect a thing. So you see, Gabby, I came here almost two years ago. I had done my homework, and I knew there were those in the region who had been involved in the Resistance during World War II. It didn't take me long to make the right connections."

Gabriella smiled. "M. Vidal, right?"

David nodded. "Yes. He helped me set up this little project with Mother Griolet and several boulangers in the region. We called it Operation Hugo—short for Huguenot. I had often seen Anne-Marie's cross. It was my idea to have the cross be the symbol of the operation. Those escaping had the paper with the cross and the date and time of departure only. Moustafa sent other information to different boulangers in France—never the same one twice in a row—in case there was ever a leak. It was like in the Resistance, *n'est-ce pas*, Mother Griolet?"

The old nun frowned. "Ah yes. Confusing everyone—keeping everyone guessing. Never knowing who was good and who was bad."

"Anyway," David continued, "the boulangers received messages including not only the cross and the date and time but also how many children were coming. Then they baked these messages into the bread, and at certain times I was to pick them up.

"Which is where you fit in, my dear." He squeezed her hand. "You kept me quite protected from Jean-Claude for a while. The first child who was to come over from Algeria in September never showed up. Something happened to him. I knew then that someone was onto the operation. So when I met you, I felt you could help me keep my cover without having to be in on the whole thing." He sighed. "It was foolish of me. I'm sorry, Gabby. I don't think I ever asked you to forgive me."

Gabriella kissed him tenderly on the forehead. "I can't complain. It has worked out so differently ... but I can't complain. And yes, I forgive you." She paused, then continued, "But what was Anne-Marie doing? And how did she and Ophélie get to Paris? Weren't they in Algeria?"

"I didn't know until Ophélie told me this morning. Anne-Marie and Moustafa and Ophélie fled Algeria—from the 'bad men,' as Ophélie puts it. They were in Paris for eight months. Then Ophélie escaped out the window of her apartment and went to live with M. Gady, an old shopkeeper whom I later found dead the night of the riot in Paris. Apparently he was a friend of Anne-Marie's who had promised to care for Ophélie should there be trouble." David paused for a breath.

"It's all quite confusing," said Mother Griolet. "I'm glad I didn't know any of this. It would have been too overwhelming."

"You're right, it's complicated," David agreed. "Ophélie said she was supposed to give M. Gady her little blue bag, but she was too afraid. So that's when all communication with us broke down. And Anne-Marie and Moustafa ended up back in Algeria. I doubt they went back of their own free will.

"In mid-October I received word that something was happening in Paris. When I went up there to find out, of course I had no idea I would return with Ophélie. Or how she fit into the puzzle. It appears that the man I was supposed to meet there was a double spy. Perhaps he was going to use Ophélie as bait, to trap me. But the whole plan fell apart when the riot broke out. And, miraculously, I ended up with Ophélie. The informant ended up in the obituaries, although I doubt very much he's dead. Spies have interesting ways of 'disappearing.'"

Gabriella interrupted him. "And when I got the wrong bread in Aix, were orphans supposed to be coming? I've been worrying about that."

"No. I checked with the boulangeries fairly often if I had not received any news. That time there would have been no message in the bread even if you had gotten the pain de seigle. But I didn't know it at the time. That's why I was so angry. I treated you badly, Gabby. I'm so sorry." David squeezed her hand.

"You were pretty awful several times. But I just knew there was something in you worth exploring." Gabriella smiled. "It was a selfless act, a huge sacrifice of your time—not to mention the danger—for you to set up this operation."

David reddened. "I suppose there were some decent intentions mixed in with the bad. But don't flatter me, Gabby. I have much to learn about selflessness." He turned to gaze out the window and spoke with a catch in his voice. "There was something appealing, satisfying about saving innocent children who were being targeted for no crime of their own—they just happened to be the wrong race." His eyes were misty as he turned to face the women. "I could understand their suffering. I had to help.

"But I've strayed from the story," he said, rubbing his eyes. "For the longest time I had no word from Moustafa, after Hakim came—he was the one you brought news of in Aigues-Mortes."

"And Aigues-Mortes is where Jean-Claude first saw me and made the connection," Gabriella interjected. "Did he follow me to the bread store?"

"I don't think so. I think it was just your cross. He somehow knew of the symbol of our operation, and he saw your cross."

Gabriella held the cross gently in her hand. "Mother could never have imagined how much trouble this cross would get me into." She gave Mother Griolet a smile. "I suppose it all goes back to you. You bought the cross. You gave it to Mother. You were even the reason David came back to St. Joseph."

The nun raised her eyebrows. "I'm quite sure it does not all come back to me, but to God. He is the Master Weaver. He saw it all before. The cross draws us to Him first, and then it draws us together."

David met Gabriella's eyes and touched her cheek with his hand.

"And if I hadn't worn the Huguenot cross, who knows if Ophélie would have opened up to me?" Gabriella said, wonder in her voice. "And now what, David?"

He had wanted to tell her alone, to break the news gently and kiss away the worry lines that he knew would appear on her forehead. But he had no choice. Now was the moment to say it.

With difficulty he straightened up in the bed. "There is Anne-Marie. I've received word about her from this man, Moustafa. She's very ill, and he fears she will die." He cleared his throat. "She can't travel alone. Moustafa has to stay in Algeria to help other families escape. Not just those threatened by Ali, but other harki families. He's asked me to return to Algiers to bring Anne-Marie back."

At once Gabriella pulled her hand away from his and gave a soft whimper.

David fought to remain calm. He wanted to say the right words. "Gabby, my dear. I have to go. For Ophélie. If I can bring her mother back to her, surely this is right."

Gabriella was twisting her hands together, staring at the floor.

Mother Griolet stood and looked at David. "I'll leave you now. God be with you, David." She paused for a moment, resting her hand on the bent head of Gabriella. "And with you, my child." She left the room.

David motioned for Gabriella to come closer. Carefully she sat down on the edge of the bed as he put his good arm around her. He kissed her tenderly as she cried.

"Please, Gabby … please try to understand."

She laid her head on his chest. "I'm trying, David, but I can't understand why you must leave now, when things are … are so good.

We're safe, we're together. Ophélie is here." Her blue eyes were shining with tears as she looked up at him. "Don't leave me now."

He breathed out slowly. "I have to go. But don't be afraid, Gabby. Don't be afraid of her. That was so long ago, and you are now. And you know for sure that I love you."

She didn't answer.

David grappled for something to say. "What was it you told me, Gabby? Something your mother said. Our God does not make mistakes."

34

The news of the cease-fire agreements coming from Évian spread quickly across the city of Algiers on the morning of March 19. Effective at noon. The gray skies echoed the mood that many felt: the cease-fire was necessary, but there was no victory. A war that started with a handful of extremists on All Saints' Day in 1954 had cost the French and Algerians hundreds of thousands of lives over the past seven years. In three months the Algerians would hold a referendum to vote for independence. The agreement written up between the FLN and de Gaulle's men specified plenty of precautions for the pied-noirs, but Anne-Marie knew what would happen. The pied-noirs would leave—leave their homes, their land, their cities to go to an unfamiliar and perhaps even hostile country where legally they were citizens.

It would not be easy. But she didn't care. Nothing could be worse than the nightmare she had lived through over the past two years. And she would be with Ophélie. Tomorrow, perhaps, David Hoffmann would walk back into her life and carry her to France. She forced herself to stand and limped across the room. At least she was walking. The bandages that had surrounded her legs for six weeks were finally off.

Moustafa came into the room and fell onto the bed with a sigh. He shook his curly hair, eyes solemn. "Cease-fire, Anne-Marie. Thank God the last children are gone. Because now is when the trouble really begins."

"Don't say it, Moustafa. Please. Surely now there will be peace!"

"And you think those French terrorists in the OAS will sit placidly by and not lift a finger? Fireworks are coming. Plenty of them. And not in celebration…." He stood up and grabbed Anne-Marie's hands. "But you will be gone from this mess, my *habibti*. You and Ophélie will be safe."

Anne-Marie frowned. "Tell me when you will come to France, so I can hope. I can't leave without knowing."

His eyes looked dull, the chocolate brown without sheen. He kissed her tenderly, and Anne-Marie closed her eyes. The kiss gave her strength. She felt a flash of passion, but suddenly Moustafa was holding her away.

"We have known all along it was impossible. For these months I have had you, and knowing that, I have hoped. But, Anne-Marie, I can't tell you when or if I'll come back to France. I know things…. And I am needed."

He pulled her close to him, and Anne-Marie could feel his heart beating.

"We have made it this far," he said. "We've shared a love I only hoped for months ago. Surely, somehow, it will carry us through. But I won't ask you to wait for me. I only ask that you call out to the heavens and pray that the harkis be spared further loss."

"Kiss me again, Moustafa," she whispered. "As if for the last time, something I can remember and hold on to." When he released her, she touched her lips as if to seal in the wonder—wonder that a war and another man she had once loved wouldn't erase.

"Ophélie," she said out loud. "Wait only a little longer. Mama is coming home."

Papa was leaving tomorrow to get Mama in Algeria. Ophélie could not decipher her feelings. Fear, excitement, love, anger. They were all colliding in her mind. She opened her chest of drawers and took out the blue bag. She cradled it in her hands, then carefully pulled apart the strings. Her small hand reached inside, as it had done so many times before, and pulled out the contents. Everything was there. She picked up Mama's letter and read it again. *I never wanted for us to be apart. But for now, my love, it's necessary.*

Mama had said it, and now Papa was saying it too. Just for a while. Then Papa would bring her back and they would be a family, like other families. Papa, Mama, Gabriella, and her.

Ophélie frowned. No, somehow that would never work. She sighed as she stared at the tiny photo of her with her mother. Why couldn't Papa love Mama *and* Gabriella? Why did he have to choose?

She kissed her mother's picture and whispered, "Mama, I can read and write, and I have found Papa. Everything is almost perfect. When you get back, then it will be like a fairy tale and we will live happily ever after."

She pulled out the top drawer, where she had stored a few blank sheets of paper and colored pencils. Mama needed to know she was waiting for her. Leaning on the top of the chest of drawers, she wrote slowly in her best cursive. *Je t'eme, Mama. Vien me voir vite. Je t'attend. Ophélie.*

She checked it over. Maybe there were a few spelling errors, but surely Mama would understand: *I love you. Come see me soon. I'm waiting for you.* Over her words she drew a large rainbow, its many-colored arc filling the page.

She tucked the note into the pocket of her black wool skirt, kissed the little photo, and replaced the blue bag in the drawer.

Now Mama would see for herself that she could write. And she would hurry to come here, to this place that had become Ophélie's home.

Mother Griolet had kindly insisted that good-byes be said in her apartment while she cared for the children in the basement. The little threesome sat in awkward silence, dreading the minutes that ruthlessly ticked by. David swallowed several times. His throat felt closed and dry. He motioned to Ophélie, who was standing solemnly by the window. Slowly she walked over to her father.

Gabriella bit her lip. He read the pain in her eyes.

David held Ophélie on his lap, rejoicing in the smell of her freshly washed hair and the feel of her soft skin, so young and alive and unblemished. "My dear, my daughter." His tone was gentle. The morning light seeped through the window and engulfed them.

"Ophélie, I'll go and find Mama and bring her back to you, to us." For a brief moment he glanced over to Gabriella, with all the love and hurt of the world in his eyes.

"You won't take me with you, Papa?" she begged.

"No, no. It's much too dangerous. You must stay here with Gabby. She'll take care of you." He turned to Gabriella, who was standing partially in the shadows. The sun tinted her hair, and it glistened thick and red, tumbling over her shoulders. He felt a hollow pain in his stomach. "You'll look after Ophélie, won't you?"

"Of course I will." She waved the child into her awaiting arms.

Ophélie reached into her pocket. "Papa? I have something for Mama. Will you take it to her for me?"

David took the folded paper. He was beside them at once, stroking Gabriella's hair and softly saying, "You have told me before. A God bigger than us is in control. I believe it now. Will you let me go?"

Gabriella nodded and turned her head down. He lifted her chin with his good hand. He contemplated kissing her. Instead he put his warm, strong hand around hers and squeezed it hard. Ophélie held him tightly around the waist. He pulled them close to his chest and with a heavy sigh whispered, "I love you both."

He could not say anything else, although he thought of a hundred different things he wanted to tell Gabriella. But they were things to be said by candlelight, nestled in the back of a charming little restaurant.

Finally he broke the tortured silence. "I'd better go." He had no heart for small talk. He simply hugged Ophélie and Gabriella as tightly as he could manage with one arm. He briefly pressed his lips against Gabriella's forehead, then left the room.

From the window in the den, Gabriella and Ophélie watched David walk to the street below. He paused to wave at them, and Gabriella's heart skipped a beat. He looked vulnerable, with wisps of black hair falling across his forehead and a half smile crossing his face. His dark brooding eyes caught Gabriella's, and all she read in them was love.

One arm of his leather jacket hung limply to the side, concealing the bandaged shoulder. Under his good arm he held a briefcase, and he clutched a small suitcase in his hand. It was the picture of David she would keep in her mind afterward.

"Bribri, are you all right?" Ophélie's face was shining with tears. "You love him so, Bribri. And he loves you. I know it. You won't pray that Mama dies, will you?"

Gabriella frowned for a moment. Then she scooped Ophélie up in her arms. "I will never pray for that. There is a God bigger than us who sees our hearts and understands, just as your papa has said. God has already worked everything out. You'll see, precious child. I'm sure we'll see."

The noise from the classroom was deafening as Mother Griolet entrusted the children to Sister Rosaline and Sister Isabelle. "It may be that lunch is late. Don't worry. Just try to calm them down now while I check out the bedrooms."

Her head was throbbing from the noise. Nine new children. Wild-eyed, terrified little harki children. Crying, screaming, clutching.

"I know they should be here, Lord. But I don't know how to do it. I will need more help, more room."

She was out of breath by the time she reached the dormitories. The nuns had squeezed three extra bunk beds into the girls' dorm, on loan from a neighbor for as long as Mother Griolet needed. "Thank

You, Lord, for kind, simple women who don't ask too many questions," the nun said.

She paused for a moment, then walked into the boys' dorm. Three cots from the hospital were neatly made. "Bless you, Sister Rosaline. How that good woman found enough sheets, I have no idea. *Merci, Seigneur.*"

Satisfied that each child would have a place to sleep that night, she left the dormitories and walked back through the courtyard and into the basement. The din from the classroom had quieted, and Sister Rosaline was animatedly telling a story.

"Bless you," Mother Griolet whispered again as she trotted through the hall and up the steps, letting herself into her apartment. Jean-Louis sat in front of her desk.

"Jean-Louis, forgive me for keeping you waiting," she said, sitting down with a long sigh.

He rose slightly and nodded. "Have you seen the paper this morning? The cease-fire goes into effect at noon."

"*Dieu merci*, it's over. And the children are safely here. Did you have any trouble in Marseille?"

He laughed. "It went as smoothly as you could expect with nine little ones. I do believe I'm getting a little old for this." He rubbed his bloodshot eyes. "And you, Jeanette? Do you have everything you need?"

The old nun cleared her throat. "I need your prayers. Many prayers, Jean-Louis." She thought for a moment. "Are you sure you can keep on with M. Hoffmann's class until he gets back?"

Jean-Louis grunted. "It's the least I can do. I can't believe he's going to Algeria at this time. You should have forbidden it, Jeanette. To keep him alive."

"God has provided me with another capable teacher," she said, winking at him. "And who am I to forbid what the Lord ordains? We must pray, simply pray."

"*C'est compris,*" he said. "You've done a good job, dear woman."

"*Toi aussi, mon ami.*" Then, almost timidly, she asked, "Do you think … do you think this is all of the children?"

He shuffled his feet and looked to the ground. "In my opinion, it will get a lot worse over there before it gets better. I don't think we're done. But as far as Hugo goes, mission accomplished." He grinned. "Oh, and you have two visitors in your den."

They touched hands lightly and left the office together.

In her den Mother Griolet found Ophélie sitting on Gabriella's lap, both of them staring out the window, both of them crying. Mother Griolet cleared her throat softly. "Excuse me for interrupting you.… You didn't wish to see him off?"

Gabriella shrugged and nodded toward Ophélie.

Understanding, Mother Griolet came beside them. "Ophélie will stay with me for a while, won't you, dear?"

The child bit her lip, holding her pink pony close.

"You'll see, children. Life goes on, and there is hope."

Ophélie quickly pulled the cross from around her neck. She offered it to Gabriella. "If you're going to Papa, take him my cross. Then he'll be safe. He'll understand."

Gabriella took it and replied softly, "You know, Ophélie, that God will protect him—not because he wears a cross, but because he has the Lord in here." She pointed to her heart.

"I know, Bribri. But still, it will help remind Papa of God … and of me. He needs to have it."

"Very well then. I will take it to him." Gabriella unfastened the chain and slipped it around her own neck. As she did, a ray of sun came in, and Mother Griolet watched the splashes of light dance through the room. The crosses hung together, touching lightly.

No one said a word for several eternal seconds.

"Go on with you now," Mother Griolet urged Gabriella. "Go quickly."

Once convinced, Gabriella raced down the steps of the parsonage and out into the cool, ethereal spring day. Her hair flying out behind her, she tripped on the cobblestones, regained her balance, and dashed around the corner, past the olive tree that brushed against her bedroom window, past the fountain that sprayed gustily, and toward the bus stop. David stood with his back to her. Two older women sat with stone-faced expressions, waiting for bus 11.

Gabriella hesitated when she was still several yards from him. Then she called out, "David!"

He whirled around, catching sight of her, an expression of delight and surprise crossing his face.

"Gabby!" He laughed and ran toward her. Picking her up with one arm, he kissed her hard on the mouth. "I'm glad you came," he mumbled between kisses.

"We'll be the talk of the town now," she said, giggling.

David grinned. "It was bound to happen one way or another." He glanced at his watch. Taking her hand, he led her away from the bus stop, across the street, and behind a row of stores.

"I have this for you," Gabriella said, taking the cross from around her neck. "Ophélie wanted you to wear it, so you will remember that God is protecting you." Her voice caught, and a cool shiver ran down her spine. He was really going. The minutes were ticking by, and she suddenly realized that she had not given him anything at all.

"I wish I had something for you—" she began, but he put a finger to her lips.

"Don't say it. Do you think I will forget you, beautiful Gabby? I have the Book you gave me. And now I have the cross. It's all I need."

His hand was on her shoulder as he looked down at her, his black eyes soft. "I will never forget all you have shared with me. Never."

She didn't like the way he said *never*. "You are coming back, aren't you? You won't be gone too long?"

He touched her face, brushing her cheek with his fingers. "I'll be back. Pray for me, Gabby. I'll come back." He fumbled with the lock on his briefcase. "I forgot to give this to you. I was going to mail it from Marseille, but since you're here—" He held out a white envelope. "Your exam," he said with a wink. "You did very well, my dear."

He pulled her to him once more and kissed her for a long moment. "I have to say good-bye now, Gabby."

They held hands and crossed back toward the bus stop. The number 11 bus was slowly crawling up the street.

"Good-bye, David." Her voice was choked with emotion. "I love you."

When he looked back, he seemed poised forever on the step of the bus, his dark eyes studying her, his good arm holding his black leather suitcase and briefcase. He set the luggage down and waved once. He boarded the bus, the doors closed, and he was gone.

Yvette and Monique watched the young couple's good-bye from the window of Monique's apartment.

"*Ooh là là.* Young love is *difficile.*" Yvette sighed, shaking her head.

"*Triste, oui, mais alors!* It is a beautiful story. They must be strong and brave. If fate and *le bon Dieu* are on their side, *alors* all will turn out fine," Monique reassured her friend.

"The good Lord, yes. Surely He is with them. And who knows? There may be a wedding yet, one of these days."

Monique rolled her eyes and picked up a potato to peel. "You never know. Life is full of surprises, *n'est-ce pas?*"

Gabriella didn't walk back to St. Joseph immediately. She followed the road past Mme Leclerc's and out toward the countryside. She remembered the time she had strolled this way with David in early December after their friendship had been reconciled. The vines had been naked then, but now tiny sprouts of green were appearing on the twisted branches.

She ripped open the envelope and removed four folded sheets of paper. They rustled in the breeze, and she looked down to read them, but her eyes were blurred. She wiped the tears away.

Across the top of the exam David had scribbled *Excellent work, Mlle Madison*. There was no grade. She felt an edgy disappointment. It looked as if he had made no other comment on the exam. She had hoped for a word, another phrase. Something she could keep from him.

Turning to the last page, she saw something written at the very bottom.

> *I'm sitting in this hospital bed, barely able to write, and thinking of you, Gabby. When you wonder, when you begin to question, read this exam again and know that I meant every word.*
> *Je t'aime,*
> *David*

Gabriella touched the words with her hand, then held the pages to her breast. She gazed out into the distance and said, with a soft confidence in her voice, "The Lord shall preserve thy going out and thy coming in from this time forth, and even for evermore."

Far across the field she saw a lone poppy quiver in the early spring breeze, bending back and forth, holding its bright-red face to the sun.

... a little more ...

When a delightful concert comes to an end,

the orchestra might offer an encore.

When a fine meal comes to an end,

it's always nice to savor a bit of dessert.

When a great story comes to an end,

we think you may want to linger.

And so, we offer ...

AfterWords—just a little something more after you

have finished a David C Cook novel.

We invite you to stay awhile in the story.

Thanks for reading!

Turn the page for ...

- **A Historical Note about the Huguenot Cross**
- **The Opening Scenes from *Two Testaments*,**
  the Sequel to *Two Crosses*, available now!
- **About the Author**

The Huguenot Cross

Protestantism began in France in the midsixteenth century. The first French Protestants were called Huguenots. Despite almost continual persecution from the Catholic Church and the kings of France, the Huguenots grew in number and influence. In 1598, Henri IV granted them religious freedom under the Edict of Nantes. However, in 1685, Louis XIV revoked the edict. The ensuing persecution forced hundreds of thousands of Huguenots to flee to England, Ireland, Scotland, Holland, Germany, Switzerland, Russia, and North America. Many thousands who remained in France were martyred for their faith.

The Huguenot cross is believed to have been created by a goldsmith in Nîmes around the year 1688. It was crafted in the form of a Maltese cross and strongly resembled the military decoration called the Medal of the Order of the Holy Spirit, created in the late sixteenth century by Henri III as a military distinction for excellent warriors.

The Huguenot cross comes in many different forms today. Originally it was made up of four equal, thick branches, each branch in the form of an arrow turned inward, with two little "balls" on the outer points of each arrow. Four fleurs-de-lis were embedded in between the branches of the cross, and a dove, symbolizing the Holy Spirit, hung with its head turned downward from the lowest branch.

The cross is popular among Protestants in France today.

Opening Scenes from
Two Testaments

March 1962
Castelnau, France

Poppies were springing up in the fields beyond Castelnau like bright-red drops of blood staining the countryside. Seeing the flowers, Gabriella Madison took a deep breath. Lifeblood and hope eternal.

She closed her eyes and felt a stinging sensation inside her chest. Poppies reminded her of David. And poppies reminded David of her. But now he was in Algeria, perhaps already in the company of Ophélie's mother, Anne-Marie. How Gabriella wished he were standing here beside her instead.

Ophélie's voice interrupted her thoughts. "Bribri, do you think it will be today that Papa and Mama get back?"

Gabriella shook her head, her red hair glistening like sun on the river. "Not today, Ophélie. But very soon."

Were they even now laughing together, reliving old times, catching up on seven lost years? Was David explaining what had been happening here in lazy Castelnau? Had he even mentioned her name to Anne-Marie?

They had been walking, Gabriella and a whole troop of children, toward the edge of Castelnau, where the village fanned out into farmland and vineyards. The children trailed behind their young *maîtresse* in pairs, holding hands and chattering excitedly. Gabriella glanced back to see Sister Rosaline, red faced and out of breath, waving from the end of the line.

"All here," the nun called out happily in her singsong French. "All forty-three."

Gabriella waved back, smiling at the children. "Do you want to go a little farther? We're almost to the park."

A chorus of *Oui, Maîtresse* sang back to her, so they proceeded down a narrow dirt road into a grassy sanctuary enclosed by tall cypress trees. At the far end of the field were several seesaws, some monkey bars, and an old swing set.

This walk outside the orphanage had become a daily ritual after lunch, weather permitting. Mother Griolet had hesitated at first. What if people began to question? After all, the population of the orphanage had doubled in a few short months. But Gabriella and Sister Rosaline had insisted. The new arrivals were loud, afraid, and restless. Together the children acted like pent-up animals, and they needed to be uncaged in a space larger than the courtyard inside St. Joseph.

In truth, Gabriella worried for Mother Griolet. With David away and all the new children here, the old nun's predictable schedule had come tumbling down.

"It's always this way at first," she had reassured Gabriella. "During the Second World War we scrambled for a while, but we eventually settled into a routine."

But Gabriella was not convinced. Over fifteen years had passed since that war, and Mother Griolet was no longer young. Still spry, yes, but she was suddenly looking quite old beneath her habit. Her face looked more wrinkled, and her green eyes had lost some of their sparkle.

Forty-three orphans and forty-two American college women would be plenty for an energetic young woman to handle. Perhaps too much for a woman of seventy-two.

Presently Ophélie left her friends to join Gabriella.

"Bribri," the child began, fiddling with Gabriella's long red curls, "what will it be like when Mama, Papa, and you are all here together?" She scrunched up her nose, her brown eyes shining and sincere.

Gabriella cleared her throat and stroked Ophélie's hair. "It will be a wonderful reunion, Ophélie. An answer to prayer."

"And who do you think Papa will choose? You or Mama? And who will I live with?"

Gabriella bent down beside the little girl. She hoped her voice sounded light and carefree. "Dear Ophélie. Your papa will not choose your mama or me. He will choose *you*! He will pick you up and swing you around, and the whole orphanage will ring with your laughter. Don't you worry now. Don't worry."

Take your own advice, Gabriella thought as she sent Ophélie off with a soft pat on the back. Two days ago David Hoffmann had kissed her—really kissed her—and then he had left on a humanitarian mission to a country gone mad. She did not want to dwell on it, for the possibilities were too frightening. Better to think of the children.

A fight broke out between two boys, and Gabriella dashed over, yelling, "*Eh! Ça suffit!*" She pulled the children apart, scolded them playfully, and began chasing several of the smallest boys, tagging one and calling, "You're it!" A few minutes into the game she stumbled, out of breath, to the side of the field, crushing a red poppy beneath her feet.

Marseille, France

David Hoffmann stood at the bassin de la Joliette in Marseille. Amid the huge ferries, *paquebots*, and steamships, he spied a comparatively small black-and-white sailboat. The *Capitaine* was empty now, except for a grisly old Frenchman at the helm.

The wharf was awash in families debarking with trunks and suitcases. Adults and children alike looked confused, sad, hopeless. David shook his head. One little orphanage in the south of France sheltering a handful of *pied-noir* and *harki* children was a drop in the bucket. These people were French citizens, but where would they go? Did France want them? David knew the answer was no.

He slipped onto the *Capitaine* and greeted the rough sailor with a handshake.

"*Bonjour*," Jacques replied. "You sure you want to go back there now? It's a bad situation and is only going to get worse."

"Yes, I'm sure. I have to go."

Jacques looked at the ground. "I can't go back, M. Hoffmann. There's nowhere for me to dock. The ferries are taking up all the room. Thousands of pied-noirs are running away faster than the

mistral gusts down the Rhône. If you're sure you have to go back,
I advise you to take a ferry. It'll be a lot safer, and I guarantee you
there'll be room—nobody's going *back* to Algeria."

David frowned, contemplating the sailor's words, then shrugged.
"I understand, Jacques. Thank you for all your help. There are many
children in Castelnau who are grateful to you."

The two men shook hands.

"*Bonne chance*, M. Hoffmann. You be careful now. Raving crazy,
that country is. Raving crazy."

David stood on the deck of a huge empty ferry, his tall frame silhouetted against the night sky. The wind whipped across the sea. His
hair blew back, his eyes squinted against the wind, and his jacket
billowed and filled with air. He gripped the railing with his good
hand, his other shoulder and arm bandaged and tucked inside his
leather jacket.

The whitecaps rose up to touch the sky, and a thousand stars
blinked back, as if flirting with the water. The sea air smelled fresh
and strong. He wished briefly that Gabriella were snuggled beside
him, then pushed the thought away.

He had twenty-four hours alone before he would step into a
world of chaos, and he wanted to spend this one night well. The
scene before him reminded him of a night on the beach one month
ago. The night of his surrender, he called it in his mind. His surrender to the God of Gabriella.

There was no doubt that something inside of him had changed.
In that moment he had actually felt forgiven, and too many

coincidences had happened lately to deny intellectually that God seemed to be up to something in his life. He was twenty-five years old, yet he was somehow new. A new man. A new conscience. A Presence was with him. He had a suspicious feeling he would never be able to get rid of this God now even if he wanted to.

Algiers, Algeria

It was midafternoon at the Place du Gouvernement in downtown Algiers. The great Cathedral of Saint Philippe formed an imposing barrier between the steep, narrow roads of the Casbah and this tree-filled square that teemed with people shopping, sipping mint tea at a *café*, and milling about in carefree jubilation. There was a feeling of peace and security among the population of Algiers. The cease-fire to end Algeria's seven-year war for independence from France had gone into effect two days before.

The noise from the square was merry, loud, jovial. This was the Algiers Hussein remembered and loved. Seven years of war had stolen his boyhood away. At fourteen, he had seen more violence than many a soldier. He secretly longed for peace. Beyond the war, beyond the hatred.

Now was the time to breathe openly, to relax, to hope. No pied-noirs had ventured out into the sunshine today, Hussein mused with grim satisfaction. Ali had predicted they would leave *en masse* before official independence was declared on July 2. Algeria would be rid of the filthy French and their colonial ways.

Yet Hussein still wished he could find the woman, Anne-Marie, to placate Ali's fury. Ali Boudani was a man obsessed with revenge. He was at one moment delirious with joy, the next moment brooding with contempt. Algeria was independent, but Ali's personal mission was not over.

Hussein glanced up at the sky, hearing a noise that sounded like a plane overhead, or maybe a missile being launched. Then his body tensed. He stood transfixed in the shadow of a building as, above him, one, then two bright flashes exploded with a terrible boom in the center of the Place du Gouvernement. Debris from the street, chairs from cafés, and bodies seemed to dance on the tips of the bright flames before his eyes. For a brief moment the deafening roar of the explosions silenced the screams coming from everywhere in the square.

Clutching one another, panic on their faces, people clambered toward the shadows of the buildings, some fleeing in the direction of the cathedral. Dead and maimed lay in the center of the square; a shrill cry of agony pierced through the din of confused voices. Everyone stopped; no one dared move. Would more bombs follow?

Then almost at once, the masses surged forward to help the wounded. Arab FLN terrorists worked alongside the French police for perhaps the first time in Algiers' bloody history. Hussein watched it all. An old woman, bloodied and disfigured, collapsed against the stones of a building. Three men lay dead. The peaceful leafy square of five minutes earlier resembled a battleground. Hussein turned on his heels and fled.

It was a lie! There was no peace for Algeria! Up the layers of tangled, dilapidated buildings of the Casbah Hussein ran, until he stumbled into the one-room office where Ali sat.

Already the Casbah was ringing with cries of indignation and fury.

"Ali! The Place du Gouvernement! Explosion!" Hussein choked on his words and took in gulps of air, his lungs burning.

Ali rose and stepped into the street as young men poured forth from their whitewashed stalls.

Other members of the FLN were already holding men back, some of them forcefully.

"Not yet! Don't run to your deaths. This is what the OAS is waiting for. Hold your ground. It's their last effort to win back Algeria."

Ali grabbed Hussein by the shoulders. "It's not over yet. You aren't afraid of bloodshed, my boy?"

Hussein gazed at him and shook his head, knowing all the while that the fear in his eyes betrayed him.

"Go then, and tell me what you see. Go to Bab el-Oued and wait. Take it all in. We must be ready."

Hussein turned and escaped through a narrow alleyway. Tears ran down his cheeks. Oh, for peace. For even a moment of peace. Then he could play as he had when he was seven and war had been only a handful of toy soldiers on the floor of his room.

A ricochet of bullets sounded in the street below the building where Anne-Marie Duchemin was staying with fellow pied-noir Marcus

Cirou. She watched Moustafa hurry a young man into their building, and she quickly limped to the mirror that hung on the flaking wall. She felt a pang of despair as her reflection stared back at her. Her black hair drooped loosely upon her shoulders. She cringed at the way her protruding cheekbones accentuated her deep-set and dull eyes. Her skin looked pale and almost yellowish. She turned away.

A thick gray sweater hung impossibly over her thin frame, but she felt completely naked. David Hoffmann was about to walk back into her life, and she was not ready. Her heart belonged to Moustafa. With him, she was not afraid to be sick and disheveled. She read devotion in his eyes. But David! Her lover when they were but adolescents. She had not seen him in so long.

Suddenly she felt afraid. He was risking his life and wasting his time to help her. Why? Would he be angry to see what she had become? A pitiful, withered flower …

The door swung wide, and David stood in the opening and paused. Anne-Marie swallowed hard and met his eyes. His six-foot-one-inch frame had filled out so that he looked every bit the grown man he was. His black eyes were softer than she remembered, and the tenderness she saw in them scared her even more. His coarse black hair was swept back away from his face, but one wisp tickled his forehead. A black leather jacket hung loosely over his shoulders. As he leaned down to set a suitcase on the floor, she noticed his bandaged arm. He straightened up, not moving forward, as if waiting for her invitation.

His mouth whispered *Anne-Marie* without making a sound.

Oh, you are a beautiful man, she thought, fighting to stand her ground, willing herself against running into his arms, forcing herself to forget that last embrace seven years ago when he had kissed her good-bye even as the tiny seed of Ophélie was forming in her womb.

David cleared his throat. "Anne-Marie." He said it almost reverently, and then he moved toward her, slowly, taking long strides. He reached out and touched her frail hand, then brushed her face. "My dear Anne-Marie."

She heard the sorrow, the groan of pain in his voice, the hurt for her suffering. She bit her lip and closed her eyes, but she could not keep the tears from flowing. She rested her head against his chest and let his strong arm enclose her as she sobbed like a terrified child who had been rescued at last.

Somewhere inside she watched the years of horror and death, killing and running for life, the years that had followed her happiest moments with David. If only ... if only ... The questions of a lifetime swam before her in liquid reality until they ran down her cheeks. Her feeble energy was spent. And though she had not uttered a word, she had the feeling that David Hoffmann understood perfectly everything she felt.

About the Author

Elizabeth Goldsmith Musser, an Atlanta native and the best-selling author of *The Swan House*, is a novelist who writes what she calls "entertainment with a soul." For over twenty years, Elizabeth and her husband, Paul, have been involved in missions work with International Teams. They presently live near Lyon, France. The Mussers have two sons and a daughter-in-law. To learn more about Elizabeth and her books, and to find discussion questions as well as photos of sites mentioned in the stories, please visit www.elizabethmusser.com.